'There seems to be a
pensively. 'I'd like you
on my medical chair.'

'Medical chair?' the girl frowned as Larry took the candle away.

'Yes,' he smiled, helping her off the couch. 'It was designed by a university professor. Er . . . I'm afraid you'll have to take your habit off.'

'I can't do that!' the young nun protested, standing before him. 'My vows . . .'

'Mary, I know you've taken your vows, but you have a problem.'

'What's wrong with me?'

'In my considered opinion, you're suffering from a range of complaints that can be corrected, but I can't help you if you won't help me. If you won't remove your clothing I'm afraid there's nothing I can do.'

'All right,' the young woman finally conceded, kicking her shoes off. 'No one will know about this, will they?'

'Trust me, Mary. What ever happens in this room will remain our secret. Not even God will know about it.'

'He will! He's everywhere!'

'He's not in here, this is a Godfree zone. Take your habit off . . .'

Also by Ray Gordon

Sisters in Lust

Depravicus – The Sequel

Carnal Craving

House of Lust

RAY GORDON

Sex Practice

NEW ENGLISH LIBRARY

Hodder & Stoughton

This edition published in Great Britain in 2002
by Hodder and Stoughton
A division of Hodder Headline

A New English Library paperback

6

A CIP catalogue record for this title
is available from the British Library

ISBN 978 0 340 69512 8

Printed and bound in the UK by
CPI Mackays, Chatham ME5 8TD

Hodder and Stoughton
A division of Hodder Headline
338 Euston Road
London NW1 3BH

Chapter One

Larry Lickman gazed lustfully at the pretty blonde sitting facing him anxiously in his consulting room. His penis strained within his tight cords as he imagined her masturbating with a vibrator – legs splayed, juicy cunt lips gaping, cerise clitoris throbbing in orgasm. Eyeing her pert breasts, her erectile nipples pushing against her white silk blouse, he smiled. She was in her early twenties, married, unable to achieve orgasm – and delectably fuckable!

The distraught young woman had resorted to Larry's infamous private sex therapy and marriage guidance practice in despair. Her husband threatening to leave her for a *real* woman, she was desperate to respond to his intimate attention, his vaginal massaging, his clitoral tonguing, and achieve the massive multiple orgasms she naively believed all other women were enjoying.

'Some women find it difficult to climax during sexual intercourse,' Larry began, his elbows resting on his desk, his dark eyes smiling. 'You're far from unique, believe me!'

'But I've read about women screaming and writhing, their nostrils flaring, their eyes rolling and . . . why can't *I* do it?' the nymphette asked despairingly, her sea-blue eyes tearful, her lavish red lips quivering. 'Why can't *I* have multiple orgasms?'

1

They're probably the women I've fucked! Larry reflected, manoeuvring his painfully solid penis into a more comfortable position. 'Worry not. You'll soon be screaming and writhing in the grips of multiple orgasms, Tina,' he reassured her. *Especially when I get my tongue between your luscious folds!* 'What I want you to do is lie on your bed, naked, and masturbate four times every day with a powerful vibrator.'

'But I don't have a vibrator!' the young woman gasped, shocked by the doctor's suggestion.

'No problem. I do a nice line in vibrators. I take Access, Visa . . . and cash, of course.'

'Doctor Lickman! I really don't think . . .'

'Vibrators are ideal for women in your situation, Tina.' *And pretty good for men, too!* 'You'll have no choice other than to surrender to your wonder – wondrous body. The vibrations coursing through your clitoris will force out one mind-blowing orgasm after another.' Pausing, he frowned at his flushing client. 'You do want to scream and writhe and have massive multiple orgasms, don't you?'

'Well, yes, but . . .'

'There we are, then. You might well be suffering from *clitoris nonresponsus*. Using a vibrator will cure the dreadful condition. OK, as this is only your second visit I'll need to know a little more about your sex life, your sexual history, so to speak. Firstly, are you a Roman Catholic?'

'What's religion got to do with sex?'

'Everything! Take Catholic priests, for example – they're all perverted, incestuous homosexual hedonists. You're not a Catholic priest, are you?'

'No, of course I'm not!'

2

'A priestess?'

'No!'

'Have you ever attended the Devil's Mass?'

'The Devil's . . . no!'

'That's a relief! Tell me, do you enjoy oral sex?' Larry asked unashamedly. *Do you relish a tongue licking inside your wet cunt?*

'I . . .'

'Come on, Tina – if I'm to help you, then you must open up.' *Open up your cunt!*

'Well . . .' she began softly, her face flushing deeper with embarrassment as she twisted her long blonde hair nervously round her fingers. 'I'm not used to talking about such intimate things, doctor.'

I am! 'I know you're not. Just relax, Tina. Imagine that I'm not here.'

'Why?'

'It will be easier for you to talk.'

'Where shall I imagine you to be?'

'What?'

'If I'm to imagine that you're not here, then I'll have to imagine you to be elsewhere.'

'Why?'

'Because you have to be somewhere. You think, therefore you are.'

'I am, therefore I think.'

'You can't suddenly disappear, become extinct – non-existent!'

'Well, I'll be here in reality, so . . .'

'But you said . . .'

'No, no! *Imagine* that I'm not here! You don't have to

3

imagine me to be elsewhere, just pretend that I'm not here – imagine that you're talking to yourself.'

'Only lunatics talk to themselves!'

'What do you know about the ranting and raving of lunatics?'

'Nothing, I suppose.'

'Then you're not in a position to discuss them. Let's not deviate – we're not here to talk about lunacy. Try it, Tina – pretend that I'm not here and chat about your sex life, the things you get up to in bed with your husband.'

'Well, we . . .'

'I'll break you in gently. What does he do for a living?'

'He's in espionage.'

'Admirable! My father was a spy.'

'Really?'

'Yes, he wanted me to follow in his footsteps but I had a calling to help women with sexual problems. The calling came when I was fourteen years old.'

'What happened?'

'A girl at school pulled her knickers down and showed me her vaginal crack. After that, I knew where my destiny lay.' *In girls' knickers!*

'That's miraculous!'

'Indeed it was! I believe her to have been sent by God to show me the light – and her vaginal crack.'

'Are you a religious man, doctor?'

'I'm a pagan at heart.'

'I admire that in a man.'

'It's often been said that I'm an admirable man. So, let's get back to your sexual problems. Sixty-nine?' Larry probed, his fathomless eyes locked to hers.

'Sixty-nine what?'

'Soixante-neuf?'

'Who?'

'Sixty-nine is . . . we'll come to that later. How do you feel about your body?'

'How do I feel about it? What do you mean?'

'Let's talk about your body, Tina. I want you to feel comfortable with your body.'

'I *do* feel comfortable.'

'Cunt!'

'Oh, Doctor Lickman!'

'There, you're not at all comfortable!'

'That's a terrible word!'

'It's the proper anatomical term for that particular part of your body, for your sex crack, your vaginal slit, your girlie crack . . . er . . .'

'Is it? I'd always considered it obscene!'

'That's a myth created by the upper classes to have vulgar tradesmen remain vulgar tradesmen.'

'I don't understand.'

Neither do I! 'Tradesmen like using the word cunt because they believe it to be obscene, they like to shock. If they knew the truth, they'd rise above the rank of tradesmen and threaten the upper classes.'

'Oh, I see.'

'The word *cunt* originates from the word *cot*, meaning a small sheath. Your cunt is akin to a small sheath, is it not?'

'Well, yes. But I thought it was a modern word.'

'Good grief, the word's as old as the hills! Older, more than likely. I wonder why people say that?'

'Say what?'

'As old as the hills. They could say, as old as the dales. Anyway, we mustn't bog ourselves down with phraseology. May I have a look at your knickers?'

'My . . . Doctor Lickman!'

'It was just a passing fantasy. I'm sorry, I couldn't help myself. Let's get down to basics, Tina – let's not be shy, prudish, bashful and . . . piss flaps!'

'What are they?'

'Inner lips – wet, pink, inner cunt lips.' *God, I'm stiff!*

'Please, Doctor Lickman!'

'This is a necessary ingredient of the therapy session, Tina. It will help you to relax and open up. Obviously, you're not at all at ease with your body, with your naughty bits. Had I said, *arm* or *foot*, you'd not have flinched an eyelid, would you?'

'Well, no.'

'Shoulder.'

'What?'

'That proves my point. I want you to feel relaxed with your body – at ease with your sexy bits. Repeat after me – wet fleshy cunt lips.'

'Wet fleshy . . . are you sure that . . .'

'Wet fleshy cunt lips, Tina!'

'Wet fleshy cunt lips.'

'Good girl! There, now you're far more comfortable! It stands to reason, if you can't even bring yourself to talk about your cunt, then how do you expect to achieve orgasm? Right, try this one – solid clitoris pulsating in orgasm.'

'Solid clitoris pulsating in orgasm.'

'Excellent! I'll bet you're feeling good about your cunt

now, relaxed, at ease. OK, try another one – stiff throbbing knob sperming in my spunk-thirsty mouth.'

'Stiff throbbing knob sperming . . . Doctor, is this *really* helping me?'

'Yes, of course it is! We're re-educating your subconscious. Right, carry on.'

'Stiff throbbing knob sperming in my spunk-thirsty mouth.'

'Perfect! You're feeling much better now, aren't you? You're feeling loose, promiscuous, immoral, really horny . . . er . . . I mean, free of inhibitions.'

'Well, I suppose so.'

'Good. Talking about your cunt will strip you of inhibitions and allow your suppressed, deep-seated, rampant sexual cravings to surface. We'll try one more. I love having a stiff cock spunking deep inside my juiced-up, tight, cunt hole.'

'I love having a stiff cock spunking deep inside my juiced-up, tight, cunt hole.'

'Superb! When you masturbate, I want you to keep repeating – I love fingering my hot, tight, wet cunt and licking my girlie-juice from my sticky fingers. Try it now.'

'I love fingering my hot, tight, wet cunt and . . . Doctor Lickman, is this *really* necessary?'

'Psychology, Tina. I won't bewilder you with the technical details, suffice to say that it's a well tried and tested method of freeing the mind of inhibitions and allowing orgasms to come. Actually, I've written a paper about it for the *BMJ*. OK, try it again.'

'I love fingering my hot, tight, wet cunt and licking my girlie-juice from my sticky fingers.'

7

'Well done! My star pupil! Female masturbation is extremely important. It's a little known fact, but it's even mentioned in the scriptures.'

'Is it? Are you sure?'

'Oh, yes! For some reason, Moses kept it to himself when he came down from Mount Sinai with the stone tablets, but there was an eleventh commandment – women shalt masturbate habitually to juice their loins.'

'Goodness me!'

'Going back to Catholic priests, do you know why they have Mass?'

'No, come to think of it, I don't.'

'Mass is a code word, it's short for masturbation. It all began centuries ago when they had midnight masturbation sessions. High Masturbation was, and still is, where the lower members of the Church masturbate the higher members, such as bishops and the like.'

'I didn't know that!'

'The Church hierarchy like to keep it a secret. During High Masturbation they use incense, another code word. What they really mean is *incest*. Why do you think choirboys are dressed in frocks? Er . . . we won't go into that. How do you feel about your cunt now, Tina? Would you consider squatting over a mirror, pulling your vaginal lips apart and having a look inside your cunt?'

'Well . . .'

'It's the finest way to familiarize yourself with your inner cuntal flesh. Would you do that?'

'No, no, I wouldn't!'

'Oh, dear! I can see that we're going to have to work a little harder on your sexual problems. Repeat after me – if

I were able, I'd love to lick inside my cunt and lap up my girlie-come.'

'I'd love to lick inside my . . . my cunt and lap up my . . . my girlie-come.'

'Wonderful, Tina! When you get home, squat over a mirror and examine your fleshy folds, it'll help you to bond with your cunt. Cuntal bonding is most important – I do it whenever the opportunity arises.'

'Think of the mess.'

'Use a towel. OK, you mentioned earlier that your husband makes unreasonable sexual demands – what are they, exactly?'

'He wants to hang my naked body upside down from chains fixed to my ankles, with my legs wide open, and use two cucumbers . . .' Her words tailing off as shouting and banging resounded throughout the building, Tina looked at the doctor in bewilderment.

'What on earth's going on!' Larry gasped, leaping to his feet as the shouting grew louder and something crashed to the floor.

'Get your fuckin' 'ands off of me, you fuckin' bitch!'

The obscene words emanated from reception. Larry forced a smile. 'There . . . there seems to be a slight problem!' he began hesitantly, his forehead lined as he shook his head in despair.

'Excuse me, Doctor Lickman,' an exquisite auburn-haired girl smiled as she put her head round the door.

'What is it, Brigit? You know I'm not to be disturbed when I'm trying to get my hands up . . . when I'm with a client. What on earth's going on out there?'

'There's a bit of bother in reception, doctor.'

'A bit of bother?'

'Yes, if you could come and . . .'

'Excuse me, Tina,' Larry smiled at his puzzled client, moving swiftly to the door as screamed expletives reverberated around the building. 'I'm sorry about this, I won't be a minute. I must exert my authority – it's a burden that comes with the position of proprietorship.'

Hurrying down the hall to reception, Larry turned to his pretty secretary. 'Brigit, what the hell's happening? I was just prising some juicy details out of that little slut about her sex life when . . .'

'I don't think you should call the clients sluts!'

'They're *my* clients, so I'll call them what I like! Now, what the hell's going on?' he cried, entering the foyer to find his receptionist, Monica Moodie, brawling with a young blonde client. 'Monica! What on earth's happening?' he bellowed, separating the fighting women. 'Miss Peabody, did you smash the pot plant?' he demanded, turning to the distraught blonde. 'I will not tolerate the mindless smashing of innocent pot plants! It's bad form!'

'Doctor Lickman!' the young tart cried, adjusting her tatty microskirt. 'That fuckin' bitch attacked me!'

'Do you have lesbian tendencies?' Larry frowned, turning to Monica. 'Do you normally attack members of your own sex?'

'I didn't attack her!' Monica returned indignantly.

'You fuckin' did!'

'Please, ladies!' Larry interceded, brushing back his dishevelled dark hair as he gazed at Sally Peabody's firm, braless breasts ballooning her ridiculously tight T-shirt.

Lowering his eyes to her laddered fishnet stockings and scuffed six-inch red stilettos, he frowned. *My God, you're a dirty little slut!* 'What *is* this all about, Sally? What are you doing here? Your appointment is for Thursday.'

'Yeah, I know, but . . . I 'ave to see you *now*, Larry! Oh, shit! I mean, Doctor Lickman.'

'She was going to burst into your consulting room, doctor!' Monica boomed, her tousled brown bob framing her anger-flushed face. 'I had to dive over the counter and stop her!'

'I weren't gonna burst in nowhere, you stupid fuckin' bitch!' Sally spat, poking her tongue out obscenely.

'How *dare* you speak to me like that!'

'I'll speak to you 'ow I like, you cuntless old hag!'

'Well, I have never . . .'

'Ladies, please!' Larry intervened despairingly.

'Huh! She's no lady!' Monica sneered.

'You ain't no fuckin' lady neeva!'

'Sally, please try and curb your disgusting language! Now, what's the urgency to see me?'

'I'm fuckin' well pregnant!'

Jesus bloody Christ! 'Er . . . *uterinus foetus inhabitus?*'

'What?'

'You're pregnant?'

'Yeah, and you're the fuckin' fath—'

'Good grief! Er . . . go to the waiting room, I'll be with you shortly,' Larry interrupted the girl, his face reddening as he propelled the shameless slut through the door. 'OK!' he grinned sheepishly, banging the door shut and turning to Monica. 'Back to work, the fun's over!' Chuckling nervously, he tried to make light of the real mess. 'Er . . . Monica, would

you be good enough to clear away the smashed pot, please? Brigit, would you be so kind as to find Lily and have her deal with my client while I speak to Miss Peabody?'

'What, now?' the girl asked morosely.

'Preferably.'

'But . . .'

'Is there a problem, Brigit?'

'Well, I was going to have my tea break and . . .'

'Clients are far more important than cups of tea, Brigit!'

'Yes, I suppose so,' the reluctant redhead sighed, wandering down the hall, her miniskirt revealing the contours of her fleshy rounded buttocks, her firm youthful thighs.

'Doctor Lickman!' Monica began, her generous bust heaving, inflating her navy-blue cardigan. 'Do you *have* to have that despicable female as a client? Miss Peabody is no better than a common slut who's crawled out of the filth in the gutter! Never in my life have I . . .'

'Don't concern yourself, Monica!' Larry interrupted the middle-aged prude. 'In my position as proprietor of this practice, I'll decide who to have as clients. I realize that Miss Peabody is somewhat lacking on the decency front, a little deficient when it comes to etiquette and eloquence, but she's my client and . . .'

'She's a common strumpet!'

'What's that smell?'

'Smell?'

'Don't you have some filing to do, Monica?'

'No, I don't!'

'Well, some other office duties, then? We must keep busy. Look at the mess on the floor. Idle hands make light work.'

'No, they don't!'

'Don't they? Oh, no, of course they don't! Many hands . . . we must keep ourselves busy.'

'I'm always busy!'

'Ah, but busy doing what, Monica – fighting with the clients?'

'Working!'

'Good! Members of staff such as you keep this place running efficiently.'

'I'm the *only* member of staff who keeps this place running efficiently!'

'There we are, then! What's that saying about the Devil and idle hands?'

'I have no idea. Doctor Lickman, I'm not one to tell tales, but I feel it my duty to inform you that I caught Brigit bending over earlier.'

'Forward or backwards?'

'Forward.'

'Heavenly! Er . . . what's wrong with that? She was probably picking something up. I wonder what it was?'

'She wasn't wearing any knickers! And her buttocks had pink lines across them! I think someone must have whipped . . .'

'Christ, I must take a look! I mean, take a word . . . have a word. Er . . . yes, I'll have a word with her about it, Monica. She probably had cause to slip her panties off and rinse them under the tap.'

'Disgusting!'

'Were they? Perhaps she'd soiled them?' *Creamed them with cunny juice.*

'Don't you find it disgusting?'

13

'I didn't see them, so it's impossible for me to comment. And I'm not prepared to hazard a guess as to the state of Brigit's panties.'

'No! I mean, it's disgusting going around without knickers!'

'It's wonderful! Well, not wonderful, exactly. Er . . . what's the word I'm looking for?'

'Disgusting!'

'Oi, Larry!' Her head peering round the waiting room door, Miss Peabody appeared agitated. 'Are you going to come and talk about our fuckin' kid or what?'

'*Please*, Miss Peabody! I'll be right with you.'

'*Our* kid?' Monica echoed, her piercing eyes glaring at Larry accusingly. 'What have you done?'

'Done? I've done nothing! You shouldn't have impure thoughts, Monica – it doesn't become you.'

'She said *our* kid.'

'She means *their* kid, her and her boyfriend. One would say *our* kid when referring to one's child. As in one's and one's partner's child, one would say *our* child, would one not?'

'No, one would not!'

'Yes, one would! If one had two children, when referring to them one would say one's and one's partner's two children, would two not . . . one would not . . . I mean, would one not?'

'What?'

'One's sorry – one seems to have confused one's brain!'

'You're behaving like a child!'

'I'm thirty-five.'

'That's as maybe . . . I know what you get up to, Doctor Lickman! And I'm not going to stand by and watch you . . .'

'The phone's ringing!' *Saved by the bell!* 'As you're an extremely efficient receptionist, an indispensable asset to the practice, I think you'd better answer it, don't you?'

'I'm going to expose you, Doctor Lickman!'

'Expose me?' *I'd like to expose your cunt . . . on second thoughts!*

'I know far more than you realize! I've been offered a job at Gina Cology's clinic. Unless things change here, I might be tempted to take it.'

'Why don't you take the job, Monica? You might be happier working for that inorgasmic slag of a bitch.'

'She's a very nice woman. She runs her practice in a professional manner, unlike you.'

'Yes, and she's losing money because I'm taking all her clients! Telephone, Monica!' *Bloody woman!*

Slipping into the waiting room, Larry closed the door to confront his wayward client. His dark eyes frowned as he scrutinized Sally Peabody's dishevelled peroxided tresses, her smudged lipstick. Standing with her long legs apart, her stockinged thighs revealed by her almost nonexistent skirt, Larry imagined her panties, bulging with her labia. The ultimate tart, he surmised, watching her take a packet of cigarettes from her red plastic handbag.

'Now, Sally, what's all this nonsense about you being . . .'

'It ain't fuckin' nonsense! I'm fuckin' pregnant!' she hissed, lighting a cigarette and blowing smoke high into the air.

'Well, don't look at me!' Larry returned, nervously straightening his tie and clearing his throat. 'Is it still raining? We're not having a very good summer, are we?

15

I blame the Chinese, they shouldn't be allowed to pollute the air with steam from their laundries.'

'You fuckin' well stuffed me up the duff!'

'Shush, don't shout! And I wish you'd stop swearing, it's unladylike.'

'Are you sayin' I ain't no lady?'

'Yes, *no*! Let's be sensible about this, Sally. I mean, it could have been one of a hundred men – a thousand men, even! A million!'

'I ain't no fuckin' tart!'

You're the epitome of tarts! 'I'm not saying that you're a tart, Sally. All I'm saying is . . . hang on a minute, we've never copulated.'

'Eh? We ain't never done what?'

'You have a wonderful way with words, Sally – did you attend the Sorbonne? Have you considered elocution classes?'

'What? What ain't we never done?'

'We ain't never done . . . God, you've got me at it now! We've never done it, we've never had intercourse.'

'We fuckin' 'ave!'

'Sally, I've only ever come in your mouth, so how on earth could I be to blame?'

'I know you spunked in me mouth, but you done it up me bumhole a couple of weeks back!'

'Shush! Don't you know anything? To make you pregnant, I'd have to spunk up me pussy . . . I mean, up *your* pussy. And you know I would never do that because I don't know where your pussy's been.' *I dread to think!*

'Me cunt ain't been nowhere! It's always been between me fuckin' legs!'

'No, what I mean is . . . oh, never mind. You really should stop swearing, Sally.'

'Why the fuck should I?'

'Well, because . . . look, why don't you go and tell your boyfriend the unhappy . . . the happy news?'

'Oh, yeah, I 'adn't thought about that drunken fuckin' bastard! I wonder if 'e's the fuckin' father?'

'Christ only knows who the fucking . . . of course he's the father, Sally.'

'Yeah, it could be 'im – 'e's been givin' me a lot of shags lately.'

'There you are, then. Right, off you go!'

'I don't suppose you've got time to give me one up me arse?' the girl asked, provocatively licking her smiling lips. 'I like your cock spunking up me bum!'

'Shush! Monica will hear you, for goodness sake! As it is, she knows far too much of my escapades. I have a lot of work to do so . . . Thursday, I'll see you on Thursday, as usual.'

'Oh, right. I'll go and tell me boyfriend about the fuckin' brat. Shall I bring the fuckin' milk bottle and the fuckin' Vaseline with me?'

'Yes, bring the fucking . . . I mean . . . good grief! I'll see you on Thursday, Sally.'

Breathing a sigh of relief as the tart left the building, Larry walked across the foyer to reception. 'Everything in order, Monica?' he humoured the grumpy woman.

'As well as can be expected for a place like this!'

'Good, good! It makes me so happy to see you enjoying your work.'

'I'm not enjoying my work! I'm not a skivvy! I wasn't employed to clear up smashed pot plants!'

'No, you weren't, but it just goes to show what an adept all-rounder you are.'

'Dogsbody, more like!'

'Have you always been of such a happy and joyous disposition, Monica, or was it an attribute you picked up during your long and tedious journey through life?'

'What?'

'Have you always been so cheerful?'

'I'm not cheerful!'

'Oh! And there was me thinking how happy you were! Hormones, I would imagine. Terrible weather for the time of year, don't you agree? Right, I'd better see how Lily's getting on. You know what these trainee sex therapists are like.'

'What are they like?'

'Er . . . ah, telephone, Monica.'

'What about it?'

'It's ringing.'

'No, it's not!'

'Oh, my mistake. Any luck with the schoolgirlies?'

'Schoolgirlies?'

'Yes, the sixth-formers. Has the headmistress phoned about . . .'

'Oh, yes, she did phone. She didn't seem to think your idea acceptable.'

'Really? You *do* surprise me.'

'She said that eighteen-year-old schoolgirls shouldn't need to see a sex therapist.'

'That's as maybe, but I need to see eighteen-year-old schoolgirlies! Er . . . I explained in my letter that . . .'

'She's giving it some thought, she said she'd phone back.'

'Excellent! I can't wait to get my hands on . . . to talk to the little girlies . . . I mean, young ladies.'

'You don't plan to touch them, do you?'

Of course I do! Hot, tight, wet, juicy . . . 'Monica! What *are* you suggesting?'

'You know very well what I'm suggesting.'

'My gast is flabbered! How can you have such immoral thoughts? I always thought you to be virtuous, wholesome, upright.'

'I *am*! It's you who's . . .'

'Do you honestly think that I'd soil and defile . . .'

'I don't think, I *know*! What's in that room at the end of the hall?'

'Which room?'

'The one you keep locked.'

'Oh, this and that – nothing of interest to you, or the police. Well, I'd better go and check up on Lily. I'll leave you to carry on with the good work, Monica.'

Entering his consulting room, Larry closed the door and smiled at Lily. 'Everything all right?' he asked the appetizing young blonde.

'No, not really,' she whimpered, her expression mirroring her anxiety, her blue eyes tearful.

God, now what? 'What's the problem, Tina?' he asked, turning to his bemused client. 'What's happened?'

'I was telling her about hanging upside down from chains with my legs open, and she burst out crying!' the young woman gasped, perplexed by Lily's incessant wailing.

'There's no need to cry, Lily!' Larry consoled the girl,

patting her shoulder. 'We're here to *help* our clients with their problems, not *cry* over them!'

'I'm sorry, Doctor Lickman. It wasn't the chains, it was her breasts!'

'Tina's breasts? What about them?'

'Her husband sucks them!' Lily sobbed uncontrollably.

'That's what they're for. There's nothing wrong with that, Lily. Mouthing breasts and sucking nipples is all part and parcel of a disgusting . . . of a healthy sex life. You must get rid of this phobia concerning female breasts, you *really* must!'

'I live in perpetual dread of my breasts!'

'Er . . . Tina, I think that had better be enough for today,' Larry smiled. 'Ask Monica to make you an appointment for next week. And remember to repeat the words during . . . and don't forget to place a mirror on the floor.'

'What about a vibrator?'

'Oh, yes. See Brigit on your way out, she'll fix you up. Ask her for a King Dick – they're expensive, but most effective. Until next week, Tina.'

'Yes, doctor,' Tina smiled, rising to her feet. 'I hope Lily will be all right.'

'She'll be fine!'

'And I thought *I* had problems!' Tina sighed as she breezed from the room.

Perching himself on the edge of the desk, Larry passed Lily a handkerchief. 'What is it about breasts that distresses you so?' he asked the tormented girl as she wiped her eyes.

'They're evil!' she wailed, her bottom lip quivering. 'They're like evil one-eyed monsters! They lurk beneath my quilt in the dark of the night, peering out at me! When I'm in the bath they surface like monsters from

the deep and stare at me! They're waiting to get me, I know it!'

'Lily, Lily! They're not waiting to get you!'

'Yes, they are! The other evening I was sitting on the sofa in my dressing gown watching television and the left one popped out. Its horrendous brown eye leered at me! They despise me! They're in league! They're working together, planning to get me!'

'Good grief, Lily! When did this peculiar phobia first arise?'

'When they arose from the depths of my chest. I was twelve when they sneaked up in the night and clung like leeches to me. They grew and grew, feeding on my fear until they were big and strong! Now I'm eighteen, they're big enough and strong enough to get me!'

'I'll have to give you regular therapy sessions, Lily. I think we'll start the sessions this afternoon. How's your phobia of penises, still bad?'

'Terrible! Like long slippery snakes, ugly pink slugs, they lie in wait! They have purple heads with one eye! They retract their pink helmets and stare at me!'

'From where did this incredible phobia originate?'

'At school. A boy showed me his penis and I stroked and rubbed it – and it spat venom at me!'

'Lily, I'm going to show you my penis. It's a fine specimen and . . .'

'No!'

'Yes! You must get over this ridiculous phobia! How can you have a normal sex life if you're afraid of your breasts and men's penises? I want you to hold my penis, get to know it intimately, fondle it, kiss it and . . .'

21

'No, I don't want to see it!' the distressed girl cried, fleeing the room. 'Argh! A disgusting, horrible, sluglike one-eyed monster!' she wailed, dashing down the hall.

'Lily! Lily, come back!'

Shaking his head in despair as the phone rang, Larry grabbed the receiver. 'Ah, Monica, everything all right on the western front?' he enquired jovially.

'Lily Dyke has just run out of the building screaming about one-eyed monsters!'

'Yes, I know. It's nothing to concern yourself with, she has a natural tendency to run out of buildings screaming about one-eyed monsters. Her peculiar psychological disturbance stems from an atrocious childhood experience.'

'You shouldn't employ her, you know she's a lesbian – and mentally unstable!'

'She's bisexual. Are you bisexual, Monica?'

'Certainly not!'

'That accounts for it, then.'

'Accounts for what?'

'Nothing.'

'Anyway, I'm not calling to discuss Lily Dyke. There's a man at reception to see you.'

'Oh, right. What does he want, do you know?'

'He wouldn't say.'

'Would you say he looks like a civil servant?'

'Why would I say that?'

'In your considered opinion, would you say he looks like a civil servant?'

'How would I know?'

'By considering your opinion, Monica.'

'Stop trying to confuse me!'

22

'You don't need my help to confuse yourself! Is he carrying a briefcase?'

'No, he's not.'

'Thank God for small mercies. OK, send him along.'

Bidding his visitor enter as a loud knock sounded on the door, Larry smiled benevolently. 'Good morning, I'm Doctor Larry Lickman. What can I do for you?'

'You told my wife to masturbate with two vibrators!' the bristling, balding man yelled.

'Er . . . Mr . . .'

'Schmidtbag.'

'Ah, yes, Mr Schmidtbag. What an unfortunate name. Are you of German descent?'

'Certainly not! I'm British through and through.'

'Have you ever considered deed poll? I have it from a reliable source that it's inexpensive.'

'I have not come here to discuss my name! You sexually assaulted my wife!'

'That's quite an accusation, Mr Schmidtbag! I find your effrontery most displeasing!'

'Well, I'm waiting!'

'You're not asking me to sexually assault *you*, are you?'

'Don't be ridiculous! I'm waiting for an explanation.'

'Aren't we all, Mr Schmidtbag – aren't we all? An explanation as to why we're here. We're just grains of sand in a vast desert . . .'

'My wife told me that you . . .'

'Er . . . your beautiful wife, Gale, has deep-seated sexual problems. She's suffering from a rare condition known as *clitoris inactivus*. Using vibrators will . . .'

'You interfered with her anal canal!'

'Interfered with her anal canal?'

'You took her into a room, locked the door, and forced her to remove her clothes!'

'I might well have had reason to examine her, yes. I probably checked her for *rectus crampus*, as I do with most clients. Haven't I seen you on television?'

'Of course you haven't!'

'I could have sworn that I've seen a photograph of you on Crimewatch.'

'What *are* you talking about?'

'Or was it a building society video?'

'A building society . . .'

'Are you in possession of a balaclava and a sawn-off shotgun?'

'What? I want an explanation! You rubbed my wife's clitoris and put your fingers into her private orifices!'

'Only in the line of duty, Mr Schmidtbag – only in the line of duty. After all, I am a qualified doctor. Doctor Larry Lickman, D.M., D.Sc., F.P.S., F.R.C.P., S.H.I.T.'

'S.H.I.T?'

'Society of Hormone Implant Techniques. I am also a highly qualified C.U.N.T.'

'You're a cunt?'

'Yes, a Cervical and Uterine Neuroma Technician.'

'I don't care *what* you are, it's disgusting! You tied my wife down to an examination couch with lengths of rope!'

'Did I? Good grief, I don't remember doing that! Are you sure your wife's not having delusions?'

'Of course she's not having delusions!'

'Hallucinations?'

24

'You're mad! What's the idea?'

'Which idea?'

'You should be struck off!'

I was never struck on! 'Er . . . Gale is unable to achieve orgasm, so . . .'

'Women shouldn't have orgasms, it's not their place to enjoy sex!'

'Why ever not? Are you a misogynist?'

'Devout! Once they begin to enjoy sex, they'll be running off getting it anywhere and everywhere!'

'Well, I wouldn't say that.'

'I'll have her fanny sewn up, that's what I'll do!'

'You can't do that, Mr Schmidtbag – you'll affect her toilet.'

'She's never coming back here! You're a sad sexual pervert!'

That's true!

'A vile, disgusting, filthy sexual deviant!'

'Excuse me, but I am *not* a Catholic priest!'

'A Catholic priest? You're mentally insane! You'll be hearing from my solicitor!' the enraged spouse stormed, charging from the room. 'I'll see to it that you're struck off!'

'Good, I enjoy mingling with fellow professionals! Good day, Mr Shitbag!'

'Problems, problems!' Larry sighed, ambling to the window to see Monica in conversation with a man in the car park. 'What's she up to now? I don't like men with briefcases, they unnerve me.' Going to investigate he found Brigit hovering in the foyer, her miniskirt revealing the gentle

curves of her naked buttocks as she bent over to scratch her knee.

'Ah, Brigit, what's Monica doing talking to that man in the car park?'

'She's talking to him.'

'Yes, I know that! Who is he?'

'Who?'

'Good grief! The man in the car park – who is he?'

'Mr Venereal.'

'Mr Venereal? Is he infectious?'

'Infectious?'

'Where's he from, Brigit?'

'He's from the health authority. I overheard Monica talking to him on the phone.'

'Yes, and?'

'She was talking to Mr Venereal.'

'Yes, but what was she saying?'

'She was saying that this place should be closed down.'

'Closed down? Is she mad? Why does she think the place should be closed down?'

'I don't know, I can't remember.'

'What else did she . . . oh, never mind. When Monica returns, send her to my consulting room, will you?'

'Send her to your consulting room. Yes, I think I can remember that.'

'Do you want me to write it down for you?'

'No, I think I can remember.'

'I hope you can!' Larry scowled, wondering why he employed the stupid girl as he returned to his room. *Because she's got a beautiful cunt, I suppose!*

The phone was ringing as he entered the office. 'Now

what?' he sighed wearily as he grabbed the receiver and perched himself on the edge of his desk. 'Dr Lickman here.'

'Ah, good morning, Doctor Lickman – Reverend Mother Barren-Womb speaking, headmistress of The Sacred Blood-ied Heart of Our Lady of the Damned Convent.'

'That's no way to speak of your convent, Mother Barren-Womb!'

'What do you mean?'

'Calling your fine educational establishment a damned convent.'

'No, Our Lady of the Damned – Convent.'

'Why is it a damned convent? Has Satan visited you?'

'It's not a damned convent, you silly man! It's Our Lady of the Damned, pause, Convent.'

'Oh, yes, I see.'

'Now I've forgotten why I'm phoning you! Oh, yes, with regard to your letter. I have given your proposal a great deal of thought and . . .'

'Good, good! And which wise decision have you come to?'

'The answer is no!'

'Oh! One would have thought it a good idea to have the girls discuss intimate sexual matters with an eminent Doctor of Sexual Fulfilment, would two not?'

'Two?'

'Yes, if I'm one and you're the other one, then you must be two. You're the second person, you see – one, two.'

'What? Two does not . . . one does *not* think it a good idea.'

'But, Reverend Mother, have some regard for the girls'

27

welfare. Think back to when you were eighteen and . . . on second thoughts, you'd better not!'

'I see no reason for the girls to discuss . . .'

'There's every reason. There are certain things about teen-age girls that you don't understand, Mother Barren-Womb. Certain mysterious . . .'

'Such as what?'

'I'm not sure, I can't remember offhand. Besides, I'm not at liberty to say – I'm sworn to secrecy by the BMA. Anyway, the girls would benefit greatly from a one-to-one talk with me. Look at the world today, there are sexual perverts on the loose worldwide! Now, surely, you don't want your girls to leave school and fall prey to such vile, debased and perverted sexual deviants, do you?'

'Well, I . . . a one-to-one talk, you say?'

A one-to-one fuck. 'Yes, a one-to-two talk in comfortable surroundings and in complete and utter confidence.'

'All right, I agree. I'll ring back later and make the appointments with your receptionist.'

'Excellent! A most wise decision, Mother Barren-Womb. You've obviously been guided by the Lord.'

'Yes, obviously.'

'Your interest in the girls' welfare has demonstrated your belief in the Lord admirably!'

'Thank you. Goodbye, doctor.'

Meditating at his desk, Larry wondered whether the time had come to dismiss the moody Miss Moodie. There was no denying she was efficient, running reception and the appointments system commendably. But she was always

prying, training her beady eye on him, her radar ear to closed doors. He'd suspected for some time that the woman was a spy sent by his rival, Gina Cology, who'd been trying to get his flourishing practice outlawed. But as yet, Monica had come up with no positive proof of her employer's debauched ways. 'If she knew half the things I get up to in the examination room!' Larry chuckled smugly as a loud knock sounded on the door.

'Ah, Monica!' he smiled as the portly woman entered the room. 'Brigit remembered, then?'

'Remembered what?'

'To tell you . . . never mind.'

'You wanted to see me?'

'Yes, yes, I did. Please, be seated.'

'I'd rather stand.'

'The prerogative's yours, Monica.'

'There's your mail,' the matron mumbled, dumping a pile of letters on the desk.

'Oh, right. Now, Monica, we've had our differences in the past.'

'I know we have!'

'Yes, of course. Er . . . who was that man you were speaking to in the car park?'

'He . . . he was lost – I directed him.'

'A wise decision. Where did you direct him to?'

'To where he wanted to go, of course.'

'Yes, yes, quite. He wasn't a private client, was he?'

'What do you mean?'

'You're not moonlighting, giving sex therapy on the side, in the car park?'

'No!'

'As you well know, moonlighting is rewarded with instant dismissal – especially in the car park. I made the rules, and I'll stick to them . . . you'll stick to them. Have you spoken to Gina Cology recently?'

'Er . . . no, not since she offered me a job last week.'

'I see. One by one, we're taking all her clients, Monica. Although I say it myself, they come to me because of my professionalism.'

'Hardly!'

'Tell me, Monica, how's life treating you?'

'Life *never* treats me!'

'How sad! How's your leg, the one you broke some time ago at the old bags' . . . I mean, the old girls' reunion?'

'What's my leg got to do with anything?'

'I was only asking after your welfare. It's my duty to care for my staff. It's unfortunate . . . fortunate that you didn't break your neck when you fell over in your drunken stupor. How is your drink problem?'

'I wasn't drunk! I'd only had two glasses of wine!'

'Yes, yes, of course you had.'

'Your next client rang to say she'll be late.'

'Who was that?'

'Miss Kneetrembler, which I very much doubt is her real name.'

'Some clients don't like to use their real names, Monica.'

'No, obviously not!'

'Change the names to protect the guilty, that's what I say.'

'You would!'

'Talking of which, how's your husband?'

'I had cause to throw him out.'

'Had you made his life difficult?'

'Of course not! He made *my* life impossible!'

'Being thrown out of the house must have been an immense relief for him.'

'It was an immense relief for *me*!'

'What had he done? Nothing illegal, I hope?'

'He had disgusting habits which . . . it's personal.'

'I'd blame myself if I were you, Monica.'

'I don't blame myself!'

'Was it sex?'

'Sex?'

'The reason for the irreparable marital breakdown – sex, was it?'

'We never had sex! I'm a Catholic.'

'Ah, say no more, Monica – say no more.'

'I must get back to reception.'

'Yes, back to work. I'm sorry to hear of your broken marriage. Still, it happens to the worst of us.'

Opening the mail as Monica flounced from the room, Larry sighed. 'The Inland bloody Revenue, Customs and Sexcise, water-sports bill, fart-gas bill, dog-and-bone bill, electricity . . . how is anyone supposed to make a bloody profit? In one bloody hand, and straight out of the other! Ah, Brigit,' he smiled as his secretary minced into the room.

'Monica said that you wanted to see me, doctor.'

'Did I? Ah, yes, so I did. Sit down, Brigit. Now, word has it that you're not wearing any panties. Is there any truth in this allegation?'

'Yes, there is.'

31

'May I ask why, Brigit? I mean, we've had complaints from clients in the past concerning your . . . how can I put it? Concerning your blatant exhibitionism.'

'I don't like wearing panties, Doctor Lickman, they chafe my pussy lips.'

'But your skirts are so short that everyone can see your . . .'

'If you remember, it was *your* idea that I shouldn't wear panties.'

'Ah, yes, so it was. But what I didn't realize was that you were going to wear skirts so short that . . .'

'I did as you asked.'

'What did you do, Brigit?'

'Do you remember saying that you were heavily into schoolgirls and you wanted me to look like one?'

'Yes, yes, I do. I must buy you a gymslip. Yes, gymslips will be our uniforms. Well, your uniform. I don't think I'd look good in a gymslip! Actually, I might. Er . . . what did you do, Brigit?'

'I've shaved my pussy, as you asked me to. Would you like to see it?'

Would I? 'Er . . . yes, definitely!'

'You were right, it looks much better without hair covering it,' the young temptress smiled, lifting her skirt up. 'Do you like it? Do I look like a schoolgirl?'

'God, yes!'

Gazing at the girl's tightly closed pinken crack, Larry gasped. Her smooth hairless sex hillocks inviting a wet tongue, he focused on her moist inner lips, protruding beautifully from her vaginal slit. *Oh, to drink the nectar of sex from your cunt!* Lifting her skirt higher, she looked

down between the swell of her firm breasts at her young luscious girl-crack and smiled.

'Isn't she wonderful?' Brigit asked, lifting her head and gazing at the doctor.

'Yes, wonderful! She's the most wonderful pussy I've ever seen!'

'Would you like to finger her?'

'Where's Monica?'

'In reception, on the phone.'

'OK, lock the door, Brigit. Miss Kneetrembler is going to be late for her appointment, so I have some time to spare.'

'Can't we go into the bondage room?'

'Yes, yes, all right,' Larry grinned, taking a key from his desk drawer.

Slipping through the hall with his select cargo in tow, Larry unlocked the door to his bondage room, ushering the pretty girl inside and bolting the door behind him. Switching the light on, he smiled at her. Her brown eyes sparkling, reflecting her burning passion for sexual gratification, she licked her lavish red lips and returned his smile.

'What would you like me to do, doctor?' she asked impishly.

'Clothes off, Brigit!' Larry ordered her excitedly.

'Oh, Larry, you *are* naughty!' the girl giggled, tugging her miniskirt down her long shapely legs, exposing her shaved girl-crack. 'What awful things are you going to do to me?'

'You'll see!' he chuckled, gazing lasciviously at her pert breasts, her dilated nipples, as she slipped her blouse and bra off. 'OK, climb onto the couch. I want you on your stomach with your legs wide open.'

'Oh, Doctor Lickman, you're not going to do anything

terrible to my bottom, are you?' laughed the sex-crazed Lolita, taking her position on the padded table, her taut, rounded buttocks covered in weals from the caning Larry had administered the previous day. 'Pretend that I'm a naughty little schoolgirl and you're my perverted biology teacher!'

'You *are* a naughty little schoolgirl, Brigit – and I *am* your perverted biology teacher! I'm going to tie you down, and then I'm afraid I'll have to give you an anal examination.'

'Oh, doctor! You're not going to stick something up my bum, are you?'

'I have to, Brigit – it's my duty as a doctor. Now, lie still and I'll bind your wrists and ankles with rope. I don't want you escaping when I push a candle up your bum.'

'Oh, I'm only eighteen! You will be rough with me, won't you?'

'Extremely rough!'

Securing the giggling girl's naked body, tying her ankles to the legs of the couch, binding her wrists, Larry ran his fingers up her inner thighs and massaged her hairless girl-lips. Her warm vaginal groove drenched with her lubricious juices of arousal, he slipped his finger into her sex valley and located the hot entrance to her tight love sheath. Driving his finger into her spasming lust duct, massaging her inner flesh, he planted a kiss on her quivering buttock.

'Now then,' he began pensively, slipping his finger out of her pussy sheath and taking a large candle from a shelf. 'Yes, I think this is big enough!' he chuckled. 'First, I'll lubricate your bumhole with some of this.' Unscrewing a jar of honey and parting her buttocks, opening her bottom crease, he poured a liberal amount of the golden syrup over her brown ring, watching gleefully as the thick liquid ran sluggishly

down between her swollen vaginal lips. 'Right, here it comes, my little beauty!' he cried, pressing the sharp end of the candle against the sensitive portal to her inner core.

Gasping as Larry drove the waxen shaft deep into her anal duct, stretching her delicate brown tissue, Brigit begged him to finger her hot cunt. 'Ah, the candle feels heavenly!' she breathed as he parted her fleshy vaginal lips, eyeing her urethral opening nestling just inside her sex duct. 'Finger me! I want to feel your fingers deep inside my cunt!'

'Who's in there?' Monica called agitatedly, hammering on the door as Larry drove three fingers into Brigit's hot sex cavern and massaged her drenched vaginal walls. 'I know you're in there, Doctor Lickman!'

Silently finger-fucking the whimpering girl, Larry grabbed the candle with his free hand and thrust the phallus in and out of her tight anal tube, causing her to quiver as the sensations of debased sex permeated her pelvis. 'Faster!' Brigit whispered excitedly, her cunt juices pouring over Larry's thrusting fingers. 'Oh, God! God, that's heavenly!'

'Who's in there?' Monica called again, her fists thumping on the door. 'Doctor Lickman! Doctor Lickman!'

'Thank God for that!' Larry breathed as the telephone resounded around the hall, sending the she-devil scurrying back to reception. 'She'll be the bloody death of me!'

'Ah, ah! And me! Oh, God, my . . . my cunt! My bum!' Brigit wailed as her orgasm welled from her rhythmically contracting womb. 'Ah, coming! Coming!'

Her leashed body shuddering violently as her climax peaked, Brigit raised her hips, projecting her tensed buttocks, offering the open sexual centre of her naked body to the doctor. Her anal ring taut around the thrusting phallus,

her rectal duct repeatedly inflating and deflating, sending electrifying sensations through her quivering pelvis, she cried out in her sexual delirium. On and on Larry pistoned his fingers into the whimpering girl's cunt, ramming the huge candle deep into her arse, bringing her the sexual gratification, the debauched sexual perversity, she craved.

Finally slowing his rhythm, allowing her to drift gently down from her paradise, he slipped his fingers from her spasming vaginal canal and licked them clean. 'Mmm, you taste nice!' he breathed, lapping up her sticky girl-come. Sliding the candle out of her hot bottom-hole, he unzipped his trousers and unleashed his erect penis. 'OK, stand on the floor and bend over the couch and I'll give you a good fucking!' he chuckled as he released the trembling girl.

Slipping off the couch, Brigit leaned over it, her feet wide apart, her cunt lips distended between her smooth inner thighs. Resting her arms and head on the couch, she gasped as Larry ran his cock up and down her dripping vaginal fissure, lubricating his knob with her copious vaginal fluid and sticky honey in readiness to penetrate her tight love-mouth. Eyeing her inflamed anal portal, the golden honey smothering her bottom crease, the curvaceous flesh of her buttocks, he drove his glans deep into her vaginal duct.

'Jesus, your cunt's hot and tight!' he gasped, his knob resting against her cervix, her cunny lips stretched tautly around the base of his rigid cock.

'God, and you're so big!' Brigit moaned, her juices decanting, marinating his heavy balls. 'Fuck me! Fuck me, I want your spunk up my cunt!' she demanded crudely, gripping the far side of the examination couch. 'Really give it to me!'

Withdrawing his knob, Larry grabbed the trembling girl's

hips and drove his glans deep into her cunt with a vengeance. His belly slapping her weal-lined buttocks, his balls smacking her fleshy mons, he took the girl to her second shuddering orgasm, her wails resounding throughout the building as his sperm gushed, filling her tight love tunnel. Again and again he drove his pulsating knob deep into her accommodating cuntal sheath, his spunk flowing, oozing from her bloated hole and running over his swinging balls, splattering her twitching inner thighs.

'Doctor Lickman! Doctor Lickman, I know you're in there!' Monica bellowed, thumping on the door as Brigit's orgasmic cries reverberated around the room. 'I know what you're up to! Who's in there with you?'

'I'm . . . I'm only looking for something!' he gasped as his balls finally drained.

'Let me in!' Monica cried. 'There's someone to see you!'

'Ah! Ah! Who . . . who is it?'

'Mr Ingram Ravenhugh.'

'Ingram . . . God, you're hot!'

'I'm not? I'm not what?'

'Nothing. I'm just coming, Monica. I've come!'

'You've won? What have you won?'

'Ask him to come back later!'

Slipping his glistening member out of Brigit's drowning pussy, Larry leaned on the examination couch, steadying himself as the girl hauled her quivering body up. 'God, that was good!' he gasped. 'You're a bloody good fuck!'

'And it was close!' Brigit giggled, kneeling before him and licking her cunny juice from his wet shaft. 'She knows what you're up to, Larry,' she warned, lapping up the heady blend of spunk and girl-cream from his bulbous glans.

'I'll have to get rid of the old bat, there's no other way!' he gasped as Brigit engulfed his knob within her hot mouth and gently sucked. 'The trouble is, she knows too much.'

'He's coming back later!' Monica hissed through the door. 'He was carrying a briefcase!'

'Jesus fucking Christ!' Larry whispered agitatedly. 'Who the hell could it have been?'

'I don't know,' Brigit murmured, slipping the meaty morsel from her mouth and climbing to her feet.

'Are you coming, Doctor Lickman?'

'I can't, not yet, anyway!'

'What?'

'Yes, yes right away, Monica!'

Composing himself, Larry zipped his trousers. About to open the door, he heard Monica dash down the hall to answer the phone. 'Saved by the bell – again!' he chuckled jubilantly.

'Quick, let's get out of here,' Brigit whispered as she finished dressing. 'This is our chance.'

'I'll stay here for a while,' Larry replied. 'You go and calm the old bat down, and I'll join you shortly.'

'Have you ever fucked Lily?'

'No, but I intend to at my earliest convenience. Why do you ask?'

'No reason. I'll see you later.'

Bolting the door as Brigit slipped out of the room, Larry reclined on the examination couch wondering who the briefcase man could be. *Either the VAT man or the tax man!* he reflected fearfully. *Unless Gina Cology has contacted the BMA!*

Chapter Two

'Doctor Lickman must have said where he was going, Brigit!' Monica snapped. 'I've not seen him for over two hours!'

'He said that he had to go out, but he didn't say where to,' the flustered girl replied, wondering what Larry was doing in the bondage room. 'Perhaps it's a secret?'

'A secret? This is ridiculous, it *really* is! Miss Kneetrembler couldn't wait any longer, there have been several phone calls . . . he has no idea how to run his practice, no idea at all! It's shambolic! I don't know who was in that room with him, but I'll find out! And where's Lily Dyke? She ran off ages ago screaming about one-eyed monsters!'

'It's no good asking me, Monica, because I don't know.'

'It's like working in a lunatic asylum! That girl's mentally insane – deranged! Well, I have a dental appointment – you'll have to hold the fort until I get back.'

'OK, I'll see you later.'

'I'll only be half an hour or so. Actually, between you and me, I'm not going to the dentist.'

'Oh? Where are you going, then?'

'I have a meeting with Mr Venereal, the man from the health authority.'

'What about?'

'I have to fill him in with a few details concerning . . . it

39

doesn't matter. I'm also going to see Gina Cology. I'll see you later.'

Sitting pretty at reception, a sticky cocktail of honeyed sperm and girl-come oozing from her inflamed vagina to stain the back of her red miniskirt, Brigit watched Monica don her plastic raincoat and leave the building. Idly slipping her hand up her skirt and toying with her wet inner lips, her insatiable erect clitoris, Brigit smiled as Larry emerged from the examination room and ambled over to her.

'What have you been doing in there?' Brigit asked, licking her sticky fingers as her boss leaned on the counter, his tanned face smiling.

'I had a kip, I was feeling tired – it's the pressure of life. Where's the old bat?'

'I can't remember. Oh, yes, I can – she's gone to the dentist.'

'That's a blessing. Let's hope he takes her tongue out!'

'Actually, she hasn't gone to the dentist.'

'Why did you say that she had, then? You weren't lying, were you?'

'She said she was going to the dentist, and then she said she wasn't.'

'An inexplicable change of mind?'

'Presumably.'

'I hope she didn't have the foresight to cancel her appointment. You know what dentists are like these days, they charge for missed appointments. So, where *has* Monica gone?'

'I can't remember. Yes, I can! She's gone to meet the man from the health authority, Mr Venereal.'

'Why?'

'I don't know. Oh, she's also going to see Gina Cology.'

'Gina Cology? Monica's up to something, Brigit, I know it. She is a bitch, she *really* is! I'll have to perform a clitectomy on her, and a nipectomy, and a . . . I believe her to be a Satanic high priestess.'

'Do you?'

'A black witch! She should be burned at the stake – naked. Come to think of it, she said she's a Catholic – I reckon she's gone to Black Mass.'

'What, with Mr Venereal?'

'No, with that sorceress, Gina Cology. She's probably the Antichrist! Or would it be the Antichristess? No, it would be the Antichrist because . . .'

'Who, Gina?'

'Yes. Gina will have me exposed if I'm not careful. I reckon Monica's in league with the cow. Did you know that Monica's thrown her husband out?'

'No, she rarely speaks to me.'

'Think yourself lucky! She reckoned that he had disgusting habits. I wonder what he got up to? Probably something as harmless as wanking over her tits while she was sleeping. Do you reckon she's got a clitoris?'

'I would imagine so!'

'If she has, I'll bet it's never brought her an orgasm. Perhaps she's a man in drag?'

'I'm sure she's a woman, Larry!'

'Are you? I'll have to check her birth certificate. Mind you, she's probably had it falsified. Presumably she had a mother and father, unless she was found under a bush. If she *is* a woman, then she's a disgrace to females the world

over. She should be stripped of her sexuality forthwith. Good God, imagine fucking her!'

'I'd rather not! Why don't you get rid of her?'

'It's not as easy as that, she knows too much about me. Murder has crossed my mind on occasion.'

'That would be a messy business.'

'What's that smell?'

'You missed Miss Kneetrembler. Apparently, she couldn't wait,' Brigit imparted, idly running her finger down the appointments book.

'Not to worry – that poor girl's beyond help, beyond redemption!'

'Oh! Mrs Jezebel will be here at twelve, and it's now five to!'

'Right, I'll be in my room,' Larry responded, dashing down the hall. 'Send her along when she arrives!'

Combing his hair and straightening his tie, Larry grinned. Young Jessica Jezebel was one of his favourite clients. Naive beyond belief, incredibly gullible for her twenty years, she'd do anything he asked of her, believing that he was giving his all to help her with her sexual problems. Her first visit to the clinic had been three months previously when she'd confessed she felt the size of her clitoris to be inadequate. Examining her, Larry had declared that he'd be more than happy to undertake remedial clitoral massage sessions to solve the problem. He'd divulged, too, that she was suffering from a rare vaginal problem and unusual anal tract condition, treatable only by the regular use of medicinal candles. Taking the girl to the examination room, the bondage room, and coercing her to endure his indecent sexual acts,

Larry relished the young housewife's weekly visits. As yet, he'd not slipped his solid penis into her tight vagina, but there was plenty of time for that!

'Come!' he called in reply to a tap on the door. *Over my face!*

'Hallo, doctor!' his pretty client trilled as she breezed into the room. 'Here I am again!'

'Yes, here you are again! Take a seat, Jessica,' he invited her, eyeing her tight minidress, her deep cleavage. *Want a pearl necklace?*

With long, jet-black hair and a sun-kissed, curvaceous young body, this filly was a rare little beauty, Larry surmised. He could not wait to get his fingers between her swollen vaginal lips, deep into her hot cunt. She'd be expecting the usual examination and sexual massage but, this week, the doctor had other exciting plans for her – debased plans!

'So, Jessica, how are you?' he asked as he sat opposite her and gazed into her big dark eyes. *Hot and wet?*

'I'm fine.'

'Breasts OK, nice and firm? Nipples looking good, long, erect?'

'Yes, better than ever since you've been massaging my breasts with your special essence of testes.'

'The white liquid is very expensive at twenty pounds a teaspoonful, but it's well worth you spending the extra money.'

'Where do you get it from, doctor?'

'Er . . . locally. I have it delivered by hand to coincide with your appointment each week. Your bottom, how's that been lately?'

'A little sore. I think it's the medicinal candle.'

43

'Yes, it will cause some inflammation of the anal duct, but don't worry about it. What about your clitoris, is it any bigger?'

'It's hard to tell, really. I've been masturbating twice a day with the vibrator I bought from you and, well, I think it's a little bigger.'

'It will take a while for the vibrations to permanently enlarge your clitoris, Jessica. I'll take you to the examination room later and have a look. Now, what about your boyfriend – are you taking him into your mouth and swallowing his sperm yet?'

'No, no, I still can't bring myself to do that.'

'Oh, dear, what a shame. But not to worry! I've just read in the *Medical Journal* about a new treatment for women who find themselves sexually restrained, women who are unable to bring themselves to commit dreadfully debased ... to commit certain sexual acts. I did leave the journal out to show you but someone seems to have taken it. Goodness me, is nothing sacred? Anyway, the treatment involves caning the buttocks, lightly, to bring about a subconscious reaction.'

'Caning the buttocks?' the girl echoed, her eyes wide, her pretty mouth open.

'Yes, a gentle caning, Jessica. I intend to begin this new and revolutionary treatment today. Apart from the immense psychological benefits, the treatment tenses the pelvic muscles, exercising and toning them. It's a highly innovative treatment for women devised by Professor Caine Flagellant – he's outstanding in his field.'

'Why is he out standing in a field?'

'No, not that sort of field. He's outstanding in his particular field, women's sexual problems.'

'Oh, how interesting!'

'I'll have to charge you a little extra for the treatment, of course, but it'll be money well spent, I can assure you. How's your husband? Is he still whining and behaving unreasonably over your boyfriend?'

'Yes, he is! We'll have been married for a year next week. He wants us to celebrate our wedding anniversary by killing my boyfriend.'

'By killing him? Would you say that your husband is demented?'

'Yes, I would! He's the jealous type, possessive, clinging.'

'Was he breast-fed?'

'Yes, I believe he was.'

'That explains it. He's probably suffering from mammary teat starvation syndrome.'

'The irony of it is that my boyfriend wants to celebrate his divorce by killing my husband. As you can imagine, I'm torn.'

'Hymen?'

'What?'

'Nothing. Decisions, Jessica – decisions! What will you do?'

'I might kill myself.'

'Well, that's one way round the problem, I suppose. Have you considered having a sexual relationship with another girl?'

'No, I haven't. Would you recommend it, doctor?'

'It can be most rewarding. Personally, I find that having sexual relationships with girls is wonderful!'

'You prefer girls to men, do you?'

'Oh, yes! They have more orifices – three, to be precise. You might consider trying it – give it some serious thought.'

'Yes, it might solve all my problems.'

'Talking of problems, how's your excessive flow of vaginal lubricant been lately? Have you been wearing your panties as I instructed you to?'

'Yes, I have. It wasn't easy at first, but I've got the hang of it now. I've been managing to push my panties into my vagina every morning to soak up the fluid.'

'You've managed to push the complete garment into your vagina?'

'Yes, I have.'

'Good girl! Stand up, Jessica. Come round here and lift your dress up for me,' Larry grinned excitedly, picturing the girl's fleshy cunny lips.

Obediently rising to her feet and standing before her mentor, the girl yanked her dress up over her stomach, exposing her knickerless dark pubic bush, her succulent vaginal lips. Probing between her fleshy folds, Larry slipped his finger and thumb inside her pussy hole and gently pulled her panties out. Her inner lips distending as the garment emerged from her vaginal duct, he parted her labia, exposing her clitoris, longing to suck the petite sex-budlette into his wet mouth.

The red panties drenched with the girl's cunny juice, he held them up to the light, scrutinizing the garment, his dark eyes grinning. 'Yes, very good!' he praised his young client, placing the dripping panties in his desk drawer. 'I'll need to hang on to them because . . . right, let's go to the examination room!' he ordered excitedly, leaping to his feet as she lowered her dress.

Closing and locking the door as the girl followed him into

the bondage room, Larry instructed her to remove her dress and lie on the examination couch. Eagerly watching as she tugged the garment over her head, revealing her firm, braless breasts, her erect nipples, he sensed his rampant penis stiffen within his trousers. Her milk-white conical mammary glands firm in youth, topped with chocolaty teats like flake bars in soft ice cream, he gazed hungrily at the feast. Lowering his appreciative gaze to the delicate curve of the girl's stomach, her young mound, he focused on her pinken vaginal crack. *Another naive little beauty to play with!*

As she climbed onto the couch and stretched out her naked body, her long nipples pointing skyward, inviting a hot mouth, Larry was impatient to begin his most unorthodox examination, his crude violation of her fresh young body. Eyeing her thick black bush, he decided that the time had come to remove her pubic veil, to strip years off her vulval intimacy, to expose it in all its feminine glory.

'Now then, I'll check your vaginal canal first,' he smiled, painfully stretching the girl's fleshy labia apart, forcing her clitoris to emerge from its pink hood, her vaginal hole to gape. 'Open your legs as wide as you can, Jessica.'

'Ouch, that hurts!'

'I'm sorry, but I have to do this. It's known in medical circles as *cuntus exposus,*' Larry imparted authoritatively, pulling her delicate crack open further, feasting his eyes past the pearl to the glistening, rubicund oyster. 'Yes, that would appear to be in order,' he breathed, slipping three fingers into her open hole.

Massaging her tight cuntal sheath against the hardness of her pubic bone, inducing a copious flow of vaginal fluid to decant from her sex nectaries, he decided to take Jessica a

step further along the path of sexual deviancy. Slipping his wet fingers out of her tight cuntal sheath, he took a tube of cream from the shelf and unscrewed the cap. 'I'm going to massage this emollient into your *mons pubis* to loosen your muscles,' he murmured, squirting the white substance over her black bush. 'There's nothing to worry about – all it will do is relax your muscles in preparation for the medicinal candle.'

Lifting her head, the trusting girl watched Larry rub the cream into her pubic mound. Relaxing, her head resting on the padded couch, she enquired whether the essence of testes had arrived.

'It will be coming shortly,' Larry asserted stiffly, wiping his hands on a towel. 'While the cream's doing its job, I'll examine your breasts.' Kneading her firm mammary spheres, her elongated, erect nipples, he smiled. 'Mmm, they're nice and hard, aren't they?'

'Yes, very!'

'And your nipples are in excellent shape! The essence of testes is working very well! Right, as usual, I'll shield your eyes from the dangerous ultraviolet rays I use to activate the essence,' he gabbled, tugging a curtain across the couch to conceal the girl's head. Draping the bottom of the curtain around her neck, he slipped his solid penis out. 'Ah, that'll be the essence!' he grinned, opening the door to Brigit. 'Right, this will only take a minute, Jessica. As usual, my assistant, Brigit, will be helping me. OK, assistant – assist me!'

Taking Larry's solid penis in her hand as he positioned his knob over Jessica's rounded breast, Brigit began her wanking motions. Watching his glans appear and disappear as she moved his foreskin back and forth, Larry began his

gasping. 'The essence is . . . is coming! Hold on, Jessica, the essence is coming by hand! I'll be splattering your breasts any minute now!'

Wanking Larry's penis faster, Brigit grinned as his spunk jetted from his pulsating knob, landing on their client's breast, spraying her areola, her brown nipple. Stifling his groans of satisfaction, the doctor grimaced as Brigit leaned over and engulfed his glowing knob within her hot mouth, eliciting his precious essence of testes. Slipping his penis out and moving over the girl's neglected breast, Brigit opened her mouth, allowing the exotic blend of white spunk and saliva to douse her other brown milk bud.

'Ah, ah, that's it!' Larry cried as Brigit sucked out the remnants of his come and dribbled the liquid over Jessica's mammary spheres. 'There, all done!' Zipping his trousers, he pulled the curtain back, his face flushed as he gazed into his gullible client's grateful eyes. 'Right, Brigit will massage the essence of testes into your breasts, and then we'll begin Professor Flagellant's revolutionary treatment.'

Spreading the natural tincture of spunk and saliva over the girl's areolae, tweaking her alert nipples, Brigit sensed her own clitoris stiffen as she gazed at her client's yawning vaginal fissure. Hungry to push her tongue into the girl's sex hole, she watched eagerly as Larry wiped the depilating cream away from her sex to reveal her baby-soft pre-pubescent flesh.

'Now, Jessica, as you'll see, your pubic hair has fallen out,' Larry imparted nonchalantly.

'Argh!' the girl screamed, propping herself up on her elbows and gazing between her sticky breasts at her hairless cunt lips, her naked *mons*. 'What have you done to me?'

'It's what you've done to yourself, I'm afraid, Jessica!' Larry replied, his eyes mirroring his insatiable lust for young girls' naked bodies. 'You see, your continual worry about sucking sperm from your extramarital partner's penis has caused this adverse reaction.'

'But, how on earth could worry cause . . .'

'The power of the mind over the body, Jessica. Your negative thoughts have had a positive . . . a negative effect upon your pubic hair follicles, resulting in premature vulval balding. What's your reaction to your hairless vulval flesh?'

'Horrified!'

'Mmm, that's a most interesting reaction – not one I expected, but most interesting. Does it make you feel like a schoolgirl?'

'Well, no, not really.'

'Shame. I only hope that this won't be followed by . . . by something dreadful!'

'Something dreadful?' the girl asked anxiously as Brigit pinched and twisted her sensitive nipples.

'Yes, I only hope that *rigor mortis* of the vagina doesn't set in.'

'*Rigor mortis* of the vagina?' Jessica gasped. 'What . . . what does that mean?'

'Stiffening of the vaginal muscles, the vaginal lips. Your entire vulval area might become petrified. There's only one preventive measure open to me – enforced vaginal dilation. Quickly, Brigit, pass me the enforced vaginal dilation candle!'

Forsaking the girl's sore nipples, Brigit snatched a massive candle from the shelf and passed it to Larry. Concealing a grin, she parted Jessica's fleshy pussy lips, exposing the

pinken entrance to her tight vagina in readiness for the huge shaft to penetrate her tight sex sheath. Whimpering as she gazed in terror at the candle, Jessica's eyes widened as Larry pushed and twisted the waxen phallus against her glistening inner sanctum.

'You'll never get that inside me!' she gasped fearfully. 'It must be at least three inches across!'

'It's the only way!' Larry returned concernedly. 'If we're to save you from *rigor mortis* of the vagina, we must push the medicinal candle deep into your vulval duct to stretch your muscles and prevent a terrible condition known as lockcunt.'

Her girl-flesh yielding as Larry forced the candle deep into her trembling body, Jessica lay her head on the padded couch, her face grimacing as her vaginal sheath bloated, stretching to accommodate the mammoth phallus. Further Larry drove the long candle into her aching vagina, gazing in awe as her pinken hole dilated, her taut flesh gripping the wax shaft. Eyeing her clitoris, an angry red after ejection from its bonnet, Larry decided that the time had come to take his client to orgasm.

'Use the vaginal muscle relaxer,' he said, grinning at Brigit.

'Yes, doctor!' she replied eagerly, grabbing a vibrator from the shelf.

'Right, switch it on to full power and massage her clitoris.'

'What . . . what are you going to do to me?' Jessica asked anxiously, her face contorting as the candle came to rest against her wet cervix.

'Massage your clitoris to prevent vaginal *rigor mortis* and

51

possible lockcunt setting in,' Larry smiled. 'Try and relax and allow the sensations to come. I just pray that this will save you!'

'Save me? Is it very serious?'

'Serious? The situation is graver than grave!'

The vibrator swelling the girl's clitoris, sending electrifying sensations deep into her contracting womb as Larry thrust the massive candle in and out of her spasming cunt, she tossed her head from side to side, her black curtain of hair dishevelled, her dark eyes rolling in her sexual delirium. 'Oh, God!' she wailed, her bronzed stomach rising and falling as her climax approached. 'God, it's heavenly!'

Stretching Jessica's vaginal slit wide open, Brigit gazed at the girl's crimson clitoris pressed against the vibrator, visibly throbbing as her orgasm welled from her contracting womb and erupted. 'Ah, ah, I'm there!' Jessica cried, her face flushing, her areolae darkening as her sperm-drenched nipples catapulted to attention. 'Oh, oh! Ah, don't stop!'

Slowing the thrusting candle to a gentle, rhythmical pistoning, Larry grinned, gazing at the girl's taut flesh gripping the waxen shaft, her creamy come pouring from her abused cunt. 'We'd better administer Professor Flagellant's treatment,' he smiled, watching Jessica's grimacing face, her gasping mouth, as her climax receded. 'I think your orgasm has warded off vaginal *rigor mortis* but I'll administer you the cane, just to make sure. Brigit, you can switch the vaginal muscle relaxer off now.'

Moving the device away from Jessica's swollen clitoris, Brigit placed it on the shelf and gently massaged the recovering organ. 'Was that all right, Jessica?' she purred.

'Yes, yes! It was . . . it was more than all right!'

'Good. I'll help you to roll over so that Doctor Lickman can administer the punishment . . . I mean, the treatment,' she said huskily, slipping her fingers from the girl's wet crack.

'I think we'd better use the restraints,' Larry suggested, nodding towards several lengths of rope hanging from a hook on the wall. 'Leave the candle in place, it will give her muscles something to grip on and prevent lockcunt.'

'Yes, doctor,' Brigit murmured, helping Jessica to roll over onto her stomach. Gazing longingly at the girl's smooth, taut buttocks, she smiled. 'I'm going to place this pillow beneath your hips to raise your bottom.'

'The treatment won't hurt, will it?' Jessica asked, lifting her middle as Brigit pushed a pillow beneath her naked body.

'No, it won't hurt,' Larry reassured her, binding her ankles to the legs of the couch with rope. 'The restraints are simply to prevent your arms and legs thrashing about during your convulsions.'

'Convulsions?' the girl echoed fearfully as Larry spread-eagled her arms and secured her wrists.

'Well, not convulsions, exactly,' he smiled. 'I'm tying you down to prevent spurious muscle spasms from hurting you. Right, Brigit – the posterior implement, please!'

Passing Larry a long, thin bamboo cane, Brigit slipped her hand between Jessica's thighs and checked the candle, easing it deeper into the tethered girl's tight cunt. 'She's ready, doctor,' she smiled, standing back as Larry raised the cane above his head and brought it down with a loud crack across his prisoner's tensed buttocks. Her wails reverberating around the bondage room as Larry brought the cane down again, Jessica tugged on the ropes, desperately trying to escape the merciless thrashing.

'Please, stop!' she screamed as the cane struck her crimson bottom-orbs again. 'Argh! No! You said it wouldn't hurt! Please . . .'

'This has to be done!' Larry cried, bringing the cane down again with a deafening crack.

'Ah, ah! Please, stop! This isn't helping me!'

'It is!' Larry breathed. 'This is Professor Flagellant's revolutionary treatment!'

Continuing the ruthless caning, Larry grinned as the cunny-wet candle shot out of the girl's spasming cunt and lay between her twitching thighs. 'Do you feel comfortable with your naked body?' he panted, striking her scarlet buttocks again.

'Of course I don't! Please, stop now!'

'Another half-dozen or so should do it!'

The pink weals fanning out across her twitching buttocks as the cane repeatedly struck her bottom-orbs, Jessica's naked body shook violently. Her vaginal juices decanting, pooling on the couch, she cried out again, begging for mercy as Monica Moodie hammered on the door.

'What's going on in there? Doctor Lickman! Doctor Lickman, what are you doing? Who's that screaming?'

'Nothing to concern yourself with, Monica!' the demonic therapist called, discarding the cane and hurriedly releasing his victim. 'Go and do some filing!'

'Who's in there with you?'

'Er . . . no one, only me!' *And the Devil!*

Bursting into the room, Monica gasped, gazing at Jessica's burning buttocks, her shaved pussy lips, as the girl rolled onto her back. 'What have you done to her?' she cried, horrified by the lewd scene. 'What *have* you done to the poor girl?'

'I thought the door was locked!' Brigit gasped. 'I'm sorry, I . . .'

'Everything's in order, Monica,' Larry grinned sheepishly, helping Jessica off the couch. 'How was your dental appointment? No extractions, I hope. Your tongue's obviously still in working order.'

'This is most unethical!' Monica bellowed. 'I didn't know that you had an examination room! My God, you've tortured the poor girl!'

'Tortured her? You weren't tortured were you, Jessica?' Larry asked the whimpering girl. 'Do you feel tortured?'

'You caned me! You tied me down and thrashed me!'

'That wasn't torture, it was Professor Flagellant's treatment. I saved you from lockcunt, from vaginal *rigor mortis*!'

'Vaginal what?' Monica boomed, glaring at Larry as Brigit slipped unnoticed from the room.

'*Rigor mortis* of the vagina,' Larry enlightened the shocked woman.

'There's no such thing!'

'As you're not a qualified doctor, Monica, I wouldn't expect you to understand the intricate workings of the vagina and its associated muscles.'

'I understand only too well!'

'Are you a woman of great vaginal understanding?'

'Yes, I am!'

'Then I fail to see why you don't understand. Now, if you'll leave my client to dress, I'll . . .'

'My buttocks are stinging like hell!' Jessica sobbed, clutching her burning bottom-globes. 'And my pubic hair's fallen out!'

'I'll apply a little cooling cream to your bottom,' Larry smiled. 'Would you mind leaving us, Monica? I do believe the phone's ringing.'

'This isn't the last you'll hear of this!' the woman hissed through gritted teeth as she stormed out of the room and slammed the door shut.

'She can be so awkward at times! Now, Jessica, get onto the couch and I'll apply some cream to your bottom,' Larry soothed, gazing at the girl's succulent inner labia emerging between her hairless cunt lips.

'Why did you thrash me?' she whimpered as Larry tended her crimsoned orbs.

'I knew the caning would hurt you, but it had to be done. Had your vaginal muscles locked, I'd have been forced to perform a cuntectomy, and you wouldn't want that, would you?'

'A cuntectomy? What's that?'

'Removal of your vagina.'

'I've never heard of . . .'

'Would you be so good as to tell Monica that you consented to the treatment?' he asked, massaging lotion into the girl's scarlet buttocks, her yawning anal crease. 'She seems to think that I forced you to endure the punishment . . . the treatment.'

'Yes, yes, all right. I didn't realize that the treatment was saving me from . . .'

'I quite understand, Jessica. There, that should do it – get dressed now and have a word with Monica on your way out.'

'Thank you, doctor,' the abused girl smiled, slipping off the couch. 'I'll see you next week, as usual.'

'Yes, until next week. I hope the stinging wears off soon.'

'Will you be administering Professor Flagellant's treatment again?' she asked as she tugged her dress over her head and veiled her technicoloured body.

'I might have to – it all depends, Jessica. I'll see you next week.'

'All right, then. Goodbye,' she said resignedly as she hobbled off to make Larry's feeble excuses at reception.

Installed at his office desk, Larry awaited Monica's inevitable arrival – her screamed threats and accusations. *If only Brigit had locked the bloody door!* He'd enjoyed the caning, taken great pleasure from luring his clients into the bondage room and sexually abusing their naked bodies. But now Monica knew of his depraved escapades, the cat was out of the bag – the pussy out of the knickers!

'Ah, Monica!' he grinned as the sex-sleuth flung the door open and stormed into the room. 'When's the next client due to arrive?'

'Next victim, don't you mean?' she hissed, her clenched fists on her hips.

'Victim, Monica? I'm sorry, I'm not with you. Are you feeling ill? Perhaps you require a little light refreshment? Have you eaten today?'

'You caned that poor defenceless girl!'

'Roughage, Monica – are you having enough roughage?'

'I could hear her screaming from outside the building!'

'Not too much roughage, mind. We don't want your colon clogged up, do we? I'd hate to have to give you colonic irrigation with a garden hose!'

'Don't be so vile! I'm going to report you for tying that poor girl up and caning her!'

I'll cane you if you're not careful! 'Monica, you know nothing about the workings of the human body. The muscles within the pelvic region tend to seize up and . . . What's that smell?'

'On her way out, she told me that she'd consented to the caning. You put her up to that, didn't you? No doubt you'd threatened the poor girl with murder, with a gruesome death!'

'Of course I didn't threaten her!' *You'll meet with a gruesome death in a minute!* 'Listen, Monica, in this business . . .'

'Why did you remove her pubic hair?'

So I could see her cunt! 'I didn't! Some women prefer to have their vulval flesh free of vulval hair. It's Jessica's choice and it has nothing to do with us – it's her prerogative. Has it stopped raining?'

'I've just been into that room again. I discovered a towel covered with cream and pubic hair!'

'Do you shave your vulval flesh, Monica?'

'My God, you disgust me! There are ropes tied to the legs of the examination couch, there's a wet candle on the couch and a cane on the floor. That explains Brigit's buttocks, the weals!'

'What did you have for breakfast, Monica?'

'What did I . . . I'm going to report . . .'

'Someone's ringing the reception bell, Monica. Let's put this behind us and get on with our work, shall we? Has Lily returned yet?'

'I'm not putting anything behind me!'

I'll put the fucking cane behind you in a minute!

'You're running a sexual torture chamber, and I'm not going to . . .'

'Monica, I wouldn't want to have to dismiss you for insubordination!'

'You can't dismiss me! I'd go straight to the newspapers and expose you! What have you got to say about that, *Doctor Lickman?*'

'How old are you, Monica?' *Eighty? Ninety?*

'Forty, why?'

'Ah, forty. Yes, that explains it.'

'Explains what?'

'Your irrational behaviour, your peculiar mental state, your derangement. Obviously, you're near-menopausal. I do wish the weather would brighten up, don't you? The cereal crop will suffer and there'll be a roughage shortage.'

'I am *not* near-menopausal!'

Post-menopausal, then! 'The bell's still ringing, Monica. Send the client in and then you might as well take your lunch break. Don't get yourself run over when you come staggering back from the pub, will you?'

'I've never been into a public house in my life!'

'You have a history of heavy drinking, Monica! Take your broken leg, you . . .'

'I've been to the health authority and told them about this place, the things you get up to! You have a bottle of whisky in your desk drawer, no doubt for plying the innocent clients. I'm going to tell Mr Venereal about . . .'

'Yes, I was talking to Mr Venereal on the phone earlier. He suggested that I refer you to a psychiatrist at my earliest convenience.'

'Of course he didn't!'

'How are your breasts these days, Monica? Still resemble two shrivelled-up empty leather bags, do they?'

'You're a disgusting . . .'

'It can't be easy, sleeping on your back with your hairy nipples in your hairy armpits.'

'I've a good mind to . . .'

'Sleep on your side? Yes, that's one way round the problem. There'll be room for your tits to lie next to you now that your husband's gone. A little light caning would firm your breasts up. For a small fee, I could . . .'

'Right, I'm going straight to the . . .'

'A very good friend of mine is a psychiatrist and he'd be only too willing to certify you insane, Monica!'

'Don't be ridiculous!'

'Your husband rang me this morning. He said that he'd be more than willing to testify as to your dreadful mental instability. By the way, he told me that he's never been happier since he left you. Apparently, he's taken up with an eighteen-year-old girl.'

'He can't do that!'

'He's done it! Beautiful, he reckons – sex-crazed, with hard tits and long nipples. Heavily into the kinky stuff, she is. Bondage, caning, sixty-nine . . .'

'I'll divorce him for adultery!'

'You threw him out!'

'He's still my husband!'

'Null and void, that's what your marriage is now. Send the next client in, please.'

Watching his distraught receptionist leave the room, Larry sighed. What the health authority would do if

they discovered that he had no qualifications at all, he dreaded to think! And if Gina Cology were to discover his antics . . .

Deciding to take Monica prisoner, keep her tied up in the bondage room and defile her plump body, he smiled as an attractive woman in her mid-thirties timidly tapped on the open door and stepped gingerly into the room.

'Ah, Jane!' he greeted her as she closed the door. 'Please, take a seat.'

'Thank you, doctor,' the woman replied, wringing her hands nervously as she sat down.

'So, how's the relationship?' Larry asked, eyeing her open blouse, her cleavage.

'In ruination!' she sighed despondently.

'Oh, dear! The last time we met you said that things were improving.'

'Yes, they were. But Lesbia and I are incompatible, I'm afraid.'

'Incompatible? Mmm, that might present a problem.'

'*Might*? It *has* presented a problem!'

'Tell me, Jane, this incompatibility . . . how was your childhood?'

'Harrowing! My father left my mother for another man when I was twelve.'

'For another man? Well, that explains your incompatibility. You were sexually confused by your father's unorthodox behaviour. Did it drive you to rampant masturbation?'

'Yes, I'm afraid it did.'

'There's no need to be afraid, Jane. It's a classic situation – in my line of work, I come across it time and time again. Father leaves mother and twelve-year-old daughter for

another man – daughter resorts to excessive masturbation, desperately seeking comfort from her orgasms – mother . . . how did this terrible event affect your mother?'

'She took to caning me every night.'

'I thought as much. She was taking her revenge out on you, venting her hatred for her husband on you. How did you feel when your breasts developed?'

'I wrapped bandages around my body to flatten them. I was ashamed of my bumps.'

'A subconscious fear of growing up, I've seen it before. At what age did your pubic hair grow?'

'Twelve.'

'That figures. You see, all this coincides with your father's coming out. How did you feel about your pubic hair? What was your emotional reaction to the arrival of your vaginal curls?'

'I shaved them off.'

'And you still do?'

'Yes – how did you know?'

'Experience, Jane – years of vulval experience. Did you sexually abuse your body?'

'Yes, I . . . I used to stick things up my bottom. I . . . I still do. Are you shocked?'

'No, no, not at all! I don't shock easily. Sticking things up your bottom was your way of coming to terms with your father's homosexuality. What sort of things did you stick up your bottom?'

'I started with toothbrush handles and progressed to . . . I now use well-greased candles – big ones.'

'You're unconsciously seeking refuge in religion.'

'No, I don't think I am.'

'Yes, you are. The candles represent the church, you see. Has there been a death in the family?'

'Yes, my cat.'

'I thought as much. Light a candle for your cat. Not while it's in your bottom, though, it would be perilous. The candle, I mean – don't try and put the cat into your bottom and set fire to it. Apart from anything else, I believe it's illegal. Is there a history of death in your family?'

'Yes, there is. All my relations over ninety years old are dead.'

'Good grief, you poor child!'

'I've learned to live with it.'

'How terrible! So, you have no living ancestors at all?'

'None.'

'You poor, sad, neglected, ancestorless girl. Going back to your present relationship, the incompatibility – in which areas are you incompatible?'

'Lesbie wants me to have a sexual relationship with her, but I don't feel that I'm ready. I'm still torn between male and female.'

'Between your anal and vaginal orifices?'

'No, I don't think so.'

'Yes, you're torn between your two sexual orifices. You see, on the one hand you're yearning for a penis to penetrate your vagina, and on the other hand, your father's homosexuality has caused you to question your bottom-hole – its sexual function.'

'I don't understand. My partner wants me to pleasure her vagina, so why would I be torn between . . .'

'To you, her vagina represents your father.'

'Why?'

'Ask Sigmund Freud. Oh, you can't, he's dead. It's a psychological response, Jane. I'm sorry to have to use this dreadful word but – you feel that your father is a cunt.'

'Oh! Yes, I do!'

'I'd call my father a cunt if he ran off with another man, it stands to reason. So, we have three components to deal with – the vagina, the bottom-hole, and the penis. You're terribly mixed up as to which two go together, as to which two should be joined in sexual ecstasy. It must be most distressing for you.'

'It is, doctor! I have nightmares, horrible nightmares about bottom-holes, penises and vaginas. They drift around me in circles, beckoning me!'

'I'm going to suggest something, Jane. This might seem somewhat unorthodox, but it will knock you off the fence of indecision. You'll land one side or the other, with your problem solved.'

'Really? Oh, if only!'

Rising to his feet, Larry crept across the room to the door. Slowly turning the knob, he yanked the door open. 'Ah, Monica!' he boomed. 'What are you doing kneeling on the floor? Looking for something? Your clitoris hasn't dropped off, has it? Or were you calling on Satan?'

'Doctor Lickman! I was . . . I tripped and fell!' the flustered woman stammered as she climbed to her feet.

'You're not drunk *again*, are you?'

'Certainly not!'

'You really must lay off the meths! Haven't broken anything, have you? Your neck, for example!'

'No, no . . . I . . .'

'What a shame! When you've found your clitoris, would you send Brigit in, please?'

Closing the door, Larry returned to his client and smiled. 'Sorry about that. She has a tendency to spy on people. Her strange obsession with gazing through keyholes comes from a terrible childhood experience. She happened to look through a keyhole and saw her mother masturbating with a cucumber. It's had a deep-seated and long lasting psychological effect – it completely unhinged her mind.'

'Oh dear, the poor woman! I blame the parents!'

'Yes, you would – your father in particular, cunt that he is!'

'What about knocking me off the fence?' the woman asked eagerly.

'Yes, Brigit will be here in a minute and . . . ah, Brigit! Come in and lock the door. This is Jane – she has a problem that I think we can help her with.'

'Hi, Jane!' Brigit trilled, shaking the woman's hand. 'What's the problem?'

'I can't decide between male and female,' she confessed softly.

'We're going to knock her off the fence of indecision!' Larry beamed. 'Brigit, would you lie on your back across the desk with your skirt up over your stomach and your legs wide open, please?'

'Yes, of course, doctor,' the girl smiled.

Sitting on the desk, Brigit yanked her skirt up and reclined, her shaved pussy crack blatantly displayed to the client's wide eyes as she opened her legs wide. Tugging his trousers down, Larry lay beside his assistant, his erect penis pointing to the ceiling. Stunned by the pair's strange behaviour, Jane

leapt to her feet, holding her hand to her open mouth in horror.

'Doctor Lickman!' she cried, gazing at his rolling balls, his purple glans, as he pulled his foreskin back. 'What *are* you doing?'

'I want you to place your chair between Brigit's legs and lick her vaginal crack, Jane. When you've had enough of that, move between my legs and suck my glans.'

'But, doctor! What sort of conduct is this? I have never seen such . . .'

'This is a well-tried and tested method of determining the sexual leanings of women. This will knock you off the fence, Jane. It's the only way you'll discover what you want, which sex you prefer.'

'Well, I really don't know whether I should . . .'

'You see, you're of an indecisive nature. You're sexually confused by your father's homosexuality. This will cure you, Jane – send you tumbling off the fence!'

'But . . .'

'Come on!' Brigit giggled, pulling her cunny lips wide apart, forcing her erect clitoris to pop out from beneath its pinken hood. 'Give me a good licking out, and then suck the doctor's penis! Keep moving between us, licking me and sucking him, until you've decided which it is you want – a man or a woman.'

'Until you've fallen off the fence!' Larry chuckled, pulling his foreskin back further.

'My God!' Monica cried, her nose pressed to the window. 'Doctor Lickman! Brigit! What *do* you think you're doing?'

'Jesus fucking Christ!' Larry gasped, leaping off the desk,

his penis wavering before Monica's astonished eyes. 'Is there no peace for the fucking wicked?'

'Shit!' Brigit gasped, slipping off the desk and tugging her skirt down.

'I've seen everything now!' Monica screamed hysterically. 'I'm going to call the police!'

'Sorry about this, Jane,' Larry grinned as the girl moved nervously towards the door. 'Please, don't go!'

'I . . . I must!' she stammered, her face flushed, her hands trembling. 'I have . . . I have never . . .'

'Please, don't go!' Brigit called as the horrified woman opened the door and fled down the hall. 'You haven't tasted my cunny juice yet!'

'Fuck it! I'd better go and stop the old hag from calling the law!' Larry breathed, zipping his trousers. 'The last thing I need is the cops sniffing around. Wait in the bondage room, I'm going to lure the old bat there and thrash her! When she enters the room, lock her in.'

'OK, Larry.'

Running down the hall to reception, Larry could see that he was too late. Replacing the telephone receiver, Monica grinned at him triumphantly. 'They're on their way!' she growled. 'You'll have some explaining to do, *Doctor* Lickman!'

'Monica, Brigit wants a hand in the examination room,' he smiled nonchalantly.

'Oh, no! You're not going to lure me into that torture chamber of yours!'

'Brigit wants you to give her a hand to clear up, that's all. We can't have the police seeing the mess in there, can we?

They'd think you an inadequate, disorderly and incompetent member of staff. Is that what you want the constabulary to think? It might even get a mention in the local paper. What would your neighbours say?'

'Well, I . . . I suppose they'll be a while yet,' Monica relented, heading off towards the bondage room – her cell!

Leaving the building, Larry hovered in the car park, his plan formulating as a police car drew up. 'Ah, a timely arrival, I must say!' he beamed as two officers climbed out of the car. 'A woman had the cheek to use my phone! I just happened to walk down the hall to reception, and there she was, replacing the receiver and dashing out of the building!'

'Which way did she go?' one officer asked.

'By the time I came out here, she'd gone. It's incredible! The cheek of it!'

'We've just had a call from a woman complaining about a blatant act of gross sexual indecency taking place in your clinic.'

'Oh, that explains it, then!' Larry laughed. 'She was obviously a nutter!'

'Yes, obviously. Perhaps we'd better have a look round, just to . . .'

'Everything's in order, officer,' Larry smiled. 'If there had been any acts of gross sexual indecency taking place in my establishment, I'd have been aware of them – it stands to reason.'

'Yes, I suppose it does. All right, we'll leave you in peace, sir. Good day.'

'Good day,' Larry smirked, before light-footing it back to the clinic. *Right, Monica Moodie – now you're in for a thrashing!*

68

Striding purposefully down the hall, he smiled at Brigit. 'Everything go to plan?' he winked.

'Yes, she's locked in – and she's furious!'

'There's no need to tell me that! Her mental state is easily determined by her hysterical screaming and incessant hammering on the door. At least she can't go running to Gina Cology now. I'll give her an hour or so to exhaust herself, and then I'll slip in and tie her to the examination couch and shag her arse!'

'Here comes Lily!' Brigit cried, gazing through the window to see the screwed-up blonde bombshell gliding across the car park.

'Ah, good! Right, you man reception, and I'll have a word with Lily. Send her to my room, will you?'

'Right, see you later,' Brigit smiled as Larry dashed down the hall.

Sitting at his desk as the morose girl wandered into his room, Larry smiled. 'Nice to see you, Lily. Take a seat, and we'll have a chat.'

'What's all that banging and screaming?' the girl asked.

'The wind. Now, Lily . . .'

'You . . . you won't get your penis out, will you?' she asked fearfully as she sat down.

'No, I won't get my penis out, Lily. But I do want you to show me your breasts.'

'No! Please, I couldn't possibly bring myself to . . .'

'Open your blouse and lift your bra up, Lily. You'll be all right, I'll be here to protect you should your breasts become aggressive and make a move to attack you.'

'Come and stand next to me, then. I want you close

in case they try anything. They're in a terrible mood today.'

Kneeling before the girl as she unbuttoned her blouse, Larry grinned. 'This is the finest way to familiarize yourself with your breasts, Lily. That's it,' he breathed as she slipped her blouse over her shoulders. 'Now, lift your bra up. By doing this, you'll overcome your fear of your breasts. It's a well-tried and tested way of . . .'

'You say that to *all* the clients!'

'I have an inclination towards repetitiveness. It stems from my early days of uncontrollable childhood masturbation.'

'You have problems, too, then?'

'We all have deep-seated psychological problems, Lily. I'm afflicted by many, but I've learned to accept them. OK, are you ready to show me your breasts?'

'Yes, I think so.'

Turning her head and squeezing her eyes shut, the girl yanked her bra up, her firm young breasts tumbling from the red silk cups, her nipples standing proud before Larry's wide eyes. Taking her firm mammary spheres in his palms, he weighed them, stroking her long brown nipples with his thumbs. Her areolae darkening as her breast buds became fully erect, he smiled.

'I want you to look at your breasts, Lily,' he coaxed gently. 'Just take a quick look to familiarize yourself with them.'

Turning and lowering her head, the girl opened her eyes and focused on her long nipples. 'They're . . . they're looking at me!' she cried.

'No, they're not! Look, I'm squeezing them, pinching your nipples. Does it feel nice?'

70

'Yes, yes, it does! No one's ever done that before, it's very nice.'

'You do it, Lily – squeeze your nipples.'

'No, no, I'm not ready to go that far yet. I'm nervous.'

'All right, I won't push you. I'm going to suck them, lick and suck your nipples.'

'All right,' the confused siren replied, turning her head away and taking a deep breath.

Taking the girl's nipple into his wet mouth, Larry sucked hard, stiffening her milk bud, bringing her beautiful sensations of sex. Looking down, she watched him suckling, her fear slipping away as she began to breathe deeply. Moving to her other nipple, Larry closed his mouth over her chocolate budling, gently sucking the brown protrusion.

'It's very nice!' Lily gasped.

'Why don't you try it?' Larry coaxed, slipping her teat from his hot mouth. 'Cup your breasts in your hands and suck your tits into your mouth.'

'No! No, I'm nowhere near ready to . . .'

'All right, don't distress yourself, Lily!'

'May I dress now?'

'Do you feel uncomfortable?'

'No, I'm not used to displaying my breasts. Nakedness frightens me.'

'Is there something missing in your life, Lily?'

'Yes, there's a void. May I dress now?'

'Yes, you may. That was a good start, Lily. You did very well. What I want you to do is . . .'

'I'm sorry I ran away,' she interrupted as she dressed. 'But I didn't want to see your penis.'

'We'll deal with your phobia of the penis when we've

dealt with your fear of breasts, Lily. Try and be positive about . . .'

'Larry!' Brigit yelled as she burst into the room. 'She's escaped!'

'Who has?' Lily asked fearfully, turning to face Brigit.

'I can't remember. Oh, yes, Monica – she's gone!'

'Oh, shit!' Larry breathed. 'How on earth did she get out?'

'Through the window!'

'How the hell did she learn that neat little trick? She must have seen it done on television, damn it! Perhaps she was a POW and felt it her duty to try and escape. Well, there's nothing we can do other than wait for the consequences. OK, you two, busy yourselves – I have some serious thinking to do!'

Flopping into his chair and resting his head in his hands as the girls scurried out of the room, Larry sighed. Monica Moodie would bring in the police, the health authority, Gina Cology, and Christ knows who else! 'Right, formulate a plan!' he breathed, grabbing the bottle of whisky from the desk drawer and taking a swig. 'Concoct some lies! And get seriously pissed!'

Chapter Three

Expecting Larry to be suffering from depression as she breezed into reception, Brigit was surprised to find him singing. 'Oh, what a terrible morning! Oh, what a terrible day! I have a horrible feeling, everything's fucked up today!'

'You're in a good mood this morning, Larry!' she giggled. 'You won the lottery or something?'

'I don't know whether to sing or cry!' he sighed, leaning on the counter. 'Do you ever question your sanity?'

'Er . . . no, I don't!'

'*I* do, Brigit – every day I question your sanity. Where's Lily?'

'In the toilet.'

'The best place to be when there's trouble brewing. Retreat to the toilets!'

'She has a thing about toilets.'

'Yes, the poor child. It's a mysterious affliction that I have no explanation for, I'm afraid – other than complete and utter lunacy of lunatically frightening proportions. I'll bet Monica's . . .'

'Doctor Lickman?' Wandering over to the counter, an official-looking man carrying a briefcase interrupted them.

'Where?' Larry smiled.

'Where what?'

'Where's Doctor Lickman? I thought you were talking to him?'

'Aren't you Doctor Lickman?' the man asked confusedly.

'Er . . . no. Do I look like him?'

'I wouldn't know, I've never met him.'

'I find that most peculiar!'

'Why?'

'Well, coming here asking to see a man you've never met. Is it your wont to go round speaking to people you've never met?'

'My wont? I . . . Can you tell me where I might find Doctor Lickman?'

'Where you *might* find him, or where you *will* find him?'

'What? Just tell me where he is!'

'Who are you?'

'My name's Fullcrack – I'm from the health authority.'

'Shit!'

'I'm sorry?'

'Er . . . ship. Doctor Lickman is aboard ship.'

'Oh?'

'Yes, he . . . he's on a day trip to France. Vive la France!'

'You're not patriotic, then?'

'Vive l'Angleterre!'

'Er . . . yes, quite.'

'May I ask what business you have with Doctor Lickman, Mr Fullcrack?'

'We've received a complaint of a most serious and disturbing nature concerning Doctor Lickman's ethics.'

Oh, fuck! 'Really? Has he not behaved himself on the

ship? Good grief, you're not suggesting that he's a lager lout, are you?'

'On the ship? No, no, I'm talking about his practice, the way he treats his clients.'

'Ah, oui, oui!'

'Are you French?'

'Certainly not! I'll have you know that my father was Lickuanian. I'm Doctor Lickman's assistant, his right-hand man, and his left-hand man – his handyman, so to speak. My name's . . . my name's Throbber, Knobby Throbber.'

'Mr Throbber, yes. Er . . . I wish to take a look at Doctor Lickman's records, his clients' files. Does he keep computer records?'

'Well, yes, he does, but . . . the weather's much better today, don't you agree?'

'Er . . . yes, I do. Where's the computer, Mr Throbber?'

'A fine day for sailing across the good old English Channel to stock up on cheap booze and fags and flog them on the black market.'

'Indeed. The computer, Mr Throbber.'

'Oh, yes, the computer. Hold the fort while I fill in Mr Fullcrack, Brigit. This way, Mr Fullcrack,' Larry smiled, leading the way down the hall to his consulting room. 'I can show you where the computer is, but it won't do you much good as I don't know how to use it – sadly, I'm illegitimate.'

'The marital status of your parents when you were conceived is of no concern to me, Mr Throbber! I suggest you take the matter up with the registrar of births, marriages and deaths.'

'No, I meant computer-illegitimate . . . I mean, illiterate.'

75

'I can control computers competently, Mr Throbber.'

'Shit!'

'I beg your pardon?'

'That's a mouthful!'

'What is?' Fullcrack asked irritably.

'Control computers competently. A tongue twister. Try saying it faster.'

'Control computer comp – competent computer controls . . . please, Mr Throbber! I don't have the time to play games!'

'You should *make* time! Work hard and play hard, that's what my father says,' Larry grinned, showing the way into his consulting room.

Watching the man open the files on the computer, Larry winced. He should have realized that all the evidence required to nail him was there for the taking. Dates, names, addresses, unorthodox treatments, not to mention his vulgar comments concerning his clients' naked bodies – and a record of the vile acts of debauchery he'd committed on them!

'Are you able to explain this?' Fullcrack asked, pointing to the screen.

'I doubt it! My inability to explain is an inherent weakness of mine inherited from my grandfather. Er . . . let me think, Miss Scrubbings – yes, she's a client.'

'What does this mean?'

'What?'

'The letters and numbers following her name, TF fifteen.'

Times fucked – fifteen! 'I really don't know!'

'What about this?'

'Er . . . the letter S.' *Shaved!* 'I have no idea, Mr Fullcrack.

76

It might be a code. Do you think Doctor Lickman is a Russian spy?'

'Don't be ridiculous!'

'Perhaps Miss Scrubbings is a Russian agent.'

'What's this?'

'AD. Er . . . after death?' *Arse done!*

'BC five, what does that stand for?'

Bondage and caning. 'Presumably it refers to a client Doctor Lickman saw five years before Christ was born.'

'Five years before Christ . . .'

'Well, I have no other explanation.'

'How on earth could Doctor Lickman have seen a client five years before the birth of Christ?'

'Perhaps he's in possession of a time machine?'

'Are you feeling ill, Mr Throbber?'

'No, I feel fine. I've got it! It must have been before Christmas. Yes, that's more logical – five days before Christmas.'

Bringing another client's notes up on the screen, Fullcrack frowned. *'The horny little bitch loves it up her bum!* Rather an odd comment to make concerning a client, wouldn't you agree?'

'No, not at all! Doctor Lickman deals with a wide range of women's sexual problems. You'd be taken aback to hear some of the weird and wonderful . . .'

'Miss Shafter – AD six. The little cow is so retarded that she actually believed that my spunking up her arse will help to enlarge her breasts. Is that the sort of comment you'd expect a doctor to make about a client?'

'No, no! That's what the woman's boyfriend said to Doctor Lickman. I remember him well, a right yob he was

– a lager lout. He came here to talk about Miss Shafter's sexual problems – that was a lewd comment he made about the woman. Due to the psychologically disturbing nature of the comment, Doctor Lickman felt it worthy of a mention in her notes.'

'I see. Well, I'll come back and see Doctor Lickman tomorrow.'

'Er . . . he'll be away for at least three weeks, if not four, or five, even.'

'But you said that he'd gone on a day trip to France!'

'Did I? Oh, yes, so I did! What I meant was, he's gone on a day trip to France, and then he's going on to Spain. He might even look in on Portugal, I don't know. He has friends in Morocco – whether he'll be nipping across the Strait of Gibraltar to see them or not, I can't say. What is all this about Doctor Lickman's ethics?'

'We've had a complaint from a gentleman accusing Doctor Lickman of sexually abusing his wife.'

'Oh, you've not heard from Monica, then?'

'Monica?'

'Has Gina Cology been in contact with you about me? I mean, about Doctor Lickman?'

'Yes, but that's another matter. My boss, Mr Venereal, is dealing with that. No doubt Doctor Lickman will be hearing from him in due course.'

Fuck it! 'Ah, you've had a complaint from Mr Schmidtbag, no doubt.'

'Yes, as it happens, we have. How did you know that he'd contacted us?'

'He suffers from . . . how can I put it? He's mentally ill, Mr Fuckcrack . . . I mean, Fullcrap . . . Fullcrack. The poor

man came here accusing Doctor Lickman of tying his wife down to the examination couch with lengths of rope! Would you believe it?'

'Yes, I did believe Mr Schmidtbag.'

'Did he say that Doctor Lickman had forced his wife to have sexual intercourse with two men at the same time, one in front and one behind?'

'Good God! No, no, he didn't mention that!'

'Totally mad! He actually accused Brigit Biways, the secretary, of having a filthy lesbian relationship with his wife! He's soon to be certified insane.'

'Is he?'

'Yes, the necessary documentation is being prepared by an eminent psychiatrist of psychiatric psychosis, as we speak. The straitjacket's been ordered.'

'Oh, well, in that case I'd better get back to the office and . . . thank you for your time, Mr Knobbing.'

'My name's Throbbing, I mean, Knobber . . . Throbber.'

'Yes, quite. Well, thank you for your time.'

'Not at all, Mr Fartcrack . . . Fullcrack. If there's anything else, please do hesitate to ring me.'

Perching on the edge of his desk as Fullcrack disappeared, Larry held his head and sighed. 'Jesus fucking Christ! That was close!' Wondering why Fullcrack hadn't mentioned Monica, he grabbed the receiver as the phone rang. 'Doctor Lickman.'

'Larry, I have a woman on line two who wants to make an appointment to see you,' Brigit enlightened him.

'Make her an appointment, then! Can't you deal with a simple task like . . .'

'She wants to see you in about ten minutes.'

'Ten minutes? Oh, all right then. Tell her I'll have to charge her double for an emergency booking. I don't see why I should see people without proper notice!'

'She says it's very urgent.'

'All right, I'll see her.'

'OK, bye.'

Returning to the computer, Larry began the laborious job of deleting the lewd remarks from his clients' files. Knowing only too well that Fullcrack would return after he'd spoken to Schmidtbag, he wondered when Venereal would be in touch concerning Gina's allegations. Deciding to give Monica a ring later, he smiled graciously as Brigit showed a buxom young woman into the consulting room.

'This is Mrs Cravings,' she introduced the woman.

'Ah, Mrs Cravings, how pleasant it is to meet you!' Larry smiled as Brigit left the room and closed the door. 'Please, do sit down.'

In her mid-thirties, with cascading chestnut hair framing an enchanting face, the woman was a real stunner, Larry surmised, sensing his penis twitch in anticipation. Her heady perfume filling the room, her succulent red lips furling into a pouting smile, he gazed into her hazel eyes, speculating on her great urgency to see him. What could be her problem? Inorgasmia? Torn between male and female? Marital problems? *Why's she carrying a camera?*

'I had to see you as a matter of extreme urgency, doctor,' the woman began, sitting opposite him and placing her camera on the desk.

'I see,' Larry smiled, eyeing her loose-fitting blouse, the deep valley of her mammary cleavage. *I'd like to spunk over*

your tits! 'What's the problem? How can I be of carnal assistance in your time of great carnal need?'

'I have a desperate yearning to commit a vile and disgusting sexual act,' the siren confessed. 'A most debased, vile and disgusting sexual act.'

Christ, so have I! 'Er . . . a vile and disgusting sexual act?' he echoed surprisedly.

'Yes. You see, I have just discovered that my husband has cheated on me, betrayed me, and I wish to betray him in return. *He* committed a most vile and disgusting sexual act with our Swedish au pair and, if our marriage is to survive his infidelity, then *I* must equal his act of filth and depravity.'

'Two wrongs don't make a right, Mrs Cravings!'

'An eye for an eye, Doctor Lickman. A tooth for a tooth, an orgasm for an orgasm. He cheats, I cheat, and we're equal. Neither can blame the other because both would be equal in their adulterous debauchery.'

'I see. Well, I don't know how I can help you.' *Apart from fuck your cunt!* 'Might I suggest that you . . .'

'Might *I* suggest that you defile my body without further delay?'

'Er . . . defile your body? Well, I . . . Mrs Cravings, I think we should discuss your problem before we do anything rash. Tell me, your husband, has he misbehaved before?'

'I've been able to control him in the past. I use a cane to thrash him whenever I sense that he's close to misbehaving. Unfortunately, I was away for a few days attending a dominatrix course and he took advantage of my absence – and the au pair!'

'Well, I could take you to my examination room and . . .'

81

Ray Gordon

'Right!' she interrupted eagerly, rising to her feet and grabbing her camera. 'Lead the way!'

Stunned, Larry opened the door and showed the woman to his bondage room, wondering about her logic – her sanity! *An orgasm for an orgasm?* Why not? he reflected, closing the door behind him as his surprise client gazed at the examination couch. Her hazel eyes reflecting her burning desire to commit a debauched adulterous act, she placed her camera on the couch and unbuttoned her blouse, slipping the garment off her shoulders and tossing it over a chair. Her full breasts heaving within her straining lace bra, she reached behind her back and freed the hook, allowing the generous mammary boulders to tumble from their confines.

'You'll notice that I have a nice bust – size forty-eight,' she smiled shamelessly. 'My breasts are ample, but surprisingly firm for their size.'

'Indeed, you *do* have nice breasts, Mrs Cravings!' Larry conceded, focusing on her udder-like nipples, the chocolate-brown plates of her areolae.

'My nipples are long and extremely sensitive. That's because I rub ice cubes over them three times a day and suck them regularly.'

'They really are fine specimens!'

'I'm very proud of my breasts, as you can imagine. Our au pair's tits are nothing in comparison.'

'You've seen them?'

'Yes, trying to understand my husband's disgusting behaviour, his wanton lust for the girl's naked body, I ordered her to strip off and show me what she's got. Her breasts are mere plums compared to my fine melons!'

'I'm sure they are!'

'Are you into breasts, doctor?'

'Yes, very much!'

'Would you say mine are the best you've ever seen? Be honest, now – I can take criticism.'

'Er . . . yes, they're definitely the best I've ever seen!'

Tugging her skirt down her shapely thighs, she dropped the garment to her ankles, kicking it aside along with her shoes. Standing before Larry, her pink panties visibly damp, the triangular patch of silk between her thighs bulging with her ample sex, she ordered him to unveil her femininity.

'You'll observe that I have large vaginal lips,' she said smugly as he knelt before her and tugged her panties down, displaying her full fleshy sex hillocks. 'My inner lips are ample, too. I've looked after my vulva, regularly masturbating with a body massager to keep my muscles firm, my labia full – my clitoris sensitive, responsive.'

'You're very proud of your body, aren't you?' Larry observed, gazing at the opaque fluid oozing from her yawning pussy crack.

'Yes, I am. Why my husband defiled that slag-bag of an au pair, I'll never know! I order him to abuse my naked body daily, so he doesn't go short. How do you intend to defile me, doctor?'

'We'll have sexual intercourse.'

'No, that's not good enough! I'd hardly call sexual intercourse defilement! Can't you think of something depraved, something vulgar?'

'Er . . . anal intercourse?'

'Mmm, that's a little better. You'll notice that I've brought my camera with me.'

'Yes, I did notice.'

'I want you to take photographs of me, of my abused body. I'll need proof of my wanton adultery, you see.'

'Proof, yes, of course.'

'Ah, you have a fine collection of candles! I'll bend over the couch and you can stick a candle up my bottom. Take a couple of pictures, ensuring that my face is in frame, as well as my abused bottom-hole.'

'Er . . . yes, right,' Larry smiled, taking a large candle from the shelf as Mrs Cravings stood with her feet asunder and leaned over the couch.

Dipping the end of the candle into the jar of honey, Larry parted the woman's ample buttocks, exposing the dank entrance to her bowels. Grinning, he pressed the sticky end of the waxen phallus against her sensitive tissue and gently pushed and twisted. Her sphincter muscles yielding, she gasped in her perversity as the candle opened her anal portal and glided deep into her rectal sheath.

'Ah, yes, that's heavenly!' she cried. 'Push it in as far as you can and then take some photographs!'

'I'll have to leave a couple of inches sticking out, otherwise it won't be seen,' Larry replied, taking the camera and focusing on the woman's brown anal ring, taut around the huge shaft.

'Be sure to get my face in shot!' she ordered, turning her head and grinning salaciously at the camera. 'This will show my husband that two can play the debauchery game!'

Taking a couple of shots, the flash lighting up the candle, the woman's wicked grin, Larry placed the camera on the couch and took another candle from the shelf. 'Might as well do the job properly!' he chuckled, parting her engorged vaginal lips and driving the huge waxen shaft deep into her

tight sex duct to the accompaniment of her gasps. Taking several more photographs, he asked her what else she'd like him to do.

'God, that feels heavenly!' she wailed, reaching behind her quivering body and thrusting the candle in and out of her anal passage. 'I want you to shove your cock up my bum and take several photographs of my wanton adultery!' she breathed, slipping the candle out of her inflamed bottom-hole.

Unzipping his trousers, Larry stood behind the woman, his solid penis in his hand as she yanked her buttocks apart, opening her sticky brown hole. 'Defile me! Penetrate my bottom-sheath! Impale me! When you're about to come, pull it out and splatter my buttocks with your sperm!' she giggled wickedly. 'That will show my husband that he's not the only one who can spunk over my bum!'

Presenting his bulbous knob to her brown ring, Larry pushed against her defending muscles, driving his penis deep into her anal tract as she let out long low moans of satisfaction. Grabbing her hips, he began his anal fucking, sliding his shaft in and out of her tightening lust duct, taking his mount to shuddering heights of sexual ecstasy.

'Take some pictures!' she cried, her body shaking violently with the anal pummelling.

'In a minute!' Larry gasped, gazing at his penile shaft emerging repeatedly between the woman's wobbling buttocks to drive deep into her tight rectum.

'God, you're bigger than my husband!'

'Does he do this to you?'

'Yes, and I do it to him!'

'What? You fuck his arse?'

'I have a strap-on dildo!'

'Fuck me!'

'No, fuck *me!*'

His climax quickly approaching, Larry drove his knob harder into the woman's rectal hole, quickening his rhythm as she reached between her thighs and pistoned her spasming cunny hole with the candle. His spunk suddenly gushing from his exploding glans, he slid his cock out of her tight anus and wanked over her buttocks, splattering her trembling flesh with his jetting jism.

'Take a picture!' she gasped.

'Christ!' Larry cried, grabbing the camera, his trembling hand clicking the shutter to capture his gushing spunk splattering the sex-fiend's quivering buttocks. 'It's . . . it's not easy!'

'Get my face in the picture!' she ordered, turning and grinning at the camera. 'Wank over my face and take a photograph!'

His sperm still spraying from his pulsating glans, Larry positioned his knob over the woman's face as she slipped off the couch and knelt before him. His white liquid running down her cheeks, dripping into her open mouth, he clicked the shutter, catching her depraved, adulterous act for posterity. His orgasm finally receding, he massaged the remnants of his spunk from his swollen knob and sank onto the couch, gasping in the aftermath of his climax.

'Perfect!' Mrs Cravings cried, rising to her feet and slipping the candle out of her drenched pussy hole. 'Now I have proof of my adulterous behaviour! My husband and I are equal!'

'Indeed, you are!' Larry gasped, concealing his spent penis within his trousers as the woman grabbed a towel from the

shelf and wiped the sperm from her face. 'I hope you enjoy a happy marriage now.'

'Indeed, I will! How much do I owe you, doctor?' she asked as she hurriedly dressed.

'Er . . . two hundred pounds, that's double my usual fee.'

'Ah, yes, the emergency booking.'

'Pay at reception, on your way out.'

'I must say that it's money well spent, you did a fine job!' she praised him.

'I aim to please.'

'Thank you for seeing me at such short notice,' she smiled, grabbing her camera and leaving the room.

'The pleasure was all yours!'

'You've saved a marriage!' she called.

'That's comforting. Goodbye, Mrs Cravings.'

'Goodbye, doctor!'

Replacing the candles on the shelf, Larry smiled to himself. *If only all my clients were like Mrs Cravings!* he reflected. Tidying the bondage room, he gazed at the window, imagining Monica making her escape, her ample buttocks ballooning as she climbed through. *Better ring the old hag and find out what she's up to!* he decided, heading for his consulting room.

'Hi, Monica, it's Larry,' he breezed, sitting on the edge of his desk as she answered her phone.

'What do *you* want?' she asked angrily.

'I was just wondering why you didn't come in today. Are you ill?'

'Ill? Of course I'm not ill! After what happened yesterday, do you honestly expect me to come back?'

'What happened yesterday?'

'You know very well! Brigit locked me in that disgusting room of yours!'

'Did she? This is the first knowledge I have of the alleged incident.'

'You didn't know?'

'No, I didn't. She must have inadvertently locked the door, not realizing that you were in there.'

'Inadvertently?'

'You know how forgetful she can be, Monica.'

'Yes, yes, I know.'

'She suffers from retention loss. Also, the door has a tendency to lock itself. I really must get it seen to, I spent three weeks in there once.'

'Three weeks? Why didn't you climb out of the window?'

'I don't have your ingenuity, your resourcefulness. Were you a desert rat?'

'My grandfather was.'

'That explains your ability to survive and escape imprisonment.'

'You were extremely rude to me! You said that my breasts were like two shrivelled-up empty leather . . .'

'That was only my little joke, Monica! You know what I'm like, always cracking disgusting jokes at other people's expense and revelling in their plight. Come back and we'll sort things out.'

'I don't know whether I should. You threatened to have me certified insane!'

'Another silly joke. You're the epitome of sanity.'

'What did the police say?'

88

'They said that we have a fine establishment here. I told them that it was your doing – the efficiency, the methodology.'

'Obviously you didn't show them your secret room.'

'Yes, I did. They were most impressed by the fine range of equipment we have. They praised your work – said that you might be in line for an OBE.'

'Of course they didn't!'

'They did! We miss you, Monica – please, come back. The place won't run efficiently without you. I'll double your salary, how's that?'

'Well, I do need the money. All right, I'll come back now.'

'Good! It will be so good to see you again. I'll go and tell Brigit.'

'All right, I'll be there soon – goodbye.'

Banging the phone down, Larry dashed to reception to find Brigit. 'Monica's on her way here!' he cried excitedly.

'Monica? What, after all that's happened?'

'Yes! This is our chance to imprison her!'

'But . . . Larry, I don't think it a good idea to lock her up! It's illegal!'

'Yes, that's the brilliant part of the plan, the illegality of it! Never again will she be able to cause me problems! I'm sure she's been spying for Gina Cology.'

'Why not have her working in reception, as she did, and be a little more discreet about your sexual antics?'

'But that's not as much fun as tying her to the examination couch and thrashing her bum with the cane!'

'It might not be as much fun, but you can't keep her locked up forever. What about the cost of feeding her?'

'I hadn't thought of that,' Larry sighed.

'There's the heating, too. We'd have to keep it on all night in the winter.'

'That would be expensive. And I suppose we'd have to give her Christmas dinner.'

'We'd have to escort her to the loo. It would be like having to look after a child!'

'Yes, you're right, Brigit – it would cost a small fortune in toilet rolls. All right, I'll keep my escapades a secret from now on. How's the appointments book looking?'

'Er . . . you have a schoolgirl from The Sacred Bloodied Heart of Our Lady of the Damned Convent arriving shortly.'

'Really? Oh, Good! Right, I'll be in my room. Should Monica arrive while I'm interfering with . . . talking to the girl, keep her well away from my room, OK?'

'OK, Larry. I hope you're not going to put your hand up the girl's skirt!'

'No, no! My cock, yes – but not my hand!'

'God, you're a pervert!' the girl giggled. 'I wonder why women aren't as sex-mad as men?'

'Some are.'

'Yes, but some are prudes.'

'The height of the libido in females is determined during the early teens. Women who masturbate frequently in their early teens usually grow up to become nymphomaniacs.'

'That accounts for my insatiable craving for orgasms!'

'Indeed, it does! I'll see you later.'

Dashing into his consulting room, Larry took the bottle of whisky from the drawer and placed it on the desk along with two glasses. *Try and get her drunk!* he thought in his devilry,

imagining slipping his hand inside her navy-blue knickers and defiling her virginal pussy sheath. The preparations done, he sat on his desk, eagerly awaiting the young girl's arrival as he rehearsed his lines. 'Do you frig your clitty to orgasm? No, no, that's not right! Er . . . have you ever felt the urge to rub between your cunt lips? Oh, fuck it, play it by ear, I suppose!' His penis stiffening as he heard a young female voice at reception, he leapt off the desk and straightened his tie. *This is it!*

'Doctor Lickman, this is Jenny,' Brigit introduced the pretty sixth-former as she ushered her into the room.

'Good morning, Jenny!' Larry greeted the girl, eyeing her short skirt, her long naked legs. 'Please, take a seat.'

'Thank you, Doctor Lickman,' the fresh-faced schoolgirl replied sheepishly, sitting at the desk.

'Right, that will be all, Brigit.'

Seating himself opposite Jenny, Larry poured the whisky. The girl's crisp white blouse outlining her small firm breasts, her young milk teats, he had a job restraining himself. How to begin? he wondered, eyeing her succulent red lips, her big blue eyes. Wondering whether she was a virgin, he smiled amicably.

'Now then, Jenny . . . here, have a drink.'

'Whisky? I don't drink whisky!'

'It'll do you good, relax you.'

Taking the glass, the girl knocked back the drink in one and grimaced. 'Argh! It's disgusting!' she complained as Larry refilled the glass.

'It's lovely! Er . . . now then, Jenny, I'm a sex therapist. Do you know what sex therapists do?' *Apart from sexually abuse schoolgirlies!*

Brushing her lank blonde hair back, she shook her head. 'No, I suppose I don't,' she admitted softly.

'Tell me, what do you know about masturbation?'

'Masturbation?' she echoed, her expression one of puzzlement and shock. 'Well, I . . . I know what it is.'

'That's a good start. Masturbation is an important part of growing up. Most girls start masturbating regularly from an early age and a good majority of them continue to masturbate throughout their lives.'

'Do they?' she gasped in astonishment, taking the glass and again downing the whisky in one gulp.

'Oh, yes! Most of the girls at your convent would have been masturbating with candles and cucumbers since they were about eleven years old – younger, even.'

'Eleven? I can't believe that my friends have been . . .'

'When did you discover masturbation, Jenny?'

'I didn't!'

'What? You mean, you don't do it?'

'No, I don't!'

'Oh, dear! You obviously don't realize that . . . do you know what and where your clitoris is?'

'Well, yes.'

'That's something! Can you honestly say that you've never masturbated, never rubbed your clitoris to orgasm?'

'Yes, honestly! Oh, I feel dizzy!'

'Here, have another drink.' Refilling the glass, Larry frowned. 'A clitoris neglected is a clitoris vulnerable to . . .'

'Vulnerable to what?' Jenny asked, her blue eyes sparkling as she sipped her drink.

'Don't they teach you *any*thing in the sixth form? If

you neglect your clitoris, it could well be irreparably damaged.'

'How?'

'The clitoris has one sole function, to bring you sexual pleasure – orgasms. If the organ is neglected, never rubbed to orgasm, it will become dysfunctional and . . . I don't want to worry you, Jenny, but . . . your clitoris might recede, leaving you sterile for life.'

'Sterile? No, no, I don't want that!'

'Of course you don't! How old are you?'

'Just eighteen.'

'Mmm, there might be time to save you. It's a great shame that I wasn't able to get my hands on you when you were sixteen, or when you were . . . no, that's illegal. Finish your drink and come to my examination room, Jenny. I'm most surprised to find a girl of your age who doesn't masturbate!' he gasped concernedly, rising to his feet and flinging open the door. 'Come with me. I only hope that it's not too late!'

'What are you going to do to me?' the girl asked, staggering down the hall and following Larry like a lamb into the bondage room.

'Examine you, for starters.'

'But Mother Barren-Womb said that . . .'

'Yes, but what she didn't realize was that you might be suffering from clitoral deflation, leading to ovarian paroxysm, causing permanent oviduct tissue damage.'

'What does all that mean?'

'That you might never conceive.'

'So, you want to look at me, *down there*?' Jenny asked, leaning on the examination couch to steady herself as Larry closed and locked the bondage room door.

'I have no choice, Jenny. With the knowledge that you might well need treatment, as a doctor, I'm obliged to examine you. It's my duty, I'm bound by law, you see.'

'I'd better tell my parents before . . .'

'Good grief, there's no time for that, child! Besides, the last thing you want to do is tell your parents! They'd blame themselves, it stands to reason!'

'Would they?'

'Yes, of course! It's their responsibility to inform you of masturbation techniques. Has your father ever sent you to night-school wanking classes?'

'Of course he hasn't!'

'That's most unusual.'

'He's an unusual man.'

'Is he?'

'He dresses up in my mother's clothes while she's out. I haven't told her, it would be too upsetting for her.'

'Indeed, it would! Have you confronted him?'

'No, I can't bring myself to say anything. Do you think I'll be all right, doctor?'

'I hope so. Quickly, onto the couch, skirt up and knickers down. Time is of the essence!'

Cautiously climbing onto the couch, Jenny reclined with her legs squeezed together, her bleary eyes trying to focus on her medic. Gently but firmly parting her legs, Larry lifted her gymslip up over her stomach and gazed longingly at her knickers, the soft, navy-blue material taut over the contour of her young sex. Instructing her to raise her buttocks, he pulled her knickers down and slipped them over her ankles, his penis solid as her tightly closed vaginal groove seemed to smile at him. Focusing on the crotch of her knickers,

'Oh, oh!' she cried as her climax erupted within her pulsating clitoris. 'Oh, that's absolutely ... absolutely beautiful! Ah, ah, it feels ... ah, ah!'

'You'd better come and see me every week,' Larry grinned, slipping two fingers into her tight vaginal duct.

'Ah, yes, yes!'

'Keep it coming!' he ordered the convulsing girl, thrusting his fingers in and out of her virginal cunt hole. 'Keep it coming!'

Her ground-shattering climax gripping her young body, bringing her unknown sexual ecstasy, Jenny tore open her blouse and yanked her small bra clear of her petite breasts. Tweaking her erect niplettes, pulling and twisting her young breast buds, she cried out, singing her appreciation for the new sensations of sex. Her clitoris receding as she gently drifted down from her sexual paradise, she kneaded her mammary globes, her body becoming rigid as her pleasure bud swelled and pulsated again, taking her to another shuddering climax.

Holding the vibrator between her reddening girl-lips as he thrust his fingers in and out of her gripping cunt, Larry watched the girl's face contorting as she trembled and screamed in the grips of her mind-blowing release. 'No more!' she gasped. 'Please, no more!' Ignoring her cries, Larry pressed the vibrator harder against her throbbing cumbud, bringing out yet another series of orgasmic shockwaves. 'No, no! Ah, ah!'

Finally releasing the girl from her carnal heaven, moving the magical vibrator away from her inflamed clitoris and slipping his fingers out of her drenched cunt, he grinned. 'Well, I think that worked!'

'Oh, oh!' she whimpered, her hands between her thighs, her inquisitive fingers discovering her girlhood. 'Ah! Ah, what happened?'

'You experienced an orgasm, Jenny,' Larry replied softly, licking her girl-juice from his fingers. 'Your first-ever orgasm.'

'It was . . . it was heavenly!' she breathed, reaching beneath her leg and slipping a finger into her vaginal hole, tentatively exploring her drenched sex duct. 'I've never known such . . . do it again! Please, I want the feeling to come again!'

Parting her fleshy labia, Larry pressed the buzzing vibrator against her swollen clitoris, watching the girl's finger pistoning in and out of her cuntal sheath as another orgasm quickly welled from her trembling pelvis. Her climax erupting, her mouth open, gasping, she uttered her moans of sexual satisfaction as waves of pure sexual ecstasy ravished her consumed body.

How many times will she come? Larry wondered as her clitoris deflated, only to balloon again and burst in another series of seismic orgasmic pulses. Her young cunt defiled, yawning, crimsoning in her heightening sexual pleasure, he decided that the time had come to strip her of her virginity – to fuck her! Finally released from the grip of her epic climax, she lay trembling, her finger deep inside her hot, wet hole as Larry switched the sex-aid off and placed it on the shelf.

'Jenny,' he said softly as the girl tossed her head from side to side, her blonde hair tousled, matted with the perspiration of sex. 'Jenny, I'm going to fuck you.' Hauling his solid penis out as he climbed onto the couch and positioned himself between her coltish legs, he repeated his statement. Her eyes rolling, she was lost in her sexual delirium, dizzy in

her post-orgasmic, alcoholic haze. Taking her hand and slipping her finger out of her vagina, he pressed his purple glans between her rubicund labia and gently drove his knob into her yielding cunt.

Gasping, kneading her young breasts as her vaginal lips rolled along his penetrating rod, she whimpered incoherent words of satisfaction, at her deflowering. Penetrating her, sliding his ravenous cock inch by inch into her surrendering cunt, Larry's glans finally came to rest against the softness of her cervix. Looking down at her swollen labia, tautly gripping the root of his organ, her clitoris forced from its hide, Larry withdrew his solid girl-wet shaft and entered her again. Her stomach rising with every impaling thrust, she gripped the sides of the examination couch, her knuckles whitening, her back arching, her hips bucking to meet him.

Quickening his fucking action, Larry took the girl on her incredible journey to her first penis-induced climax, shafting her spasming young cunt with a vengeance. His shaft glistening with her girl-come, his knob repeatedly appearing between her rubicund inner petals and driving into her hot hole, he fucked her until his sperm pump triggered and his glans throbbed in orgasm. Slipping his cock from the girl's gripping sex sheath, he massaged her pulsating clitoris with his throbbing knob, splattering his spunk over her pubic hair, her inflamed girl-crack.

'Wank me!' he gasped, grabbing her hand. Following his instruction, the girl lifted her head and watched his spunk jet from his cock as she massaged his throbbing glans. 'Ah, ah! Don't stop!' he breathed, gazing down at his jetting spunk as she massaged her solid clitoris with his glans. 'Keep wanking me!' Moving her hand faster up and down

his veined shaft, massaging her clitoris with his swollen knob, bringing out his come, her eyes widened with glee as her own climax heightened, sending electrifying sensations through her abused body. 'That's it, that's good!' Larry praised his young pupil. 'Ah, ah! Keep wanking me until there's no more spunk!'

His flow finally ceasing, he placed his hands either side of her young body, his weight on his arms, his mouth open, gasping in the aftermath of his climax. 'That was good!' he panted, leaning forward and sucking the girl's startled niplette into his hot mouth.

'It was!' she breathed, massaging his spent cock, exploring his drained balls with her slender fingers. 'It was wonderful! Do it to me again!'

'In a minute, in a minute! I need to rest!'

'Please, use that electric thing on me – give me the feeling again!' she pleaded in her unquenchable thirst for sexual satisfaction.

'All right, all right!' Larry sighed, climbing off the couch and grabbing the vibrator from the shelf. 'Bring your knees up, place your feet by your buttocks and part your knees as wide as you can. That's it, now hold your cunt lips open for me.'

The girl's pussy crack spewing out its sticky cocktail of lust juices, she parted her outer labia, opening her burgeoning sexual centre for the vibrator to orbit her to paradise again. Placing its buzzing tip over her clitoris, Larry grinned as she inhaled sharply, her face serene, her body jolting in response to the incredible sensations permeating her pelvis.

'Ah, ah, it's beautiful!' she sang, stretching her cunt lips further apart, presenting the full length of her solid clitoris to the sex machine. 'God, it's heaven!' Running the tip of

the vibrator around her swelling pleasure bud, Larry brought out another mind-blowing orgasm. Arching her back, the girl reached beneath her thighs and slipped three fingers into her decanting love mouth, finger-fucking her cunt as her climax rolled on. Delirious, her head swimming, she rolled her eyes as the sensations peaked and her cunt gripped her pistoning fingers.

Well and truly deflowered, her virginity stripped away, she'd rocketed from girlhood to womanhood. Gazing at her heaving breasts, taut, unblemished in youth, Larry smiled. This was his role in life, he mused – waking the dormant sexual desires of females, taking them to orgasm, teaching young girls how to pleasure their beautiful bodies. And there were more girls to deflower, he reflected. The convent was brimming with young virgins!

'Enough!' Jenny finally gasped. 'Ah, ah! Beautiful! Heavenly! Stop now!' Switching the vibrator off, Larry watched the girl pull her cunt-wet fingers from her steaming sex duct. Her arms limp by her sides, she straightened her trembling legs and relaxed in the aftermath of her enforced sexual awakening. Cupping her breasts in her bra and buttoning her school blouse, Larry was about to pull her navy-blue knickers up her long legs when he had an idea.

'I'll cleanse your cunt,' he said softly, parting her legs and leaning over her curvaceous body. Sweeping his tongue up her inflamed girl crack, he lapped up her pussy juice, stiffening her clitoris yet again. 'Like it?' he breathed, opening her thighs further and slipping his tongue into her youthful cunt.

'Mmm!' she moaned through her nose, her face reddening as sensations of oral sex shook her young body. 'Mmm, lick me all over!'

His tongue irrigating her vulval pasture, her swollen hillocks, her mound, the crevices of her young thighs, Larry cleansed the shuddering girl, lapping up his spunk and her creamy lubricant. Parting her fleshy folds, he drove his tongue into her tight vagina again as she gasped with delight.

'Larry!' Brigit called, tapping softly on the door. 'Larry, Monica's back!'

'OK, OK!' he panted, standing upright. 'You'd better put these on, Jenny,' he smiled, passing the trembling girl her school knickers.

'I thought you were going to give me another feeling!' she sighed disappointedly, tugging the erotically asexual garment up her legs and concealing her abused cuntal slit.

'You can come and see me again, if you want to,' he smiled, straightening his tie.

'Oh, yes, please!' Jenny beamed appreciatively, slipping off the couch and adjusting her school uniform.

'OK, let's go.'

Leading the staggering girl through reception, Larry flashed a smile at Monica as he showed the flushed-face nymphette out of the building. 'I'll see you again,' he whispered, patting her rounded bottom cheeks. 'Call in any time.' Returning to reception, he took a deep breath before confronting Monica, winking at Brigit as she stood behind the woman making odd facial expressions.

'Was that one of the girls from The Sacred Bloodied Heart of Our Lady of the Damned Convent?' Monica asked, her accusing eyes frowning.

'Yes, yes, she was from the bloody damned convent,' Larry grinned.

'Why was her face flushed?'

'It's hot in my consulting room. It's a hot day, unlike yesterday, don't you agree?'

'Yes, I suppose it is. Why was her blouse buttoned up wrongly?'

'She . . .'

'Why was she staggering all over the place? You didn't do anything to her, did you?'

'Yes, as a matter of fact, I did.'

'Doctor Lickman! After the episode in your torture chamber yesterday, I'd have thought . . .'

'It's not a torture chamber, Monica! Ask me what I did to the girl.'

'What did you do to her?'

'I talked to her, that was all. You must stop jumping to the wrong conclusions.'

'You fraternize with sex every day! All you ever think about is sex, it's unhealthy!'

'I have to, it's part of the job – it's my duty. Er . . . Brigit, where's Lily?' Larry asked.

'Er . . . Lily? She's . . . yes, she's still in the toilet.'

'*Still*? Good grief, she's been in there a long time!'

'She won't come out.'

'Why ever not?' Monica snapped, turning to Brigit. 'Has she gone off into one of her mental states again?'

'I . . . I don't know. I banged on the door and she said something about a pink snake with one eye chasing her.'

'Oh, no!' Larry sighed. 'All right, you two carry on and I'll go and have a word with her.'

*　　*　　*

Hurrying through the hall to the ladies' toilets, Larry tapped on the cubicle door. 'Lily, Lily, are you all right?' he asked. 'Open the door!'

'Shan't!'

'Open the door Lily!'

'Shan't!'

'Look, I can't be doing with this sort of behaviour! Open the door this instant or I'll call a psychiatrist and have you certified insane!'

'All right,' she replied, sliding the bolt back.

Entering the cubicle, Larry frowned. 'Lily, why are you naked?' he asked, eyeing her vaginal slit peering through a bush of blonde pubic hair. 'Why are you standing on the toilet, naked?'

'I . . . I was trying to get my foot up my pussy,' she confessed. 'And I was fondling my breasts, trying to familiarize myself with them.'

'I can understand you fondling your breasts to acquaint yourself with them, but why put your foot up your pussy?' Larry asked surprisedly, gazing at her cunny-wet toes.

'I . . . I don't know. It's something I've done ever since I can remember. Do you find it shocking?'

'No, not shocking, Lily. But I do find it unusual.'

Locking the cubicle door as he heard Monica bellowing at Brigit, Larry leaned on the wall, gazing at the girl's inner lips protruding invitingly between her full outer sex cushions, the sexual centre of her naked body at eye-level. *Trying to get her foot up her pussy?* he pondered, wondering what weird psychological problem lay behind her peculiar act.

'Lily, have you ever *succeeded* in getting your foot into your pussy?' he probed.

'Oh, yes! Well, my toes, at least. I'm somewhat of a contortionist.'

'Yes, as was my mother.'

'Oh, was she?'

'Yes, but I won't go into that now. What drives you to do such a dreadful thing?'

'I don't know.'

'Did your mother have a difficult birth?'

'Yes, apparently I took hours to come out.'

'Ah, that explains it!' Larry grinned triumphantly as he dreamed up an explanation for her strange behaviour. 'You see, you didn't *want* to come out, and you're now trying to get back into the womb, albeit your own womb. The condition is known as uterine regression.'

'Oh, I see! What can I do about it, is there a cure? I wonder why I didn't want to come out?'

'There might be a cure, yes. I'll come to that in a minute. I would imagine the reason that you didn't want to come out was because it was warm and cosy in there. Was your mother warm during her pregnancy? When were you born?'

'In May.'

'Ah, so your mother was pregnant throughout the winter months.'

'Yes, and the house was always very cold.'

'That's it, then! Now, the cure. Er . . . allow me to give you a quick internal examination,' Larry smiled, parting the girl's succulent sex cushions. 'Bend your knees and open your legs for me.'

Slipping three fingers deep into her vagina, he looked up

at her pretty face and smiled. 'You have what we call, in the trade, *cuntum constrictum.*'

'What does that mean?'

A tight cunt! 'Er . . . it means that your vaginal duct is . . . Lily, I'm going to try to get my fist into your vagina to check your *ductus vaginus capacitum.*'

'What's that?'

How big your cunt is! 'Er . . . nothing for you to concern yourself with.'

Straightening his fingers, Larry managed to push them into the girl's yielding cunt, her swollen vaginal lips taut around his knuckles as he gently opened her sex duct. He drove his fingers further into her trembling body, managing to force half his hand into her hot cavern to the accompaniment of her gasps. Bending her knees, lowering her sexual centre, Lily grimaced as Larry clenched his fist, her labia finally stretched tautly around his wrist.

'There, I've done it!' Larry gasped excitedly, gazing at the girl's abused vaginal lips gripping his arm. 'How does it feel?'

'God, it feels . . . it feels great!'

Twisting his fist, massaging her stretched inner flesh, he jumped as Monica hammered on the door.

'Doctor Lickman!' she called. 'Is Lily all right? What are you doing?'

'Lily's fine!' Larry replied, trying to pull his fist out of the girl's hot cunt. 'Lily, I can't get my hand out!' he whispered. 'It's stuck!'

'What's stuck?' Monica asked agitatedly.

For Christ's sake! 'Nothing, Monica! Man reception!' *While I unman Lily!*

'Can't you pull it out?' Lily asked anxiously, gazing down at her distended labia.

'No, I can't! I'm being sucked in. There's a vacuum.'

'What shall we do?'

'Monica!' Larry called through the door of the cubicle. 'Go and get the enema syringe and a length of rubber pipe!'

'What for?'

'Er . . . there's a problem with the plumbing!'

'Are you a plumber?'

'No, no! Just go and get me the . . .'

'Mr Ingram Ravenhugh is on the phone. He wants to see you.'

Fuck! 'Er . . . I'll be out in a minute. I'm giving Lily some therapy. Make an appointment for him, Monica.'

Taking his pen from his jacket pocket, Larry unscrewed the top and pulled the refill out. 'I hope this works,' he breathed, slipping the hollow pen alongside his wrist into Lily's bloated cuntal sheath. The air suddenly rushing in, he managed to slip his drenched fist out of her cavern. 'Done it!' he cried triumphantly, watching the girl's swollen vaginal lips recede. 'You'd better get dressed, Lily. And let's not have any more of your nonsense!'

Jumping off the toilet, Lily grabbed her clothes from the floor and hurriedly dressed, apologizing profusely as Larry slid the bolt back and cautiously opened the door. 'Lock the door behind me,' he said, grinning as the girl concealed her beautiful body. 'I'll go to reception and calm the old bat down.'

Leaning nonchalantly over the reception counter, he smiled at Monica. 'Mr Ingram Ravenhugh? What's he want, do you know?'

'He wants to speak to you about income tax,' she returned, frowning as she focused on Larry's wet hand. 'And national insurance contributions.'

'When's he coming?'

'I've made an appointment for this afternoon. By the way, the Reverend Mother Barren-Womb rang. She's not at all happy, Doctor Lickman! She said that Jenny returned to school drunk!'

'Drunk? Good grief!'

'She's coming to see you tomorrow. Most disgruntled, she was.'

'Tomorrow, right. Er . . . I'll be in my consulting room, I need a rest!'

Recuperating at his desk, Larry swigged from the whisky bottle, wondering how to explain Jenny's drunkenness to the old hag. *Jesus, I've never had a Reverend Mother before! I wonder whether she fucks?* Gulping from the bottle again, he sighed. 'Unless I can convince her that the girl wasn't drunk, she'll not be sending me any more little beauties!' *Oh well, might as well get pissed!*

Chapter Four

'Larry, why are you slumped over your desk?' Brigit asked agitatedly, shaking his shoulder. 'Have you been here all night? God, you're not drunk, are you?'

'I was just . . . oh, fuck, I seem to have finished off the scotch! Shit, I've been drinking all night!'

'The Reverend Mother Barren-Womb is here!'

'Fuck and double fuck! Er . . . Jesus, my head!'

'Hide the bottle and smarten yourself up. I'll show her in.'

Dropping the empty bottle into the desk drawer, Larry straightened his tie and staggered to his feet. His head spinning, he leaned against the desk for support as Brigit showed the behabited woman into the room. Her scowling face framed by her crisp white linen wimple, her arms folded aggressively, she glared at Larry, demanding to know why the room reeked of whisky.

'Er . . . whisky? I've just had the cleaner in, I think you'll find it's the special malt polish she uses on my desk,' he smiled, offering her a seat as he stumbled around the desk and collapsed into his chair, his dishevelled hair cascading over his lined forehead. 'Now, Reverend Mother-Womb . . . Barren-Mother. What's all this nonsense about Jenny being spunk . . . drunk?'

'Did you ply her with whisky?' the suppressed woman growled as she seated herself.

My God, you look like an old man! 'Sly her with piss . . . good grief, no! Were you made in the image of God?'

'What?'

'Man was made in the image of God, I just wondered in whose image you were made.' *A ghoul's?*

'Don't try to change the subject! The girl's blouse was incorrectly buttoned when she came staggering back to the convent!'

'Her buttons were incorrectly bloused? What do you mean?'

'Her blouse had been interfered with!'

'I've never heard of anyone interfering with a blouse. Is it some kind of new and disgusting sexual fetish conceived by Catholic priests to . . .'

'Don't be ridiculous! I had cause to examine the child's clothing, and I discovered that she'd been tampered with!'

Fucked, more like! 'Tampaxed . . . tampered with? I don't understand. What do these terrible allegations have to do with me, Reverend Brother? I don't see your logic in connecting the girl's dishevelled attire with me.'

'I interrogated her!'

'Do you suspect her of being a spy? You're not a descendant of Philby, are you?'

'What? What *are* you talking about?'

'Spies. Did she break down and confess under torture?'

'She informed me that you'd examined her.'

Shit! 'Ah, yes, so I did. I *am* an eminent Doctor of Sexual . . .'

'You sullied her virginal body! It's a cardinal sin!'

'I did nothing of the sort! She left here as unsullied as the driven snow.'

'You removed her underwear!'

'Well . . . yes, that's true.'

'You can't remove schoolgirls' knickers! It's immoral! Saint Peter will send you to hell! God have mercy on you!'

'Oh, good, I'll meet all my old friends! Anyway, I *can* and I *did* remove her knockers . . . her knickers. She was suffering from *hymen constrictum.*'

'What's that?'

'Constriction of the hymen. It's a common complaint in teenage girls. You'd never believe how many hymens I've come over . . . I mean, come across. I had to dilate her hymen with my . . . with my hymen-dilation tool. It's a good job she came in time.'

'Came in time?'

'Yes, to see me. Had it been left any longer . . . well, the consequences could have been dire. The fate of her vagina would have been in the hands of the gods.'

'Blasphemy!'

'Satan.'

'You'll be struck down! Have you no fear of God's wrath?'

'Does He upset easily?'

'Very easily! Especially when there's talk of Satan!'

'Satan was near, Reverend Lover. I sensed him constricting the girl's hymen. She harboured sexual demons – I saved her from the eternal fires of . . .'

'Please, stop referring to the Devil and demons!'

'The girl's vulval tissue was traumatized by sexual demons.'

'What *are* you talking about? Can you explain her drunkenness?'

'Ah, no, no, she wasn't drunk. You probably mistook the effect of the anaesthetic for rampant alcoholism.'

'Anaesthetic?'

'Yes, I had to anaesthetize her vulval tissue by performing a copulatory penile injection.'

'What's that?'

'A spermatozoic injection into the cervical os. She'll be all right now.'

'Oh, well . . . I appear to owe you an apology, Doctor Lickman.'

Fucking right, you do! 'No, not at all! I'm pleased to see that you have the welfare of the girl at heart, Reverend Father. I must stress the importance of my seeing *all* the sixth-form girls.' *The importance of my fucking their tight cunts!* 'After uncovering Jenny's complaint, it's of the utmost importance that I see the other girls at my earliest inconvenience.'

'Yes, of course. But I have to stress that, in my position as Reverend Mother of the convent, I'm responsible for the girls. The Lord has charged me to protect them from the wicked ways of the world.'

'Goodness me, you had to pay the Lord?'

'No! He charged me, commanded me.'

'Oh, I see. Tell me, Reverend Smother, when did you get the calling?'

'Ah, the calling from the Lord! He came unto me.'

'He came into you?'

'He came *un*to me, not into me. I remember it well, I was fourteen years old at the time of my calling. I was in the bath, and He came unto me. I was staggered, as

any young girl would be to see the Lord standing by her bath.'

'He stood by the bath?'

'Yes. There I was, meek in all my nakedness, and . . .'

'Blessed are meek fourteen-year-old girls for they shall inherit my . . . what did the Lord look like?'

'There was a lot of steam in the bathroom and His head was shrouded in a white sheet. I couldn't see properly, only His eyes were showing. He reminded me very much of my father.'

'Goodness me!'

'My father swore blind that it wasn't him when my mother confronted him. He said that I must have seen the Lord. In my heart of hearts, I knew I'd had a vision.'

'What did the Lord say?'

'He asked me to get out of the bath and stand naked before Him.'

'Then what happened?'

'He knelt before me and blessed me.'

'How?'

'He touched and kissed me. He said that he'd take my virginity as he'd omitted to take Mary's.'

'What happened next?'

'I . . . I can't tell you, I'm sworn to secrecy. He said that I should tell no one as the act might be liable to misinterpretation.'

'Indeed, it might!'

'Well, thank you for your time, Doctor Lickman.'

'You're most unwelcome!' Larry smiled, holding his aching head as he staggered to his feet and led the penguin

down the hall. 'I'll look forward to seeing the rest of the girls very soon.'

'It's good of you to take such an interest in the girls. Actually, there's a young nun I'd like you to see. She's been complaining of dizziness, which I find worrying.'

'Yes, of course. Phone reception and make an appointment for her. I'd be only too pleased to take a look up her . . . a look at her.'

'Thank you. Well, good day, doctor.'

'Good day, Mother Barren-Room,' Larry smiled, seeing his appeased visitor out of the building.

Grinning triumphantly at Monica as he entered reception, Larry leaned over the counter. 'A little misunderstanding!' he chuckled. 'The Reverend Mother Barren-Womb had grabbed the wrong end of the dick.'

'A misunderstanding? You defiled a schoolgirl!' the woman returned, her face flushing with her rising anger. 'It's illegal! You should be put behind bars!'

'It's not illegal!'

'Of course it is! It's disgusting, subjecting the girl to . . .'

'Monica, Monica! Why is it that you perpetually think along such vile and debased lines? Are you deranged? It seems to me that all you ever think about is perverted sex! Your mind's rife with thoughts of indecent, perverted sexual acts!'

'It's not! Why was the girl staggering? She could barely walk!'

'She was exhausted after a heavy bout of chemistry homework. Anyone would stagger after such an ordeal, it weakens the thighs.'

'Rubbish! Look what you did to that poor Jessica Jezebel!'

'I was firming and toning Jessica's pelvic muscles, and you accused me of caning the girl – torturing her!'

'You *had* caned her! And it *is* torture, there's no other word for it!'

'Professor Flagellant's revolutionary . . . look what happened when Jane was in my consulting room. I was using a tried and tested method to help her off the fence of indecision, and you were spying at me through the window! As usual, you grabbed the wrong end of the cane . . . of the stick.'

'I saw you and Brigit lying over your desk half naked!'

'Yes, but it was all in keeping with the treatment, the therapy session, Monica.'

'What, exposing your genitalia?'

'What I was doing is called gender preference therapy. It's not only recognized by the BMA but highly recommended by them.'

'Of course it isn't! Do you think me stupid?'

'Yes, I have to say that I do think you're stupid, Monica. You know nothing of today's modern techniques. You cannot accuse people of sexual debauchery if you don't know the facts. If I were to come across a man and woman naked in a cornfield, my mind wouldn't immediately jump to the conclusion that they were involved in some sort of indecent sexual activity, as your mind would.'

'Why else would they be naked in a cornfield? It's unnatural! And it's illegal!'

'It wouldn't be illegal if they owned the cornfield, would it?'

'What on earth would they be doing other than . . .'

'They might be sunbathing.'

'What, naked?'

'There's little point sunbathing in a cashmere overcoat, a scarf and wellington boots! If you saw two men enter a public toilet cubicle together, no doubt you'd immediately think them bent.'

'As would any decent person! It's obscene!'

'There's a simple explanation for two men entering a public toilet cubicle together.'

'There's only one explanation in my book!'

'Plumbers!'

'Where?'

'My fictitious men are plumbers, Monica! One's married with four kids and the other is married with two kids – they're decent husbands and fathers. They work hard at their job. They have to, especially the one with four kids because his mortgage is . . .'

'It doesn't take two plumbers to repair one toilet!'

'Yes, it does – a plumber and his mate. You see, you don't stop to think, do you? Take Jenny, the schoolgirl. You asked why her face was flushed, no doubt thinking that some vile sexual act had occurred in my consulting room, when the explanation couldn't have been more innocent – the poor child was hot! You asked why she was staggering, you said that her blouse had been incorrectly buttoned . . . again, your thoughts were centred on vile sexual acts.'

'Well, I . . .'

'Having lost a button on her blouse, she had to button it up incorrectly to compensate for the missing button – to conceal her virgin breasts, her unsullied milk teats. You see, it's as simple as that. No one was trying

to get at her body to commit a beautiful ... a dirty sexual act!'

'I didn't realize that she'd ...'

'That's exactly my point! You're leaping before you've looked. If you feel that you're in need of psychiatric help, I'll be only too willing to ...'

'I don't need *your* help! I'll admit that I have a suspicious mind, but that's perfectly normal, given the circumstances.'

'What circumstances?'

'Well, working here, among all these people with sexual problems.'

'If you're not up to the job, Monica, then ...'

'I am up to the job. I want to work here, especially now that you've doubled my salary.'

'I believe your suspicious mind stems from your childhood.'

'I had a very happy childhood, Doctor Lickman! My mother was one of the best, and my father was ... well, he did his best, considering the unfortunate circumstances.'

'Weren't you psychologically disturbed?'

'No, not at all! Why should I have been?'

'Did the Lord come all over you?'

'The Lord? I had a decent Catholic upbringing. My childhood was remarkably undisturbed.'

'That proves my point – your childhood was completely and utterly abnormal.'

'What makes you say that?'

'All kids are psychologically disturbed, especially girls. It's a natural part of growing up, it stands to reason.'

'Does it?'

'You never had children, did you, Monica?'

'No, I didn't. It's against my religion.'

'What, having kids?'

'No, sexual intercourse. The Pope says . . .'

'Surely you don't listen to an old git who goes around kissing the ground and posing as God?'

'Well, I . . .'

'It's insanity! If all women remained barren, the world would become devoid of human beings! Imagine what it would be like.'

'Quiet and peaceful, no pollution.'

'Who would that benefit?'

'The few people left waiting to die – and the animals.'

'The notion's crazy! Let's make a new start, Monica. Now, be honest with me, what does this Venereal man want? What have you told him?'

'I . . . I told him that the practice isn't run in a correct and proper manner.'

'And all because you keep jumping to the wrong conclusions! I think you'd better contact him and tell him how very wrong you were, don't you?'

'Er . . . yes, Doctor Lickman. I'll do it right away.'

'Good. Ah, Mr and Mrs Crotcher!' Larry beamed, glancing at his watch as a middle-aged couple wandered across the foyer. 'Dead on time, as usual. Er . . . Mrs Crotcher, would you be so good as to pop along to the waiting room? I'll have a chat with your husband and then I'll see you. Monica, a cup of tea for Mrs Crotcher, please. Right, Mr Crotcher, this way, this way.'

* * *

Offering his client a chair, Larry sat opposite the man and rested his elbows on the desk. 'So, how are things?' he asked, thankful that, at last, he'd put Monica in her place.

'Awful, doc! She ain't got no better since we first come 'ere two weeks ago!'

My God, you're common! 'Surely, there's been some improvement?'

'No, there ain't been none at all! Like what I said last time, I'm a normal kind of bloke – you know, I like a bit of the old dirty stuff. I bought some 'andcuffs, and she won't even look at the fuckin' things, let alone . . .'

'Er . . . yes. I thought you were going to gently ease your wife into . . .'

'I was! Last night, I was feelin' really 'orny – you know, bollocks full, knob as 'ard as bleedin' granite . . . anyway, we goes to bed, and she bleedin' well rolls over! Daft bitch that she is! She's lucky I never stuffed it up 'er arse! I told 'er – Mary, I says, remember what the doc said? She turns round and goes "I don't give a damn what 'e said, I'm tired!" '

'I see. Have you been touching, fondling, easing her into foreplay, as I suggested?'

'She won't let me get me 'ands nowhere near 'er. The other night we goes to bed and she goes "If you don't get that thing out of me back, I'll kip on the sofa!" That's a fine way to talk about me knob, I must say!'

'Right, Mr Crotcher. Go to the waiting room and send your wife in. I'll have a word with her and then I'll speak to you again.'

'OK, doc. Tell 'er to open 'er bleedin' legs.'

'Er . . . yes, yes, I will.'

Holding his head, Larry sighed. There was no way he

could help the couple. Mrs Crotcher was frigid beyond belief and her husband didn't have the understanding of a pubic louse! Wondering whether the desperate man would be willing to pay for sex with Brigit, he smiled as the harried woman entered the room.

'Ah, please sit down, Mrs Crotcher.'

'Thank you, doctor,' she replied, brushing her mousy hair away from her pale face.

'According to your husband, things aren't too good on the sexual front?'

'The things he wants me to do are . . . are disgusting! He's abnormal, that's what he is! How could he sink so low? I've always led a decent life. Whatever have I done to deserve a perverted sex maniac like him?'

'Perhaps you were a wanton hussy in a past life?'

'I have it on good authority that I was an Egyptian monk.'

'Oh! Has your husband ever felt a need to turn to the church?'

'Why do you ask that?'

'Well, that would explain his sexual deviancy. Sexually deviant men tend to congregate in churches. Was his father a Catholic priest?'

'No, he was a drunkard! I have never met anyone as disgusting as my husband. The things he asks me to do are vile, obscene, debased! Would you eat bananas from your wife's . . . from her bottom? Apart from disgusting, the act is illegal!'

'It's not illegal.'

'Well, it should be! What sort of government condones such a disgraceful act? We should have a dictator running the country, not a wimp! Would you eat bananas from . . .'

120

'Well, I don't have a wife so . . .'

'Any woman's bottom, then?'

Not from yours, that's for sure! 'Er . . . I don't like bananas so the question doesn't apply. What else does he demand of you?'

'He wants me to dress up in clothes that only cheap prostitutes would be seen in!'

'Cheap prostitutes? Was his mother a prostitute?'

'I don't know – why?'

'I'm wondering what the reason is for him wanting to portray you as a cheap prostitute. He obviously has leanings towards streetwalkers. In my considered and unprofessional opinion, I'd say that he was breast-fed for far too long – possibly until he was fifteen or sixteen.'

'He's always been unhealthily close to his mother.'

'I thought as much. Describe the clothing he wishes you to wear.'

'He bought me a red leather bodysuit with holes in it. Disgusting, that's what it is!'

'It has holes in it?'

'Yes, holes for my breasts and a hole . . . well, you know, *down there*.'

God forbid! What a sight! 'Er . . . some men find dressing their women in kinky clothes sexually exciting.'

'What would the neighbours say?'

'They wouldn't know.'

'They might knock on the door for a cup of sugar.'

'Don't answer the door.'

'A bag of flour, even.'

'Ignore the doorbell.'

'I always answer the door, it's mannerly.'

'Do you have a peephole bra, Mrs Crotcher?'

'What's that?'

'A bra with holes for your . . .'

'All my bras are in pristine condition! Holes? If my bras were holed, I'd bin them!'

'Yes, quite. Do you know what your nipples are for?'

'Yes, they're . . . they're for . . .'

'Sucking.'

'Well, yes. They're for feeding . . .'

'Exactly. Now, if you were to wear a peephole bra, your husband would feel free to suck your . . .'

'I'm not letting him suck my nipples, it's not natural! He might act like a child, but he's not a baby!'

'But that's what your nipples are for. You see, as your husband was breast-fed until his mid-teens, it's left him with a craving for the mammary teat. Psychologically, he needs the motherly bonding that breast-feeding offers. The poor man's lost in a mammary void. Let's talk about masturbation.'

'Why?'

Because I like talking about masturbation! 'Because I need to discover more about your sexuality. At what age did your pubic hair begin to grow?'

'What's that got to do with masturbation?'

'Everything! When did you first shave your vulval hair?'

'I have *never* shaved my . . .'

'How old were you when you first discovered your clitoris?'

'I didn't discover it!'

'When did your breast buds swell?'

'They didn't!'

'What? You don't have breasts?'

'Of course I have breasts!'

'At what age did you first need to wear a bra?'

'I bought my first bra when I was . . . Doctor Lickman, it's my husband who needs help, not me!'

'I know. I'm helping him through you – it's a new and fascinating psychological approach. You see, if your husband is mentally ill, then I can help him by talking to you.'

'I don't understand that!'

'Is there anything about him that you find disturbing?'

'Actually, there is something dreadful about him – but I could never bring myself to discuss it!'

'Give me a clue.'

'I can't, it pains me.'

'Just a little clue.'

'No! I'll tell you this, though – the other day he asked me to . . . to take my clothes off and sit on his face!'

'Well, that's not such an unusual request for a man to make of his wife.'

'It's dreadful! What does he think he is, a chair?'

'No, he wanted . . . let's talk about lesbians.'

'Why? It's not decent!'

'No reason, I just thought we might chat about them. How do you feel about lesbians, Mrs Crotcher?'

'They disgust me!'

'You've never had tendencies?'

'What sort of tendencies?'

'Lesbionic yearnings, leanings towards your own sex.'

'Certainly not! I'm clean living, brought up properly. I said to Father Godly only last week . . .'

'You go to church?'

'Regular as clockwork.'

'Confession?'

'Once a week.'

'What do you confess to?'

'I can't tell you.'

'You must!'

'You're not a priest, so I can't.'

'Don't reveal this sensitive information to anyone, Mrs Crotcher, but I *am* a priest. I'm a Roman Catholic priest. I was ordained only last week by Father Pederast at the Church of the Unchaste Temptress.'

'I haven't heard of Father Pederast. Where's he coming from?'

'Look him up in the dictionary and you'll find out!'

'But you're a doctor!'

'And a priest. To which dreadful sin did you confess?'

'I'm sorry, Father, I didn't know that you were a priest.'

'That's all right. Anyone could make the same mistake, seeing as I'm not wearing my dog collar. Without a dog collar the profession of a priest is indeterminable. I've often been mistaken for an electrician, although I can't think why.'

'It might be your nose – you have an electrician's nose.'

'Possibly. Being a priest comes in very useful – I confess my sins to myself.'

'That must make quite a saving on travelling expenses to the church.'

'Indeed, it does. It costs a small fortune by bus these days. Now, imagine that we're in the confessional.'

'Forgive me, Father, for I have sinned.'

'What was the nature of your sin, my child?'

'I've had wicked thoughts. I've thought how nice it would be if my husband died.'

'That's perfectly normal for a woman in your difficult position. Have you considered murder?'

'Well . . . yes, I have.'

'I wouldn't recommend it, it's a crime that carries a heavy punishment. Divorce would be more appropriate, it has the added benefit of legality. I can put you in touch with a very good solicitor.'

'I'd be lonely.'

'No, he's a nice man – warm, approachable.'

'Who?'

'The solicitor.'

'No, I meant that I'd be lonely without my husband.'

'You'd be happy. What other dreadful sins have you committed?'

'I've spied on my husband.'

'Spied on him? Why?'

'He . . . he's in desperate need of psychiatric help, doctor. He has a blow-up doll.'

'Really? What does he do with the doll?'

'He blows it up.'

'How peculiar! What does he do then?'

'He . . . I can't bring myself to talk of the dreadful act.'

'You must! Remember, I'm a priest. We've been brought together by God so that I may guide you in your time of sexual confusion. What does he do with the doll?'

'He . . . he has sex with it.'

'Is this the dreadful thing you couldn't bring yourself to discuss earlier?'

'Yes, it is.'

'This blow-up doll . . . enlighten me as to the sordid details, Mrs Crotcher.'

'He has sex with its mouth.'

'Good grief!'

'The doll buzzes loudly, although I don't know why. And it talks in an awful American voice.'

'What does it say?'

'I couldn't bring myself to repeat the doll's words!'

'Write the words down for me.'

'No, certainly not!'

The door bursting open and hitting the wall with a loud thud, Larry looked up in surprise. 'It's courteous to knock, Monica!' he reprimanded the flustered woman as she stormed into the room.

'There's a disgusting sexual act taking place in the waiting room, doctor! I felt it my duty to inform you without undue delay.'

'A disgusting sexual act? Who's involved in this alleged act of sexual filth?'

'Mr Crotcher and Brigit Biways.'

'My husband?' Mrs Crotcher screamed hysterically, leaping to her feet. 'I'll murder him!'

As the woman rushed out of the room and torpedoed down the hall, Larry held his hand to his head and sighed. 'Monica, don't you have any tact at all? You've just destroyed a marriage!'

'*Me*?'

'Yes, you and your tactless, incriminating mindless words!'

'The woman has a right to know of her husband's debased infidelity.'

'No, she doesn't! Women don't have rights! Those bloody suffragettes have ruined mankind! I hope your conscience stabs you to death!'

'But I . . . I thought it best . . .'

'What was going on in the waiting room?'

'Brigit was on her knees with Mr Crotcher's . . . with his penis in her mouth. I have never witnessed such a vile and degrading act! Has the girl no decency, no respect for her femininity?'

'Of course she has! She's using her body, her mouth, to pleasure one of our valued clients. It's a woman's place to do such things to men.'

'It's not their place! I've never done such a disgraceful . . .'

'No, I don't suppose you have! I hope she intends to charge for the service. She knows the rules concerning moonlighting.'

'You'll sack her, of course.'

'Sack the girl? Why sack her?'

'Because of her disgusting, unprofessional behaviour.'

'She acted in a professional and responsible manner. Mr Crotcher was in dire need of sexual relief, and Brigit relieved him.'

'The whole episode is . . .'

'Remember that I've doubled your salary, Monica!' Larry grinned as the phone rang. 'You'd better go and see what's going on.'

Watching the distraught woman leave the room and close

the door, Larry grabbed the phone. 'Doctor Larry Lickman,' he said authoritatively.

'Ah, Doctor Lickman – Gina Cology here.'

'And how are you, Gina? Clients dropping like flies, are they?'

'I have more than enough clients, thank you.'

'How's your clitoris these days?'

'Please, try not to be disgusting!'

'Are you still masturbating heavily?'

'I'm calling because I have . . .'

'Do you like sucking your nipples while you masturbate with a cucumber?'

'I'm calling because I have a young woman here, an ex-client of yours.'

'Oh, who's that?'

'Her name's Jane. She's told me about your methods, your disgusting . . .'

'Jane who? I don't have a client called Jane.'

'I know you haven't, she's now *my* client! Her name's Jane Churcher. She told me that you and your secretary exposed yourselves to her. She said that you ordered her to suck your penis and lick your secretary's vagina.'

'Good grief! She must be mentally unhinged – deranged, even!'

'She's perfectly sane, and she's willing to testify. I also have some incriminating photographs here – photographs of you sexually abusing a client.'

'Are you mad? Has your brain suffered a seizure? You really must stop masturbating, it's destroying you! What's it like being a common slut, Gina?'

'Do you have to resort to personal abuse?'

'No, but I enjoy it!'

'You think you're funny, don't you? Well, this will wipe the smirk off your face! I sent a friend of mine along to see you.'

'Good God, you have a friend? Well, this *is* unbelievable news!'

'She used a pseudonym – Mrs Cravings.'

Bloody hell!

'Being the fool that you are, you believed her story about her husband and the Swedish au pair. You'll be pleased to know that the photographs have come out very well. I now have all the evidence I need to have your so-called sex-therapy practice closed down!'

'The pictures don't show my face, so you can't . . .'

'They show your examination room, and your . . . the mole you have is evidence enough. I do believe that I've won, don't you?'

'No, no way! There's nothing you can do to prove that it's me in the photographs. It could be anyone. It might even be the Pope.'

'Does the Pope visit your debased establishment to have perverted sex with your clients?'

'Not as far as I know.'

'Then how could it possibly be him?'

'He might have called without my having knowledge of his visit. I'll check the appointments book. What's his name, do you know?'

'Don't be ridiculous! We'll see what the BMA have to say about this.'

'Would you like me to come over to your floundering clinic and spunk down your throat, Gina?'

'Be as crude and vulgar as you wish, you're about to be history!'

'I'll cut your fucking nipples off and stuff them up your cunt when I next . . .'

'Goodbye, Doctor Lickman. And good riddance!'

Replacing the receiver, Larry ran his fingers through his hair and sighed. Hearing shouting and screaming coming from reception, he wondered whether the time had come to throw in the towel and call it a day. *Just when I'd lined up the schoolgirlies!* he reflected dolefully as Brigit swanned into the room.

'The Crotchers have gone,' she enlightened him, perching on the edge of his desk, her alluring pussy crack blatantly displayed beneath her red microskirt. 'They had an almighty punch-up, it was brilliant!'

'I'm not surprised! How much did you charge him for the blow job?'

'I've forgotten. Oh, yes, fifty pounds.'

'Good girl! What's the old bat doing?'

'She's talking to Lily in reception.'

'Oh, right. Gina Cology rang, she has Jane there – plus photographs of me with my . . . I think my end has come, Brigit.'

'Your end has come? That's nice for you!'

'No, no! The end of the practice is nigh.'

'You're not giving up, are you?' Brigit gasped, opening her legs to afford Larry a better view of her shaved vaginal crack. 'Just because that Cology woman threatens you, you can't give up!'

'She has proof of my . . . it's obviously the will of God. I'm to be eternally damned, cast into the eternal fires of Lucifer's

kingdom – I can feel it in my water. Oh well, there'll be plenty of tarts to fuck, I suppose. I wonder if the beer really is free in hell?'

'Larry, why don't I go and spy on Gina, get some dirt on her and . . .'

'She knows you.'

'I've only spoken to her on the phone, I've never actually met her.'

'Oh, right! OK, let me give it some thought. I'll come up with a plan of action.'

'If I go to her clinic, I could claim that I was sexually assaulted by her. She'd deny it, of course, but it would get into the local paper. Anyway, I'll leave you to think about it.'

'OK, Brigit. Yes, I like the idea, I'll come up with a plan. Send Lily in, would you?'

'OK, I'll see you later.'

Gazing out of the window, Larry contemplated Brigit's proposal. It might work, he reflected, imagining Gina Cology's photograph plastered over the front page of the local rag. Wandering over to the window, he turned his thoughts to Lily, deciding that the time had come to rid the girl of her penis phobia. *If I'm closed down, I might not have another chance to screw young Lily!*

'Ah, Lily,' he greeted the girl as she peered round the open door. 'I'd like you to come to my examination room.'

'Monica has been telling me that you have a torture chamber – that's not where you're taking me, is it?' she asked, her blue eyes wide.

'I don't have a torture chamber!' Larry laughed, walking past the girl into the hall. 'Come on, this way.'

Locking the door as Lily walked into the room and gazed at the examination couch, Larry grinned. The only way to have her overcome her fear of penises was to force his magnificent organ upon her, he decided. *Fight fire with fire, penises with penises!* 'Hypnosis, Lily,' he decreed, gazing at the girl's honey-blonde hair, her pretty face. 'Take your panties off and lie on the couch. I'll hypnotize you and you'll no longer have a phobia of breasts or penises.'

'Why do I have to take them off?' she asked, lifting her skirt and tugging her red silk panties down.

'I'll explain in a minute.'

'Do you think it'll work?' she trilled excitedly as she climbed onto the couch and lay down.

'I'm positive. Now, I'll have to tie you down because very often violent muscle spasms occur during the hypnotic state.'

'I didn't know that!' the girl gasped as Larry parted her legs and secured her ankles to the legs of the examination couch with rope.

'Oh, yes. It's the subconscious, you see. It doesn't like people prying into it so it retaliates by causing violent muscle spasms. Right, put your arms behind your head and I'll secure your wrists.'

The girl spreadeagled, her thighs wide apart, Larry lifted her short skirt and gazed at the swell of her vaginal lips, her sparse blonde pubes. 'This is necessary,' he smiled, running his fingertip up and down her moist sex valley.

'Why?' she asked, lifting her head in surprise. 'How is this helping me?'

'You have a fear of penises, Lily. The penis enters your vagina, among other orifices. Er, it follows that your vagina is at the root of your problem.'

'I thought it was psychological?'

'No, no. You see, your vagina sends messages to your brain whenever there's a threat of a penile invasion, vaginal penetration by a stiff penis. Now, what I intend to do is slip my fingers into your *ductus cuntus* to determine the extent of your vagina's fear of the penis.'

'Are you going to put your fist up me again?'

'That is something I might have to consider. I have a length of rubber hose pipe at hand so we shouldn't have the vacuum problem again.'

'Aren't you going to hypnotize me?' Lily asked as Larry parted her cunny lips and drove three fingers deep into her hot cuntal sheath.

'Yes, later. Oh, what's that?' he asked as his fingertips pressed against something hard.

'It's . . . it's for Brigit,' the girl confessed, her face flushing. 'It's an apple.'

'Why keep it in your pussy?'

'To warm and wet it. She likes warm, wet apples.'

'Well, you'd better push it out. I can't examine you with an apple stuffed up your pussy! Go on, push, bear down and give birth to it. Imagine that you're in the labour room. Would you prefer a boy or a girl?'

'Neither!'

Watching as the girl's vaginal lips began to part, Larry pushed on the soft flesh above her pubic mound, helping her to emit the wet fruit. The large red apple appearing, her pink girl-flesh distending as it emerged from her bloated cunt,

she squeezed her eyes shut and pushed harder, expelling the steaming fruit from her sex cauldron.

'Well done!' Larry laughed, taking the apple from the couch. 'It's a boy! You've nothing else in there, have you? Perhaps another apple, a twin?'

'No, nothing else,' Lily smiled, watching Larry take a bite from the hot apple. 'I used to keep bananas in there but they became a pulp by lunch time.'

'I'm not surprised!' he replied, slipping three fingers into her gaping cunt. 'How does that feel?'

'Well, it feels like fingers in my vagina, I suppose.'

'Good, I hoped you'd say that,' he smiled, discarding the apple and discreetly slipping his erect penis out. 'Tell me, Lily, do you masturbate?'

'Yes, I do.'

'With a vibrator?'

'Yes, Brigit and I vibrate each other's clitties – and we lick each other. I won't suck her nipples, though. With my problem, that's understandable, isn't it?'

'Yes, it is. I didn't know that you and Brigit were *that* friendly!'

'She said that I shouldn't tell you.'

'I can keep a secret. I'll say nothing, don't worry. What else do you both get up to?'

'We finger each other's bottoms.'

'You like that, do you?'

'Very much! It makes me quiver all over!'

'I would imagine it does! Right, everything seems to be in order down there,' Larry smiled.

Slipping his fingers out of the girl's wet pussy sheath, Larry moved along the examination couch and revealed

his erect penis to her fearful eyes. Screaming as he held her head and pushed his bulbous knob into her open mouth, she tugged on her bonds, desperate to escape the one-eyed monster.

'Suck it!' he chuckled. 'I'm going to fuck your pretty mouth, Lily!'

'No! No, please!' she cried, turning her head.

'Yes, yes! You must swallow my spunk!'

'Larry!' Brigit called, tapping on the door. 'Larry, open the door!'

'What is it?' he asked, letting the girl in and locking the door.

'I heard the fun, I want to join in.'

'OK, squat over her face to keep her quiet, and I'll fuck her.'

'I don't want to be fucked!' Lily cried. 'Please, I don't want to be fucked!'

'Of course you do!' Larry laughed. 'Fucked senseless!'

Protesting wildly as Brigit climbed onto the couch and placed her knees either side of her head, Lily finally quietened as her mouth filled with Brigit's wet girl-flesh. Rocking her hips, sliding her vaginal crack over Lily's gasping mouth, Brigit began her sexual whimpering. 'Put your tongue in my cunt!' she breathed, her eyes rolling as she leaned forward and kissed and licked the girl's swollen pussy lips. 'Ah, ah! Yes, that's it, lick inside my cunt!'

Untying Lily's ankles, Larry opened her legs further, bending her knees and hanging her feet either side of the couch. Gazing at her gaping cuntal crack, her unfurling inner lips revealing the pink entrance to her sex duct, he knelt down and tied a length of rope between her feet,

securing her curvaceous body in the degrading position in readiness for the vaginal fucking.

Gasping as her clitoris swelled and throbbed in response to Lily's sweeping tongue, Brigit was quickly nearing her climax. Her cuntal juices coursing over the girl's face, filling her thirsty mouth, she brought her body upright and reached between her thighs, pulling her cunny lips wide apart, exposing her wet inner flesh to her friend's caressing tongue. Watching the arousing lesbian act, Larry positioned himself between Lily's splayed thighs and pressed the purple head of his rock-hard penis between her rubicund pussy lips.

'No!' Lily protested, trying to turn her face away from Brigit's gaping cunt. Ignoring the girl, Larry pressed his penis head against her cuntal flesh, easing his knob into her hot vaginal duct. His shaft slowly sliding into her tight tube, his heavy balls rolling, he gazed at Lily's tongue sweeping up and down Brigit's lush, open netherland.

'Do you like it, Lily?' he murmured as his knob touched the girl's cervix. 'Do you like my cock up your cunt?'

'Yes, yes!' she breathed, her tongue stiffening Brigit's clitoris, taking the girl ever closer to her climax.

'I'm fucking you, Lily!' Larry gasped, withdrawing his organ and driving his knob deep into her tight cunt. 'Have you ever been fucked before?'

'No, never! Ah, ah, I like it! Do it faster!'

Repeatedly withdrawing his solid penis and ramming into Lily's trembling body, Larry locked his mouth to Brigit's, their tongues entwining as they used the tethered girl's youthful body to bring out their respective orgasms. Larry's penis deep inside Lily's tight cunt, Brigit's clitoris

sucked into Lily's mouth, Larry's tongue excavating Brigit's wet mouth, the three-way circuit complete, all three reached their explosive climaxes.

As Larry's spunk jetted from his throbbing knob, filling Lily's spasming vaginal cavern, he thrust harder into the girl's quivering body, sustaining her first penis-induced climax. Again and again he withdrew his cock and drove his knob deep into the girl's tight cunt, taking her higher to her sexual heaven. *I'll do her arse next!* he laughed inwardly as his balls drained again. *Fill her tight arse with my spunk!*

Brigit's vaginal fluid decanting, flowing into Lily's gasping mouth, their bodies trembling, they finally rested, heaving in the aftermath of their lewd sexual coupling. 'God, I needed that!' Larry chuckled, gazing at his glistening shaft as he drove it deep into Lily's cunt for the last time. Clambering off the couch, Brigit peeled Lily's inflamed vaginal pads apart, gazing in awe at the embedded root of Larry's wet cockshaft.

'Can you fuck her again?' Brigit enquired curiously, massaging Lily's solid clitoris.

'Yes, I think so!' Larry gasped. 'But you'll have to stiffen me up a bit first. Suck me off, that should do it.'

'My pleasure!' Brigit beamed, leaning forward as he withdrew his girl-wet glans from Lily's sperm-drenched cunt.

Taking his purple plum into her mouth, Brigit sucked and mouthed, savouring the heady taste of girl-come and spunk. His penis rapidly swelling, restiffening, Larry grinned at Lily. Her eyes closed, her face flushed, she lay panting, wallowing in the wake of her incredible orgasm. 'Well, you've finally been fucked!' Larry chuckled, eyeing Brigit's girlie juice running down Lily's flushed cheeks.

'Yes, yes!' she breathed, licking her lips. 'God, it was heavenly! Do it again!'

'Do you want me to fuck your mouth?' he asked as Brigit licked his solid glans.

'No, I'm not ready for that. Fuck my cunt again.'

'We'd better hurry up!' Brigit warned, licking her sperm-wet lips. 'Monica will be wondering where we all are!'

'Yes, you're right,' Larry panted. 'OK, guide me in!'

Running his wet glans up and down Lily's girl-crack, Brigit pressed his plum against the tight entrance to the other girl's vaginal duct and ordered him to push. His shaft gliding into Lily's spasming cunt as Brigit kneaded his balls, his knob gently pressed against the girl's cervix. Savouring the wet heat of her cuntal sheath, Larry slowly withdrew his shaft and thrust into her. Again and again, he slipped his penis out of her vagina and impaled her, repeatedly jolting her young body.

Her eyes shut, her mouth gasping, Lily arched her back as Brigit reached beneath her leg and located the tight entrance to her bowels. Her finger sliding into the girl's anal duct, Brigit massaged her solid clitoris, enhancing her sexual pleasure as Larry continued his vaginal fucking.

'God, I'm going to come again!' he gasped as his glans throbbed.

'Ah, and me!' Lily breathed. 'Brigit, do my bottom faster!'

'Here it comes!' Larry cried, his face grimacing as his sperm jetted deep into the girl's tight vaginal sheath. 'Ah, coming, coming!'

'Doctor Lickman!' Monica bellowed, hammering on the door. 'Doctor Lickman, what's going on in there?'

'Nothing!'

'Mr Ingram Ravenhugh is here!'

'All right, Monica, I'm coming! Ah, I'm coming!'

Making his last penile thrusts, Larry filled the girl's convulsing vagina with his spunk as her own orgasm erupted in her pulsating clitoris. Massaging between the girl's swollen pussy lips and finger-fucking her bottom-hole faster, Brigit sustained her incredible pleasure. Her body trembling as electrifying orgasmic shockwaves gripped her, Lily tossed her head, her eyes rolling, her mouth gasping as her pleasure increased. On and on her orgasm rolled, rocking her young body, taking her higher to her sexual paradise until she floated down gently, exhausted, serene – satisfied.

'You liked that, didn't you?' Brigit asked, gently massaging Lily's swollen clitoris as she slipped her finger out of her friend's hot anal tube.

'God, yes!' Lily gasped, her cunt spasming as Larry's penis slid out. 'God, it was heavenly!'

'I'd better go and see this Ravenhugh man!' Larry sighed despondently, climbing off the couch and zipping his trousers. 'I'll leave you horny lesbians to enjoy yourselves. Lock the door after me.'

Entering his consulting room, his face flushed, he smiled at the middle-aged, balding man. 'Good afternoon, I'm Doctor Lickman.'

'Ravenhugh, Ingram Ravenhugh,' the man replied, shaking Larry's hand. 'I'm from the Inland Revenue.'

Fuck it! 'I'm pleased to meet you, Mr Revenue . . . Ravenhugh. Please, take a seat,' Larry invited, sitting in his swivel chair.

'Thank you. Now then, Doctor Lickman, according to our records we've only received fifty pounds from you in the last six years.'

'As much as that!' Larry gasped surprisedly. 'That's great! Obviously, I'm in line for a tax rebate!'

'A rebate? Hardly! Apart from income tax, you've not paid national insurance contributions for the last six years!'

'National insurance contributions? Contributions are usually voluntary! National insurance robbery, more like!'

'Why haven't you paid? When did you start this business?'

'Six years ago, obviously.'

'Why obviously?'

'That's when I started the business of not paying my contributions.'

'No, I meant, when did you start practising?'

'Practising what? I don't practise anything. Well, apart from . . .'

'No! This place, your clinic – when did you open it?'

'Nine o'clock this morning.'

'You opened at nine this morning?'

'Yes, that's right.'

'I find that difficult to believe, Doctor Lickman. In fact, I find it impossible to believe!'

'Ask my staff if you want proof. I always open up at nine o'clock. I've only ever been late once, and that was because my car . . .'

'Good God! Let's *try* to communicate, please, Doctor Lickman!'

'My communication skills are admirable.'

'I'm glad to hear it! I'll try again – when did you first move into this building and open your clinic?'

'Oh, I see! Er . . . quite some time ago.'

'Yes, but when?'

'Let me see. Er . . . three years ago, Monica joined the practice. Brigit . . . she joined last year. Lily's only been with us for a short time so . . . six months ago.'

'If one member of your staff joined the practice three years ago, how could you have opened the business six months ago?'

'I didn't.'

'You just said that you did!'

'No, I didn't! I said – six months ago. I didn't say that I'd started the business six months ago. I was recalling the time when the decorators moved in to brighten up the reception area, which was six months ago. They did a good job. Do you know, they . . .'

'God help me! All right, Doctor Lickman, we'll come back to that later. Let's try another one – what was your turnover during the financial year April ninety-five to April ninety-six?'

'Which turn over?'

'How much money did your business take?'

'A fortune! Thousands and thousands of pounds, in fact!'

'Ah, now we're getting somewhere! Can you give me a rough idea as to the amount?'

'Yes, about eighty thousand.'

'In one year?'

'No, it took about three months.'

'You took that amount in three months?'

'No, I spent that amount in three months.'

'What?'

'You asked me how much the business took. It took about eighty thousand pounds to set it up. There was the plumber, the electrician . . . the building alone cost a small fortune!'

'Doctor Lickman, I don't believe you to be mentally insane.'

'Neither do I!'

'Will you tell me, in plain English, how much your business made between April ninety-five and April ninety-six?'

'I couldn't tell you in any other language, I'm afraid!'

'Good, English it is, then.'

'I know a little French.'

'English will be fine. How much did your business make?'

'Nothing.'

'Nothing?'

'That's right, it was a terrible year – no one had any sexual or marital problems at all! I blame the government.'

'How did you pay your staff?'

'Er . . . I didn't. I must say that they were very understanding.'

'You do realize that I'll check?'

'Oh, well . . . we might have made a *little* money.'

'Ah, right! How much?'

'I can't remember.'

'OK, Doctor Lickman, we'll do it your way. Write down the name and address of your bank and your account numbers.'

Opening the desk drawer, Larry pulled out his cheque book and wrote the information on the back of an envelope,

sighing as he passed the details to Ravenhugh. What with Fullcrack, Gina Cology, Venereal, and now Ravenhugh, things weren't looking good! Deciding that his only option was to close the business and do a runner, he thought of the bank account he'd opened in a false name. *At least I'll have plenty of cash!* he mused.

'You do realize that you've defrauded the Crown?' Ravenhugh asked, slipping the envelope into his briefcase.

'The crown?' Larry echoed.

'The Queen, you've defrauded her.'

'I haven't touched her!'

'All her subjects pay tax, Doctor Lickman, and . . .'

'I pay tax, too! She's had fifty pounds from me, you said so yourself! And I pay tax on alcohol and . . .'

'I'm talking about income tax, not Customs and Excise duty.'

'It's not fair! I do all the work, put in long hours, while the Queen's sitting pretty in her palace – and she wants my hard-earned money!'

'That's the way of the land.'

'Well, it's high time someone changed the way of the land!'

'You're not suggesting a revolution, Doctor Lickman?'

'Damned right, I am! Who benefits from VAT? Tell me that!'

'That's not my department.'

'Income tax, Value Added Tax, road tax, council tax, alcohol and tobacco tax, tin tacks, this tax, that tax . . . God, it's no wonder everyone's broke! Where the hell does all this money go to? Who's creaming it all off?'

'The government have to . . .'

143

'Bollocks to the government! It's tyranny!'

'For example, distribution of wealth . . .'

'Communism, you mean? Take money from the masses and distribute it among the chosen few, the elite.'

'No, it's not like that!'

'That's exactly how it is! What right have you to go poking around my bank account?'

'Every right. I'll be checking the transactions because . . .'

'Give me the details of your bank account.'

'I can't do that, Doctor Lickman!'

'As I thought, one rule for me, and another for you! I'll bet you're not allowed to look at the Queen's bank balance.'

'Even the Queen pays tax.'

'Yes, she pays it out with one hand and then grabs it back with the other!'

'This is getting us nowhere, Doctor Lickman. I'll be in touch with you when . . .'

'I might take to robbing building societies and stealing cars.'

'You can't do that!'

'Why not? What's the penalty? I'll tell you what it is – holidays, safaris!'

'You'd go to prison!'

'No, that's not the way it works, Mr Ravenhugh. I've seen it in the papers: villains are sent on holiday at the tax payer's expense. Imagine, five social workers to look after me, no money worries, good food, holidays abroad . . . yes, I might well nick a few cars!'

'I'll be in touch, Doctor Lickman,' Ravenhugh declared, glancing over his shoulder as he made his exit.

'I'll look forward to it!' Larry called from his consulting room doorway. *Fuck off!*

Flopping into his chair, he held his head in his hands, wondering how to break the sad news to the staff. *I'll miss the clients*, he reflected. *God, and all those fresh sixth- form girlies with their tight cunts and rock-hard titties!*

Chapter Five

What with Ingram Ravenhugh on his back, things were looking pretty grim, Larry reflected. He'd heard nothing from the Revenue for several days, but he knew that by now they'd have investigated him, his substantial bank account. Gina Cology had kept a low profile, even though she had photographic evidence of his lewd behaviour. What was the bitch planning? he wondered, pouring himself a large scotch and resting his elbows on his desk. And why hadn't he heard from Fullcrack?

Responding to a knock on the door, he lifted his head and smiled as Brigit showed a young nun into the room. 'This is Sister Mary,' Brigit introduced the young, pale-faced novice.

'I'm sorry we weren't able to fit you in earlier, Sister,' Larry smiled, rising to his feet as she seated herself opposite him. 'For the last few days I've been inundated with the convent schoolgirlies . . . I mean, sixth-formers. I still have a couple of dozen to . . . to examine.'

'That's all right,' the young woman replied softly, her benevolent face framed by a band of crisp white linen. 'I'm just pleased to be here, I've been so worried about my health.'

Sitting down and slipping the bottle of scotch into the

desk drawer, Larry gazed into the young nun's eyes. 'The Reverend Mother said that you suffer from dizziness,' he began, wondering whether she'd ever had the pleasure of a hard cock spunking up her wet cunt.

'Yes, that's right. I often feel dizzy in the mornings, after breakfast. My head spins and I can't keep my balance.'

'I see. How old are you?'

'Twenty-two.'

'And how long have you been having these dizzy spells?'

'Since I was about sixteen. I've always tried to push the problem to the back of my mind, but it's been getting worse lately. Have you any idea what might be causing it?'

'I'll have to give you a thorough physical examination before we go any further, Mary. If you'll come along to my examination room, I'll . . .'

'A physical examination? But I . . .'

'Mary, you're suffering from dizziness which might be a symptom of something serious. Your dizzy spells might just be the tit of the iceberg. Unless you allow me to examine you . . .'

'I'm not sure whether I should be examined. Nakedness is a sin, you see.'

'Why come to me, a doctor, if you don't want to be examined?'

'I . . . I don't know. I suppose I thought you'd be able to tell me what was wrong without . . .'

'I'm a doctor, Mary, not a psychic! Dizziness, particularly in the mornings, and especially after breakfast, sounds pretty serious to me! Add to that the fact that these spells began when you were about sixteen and . . .'

'Yes but . . . you want me to undress? I can't unveil my body, I've taken my vows. Poverty, chastity and obedience are . . .'

'When did you decide to become a nun, Mary?'

'When I was fourteen.'

'What happened?'

'I received a message from God. He said that I should remain chaste, and the only way to do that was to become a nun.'

'Didn't your parents mind?'

'Yes, my father wanted me to have children.'

'Why?'

'I don't know, he's funny like that. Doctor Lickman, I can't allow you to . . .'

'If you want me to help you, Mary, I'll have to examine you. I dread to think of the consequences should this develop into something awful. It might even lead to a condition known as RNBS.'

'Good heavens, what's that?'

'Rampant nymphomaniacal behaviour syndrome.'

'Rampant nymphomaniacal . . . I'm feeling dizzy, doctor, not . . .'

'Dizziness is often associated with deep-seated subconscious cravings for a life of perpetual lesbian-induced orgasms.'

'What?'

'Most sexually unfulfilled nymphomaniacal lesbians suffer from dizzy spells, particularly after breakfast, it's a well-known medical fact.'

'But I don't have lesbian tendencies! And I'm certainly not a nymphomaniac!'

149

'That's my point.'

'What is?'

'You have deep-seated lesbian tendencies. Taking your vows, particularly to remain chaste, has caused suppression of your natural nymphomaniacal desires, leading to post-breakfast dizziness. You really should take my expert advice and allow me to give you a thorough examination.'

'Oh, well, put like that I suppose I have no choice. I can't remove all my clothes, though. It's against my faith to . . .'

'Don't worry, Mary, you may keep your habit on. Follow me and we'll get this over with as quickly as possible.'

Ushering the young nun into his bondage room, Larry closed and locked the door, his heart racing as he imagined lifting the pretty girl's habit and yanking her knickers down. Wondering how to get his fingers into her virginal pussy, what excuse he could dream up for finger-fucking her sacrosanct cunt, he suggested that she lay on the examination couch.

'I'll start with your lower legs,' he murmured as she lay on her back. 'Dizziness is often caused by suppressed lesbian desires which cause the womb to contract, leading to poor circulation in the legs. I'll lift your habit up to your middle and start with your calves, working up to your . . . to your thighs.'

'I don't know whether . . .' the young nun began as Larry tugged her habit up, unveiling her naked legs, her shapely thighs.

'Have you ever been aware of your lesbian tendencies, Mary?'

'No, never!'

'Did you have a close friend at school, a girl you spent most of your time with?'

'Well, yes, I did. Her name was Fay, we did everything together.'

'Such as?'

'Swimming, country walks, netball ... we spent our summer holidays together.'

'I thought as much. Did you ever play around, you know, pillow fights on the bed or rolling in the hay during your country walks?'

'Of course we did. We were always playing around, having mock fights.'

'There you are, then. Lesbian tendencies, Mary, that's what you had. And you still do, although you've suppressed them by vowing to remain chaste. Just by looking at your legs I can see that there's a problem. Your upper thighs are very pale, which gives me great cause for concern.'

'They've always been pale. I suppose it's because my body is never exposed to the sun.'

'That might be the reason, Mary, but your thighs are rather *too* pale for my liking.'

Pulling her habit up further, Larry exposed her grey woollen knickers, picturing her neglected vaginal crack, her protruding inner lips as he gazed at the triangular patch of bulging material. Had her slender fingers explored between her pink cunny lips? he wondered as he massaged the firm, warm flesh of her inner thighs. Had her fingertips caressed her solid clitoris to orgasm as she lay naked in her bed, her legs wide open, her cunt crack gaping?

'I have to ask you this, Mary,' he smiled, catching her blue eyes, his trembling fingers dangerously near to her

151

bulging knickers. 'Are you a virgin?' *Have you ever been fucked?*

'Oh! Er . . . yes, of course I am!' she gasped surprisedly. 'What does that have to do with my dizzy spells?'

'Unless I'm mistaken, I'd say that you're suffering from *vaginus neglectus.*'

'Vaginus . . . what's that?'

'It's a rare condition of the vaginal walls. I'm going to have to give you an internal examination, Mary. If you'll slip your knickers off, I'll . . .'

'But . . . Doctor Lickman, I . . .'

'Mary, I couldn't live with my conscience if I allowed you to leave here without my having examined you. Should something terrible happen to you, I couldn't live with the harrowing guilt. Do you want me to spend the rest of my days worrying about you, about your vaginal health?'

'Well, no.'

'Imagine if I received news a few weeks from now that you'd undergone vulval fissure healing. I'd feel responsible, dreadfully guilty.'

'What's vulval fissure healing?'

'It's a rare condition where the vaginal labia knit together. Basically, it's healing of the vulval valley.'

'What, you mean that my . . .'

'You'd have smooth skin covering your vulval region. You would no longer have a vaginal crack, Mary.'

'I've never heard of anything like that!'

'I dread to think how you'd survive vulval fissure healing. I implore you to allow me to examine you.'

'If you're sure that it's really necessary, I suppose . . .'

'It's of the utmost importance that I give you an internal

examination, Mary. I'm not doing this for my sake, believe me!' Larry grinned as she reluctantly lifted her buttocks clear of the couch and tugged her knickers down. 'Allow me to slip them off your feet,' he coaxed, glimpsing the daughter of God's dark pubic curls nestling between her milk-white thighs as he tugged the garment over her ankles.

Carefully lifting her habit up over the slight swell of her smooth stomach, he focused on her long pussy crack, her inner lips emerging from her sex slit. Turning her head to one side as he gently parted her thighs, she closed her eyes as if trying to blot out the reality of her predicament, her nakedness, her blatant vaginal exposure. *Will she enjoy this?* Larry wondered as he eased her pussy lips apart and gazed hungrily at her moist inner flesh. Had she ever had a man's finger enter her pussy sheath? Had her own fingers ever excavated the wet heat of her inviting young sex duct?

'Do you feel all right?' Larry murmured huskily as he located the moist entrance to her tight sanctum.

'Yes, I think so,' she whispered, quivering as his finger glided into her hot sheath.

'Have you ever had an internal examination before?'

'No, no, I haven't.'

'I thought as much. You seem to be suffering from *labia majora poutus*. You should make sure that you're examined regularly, Mary. It's far better to discover vaginal problems early rather than wait until they become serious.'

'What's *labia majora poutus*?'

'Pouting of the outer labia, the outer lips. I'm going to check you for *clitoris throbus*.'

Stretching the young nun's sex crack wide open, exposing her clitoral nodule, Larry massaged her secret sex bud,

watching her pretty face out of the corner of his eye as he slowly slid his finger in and out of her vaginal canal. Her mouth slightly open, her wet tongue licking her dry lips, her innocent young body quivering, she began to breathe heavily. She was obviously enjoying the sensations, Larry observed, slipping a second finger into her neglected cunny hole. Would she allow him to take her to her sexual climax? he wondered as he quickened his clitoral massaging, stiffening her pleasure budlette. Would she, in the heat of the moment, forget her vows and allow Satan to take her to paradise?

'Are you comfortable?' he probed, bending his fingers and massaging her wet inner flesh against the hardness of her pubic bone.

'Yes, I am,' she breathed, opening her rolling eyes and gazing at the ceiling. 'Will it take much longer?' she asked apprehensively.

'Not too long now.' *Is she ready for the vibrator?* 'Your muscles are tense, preventing me from examining you properly. I'm going to relax your pelvic muscles with an electric massager.'

'Will it hurt?'

'No, no, it won't hurt. Open your legs as wide as you can and relax,' Larry instructed her, thrusting his fingers in and out of her tightening cunt as he grabbed the vibrator from the shelf. 'Open your legs as wide as you can, Mary. That's it, let your feet hang down either side of the couch to allow me better access to your *vaginus cractus*.'

Switching the vibrator on, he pressed the buzzing tip against the nun's exposed clitoris, watching excitedly as her sex button swelled, emerging fully from its protective pink bonnet. Pistoning and twisting his pussy-juiced fingers,

tightening her cunt muscles, inducing her honeydew to flow, he grinned as she desperately tried to stifle her gasps of sexual pleasure. She was going to come, he knew, as she tossed her head from side to side, her eyes closed, her mouth open, gasping. Was this the first orgasm she'd ever experienced? he wondered, pressing the vibrator harder against her pulsating clitoris.

'Oh, oh!' she gasped, her hands gripping the sides of the examination couch, her knuckles whitening as she arched her back. 'Oh, doctor! It . . . it feels strange!'

'Just relax,' Larry said softly, gazing at her swelling, rubicund vaginal lips. 'Just relax and allow the sensations to come.'

'It feels funny! Oh, oh! Please, stop now!'

'You're nearly there, Mary! Relax, concentrate on the sensations and . . .'

'Ah! Ah, what's happening to me?' the girl cried as her climax rose from her contracting womb and exploded within her solid clitoris. 'Ah! Oh, oh!'

Her outer pussy lips engorging, swelling, her milk-white thighs twitching, her firm breasts heaving, ballooning her tight habit, she gasped incoherent words of sexual satisfaction as her drenched cuntal sheath gripped Larry's thrusting fingers like a velvet-jawed vice. Biting her lip, she raised her head, gazing in awe at her crimsoned pussy lips, her yawning vaginal crack, as her orgasm peaked again, sending electrifying quivers of sex through her defiled body.

Desperate to slip his cock into her tight cunt as she rested her head on the couch, Larry moved the tip of the vibrator in circles around her pulsating sex bud, sustaining her sexual

pleasure. His penis solid within his tight trousers, yearning for the welcoming heat of her unholy cunt, he slipped a third finger into her drenched vaginal sheath, her multiple orgasm peaking again, plunging her deeper into the beautiful depths of sexual pleasure.

'Oh, please stop!' the nun sang as her enforced climax finally began to recede, leaving her quivering, gasping for breath. 'Please . . . I can't . . .'

'It's all right, it's all over,' Larry reassured her, switching the vibrator off and slipping his wet fingers out of her abused cunt. 'Did you enjoy that?'

'Yes, no, I mean . . . I don't know. I've never known such . . . such amazing feelings before!'

'You found the experience pleasant?' he asked, placing the vibrator on the shelf and gently massaging her receding clitoris with his cunny-wet fingertips.

'Yes, very! But I feel that I've sinned, doctor. It's not right to enjoy the pleasures of the flesh.'

'Satan . . . I mean, God gave you your vagina, your clitoris, for your enjoyment, Mary. He gave you your clitoris so that you might sexually pleasure yourself.'

'Yes, but . . .'

'Turn over, I need to examine your anal canal before you go.'

'But . . . but that's not . . .' she stammered, rolling over and exposing her taut rounded buttocks, the deep valley of her bottom crease.

'This won't take a minute,' Larry promised, grabbing the jar of honey from the shelf and smearing the golden liquid between her tensed bottom orbs. 'You may go after I've checked your anal duct. I might as well give you a full

examination while you're here. Have you ever had an anal examination before?'

'No, no, I haven't, doctor.'

'Have you ever inserted anything into your bottom-hole?'

'Inserted anything? What do you mean?'

'Well, a finger.' *Or a penis!*

'A finger? No, never!'

'You should insert a finger into your bottom daily. Fingering your bottom-hole will keep your anal sphincter muscles firm.'

'I couldn't bring myself to do that!'

'Use a candle, then.'

Spreading her legs, Larry grinned, eyeing the girl's full vaginal lips ballooning between her parted thighs, her cunny juice oozing from her desecrated hole. Parting her buttocks, he pressed his fingertip against the delicate brown tissue surrounding the portal to her rectal sheath, causing her to gasp and writhe as his sticky finger slipped into the dank heat of her bottom-hole. Further he drove his finger, exploring her fiery core, stretching her delicate inner tissue, waking sleeping nerve endings.

'Oh, ah! That's . . . that's nice!' she whimpered, raising her bottom, affording Larry a perfect view of her wet, gaping vaginal crack. 'Ah, it feels . . . it feels . . .'

'Just relax, Mary,' Larry smiled, catching her glazed blue eyes as she turned her flushed face to look at him. 'Just relax and enjoy the rectal sensations.'

Managing to drive a second finger into her tight anal tube, stretching her brown tissue, he grabbed a large candle from the shelf and slipped the pointed end between her swollen sex

hillocks. Slowly pushing the phallus deep into her tightening cunt, he waited in anticipation for her response, wondering what she was thinking. She'd enjoyed the vibrator, he reflected as he thrust his fingers in and out of her tight velveteen bottom-hole. Would she allow him to slip his solid penis deep into her vagina and fill her with sperm? What reason could he conjure to make her believe that she should be well and truly arse-fucked – her bowels filled with spunk?

'There seems to be a problem, Mary,' Larry began pensively, slipping his fingers out of the girl's anal duct. 'I'd like you to climb off the couch and sit on my medical chair.'

'Medical chair?' the girl frowned as Larry slipped the cunny-wet candle out of her tight, hot pussy duct.

'Yes,' he smiled, helping her off the couch. 'It was designed by a university professor. Er . . . I'm afraid you'll have to take your habit off.'

'I can't do that!' the young nun protested, standing before him. 'My vows . . .'

'Mary, I know you've taken your vows, but you have a problem.'

'What's wrong with me?'

'In my considered opinion, you're suffering from *anusus vestal*.'

'What are all these weird complaints? You seem to think that I'm riddled with problems.'

'*Anusus vestal* is fairly common in young women, but it can be easily rectified by use of a medicinal candle. *Labia poutus* can also be cured, but you'll have to allow me to administer the treatment. *Vaginus neglectus* can be corrected, but I can't help you if you won't help me. You might also be

suffering from *teatus milkus* suckle deficiency, but if you won't remove your clothing I'm afraid there's nothing I can do.'

'All right,' the young woman finally conceded, kicking her shoes off. 'No one will know about this, will they? I mean, if Mother Barren-Womb were to find out that I'd undressed and allowed you to examine me, she'd be furious.'

'Trust me, Mary. Whatever happens in this room will remain our secret. Not even God will know about it.'

'He will! He's everywhere!'

'He's not in here, this is a God-free zone. Take your habit off.'

Tugging the ungodly garment over her head, her long raven hair tumbling over her naked shoulders, the girl unclipped her bra and released her firm breasts from their white cotton cups. Eyeing her curvaceous body, her erect nipples, her most appetizing chocolatey areolae, Larry opened a large cupboard and pulled out his special chair. Gazing in awe at the round hole in the seat of the chair, Mary stood naked before her non-spiritual advisor, her hand over her open mouth.

'You want me to sit on *that*?' she asked, aghast, folding her arms to conceal her naked breasts.

'Yes, if you would. The hole in the centre of the chair is for . . . just sit down, Mary,' Larry wheedled, taking the girl's arm. 'That's it, now put your hands behind the back of the chair.'

'Why?' she asked, her eyes following him as he moved behind her.

'This will help your pelvic muscles to . . . there, that's it!' he chuckled, deftly lashing her wrists together with a length of rope.

159

'Why have you tied my wrists?' the girl gasped, trying to wriggle free.

'So that I can sexually abuse your beautiful wet cunt!' Larry laughed, kneeling down and massaging her swollen cunt lips through the hole in the chair.

'Please, you can't do this to me!'

'I *have* done it to you!'

'Mother Barren-Womb will . . .'

'You're no more a nun than I'm the fucking Pope! Did you really believe that you could fool me?'

'Fool you?'

'I know who you are – Christine Cology! I suppose this was your mother's idea, her way of trying to . . .'

'She'll come looking for me!' the girl hissed as Larry slipped his finger between her fleshy labia and drove it deep into her tight vaginal cavern.

'That's true, but she won't find you!' he laughed, slipping his wet finger out of her cunt and rising to his feet. 'You see that blank wall – do you notice anything odd about it?' he asked.

'No, no I don't.'

'Watch.'

Pressing a button concealed beneath the shelf, Larry grinned as the false wall slid slowly back, revealing another room. Her eyes wide as she gazed at the chains hanging from the walls, the handcuffs and whips adorning the room, the horizontal planks of padded wood forming an X, the prisoner turned to her sadistic master.

'What are you going to do to me?' she asked Larry fearfully.

'Many things, Christine – but the first thing I'd like to do

160

is fuck you, fuck your tight cunt hole! It seems that I'm now in a position to call the shots!' he grinned, dragging the chair into his secret room. 'All the time I have you, your mother won't be able to do a thing. Of course, I realize that Monica was behind this, telling your mother about Barren-Womb sending one of her young nuns to see me. As Monica's out at the moment she won't know that you've arrived. I'll tell her that you didn't turn up and . . .'

'I'll scream!'

'Go ahead, this room has been completely soundproofed. No one will hear anything, Christine, no one will ever know that I'm in here, fucking you, fucking your tight arsehole!'

'This is against the law!' the girl spat. 'You can't . . .'

'Which law?'

'The law of the land!'

'I abide only by Satan's laws. All's fair in lust and sex. Right, I'm going to lay you on my sex cross!' Larry chuckled, releasing the struggling girl's hands and frogmarching her to the cross. Pinning her naked body across the padded planks, he managed to secure her outstretched arms with rope. 'You came here expecting me to fuck you, so I'm *going* to fuck you!'

'I didn't come here expecting . . .' the frantic girl screamed, desperately trying to break free.

'Yes, you did! You were hoping that I'd fuck you so that you could go running back and tell your . . . wait a minute!' Larry gasped, parting her kicking legs and securing her ankles to the ends of the planks. 'You'd need proof, wouldn't you? It would be my word against yours if . . . How were you going to prove what had happened to you?'

'Monica was . . . I . . . I wasn't going to prove anything!' the

prisoner returned, her four limbs racked, her cunt crack open, yawning, her young naked body completely defenceless.

'Ah, Monica, of course! No doubt she was going to . . . hang on, she said she was going to the hairdresser. No doubt the plan was for her to come barging in and . . . and bring your bloody mother with her as a witness!'

'No, no, she . . .'

'Right, I'm going to have some fun with you! As I said, scream for all you're worth, but it won't do you any good!' Raising his hands above his head and looking up at the ceiling, Larry grinned. 'Satan, I offer you this young girl's cunt! Take her, Satan, take her cunt!'

'You're mad!'

'We're all mad, Christine.'

'You mustn't call on the Devil!'

'Why not, he's a good mate of mine.'

The planks about eighteen inches above the floor, Larry sat between the trembling girl's splayed thighs, his face level with her gaping cunt slit. Parting her sex folds, he licked her pinken flesh, sucking on her inner lips, savouring the heady taste of her sticky vaginal juices. Squirming and tugging on her bonds, the prisoner couldn't prevent her demonic aggressor from lapping at her open hole, snaking his venomous tongue into her vulnerable sex cavern.

'You'll be sorry for this!' the tethered girl screamed as Larry drove three fingers deep into her wet vaginal duct.

'You can't prove a thing!' he leered, thrusting his fingers in and out of her fiery cunt. 'Besides, I'm going to keep you here forever!'

'I'll escape and . . .'

'Christine, let's not talk about escaping! Why don't you

relax and enjoy yourself? I'm going to fuck you in a minute, I'm going to spunk up your tight cunt hole – you'd like that, wouldn't you?'

'No! If you dare to . . .'

'I'll fuck your bottom, too. I know you'll love having my hard cock spunking up your arsehole!'

'If you . . .'

'Right, I'll get my cock out and give your cunt a good seeing to!' Larry laughed, slipping his wet fingers out of her tightening pussy hole. 'Later, I'll wank over your tits. Yes, cleavage sex, I like that. I might even fuck your pretty mouth, if you're a good girl.'

'I'll bite your cock off if you . . .'

'In that case, I'll wank over your face, splatter my spunk over your mouth. But it's your lovely bumhole that I'm looking forward to! I love slipping my cock up a hot, tight, velvety bumhole!'

Pushing the hinged planks apart, painfully opening the girl's legs, her vaginal crack, Larry grinned. His sex cross was an ingenious invention, the padded planks not only able to open and close like scissors but move up and down, raising his victim's legs. 'Do you like my sex cross?' he taunted, pushing the planks further apart, the girl's cunt gaping as her thighs opened almost to right angles to her naked body.

'You disgust me!' she spat.

'Why, thank you! OK, here comes my big cock!'

Kneeling between his prisoner's thighs, Larry unzipped his trousers and hauled his erect penis out, rubbing his bulbous knob up and down her defenceless sex slit, lubricating his weaponhead with her lubricious cream. Lifting her head,

spitting expletives, Christine grimaced as Larry's knob plunged into her vaginal portal and drove deep into her struggling body. Her outer lips taut around the base of his solid member, his full balls squashed against her firm buttocks, his glans pressing against her cervix, she was completely impaled on his veined sex-staff.

Slipping his penis out of the girl's cunt, Larry drove his fleshpole into her again, causing her stomach to rise, her clitoris to stiffen in response to the vaginal pummelling. Holding her swollen pussy lips apart with his thumbs, exposing her engorging sex button, he gazed at her crimsoned girl-flesh, the sheer girth of his wet shaft as it repeatedly invaded her hot sheath and emerged, dripping with her arousal juice. Gasping, her eyes closed, the girl was obviously enjoying the enforced fucking, the penile thrusting, as Larry quickened his rhythm. Would she come? he wondered, massaging her solid clitoris with his thumb. Would she beg for more crude sex after he'd spunked up her cunt and taken her to her shuddering climax?

'There's nothing I like more than tying a girl down and using her body for obscene sex!' he chuckled as she tossed her head from side to side, her long black hair veiling her sex-flushed face. 'And there's nothing Brigit likes more than drinking sperm from a tethered girl's dripping cunt hole!'

Remaining silent, Christine relaxed, allowing the sensations of orgasm to build deep within her contracting womb. Her nipples erect, her areolae darkening in her sexual arousal, she was close to her climax, Larry observed. His balls slapping her taut buttocks as he fucked her, he gasped

as his knob throbbed and his sperm coursed its way up his twitching penis shaft and jetted from his pulsating knob.

'God, you're tight!' he cried, thrusting into the girl's convulsing cunt as she gasped in the grip of her orgasm. 'Ah, ah, your cunt's so hot, tight, wet!'

'Harder!' she wailed in her sexual delirium, her thighs twitching, her breasts heaving, bouncing. 'Fuck me harder!'

Grabbing his prisoner's hips, Larry complied, driving his orgasming knob deep into her drenched cunt, his shaft gliding over her sensitive clitoris, satisfying her lust, sustaining her climax. The remnants of his spunk pumping into her vagina, bathing her hot cervix, he finally slowed his rhythm, gently bringing the girl down from her sexual heaven. Gasping, semiconscious, her tethered body quivering, she opened her eyes and lifted her head.

'You're a bastard, you really are!' she spat, yanking on her bonds.

'God, I needed that!' Larry chuckled, slipping his semi-erect penis out of her hot, sperm-drenched cuntal sheath. 'I'll fuck your arsehole later!'

'My mother knows where I am! You needn't think that you'll get away with this!'

'What is it with women?' Larry frowned, zipping his trousers. 'Men go to all the trouble of fucking them, and all they get in return is complaints!'

'Rape, that's what it is!'

'Rape, my arse! You came here knowing full well that I'd fuck you, so how can you say that I've raped you? You wanted this to happen so that Monica and your mother would catch me red-handed – red-knobbed! Right, I'll see you later. I have things to do.'

Slipping out of the room and pressing the button, Larry watched the false wall slide across, concealing his prisoner. Grabbing the girl's habit, he stuffed it into the cupboard along with her grey knickers and regulation bra. 'Right, that should do it!' he grinned, flinging her shoes into the cupboard and closing the door.

Approaching reception, he smiled at Brigit. 'Where's the witch?' he enquired.

'She's still out,' the girl replied. 'What have you done with the nun?'

'She's no nun, she's Gina's daughter!'

'God, really? Where is she?'

'In the secret room. Ah, right on cue!' he grinned, turning to face Monica and Gina as they entered reception. 'Hallo, ladies!'

'Hasn't the nun arrived?' Monica asked, her suspicious eyes frowning at Larry.

'No, she hasn't. I do hate it when people miss appointments, it's such a waste of my time! How are you, Gina? What brings you to my highly successful and profitable establishment of sexology?'

'I was just passing when I met Monica in the street,' the pretty blonde replied, glancing around reception.

'Where could the nun have got to?' Monica fretted, her puzzled gaze catching Gina's. 'The appointment was . . .'

'God only knows!' Larry groaned. 'Anyway, I have things to do. Sally Peabody is due soon so I'd better prepare myself – you know what she can be like! Er . . . Gina, would you like me to pull your panties down and . . .'

'No, I wouldn't!' his arch rival returned, cutting short his lewd remark.

'I don't understand why the nun missed her appointment!' Monica persisted, turning to Brigit. 'Are you sure she didn't turn up, Brigit?'

'Of course I'm sure! I'd know if a nun walked in here, wouldn't I? Unless I've forgotten. You know what my memory's like.'

'I'll be going,' Gina said, forcing a smile as she moved towards the door. 'Er . . . I'll be in touch, Monica.'

'Yes, yes, all right. I'll . . . I'll let you know about . . . I'll ring you.'

'Bye, Gina!' Larry called, his dark eyes grinning. 'Mind how you go!'

Watching Monica hurry down the hall towards his consulting room, Larry grinned. The old bat knew that something was going on, that Gina's daughter would have turned up. Between them, the conspirators would have gone to a lot of trouble hiring the habit and preparing the trap – Christine wouldn't have let them down, Monica would be sure of that. Nudging Brigit as Monica peered into the examination room, Larry sniggered.

'She can't understand it!' he whispered excitedly. 'Look at her, she's sure that the girl's here somewhere, but she'll never find her!'

'How long will you keep her here?' Brigit asked as Monica turned and headed back towards reception.

'I don't know. To be honest, I don't know what to do with the girl, apart from fuck her! Er . . . are you looking for something, Monica?'

'No, no, I . . . what time's that dreadful Peabody girl due?'

'In about ten minutes,' Brigit replied, checking the appointments book.

'Right, I'll be in my room,' Larry smiled. 'Send her along when she arrives.'

Ensconced at his desk, Larry again wondered what to do with Christine Cology. He couldn't keep her prisoner for too long, he knew, but he'd imprison the girl long enough to sexually abuse her naked tethered body, cane her taut buttocks. Brigit, too, would enjoy the girl's body, her firm breasts, her tight cunt hole. *We'll commit the most debased and vile sexual acts with her, and she'll be able to prove nothing!* he gloated as female voices emanated from reception.

'Ah, Sally!' he grinned as the scruffy girl wafted into his consulting room. 'Did you bring the milk bottle and Vaseline?'

'Hi, Larry. No, I never brung it – I've got a fuckin' problem,' she confessed, lifting her red microskirt and revealing her knickerless pussy, her sparse blonde pubes, her pinken tart-crack.

'Oh, what's that?' he asked, gazing at the opaque droplets of sex fluid clinging to her protruding inner lips.

'I've got a fuckin' apple stuck up me fuckin' cunt.'

'A fucking . . . I mean, an apple? What are you doing with an apple . . .'

'I was frigging meself off and I shoved the fuckin' apple up me fuckin' cunt. Now I can't get the fuckin' thing out!'

'Sally, I do wish you wouldn't punctuate all your sentences with expletives!'

'You wish I wouldn't do what to me what with what?'

'What? Try omitting the word *fucking* from your sentences.'

'Omitting? What's that?'

'Try leaving the F-word out. Now, how long has this apple been lodged in your vagina?'

'Since fuckin' . . . sorry, since bleedin' yesterday.'

'OK, I'll take you to my examination room and try to remove it. You girls will insist on stuffing apples up your vaginas! I don't know what things are coming to!' Larry laughed, leading the wanton slut to his bondage room. 'Right, strip off and lie on the couch,' he smiled, closing and locking the door.

Tugging her microskirt down, revealing her inflamed vaginal crack, Sally kicked the scruffy garment across the floor along with her red stilettos. Yanking her T-shirt over her head she looked down at her pert young breasts and grinned salaciously. Firm, topped with long, erect nipples, they were fine specimens, Larry observed. He could hardly wait to suck them into his wet mouth!

'You ain't goin' to 'urt me, are you?' the girl asked as she lay on the couch and opened her legs wider than a ballerina doing the splits.

'No, I won't hurt you,' Larry reassured her, peeling her vaginal lips open and pushing a finger into her drenched sex hole. 'God, it's a big one!' he exclaimed, pressing the offending fruit. 'Try pushing, try squeezing your muscles.'

Her stomach concaving, her pussy lips swelling as she bore down, the young tart was still unable to eject her erotic cargo. Again, she grimaced and pushed, her cunt lips parting coyly to display an ovoid area of the shiny red apple. 'Go on!' Larry urged her excitedly. 'Keep pushing!'

'I fuckin' am!' she hissed through gritted teeth. 'It's no fuckin' good, I can't get the fuckin' thing out of me fuckin' cunt!'

'You're nearly there! Go on, push! Push!'

Her inflamed cunt lips opening wide as the sticky apple slowly emerged, she gasped for breath, her face flushing, her stomach muscles tensing as she gave one last almighty push. The apple opening her sex entrance, stretching her delicate inner lips, her body became rigid as she managed to expel the wet fruit.

'Good grief!' Larry cried, gazing at the apple. 'Look at the size of it!'

'Fuck me! I thought I was going to fuckin' well split open!' she breathed, lifting her head and gazing at her yawning pussy slit. 'Look at me fuckin' cunt, it's 'anging wide open! Shit, I think I've gone and fucked it!'

'You'll be all right, Sally. It's good practice for when you give birth,' Larry humoured the exhausted girl. 'Just relax and let your muscles recover. So, what was your boyfriend's reaction to your news?' ·

'It's OK, I worked me fuckin' dates out wrong. I ain't due on till next fuckin' week.'

'That must be a relief for you.'

'No, it ain't! I won't get me fuckin' council flat if I ain't up the fuckin' duff.'

'Sally,' Larry smiled, tweaking her sensitive nipples. 'Sally, why don't you try and change your ways, your life? I mean, there are opportunities today . . .'

'What the fuck you talkin' about?'

'I'm talking about you trying to better yourself. If you were to stop swearing and get yourself some decent clothes

. . . have your hair done and do your make-up properly, you could get a job and rent a nice flat.'

'Work? Fuck me, I can't fuckin' work!'

'Why not?'

'I wouldn't get me fuckin' dole money!'

'No, but you'd get a wage.'

'I'm goin' on the fuckin' game, then I'll 'ave plenty of fuckin' dosh.'

'Try saying one sentence without swearing, Sally,' Larry suggested, running his finger over her smooth stomach to her wet vaginal crack. 'Do you like that?' he asked, massaging her erect clitoris.

'Yes, fuckin' right, I do!'

'Leave out the F-word.'

'Yes, I like it.'

'Good. Would you like me to use my vibrator on your clitoris?'

'Yes, I want to fuckin' . . . I mean, I want to come.'

'God knows how you're able to open your legs as wide as that!' Larry grinned, grabbing the vibrator. 'They're at right angles to your body, it's incredible!'

'I've been doin' it since I was twelve.'

'Really?'

'Yes, since me cousin . . . whoops, I'd better not say nothin' about that.'

'Er . . . yes, well . . . OK, are you ready for the vibro?'

'Yes! Put your cunt clips on me and then fuckin' well bring me off!'

Reaching to the shelf, Larry grabbed two small metal clips connected to heavy weights by lengths of string. Fixing the clips to the naked girl's outer lips, he gently lowered the

weights either side of the couch, watching her vaginal lips distend painfully, her pussy slit open, exposing her cunt hole, the full length of her solid clitoris.

'OK?' he asked.

'Yes, it feels great! I like me cunt stretched open. Shove a candle up me arse.'

'You're an insatiable little girl, aren't you?' Larry smiled, taking a massive candle from the shelf.

'I'm a what?'

'Insatiable. Er . . . you can't get enough, can you?'

'No, fuckin' right I can't! Go on, shove it right up me fuckin' arse!'

'OK, here it comes!' Larry grinned, positioning the end of the candle between her splayed buttocks and pushing against the brown flesh surrounding her tight bum-hole.

Her anal entrance yielding, the waxen shaft sinking into her hot rectal tube, the girl gasped as the lewd sensations permeated her quivering pelvis. Christine would be forced to endure the candle, Larry mused as he pushed the shaft deeper into the trembling girl's bowels. The most delectable Miss Cology had endless hours of iniquitous fun and games to look forward to!

'Shove another one up me fuckin' cunt hole!' Sally demanded of Larry crudely, raising her flushed face and grinning up at him.

'OK, you're the boss!' he chuckled obligingly, taking another candle from the shelf.

'Do me nipples with your clips, and then bring me off with your fuckin' vibro!'

'You're a dirty little girl, Sally, you really are!' Larry

laughed, pressing the end of the candle against the irrigating flesh surrounding her open orifice.

The shaft driving into her hot vaginal sheath, Larry gazed at her taut girl-flesh, her stretched outer lips. The weights painfully opening her sex crack, her pelvic cavity bloated with the two massive candles, the nymphomaniacal girl was in her sexual element. Her naked body crudely abused, she again begged Larry to fix clips to her erect nipples.

'The 'eaviest fuckin' weights you've got!' she giggled as he pushed the candle fully home and reached to the shelf. 'Really 'urt me fuckin' nipples!' Fixing metal clips to her long milk teats, Larry dropped the lengths of string down either side of the couch and grabbed two heavy weights from the shelf. Connecting the weights to the strings, he gently released them, watching excitedly as the girl's nipples painfully distended, her firm rounded breasts becoming taut cones.

'Ah, yes!' she breathed, lifting her head and focusing on her elongated breast buds. 'Me fuckin' bum and me cunt feel great! And me fuckin' nipples really 'urt, I love it!'

'What else do you love?' Larry probed. 'Before I bring you off with the vibrator, is there anything else you'd like me to do to you?'

'Yes, there is. Shove another fuckin' candle up me fuckin' cunt.'

'Christ, Sally, I won't be able to . . .'

'Yes, you fuckin' will! Go on, fuckin' well try!'

Taking another candle from the shelf, Larry frowned, sure that the girl's already bloated vaginal cavern wouldn't accommodate a second wax phallus. Pressing the pointed end against her taut, reddening flesh, he gently pushed, forcing her vaginal entrance asunder. Gasping, her face

grimacing as her abused sex hole finally yielded, the girl ordered Larry to push the candle deep into her cunt. His eyes wide, transfixed on her glistening vulval flesh, he drove the candle deep into her ballooning sex pouch, amazed by the crude distension of her abused inner labia.

'Fuck me, that's fuckin' good!' Sally gasped. 'Ah, God, me cunt feels . . . me cunt feels fuckin' great! Put more weights on, I want me fuckin' nipples 'urting like fuckin' 'ell!'

'Anything you say!' Larry laughed, eyeing the girl's painfully abused nipples as he grabbed two more weights from the shelf.

Attaching the weights to the strings, he watched her nipples elongate, the metal clips painfully stretching the brown discs of her areolae. Whatever next? he wondered as she lifted her head and grinned, focusing on her conical breasts tapering to points. The metal clips biting into her sensitive nipples, her cunt lips crudely forced apart, her vagina bloated to capacity, her anal duct inflated, Larry wondered what else the young masochist would demand of him.

'Tie me fuckin' feet!' she cried, lifting her head and grinning at Larry. 'Fix ropes to me fuckin' feet and pull me fuckin' legs wide open!'

'Your legs are already wide open!' Larry remonstrated.

'No, no! I want me fuckin' legs forced apart until they 'urt, I want me feet tied so that I can't close me fuckin' legs!'

Shaking his head in disbelief, Larry took a length of rope from a hook on the wall and tied one end to the girl's left ankle. Pulling on the rope, he wound the other end around a hook on the wall, securing her leg at right angles to her quivering body. Binding her other ankle, he pulled on the rope, yanking her leg in line with

the other one and tying the rope to a hook on the opposite wall.

'Christ!' he gasped, standing at the end of the examination couch and gazing at the three candles emerging from the girl's obscenely stretched sex holes. 'You're a bloody contortionist!'

'Jesus, it fuckin' 'urts! Ah, me legs fuckin' 'urt, it's great!' she gasped. 'Now bring me off with your fuckin' vibro!'

'You're sure you're ready?' Larry chuckled. 'I mean, you don't want me to tie ropes around your tits, do you?'

'Yes, good idea! Tie ropes around me fuckin' tits, really tight so they fuckin' 'urt like fuckin' 'ell!'

Taking two more lengths of rope from the wall, Larry tied them around the base of each of the girl's breasts, pulling the knots tight, painfully ballooning her mammary globes. Surely this was enough? he thought incredulously, gazing at her long nipples, her areolae no longer discs but cones of brown flesh.

'Me arse!' Miss Masochist cried. 'I want another fuckin' candle up me fuckin' arse!'

'Sally, I really don't think . . .'

'Just fuckin' do it!'

'OK, it's your body.'

Taking a fourth candle from the shelf, Larry plunged the end into the jar of honey, certain that the girl's anal duct would never accommodate a second phallus. Leaning forward, he scrutinized her brown ring, stretched tautly around the candle deep within her rectal sheath. *Oh well, here goes!* he thought, pressing the pointed end of the candle against her inflamed brown tissue. Twisting and pushing, he watched in amazement as the girl's bottom-hole began

to yield to the second intruding shaft, stretching wide open to accommodate the candle.

'Keep fuckin' pushin'!' she breathed, her face grimacing with the pain and pleasure her abused body was bringing her. 'It's goin' in! Keep fuckin' pushin'!'

'I am!' Larry breathed, stunned as the brown ring opened to receive the huge phallus. 'My God! I'd never have thought it possible!' he exclaimed as the candle disappeared into the girl's bloated bowels.

'God, it's fuckin' wonderful! Now bring me off with your fuckin' vibrator!'

Taking the vibrator from the shelf, Larry switched it on and pressed the buzzing tip to the girl's swollen clitoris, grinning as she immediately responded by wailing her appreciation for her painfully abused young body. Her smooth stomach rising and falling as her orgasm quickly rose from her contracting womb, she tossed her head from side to side, her matted blonde tresses veiling her contorting face, her body shaking violently with her explosion of undiluted lust.

On and on her multiple orgasm rode, the waves of sexual ecstasy crashing through her rigid body. Her cunt muscles gripping the two candles, her pussy milk flowing in torrents, her distended anal duct spasming, the semiconscious girl convulsed violently. Her naked body twitching uncontrollably, the perspiration of obscene sex streaming down her scarlet face, she'd given her very soul to Lucifer, exchanged her very being for the gratification of perverted sex.

Moving the vibrator away from her inflamed clitoris, Larry shook his head, focusing on her tortured breasts, her sore nipples. Never had he known such a masochist, such an insatiable nymphomaniac. Her body twitching, convulsing

wildly, he gazed at her crudely opened sex holes, wondering at the mystical blend of pain and pleasure she was deriving from her physical abuse.

'Your cock!' Sally finally managed to gasp as she returned to consciousness. 'Spunk . . . spunk in me fuckin' mouth!'

Slipping his erect penis out, Larry stood beside the girl's head, offering his bulbous knob to her gasping mouth. Taking him inside, she sucked fervently like a starving babe at the breast, taking half his solid shaft into her wet mouth. Her eyes rolling, she swivelled her hips, bringing herself untold sexual pleasure as the irreverent candles massaged her sex ducts.

'You certainly know how to use your tongue!' Larry gasped as his glans pulsated and his shaft twitched. 'God, you're bloody good at cock sucking!'

'I want your fuckin' spunk!' the sex-vampire gasped, slipping his knob out of her mouth. 'Give me your spunk and then bring me off with your fuckin' vibrator again!'

'Yes, yes, I will!' Larry spluttered as she engulfed his swollen glans again.

His heavy balls rolling, his orgasm approaching, he rocked his hips, fucking the slut's hungry mouth as Monica's voice boomed in the hall. Not again! he groaned inwardly, and then outwardly as, watching Sally's cheeks ballooning, he thrust his knob to the back of her throat and loosed his sperm. Swallowing hard, the vampire drank from his fountainhead, delighting in her debauchery. Swivelling her hips, massaging her sex sheaths with the four candles, she slipped his spunking knob out of her mouth and tongued his glans.

His sperm splattering her face, her lips, her young body painfully abused, she was lost in her sexual deviancy, her

lewdness. She was no more than a whore to be used and fucked, Larry reflected, watching his spunk jetting over her snaking tongue. As his orgasm finally receded, he thought about Christine Cology bound to the sex cross in the secret room. Once Sally had staggered out of the building he'd fix the weights to Christine's nipples, the clamps to her pouting outer cunt lips and abuse her waiting, naked body.

'Doctor Lickman!' Monica bellowed.

Jesus fucking Christ!

'Doctor Lickman! Where are you?'

Go away, you inorgasmic, cuntless hag bag!

'Doctor Lickman, there's a problem in reception!'

Swallowing the last of his sperm, Sally slipped his throbbing glans from her wet mouth and grinned. 'Why don't you fuckin' well get the old bag in 'ere and fuckin' well tie 'er up?' she asked as Larry zipped his trousers. 'I'd like to get me fuckin' 'ands on 'er fuckin' cunt!'

'I can't do that!' Larry chuckled. 'You're not a lesbian, are you?'

'I'm fuckin' anythin' and fuckin' everythin'!' the shameless hussy giggled, squeezing her cunt muscles and ejecting the candles. 'Watch me arse, I'm goin' to shoot them fuckin' candles out!'

Moving to the far end of the examination couch, Larry focused on the girl's taut anal ring, the two candles emerging between her splayed buttocks. Tightening her pelvic muscles, she grimaced as the candles began to glide out of her rectal tube. Bearing down, her cunt juices trickling from her inflamed vaginal sheath, she pushed the candles half way out of her arsehole, her face contorting and flushing with the exertion.

'Ready?' she panted, taking a deep breath. The candles shooting across the room and hitting the far wall with a dull thud, Larry gazed in awe at the girl's gaping bottom-hole, wondering how on earth she could have accommodated the two massive waxen shafts. 'Fuck me! Me fuckin' arse feels fuckin' great!' she giggled. 'Take the fuckin' clamps and stuff off of me!'

Releasing the tortured girl and helping her to her feet, Larry smiled. She was his star client, he reflected, eyeing her stretched milk buds, her gaping vaginal slit. Of all the clients he'd ever had the pleasure of sexually abusing, Sally was the best. Watching her dress in her tatty clothes he thought of Christine Cology again, wondering what to do with her. Was there time to have Sally abuse his prisoner? he wondered as Monica bellowed again from reception. *Shit, no!*

'I'll see you next fuckin' week,' Sally imparted, slipping into her stilettos as she finished dressing.

'Yes, next Thursday,' Larry smiled as Monica screamed his name from reception. 'Right, I'd better go and face the music! Come on, Sally, let's go.'

'Will you whip me fuckin' cunt lips next week?' she asked.

'Whip your lips?'

'Yes, with a fuckin' cane. I love 'aving me cunt whipped with a fuckin' cane!'

'It'll be my pleasure!' he laughed, wondering again at the frightening depths of the girl's perversity.

'And me fuckin' tits! Cane me fuckin' tits until they're fuckin' red!'

'Ok, anything you say. Come on, let's get out of here!'

Seeing Sally out, Larry held his hand to his head as he

179

returned to reception. Standing before him, her fists on her hips, her face scowling, Monica was obviously in a bad mood. 'Everything all right?' he asked her, frowning at Brigit and Lily hovering by the waiting room door.

'No, everything's far from all right!' Monica snorted. 'What have you been doing in your torture chamber?'

'Sexually torturing Sally Peabody. Now, what's the problem?'

'You're vile!'

'Remember that I've doubled your salary, Monica!'

'Oh, yes, well . . . er . . . the nun's gone missing. She left the convent to come here, and she's disappeared.'

'That's not our problem, Monica.'

'Er . . . well, it is because she was seen entering the building.'

'Well, in that case, we'd better send out a search party!' Larry laughed, wondering why Brigit was making odd facial expressions and pointing at the waiting-room door.

'There's another problem,' Monica began. 'There's a man to see you, he's in the waiting room.'

'Oh, who's that?'

'That convent schoolgirl's father.'

'Which schoolgirl?' Larry asked, his eyes wide.

'Jenny, the one who staggered back to the convent with her blouse . . .'

'Christ! Er . . . I have to go out for a while.'

'He knows that you're here. He said that you'd deflowered his young daughter. He's having her examined to see whether she's lost her virginity.'

'Christ! Tell him that I'm away for a few days!' Larry yelped, dashing across the foyer.

Sex Practice

Bolting out of the building, he made for the local pub, wondering how to get out of this particular mess. 'Christ! The tax man, Gina Cology, Christine Cology, Fullcrack, Venereal, and now a schoolgirl's bloody father!' he cursed as he lurched wearily into the pub. Ordering a large scotch, he sat at a corner table and held his head. The end had come, he knew as he sipped his drink. Damnation!

whips we use.

"Oooo! Stop that! This is terrible. Buy if there were only too willing to agree gently to the thrashing of a young girl. Why do you..."

Chapter Six

'Monica,' Brigit whispered as Lily left the building to search for Larry. 'Monica, when that girl's father catches up with Larry, he'll wheedle his way out of it, as he always does. I think we should do something.'

'Do something? Such as what?' the portly woman asked, frowning suspiciously.

'I don't know but . . . what with the tax man and the health authority and everything, I think Larry's gone too far.'

'You're telling me he has!'

'Monica, I've never told anyone before but . . . he's sexually abused me many times, and I want to expose him for what he really is – a filthy pervert.'

'*You*? *You* want to expose him?'

'Yes, I'm going to see him pay for all he's done if it's the last thing I do! The time you looked through his consulting room window and saw . . . he made me do that, he threatened me and made me expose myself to that girl.'

'But I thought that you . . .'

'He says that he'll sack me if I wear panties to work. He whips me, too.'

'Good gracious! This is terrible, Brigit! But you were only too willing to be a party to the thrashing of that young girl. Why did you . . .'

'He threatened me. He's treated me despicably.'

'Why didn't you leave? You don't have to work here.'

'He threatened to do all sorts of dreadful things to me if I grassed on him or left the practice. I must nail him, have him locked up so that I'm free of his sexual abuse and awful threats!'

'How do you intend to do that?'

'With your help, Monica. There's a camera in his examination room. If you'll allow me to tie you to the couch and take pictures, we'll go to the police and have Larry nailed once and for all.'

'Oh, no! If you think . . .'

'No, listen! I'm on your side now. You can tie *me* down, too. Take photographs of me tied to the examination couch and we'll expose Larry. He'll worm his way out of trouble again and again and continue to abuse and threaten me, but if we have photographs, evidence of his debauchery, and we both testify . . .'

'All right, Brigit. I'm glad you've seen the light, at long last! What changed your mind?'

'He . . . he tied me down to the examination couch and . . . I can't talk about it, it's too dreadful.'

'You poor child. You should have confided in me long ago.'

'Yes, I know. I suppose I didn't know what to do, who to turn to. Anyway, there's not much time, he might be back soon. Come on, I'll tie your wrists and ankles and take a few pictures, and then you can do the same to me. Gina Cology already has some photographs of Larry with a client so . . .'

'You know the nun who was supposed to come here to see Doctor Lickman?' Monica interrupted the girl.

'Yes.'

'She's not a nun, she's Gina's daughter.'

'Really?'

'Yes, but she's gone missing. She didn't come here, did she?'

'No, she didn't turn up. Where is she, then? She must have . . .'

'I don't know where she is. As you can imagine, Gina's out of her mind with worry.'

'God, she must be!'

'Gina suspects Larry of abducting the girl.'

'Abducting her? I'd have known about it if he'd done that. I'm sure he hasn't, Monica! Besides, where would he keep her? There's nowhere to hide her here, is there?'

'No, she's not here – I've searched everywhere. If I have the opportunity, I might break into Doctor Lickman's house – Christine could be there.'

'OK, I'll help you search for her later. But we mustn't worry about that now. Come on, let's get this over with, Monica. Let's nail Larry bloody Lickman once and for all!'

Leading Monica into the examination room, Brigit closed and locked the door, ordering her to lie on the couch. Binding the woman's ankles with rope as she lay on her back, Brigit wondered when Larry would return.

'If he catches us, there'll be hell to pay!' she whispered, pulling Monica's arms behind her head and binding her wrists to the legs of the couch. 'Right, that should do it!'

'Quickly, take the photographs and let me go before he gets back! If he finds me like this, he'll . . . God only knows what he'll do!'

'OK, I'll have to lift your skirt up and pull your knickers down!' Brigit giggled. 'This must appear authentic!'

'No! Brigit, you can't . . .'

'It's all right, Monica! This is only for the photographs, to make the scene appear genuine!'

'No, don't . . .'

Pulling the woman's skirt up over her stomach, Brigit tugged her blue woollen knickers down, displaying her dense black pubic bush, the yawning gorge between her fleshy sex hillocks. Ignoring her prisoner's pleas and threats, she took a pair of scissors from the shelf and cut through the thick material, pulling the shredded garment away from the woman's flailing body.

'You have a nice cunt!' Brigit gloated, focusing the camera on her protruding inner lips. 'Let's have a look at your flabby tits!'

'You've tricked me, you bitch! If you dare to cut my . . .'

'Have you ever had a girl's tongue up your cunt?' Brigit asked, unbuttoning Monica's navy-blue cardigan. 'I'm going to lick your cunt out for you, you'll like that, won't you?'

'I have never met such a vile and wicked little strumpet as you in my life! Unless you release me now, I'll . . .'

'You'll what?' Brigit grinned, unbuttoning her prisoner's blouse and exposing her full, straining bra. 'Right, let's have a look at your big fat wobbly tits!'

Yanking Monica's bra clear of her mammary spheres, Brigit gazed appreciatively at her dark areolae, her stiffening nipples. Running her fingers up and down the woman's vaginal crack, her libido soaring, her vaginal juices decanting, she grinned wickedly.

'I'm going to remove your cunt hair!' she laughed, taking the depilating cream from the shelf. 'When Larry gets back, he'll be really pleased with me!'

'Brigit! Brigit, if you dare to . . .'

'You've got a hell of a lot of cunt hair, Monica! Obviously, you don't trim your bikini line. Mind you, with a body like yours, I don't suppose you wear bikinis. You'd be arrested for gross indecency!'

'You disgust me, Brigit! I might have known that this was a trick!'

'Yes, I'm surprised you fell for it! I'll remove your cunt hair and make you look like a schoolgirl, shall I? Larry likes schoolgirlies. When he sees your hairless cunt, he might even fuck you – if you're lucky! He's heavily into schoolgirlie lookalikes!'

'Brigit, I'll . . .'

'There, that's more than enough!' Brigit laughed, massaging the cream into Monica's mons, her fleshy outer lips. 'Now all we have to do is wait and – *voilà*. Vestal vulva!'

'I'll kill you for this! You can't keep me here forever, Brigit! When I'm free, I'm going to . . .'

'Oh, do stop complaining, Monica! All I'm doing is removing your cunt hair, for Christ's sake!'

'You'll end up in prison for this, my girl!'

'Yes, yes, I know! You'll kill me, you'll send me to prison . . . what will the charge be? Oh yes, removal of Monica Moodie's cunt hair against her will! The sentence? Well, I reckon five years' hard labour. I'm not surprised that your husband walked out on you. The poor man suffered you for too long. I don't suppose you sucked him off or let him lick your cunt out or . . . have you ever heard of sixty-nine?'

'Of course I have! Brigit, release me this instant or I'll . . .'

'Oh, I think someone's at reception. I'll leave the cream to do its job and see you later. Don't go away!'

Mincing down the hall to reception, Brigit smiled at Ingram Ravenhugh. 'Can I help you?' she asked, hoisting her red microskirt up to *inadvertently* expose her knickerless vaginal slit. Having taken Christine and Monica prisoner, there was nothing to lose now, she mused. Venereal and Fullcrack were forcing Larry into a corner, and Gina Cology was closing in fast. No, there was nothing to lose!

'Er . . . I'm from the Inland Revenue. My name's Ravenhugh,' the tax man replied, focusing on Brigit's swollen pussy lips, her open sex valley, as she projected her hips forward. 'Is Mr Throbber available?'

'Mr who?'

'Throbber, Doctor Lickman's assistant.'

'I've never heard of him. I think you must have . . .'

'I was talking to Mr Throbber the other day, he . . . Who are you?'

'I'm Brigit Biways, Doctor Lickman's secretary.'

'Oh, I see. And you've never heard of Mr Throbber?'

'No, there's no one of that name here. Perhaps I can be of assistance?' Brigit grinned, blatantly hiking her skirt up to her stomach and displaying her hairless pussy crack.

Wondering why Ravenhugh seemed oblivious to her flagrant exhibitionism, the girl frowned. Standing with her feet further apart, her cunt slit gaping, her inner pink petals hanging prettily, she decided to go for it. 'Do you like my cunt?' she demanded, leaning back and projecting the open centre of her femininity. 'You can finger my cunt hole, if you want to.'

Dropping to his knees, his mouth open, his eyes wide with astonishment, Ravenhugh gazed lustfully at Brigit's pinken girlie slit. His mouth twisting into a salacious grin as he focused on her protruding inner petals, he tentatively reached out and stroked her swollen sex hillocks.

'My God, you're beautiful!' he gasped, moving closer as she parted her outer labia with her slender fingers to offer him her open vagina. Eyeing the opaque droplets of maiden juice clinging to her inner cunt flesh, the stricken man looked up to the harlot's elfin face as if awaiting her instruction, her permission to taste her succulent sex pasture.

'Go on, finger my cunt!' the saucy temptress giggled, knowing the man's carnal craving.

'God, you're a sexy little thing!' he exclaimed, slipping a finger between her swollen sex hillocks. 'Christ, you're wet!' Driving his finger deep into the fiery heat of her tight vagina, he licked his lips, imagining his tongue lapping around her open hole, savouring her heady sex juice.

'Why have you come here?' Brigit asked softly, stretching her cunt lips further apart.

'To sort out Doctor Lickman's tax affairs,' the helpless man murmured, examining the girl's sex folds, her stiffening clitoris as it emerged from its pink hide.

'I'm sure we can come to some arrangement. Ah, that's nice, finger my cunt faster! God, you're making my clit go hard! I . . . I want your . . .'

'Arrangement?'

'Yes, an arrangement . . . ah, God! God, that's nice! A deal . . . we'll make a deal about the tax Doctor Lickman owes.'

'Well, I don't know whether . . .'

'Oh, you don't want my cunt?' Brigit asked petulantly, his finger slipping out of her hot sex sheath as she stepped back and pulled her skirt down.

'Well, it's not that I don't want . . .'

'You either want my cunt or you don't. Are you married?'

'Yes, I am.'

'Does your wife shave her cunt?'

'Good God, no!'

'You'd like to come in my mouth, wouldn't you? You'd like me to suck you off and swallow your spunk, wouldn't you?'

'Yes, very much!' the sex stooge breathed, moving forward on his knees and slipping his hand up her skirt. 'My wife . . . she . . .'

Raising her skirt, Brigit grinned as Ravenhugh's finger penetrated her juicy cunt sheath again. 'Does your wife suck your knob and swallow your spunk?' she asked impishly.

'No, she won't do that.'

'Oh, you poor thing! Does she like you licking her clitty to orgasm?'

'No, she won't let . . .'

'Surely, she loves you lapping up her cunt juice?'

'She's not into oral sex,' he replied dolefully.

'Does she like you fucking her arsehole?'

'She . . . thinking about it, she doesn't seem to like anything.'

'Oh, dear! So, what arrangement can we come to? How much tax does Larry owe?'

'Thousands!'

'You can lick my cunt, if you like. Of course, you'll have to promise me that you'll get Larry off the hook.'

'I can't write off . . .'

'You don't want me to suck you off, then? I'm the best cocksucker in town, ask anyone. Well, I don't actually mean *any*one!'

'I . . .'

'I'd like you to fuck my mouth, fuck my mouth and spunk down my throat as if it were my cunt.'

'All right, I'll work something out! It won't be easy, but I'll try.'

'You'll have to do better than that, Mr Tax Man! Come into the examination room and I'll lick your knob, just to give you a taste of what's on offer. Well, to give *me* a taste, I suppose!' Brigit giggled as he retrieved his sticky finger from her honeypot and leapt up.

Leading the way to the pussy's den, Brigit formulated her wicked plan. Larry's camera was kept in the bondage room, ever-ready for photographing young girls' fresh cunts. A couple of shots of the tax man committing vile and indecent acts with Monica would be enough to have him eating out of Brigit's hand – her pussy! The pictures might well come in useful too, should it be necessary to blackmail Monica, she reflected.

'This is Monica,' Brigit ventured, showing the way into the bondage room. 'She's having her cunt hair removed to make her look like a schoolgirl. Monica, this is the tax man.'

'Brigit! Brigit, I'll . . .'

'Ignore her, she's always complaining, never satisfied! Why don't you grab that towel from the shelf and wipe

the cream off her cunt? Do you like shaved cunts? Are you into schoolgirls?'

'You bet!' Ravenhugh enthused, his eyes gleaming. 'Although . . . she's rather old, isn't she?'

'You dare!' Monica bellowed as he reached out to the shelf. 'If you touch me, I'll see that you're taken to court and . . .'

'Oh, do shut up, Monica!' Brigit snapped, kneading the woman's ample breasts, twisting and pulling on her brown milk teats. 'For once in your life, why don't you enjoy yourself – your cunt?'

Grinning lustfully, the towel in his hand, the uncivil servant cleansed his victim's fleshy labia, exposing her smooth hairless skin, her yawning sex valley. He'd not demand a penny in income tax, Brigit rejoiced, grabbing the camera and focusing it on the letch. Clicking the shutter to the accompaniment of Monica's screamed protests as Ravenhugh sank three fingers into her hot vault, Brigit moved to the far end of the couch and focused on the woman's smooth, hairless vaginal lips, stretched tautly around the zealous tax man's greedy fingers.

'Why take pictures?' Ravenhugh panted, momentarily distracted from his unbusinesslike probing as Brigit clicked the shutter again.

'Just a little insurance should you decide to change your mind and send Larry a tax demand,' she smiled. 'Pull your trousers down and I'll suck your knob off and drink your spunk.'

'When I get out of here . . .' Monica shrieked as Ravenhugh withdrew his drenched fingers from her gaping cunt.

'Shut up, Monica, or I'll have the tax man wank himself off and spunk all over your face!'

Dropping to her knees, Brigit focused the camera on Ravenhugh's erect penis, his bulbous purple knob, as he tugged his trousers down. The flash illuminating his heavy balls, she lay on the floor, taking several more shots of his cock with his face in frame before discarding the camera and kneeling before him. Taking his solid shaft in her hand, she pulled his foreskin right back. 'Mmm, you have a fine weapon!' she breathed, opening her mouth and sucking his glans to the back of her throat.

Monica's shrieks resounding around the building, the tax man gasping, leaning on the examination couch to steady his trembling body, Brigit continued her fervent mouthing and sucking. Bending over his trussed treat, Ravenhugh licked her hairless sex slit, driving three fingers into her wet cunt again as Brigit took his knob to the back of her throat and gently sank her teeth into his twitching shaft. Kneading his brimming balls, taking him closer to his sexual ecstasy, she decided *she* wouldn't swallow his final demand. Monica would be the unwilling recipient, she concluded, slipping his wet glans from her hot mouth and licking his veined shaft.

'OK!' Brigit squealed excitedly, rising to her feet. 'Monica, how would you like the tax man to fuck you?'

Fixing the raunchy redhead with a look of hatred, Monica's bottom lip quivered. 'Brigit Biways, if you dare to . . .'

'God, here we go again!' Brigit giggled, pressing the concealed button and watching the false wall slide back. 'Hi, Christine! Welcome to the orgy!' she laughed as the

tethered girl turned her head to gaze at the blatantly excited tax man. 'I'm sure you'd like to be fucked, wouldn't you?'

'Christine!' Monica cried, lifting her head and focusing on the naked girl. 'Christine, what . . .'

'God, she's a bit of all right!' Ravenhugh breathed, turning to look at Christine. 'I'll fuck that one, but not this old hag!' he laughed, slipping his fingers out of Monica's wide canal.

'No, you'll fuck both of them!' Brigit returned, grabbing his solid dick and pulling him towards the secret room – towards her protesting victim. 'First, you'll fuck Christine senseless, and then you'll screw Monica's cunt! That's today's special offer – fuck one, fuck one free!'

'And what about you?' Ravenhugh lusted. 'Don't I get to fuck your tight cunt?'

'Oh, you are a naughty tax man! We'll see how you get on with these two first.'

Kneeling between Christine's splayed thighs, Ravenhugh looked down as Brigit grabbed his solid penis and presented the purple head to the girl's gaping vaginal entrance. 'OK, let the fucking commence!' she cried, grinning at Christine as Ravenhugh's cock slipped deep into her silky sex sheath. 'Your cock's found its haven, so now fuck the bitch rotten and fill her cunt with tax-free spunk!'

'No!' Christine shrieked, objecting as her young body rocked with the penile thrusts. 'When my mother finds out that . . .'

'Your mother will never find out!' Brigit laughed, moving to her victim's side and licking her erect nipples. 'Mmm, you've got nice tits, nice and firm. I like your body,

Christine, I might allow you to tongue-fuck my cunt if you're a good girl.'

'This is rape!'

'No, it's not, it's brilliant! You'd love to come, wouldn't you?' Brigit taunted the helpless girl, moving up her naked body and kissing her mouth.

Turning her head away, Christine pulled on her bonds. 'You filthy lesbian!' she spat as Ravenhugh increased his rhythm and began to gasp. 'You filthy bloody lesbian!'

'God, here it comes!' Ravenhugh cried, grabbing the girl's hips and driving his throbbing glans deep into her tightening cunt. 'I'm . . . I'm coming!'

Reaching down to Christine's yawning sex slit, Brigit massaged her erect clitoris, determined to take her prisoner to orgasm as Ravenhugh grimaced and pumped out his load. Driving his rock-hard cock in and out of the quivering girl's sex duct, filling her love sheath with his gushing spunk, he gasped. 'God, she's tight!' he cried. 'Christ, she's got a beautiful cunt!'

Grinning as Christine began to breathe heavily in the beginnings of her own climax, Brigit massaged the girl's clitoris faster, praying that the debauchery would ravage Larry's tax demand. She'd have to offer Ravenhugh more goodies, she mused as Christine sang out in her coming. One slice of perverted sex wouldn't be enough, she knew. She'd have to promise him the whole fruity cake – but only until Larry was off the hook. Then, just for kicks, she'd show Mrs Tax Man the photographs of her taxing husband!

Peering round the doorway, Larry frowned. *What the hell's going on here?* he thought, gazing at Christine's gasping

mouth, her tongue licking her dry lips as her mind-blowing orgasm gripped her. *Ravenhugh screwing Christine Cology? Do penises fly?*

Deciding to take some incriminating photographs, he reached out and snaffled the camera from the shelf. Focusing on Ravenhugh, he grinned. Now he had the tax man where he wanted him, he reflected, clicking the shutter – by the goolies! Oblivious to the flash, the sex-starved beast continued his adulterous fucking, his cunny-wet cock repeatedly emerging from Christine's spasming pussy sheath and driving deep into her body, pumping the last of his spunk into her spasming vagina.

This was the break he needed, Larry reflected, taking another shot as Ravenhugh withdrew his glistening penis from Christine's sperm-bubbling cauldron. If he could lure Venereal and Fullcrack into his den of iniquity and offer them the sexual delights of Brigit's and Christine's fresh young bodies, he'd come out on top – they'd all come out on top!

'I'd better be going,' Ravenhugh sighed, zipping his trousers.

'I thought you were going to fuck Monica?' Brigit asked surprisedly.

'I have an important appointment, so ... I'll be in touch.'

'In touch about what?' Brigit frowned, massaging the last pulsations of orgasm from Christine's swollen clitoris to the accompaniment of the girl's whimpers.

'About ... well, about coming here again, I suppose.'

'And why would you want to come back here?'

'To . . . to see you and . . .'

'And have sex?'

'Well, yes, if that's OK.'

'Yes, that's OK. You can see yourself out. Oh, by the way, don't forget that I have the photographs. I'm sure your wife wouldn't take too kindly to your adultery, if you get my meaning.'

'Yes, I get your meaning. It won't be easy, but I'll ensure that Doctor Lickman won't be sent a tax demand. Well, goodbye for now.'

'Bye, Mr Tax Man.'

Hurriedly slipping into his consulting room as Ravenhugh scurried through the hall and left the building, Larry rubbed his chin. That might be his tax problems sorted, he mused, but what about Christine Cology and Monica? They presented major stumbling blocks – especially Monica! Returning to the bondage room, wondering what the hell to do, he leaned over Monica and grinned.

'What are you up to?' he mocked the flushed-faced woman as he focused on her hairless vaginal lips, her long pussy crack. 'Is this how you behave the minute my back's turned? I thought you were virtuous, wholesome and . . .'

'No, it's not like that! Brigit tricked me and tied me down!'

'Larry, you're back!' Brigit beamed, deserting her trembling prisoner and joining him by the hapless receptionist's side.

'Yes, I'm back. What the hell's going on here?'

'Well, I've captured Monica, as you can see, and . . .'

'Now that you've taken her prisoner, what do you

intend to do with her? I don't think this is a good idea, Brigit.'

'What do you intend to do with Christine now that you've taken *her* prisoner?' Brigit returned.

'All right, we're quits. What we do now, God only knows!'

'Doctor Lickman!' Monica bellowed, her ample breasts heaving as she struggled to free herself. 'Release me this instant or I'll . . .'

'She's been making futile threats for ages!' Brigit laughed. 'She's becoming somewhat boring!'

'Monica,' Larry smiled, running his fingers over her fleshy sex lips. 'You seem to have got yourself into a rather difficult predicament. What I suggest we do is . . .'

'And I suggest that you release . . .'

'You're in no position to suggest anything, Monica! Now, listen to me. Brigit has dealt with the tax man admirably. Fullcrack and Venereal . . . well, I have plans for them. That leaves you and Christine, does it not? Christine won't be a problem because she'll not be able to prove a thing.'

'Yes, I will!' the girl called.

'Christine, you have no proof whatsoever, so shut up!' Brigit snorted. 'Unless you want me to sit on your face and bring myself off in your mouth!'

'That just leaves you, Monica,' Larry smiled, slipping his finger into the heat of the woman's accommodating vaginal cavern. 'As I was saying, what I suggest is this. You have no proof, apart from your shaved fanny, but that's circumcisional – I mean circumstantial – because you could have quite easily shaved yourself. You can't

prove that Brigit stole your vulval curls. So, what I'm going to do is keep you here as my prisoner . . .'

'You can't do that!' Monica cried, squirming as Larry slipped another finger into her cobwebbed cunt.

'All right, what would you suggest, then?'

'Let me go! You have no choice!'

'What, and have you go running to the police as you did before?'

'No, no I'll keep quiet, I promise you.'

'Promises are made to be broken, Monica, as are marriage vows, the vows that nuns make . . . old crumbly though you are, I'm sure I'll be able to sell you for sex. Yes, if I cover your ugly face with a piece of old sacking, I'm sure . . .'

'Doctor Lickman, unless you untie me . . .'

'Shit, someone's in reception!' Larry gasped, pressing the button and concealing Christine's tethered body. 'Quickly, Brigit, get out there and deal with it! We'll continue our chat later, Monica,' he whispered, leaving the room.

Locking the door as Brigit raced down the hall, Larry composed himself and entered his consulting room, wondering what other problems the day would throw at him. Lifting the ringing phone as he sat on the edge of his desk, he asked Brigit what was going on.

'It's Gina Cology!' the girl whispered excitably. 'She wants to see you!'

'OK, OK send her along.'

'But what about . . .'

'I'll deal with Gina, Brigit, have no fear of that! When you've shown her in, bring me a length of rope and a pair of handcuffs.'

'A pair of handcuffs?'

'Yes, you do know what handcuffs are, don't you?'

'Well, yes, but . . .'

'Just do it, Brigit.'

Exactly what he planned to do, Larry had no idea, but seeing as he already had two prisoners, he decided that a third wouldn't really make much difference. *Might as well be hung for a lamb as a sheep!* Taking a deep breath as female voices emanated from the hall, he straightened his tie and donned a huge grin.

'Gina!' he greeted the petite bombshell as she erupted into the room. 'How insufferable it is to see you again! As I hadn't heard from you for a while, I'd hoped you'd met with a gruesome death! It really is horrible to see you again!'

'Likewise, I'm sure!' Gina spat, standing before Larry with her arms folded. 'I want to know where my daughter is!'

'Where did you leave her?'

'Don't play games with me! I want to know where you're keeping Christine!'

'Keeping her? I'm sorry, I don't understand.'

'She came here and . . . what have you done with her?'

'She came here? What, she had an orgasm, here, in my insulting room?'

'Don't be ridiculous! She came here to see you and . . .'

'When did this alleged visitation take place?'

'You know very well when! She came here dressed as a nun and . . .'

'There you are, then. She's obviously found God, and I wouldn't mind betting that you'll find her praying in the nearest cuntery . . . I mean, nunnery. I'll check Yellow Pages. What would it be under? Nunneries, I suppose.'

'Don't be so stupid!'

'It could be under nuns or mother superiors or Godfearing virgins or . . . I wonder whether it's listed under cunts?'

'OK, you win. I'll give you the photographs if you . . .'

'If I what, Gina? Give you a damned good seeing to, perhaps? How would you like me to spunk up your arse?'

'My God, you're crude!'

'Oh, thank you! Crudity is a speciality of mine. Would you like to hear some more?'

'No, I would not!'

'I'd love to fuck your arse and then suck my sperm out of your bumhole, Gina.'

'I'm not listening!'

'I'd love to shave your cunt and bring you off with a marrow. Do you reckon I could force a marrow up your cunt?'

'Larry, please tell me where my daughter is!'

'Oh, it's Larry now, is it? Well, I must say, Gina, you've changed your tune a bit! Are you yearning for my cock?'

'Of course I'm not, you stupid man!'

'Aren't you in love with me? I'd have thought you'd beg me to fuck you senseless.'

'Beg you to . . . this is serious! You can't abduct young girls!'

'Who said I had? Prove it, Gina – prove that I have your daughter locked away somewhere! Prove that I've tied her naked body down and fucked her tight cunt!'

'If you've . . .' Her words tailing off as Brigit entered the room, Gina turned to face her, her eyes transfixed on the handcuffs and rope.

As if resigning herself to her fate, she did nothing to resist

as Brigit lifted her arms and cuffed her wrists. Presuming that the woman was complying in the hope that she'd be taken to her daughter, Larry rubbed his chin, eyeing her slender body, her cuffed hands clasped as if to protect her vaginal orifice. *Like daughter – like mother?* Ordering Brigit to tie one end of the rope to the handcuffs, he moved to the door.

'OK, this way!' he grinned, leading the way down the hall to the bondage room. 'Right, Gina, I'm going to allow you to see your precious daughter. If you'd be so good as to follow me,' he invited, grabbing the end of the dangling rope and opening the door. 'There's Monica, all shaved and ready to be sold for perverted sex!' he chuckled, yanking on the rope and pointing to the trussed woman.

'My God!' Gina gasped. 'What have you done to her?'

'Nothing, as yet!' Larry laughed. 'Would you like me to shave your cunt, Gina? Do you remember when you were a schoolgirlie with a hairless cunt?'

'I have never met such a debased, perverted sexual deviant as you in all . . .'

'Haven't you? Well, you should go to church more often. Churches are full of sexually perverted priests. Monica's hairless cunt reminds me of a joke. A young girl visits Santa in his grotto and sits on his lap. "And what do you want for Christmas, little girlie?" Santa asks. "Hair between my legs", she replies. "Oh, I'm afraid I can't do that! Will a beard do?" he chuckles.'

'I don't find that funny!' Gina hissed.

'No, you wouldn't!' Larry returned, pressing the concealed button. 'Talking of little girlies, there, in my secret room, is Christine!'

Gazing in horror as the wall slid back, Gina slipped the

rope and ran across the room to her daughter. Following the distraught woman, his face beaming, Larry secured the end of the rope to a steel ring set in the low ceiling and turned to face his prisoners.

'Before you ask, Gina – yes, I have fucked her!' he laughed.

'Mother!' Christine sobbed. 'Please help me! Two men have used me, forced themselves upon me and . . .'

'Oh, Christine!' Larry mocked. 'How can you say that I forced myself upon you? You begged me to fuck you.'

'I did not!'

'And you pleaded with the tax man to . . . what were your words? Oh, yes, you begged him to *shove it right up my cunt and fill me with spunk.*'

'Mother, I . . .'

'It's all right, Christine, I know he's lying,' Gina consoled her trembling daughter. Turning to Larry, her lips twisting in anger, she scowled. 'OK, you win. I'll give you the photographs if you let us go free.'

'But I haven't fucked you yet, Gina! I've fucked your daughter's tight cunt, and now I'm going to fuck yours!'

'If you come anywhere near me, I'll . . .'

Releasing the knot from the steel ring and pulling on the rope, Larry raised Gina's arms high above her head, grinning as he eyed her firm breasts ballooning her tight blouse. Securing the rope, his penis stiffening at the prospect of screwing Gina Cology's tight vagina, he knelt before his fearful prisoner. Tying lengths of rope to her ankles as Christine lifted her head and looked on in horror, Larry forced Gina to stand with her feet wide apart and secured the ropes to steel rings set in the far walls.

'There, that should do it!' he leered, standing and unbuttoning the woman's blouse. 'Let's show your daughter what your tits look like, shall we?' Remaining silent as Larry opened her blouse and lifted her red lace bra clear of her firm breasts, Gina closed her eyes, her long blonde hair concealing her flushed face as he sucked each nipple in turn. Licking her darkening areolae, gently biting her milk teats, his penis twitched, desperate for the wet heat of the woman's sex-furnace.

'OK, now let's show Christine your cunt!' he chuckled, tugging his victim's skirt down to her knees. 'Oh, red panties – and they're silk! Yes, very alluring! Brigit, why don't you unveil her cunt? You're into cunts, aren't you?'

'Yes, I am!' Brigit trilled, dancing into the secret room and tweaking Gina's long milk teats. 'She's got nice tits, hasn't she?' she gushed, dropping to her knees and gazing longingly at the triangular patch of the woman's bulging panties.

'She certainly has! Christine, you can watch your mother writhe in orgasm as Brigit licks and sucks her clitoris. You'd like to watch her come, wouldn't you?'

'I'm not going to watch anything! You're a disgusting man! I hate you!'

'I'm sure you don't hate me. You loved me fucking you, spunking up your cunt, so how can you say that you hate me? OK, Brigit, let's see what Gina's cunt looks like.'

Kissing and licking Gina's inner thighs, Brigit tugged the woman's panties down to her knees, revealing her sparse blonde pubes, the deep dividing groove between her pouting sex cushions. Slipping a finger into her juicy love hole, she licked the gentle rise of her mound, the warm flesh above

her vaginal crack, breathing in the intoxicating aroma of female sex.

'There's nothing I like more than fanny licking!' she giggled, thrusting her fingers in and out of the woman's vagina. 'But before I do that, I want her nicely juiced up. I want her sex juices flowing, pouring out of her beautiful cunt.'

'You disgust me, Brigit!' Monica cried from the examination couch.

'There are times when I disgust myself!' Brigit giggled. 'Larry, I'd like to cane Gina's bum.'

'Be my guest!' he chuckled. 'You'd better cut through her finery first, it'll get in the way.'

'No! No, you can't . . .' Gina gasped.

'I can do what I like to you, Gina, you're my prisoner! Pass me the scissors please, Larry!' Brigit giggled, withdrawing her cunt-juiced fingers from the woman's trembling body.

Taking the scissors, the young sadist began cutting through Gina's skirt, carefully snipping her way up the middle of the tight garment. The material dropping to the floor, she looked up at the horrified woman and smiled. 'You've stained your panties,' she chided, looking down and cutting through the juiced red silk. 'Your panties are covered with cunt milk.' Her eyes almost popping out of her head, Gina looked down in disbelief as Brigit scissored through her last vestige of vulval protection and tossed the garment aside.

'And now for your tits,' Brigit murmured as she rose to her feet. The audience silent, watching the enforced disrobing, she snipped her way through Gina's blouse, cutting up the sleeves until the shredded material fell away from the

woman's quivering body. Cutting her bra in two, her body now naked, Gina was ready for the thrashing of her life.

'Pass me the cane please, Larry,' the young dominatrix ordered, standing behind her victim and focusing on her taut, rounded buttocks. Her voice low, husky, Brigit turned her prisoner's head and gazed into her wide eyes. 'Have you ever had the pleasure of a good caning, Gina? Have you ever been thrashed?'

The petrified woman said nothing, praying that Brigit was joking, that she wasn't going to administer the cane. Her face flushed, her bottom lip quivering, she watched Larry pass the girl the thin bamboo cane. 'You're . . . you're not really going to . . .' she stammered.

'I like caning women,' Brigit smiled. 'I have a thing about caning women's buttocks, it turns me on. I like to see their bums turn red, scarlet, the weals appearing across their smooth skin as I cane them. I caned a girl once and it turned me on so much that I came in my panties! I came, without even touching my clitty!'

'Please!' Christine cried, gazing at her terrified mother. 'Please, you can't cane her!'

'Why can't I?' Brigit sneered, kissing the nape of Gina's neck and running her fingers over her delectable buttocks.

'Doctor Lickman!' Monica shrieked. 'If you allow . . .'

'This has nothing to do with me!' Larry remonstrated, turning to face the appalled woman. 'This is a personal matter between Brigit and Gina.'

'Please!' Gina gasped as Brigit ran the cane over the unblemished skin of her tensed buttocks. 'Please, I'll do anything! Money, I'll give you money!'

'I don't want money!' her tormentor laughed. 'I want

to thrash your bum! I want to thrash your buttocks until they're scarlet and you scream for mercy!'

'Doctor Lickman, you must put a stop to this!' Christine screamed. 'It's sadistic, it's inhuman!'

'It is!' Brigit taunted her. 'And it's your turn next, Christine! And you, Monica, it's high time you had a damn good thrashing! I'm going to cane all three of you, and then drink the juices from your cunts!'

'Brigit, I'll give you anything you want if you . . .' Gina began, her fear soaring as the stark reality of the situation hit home.

'Anything I want? I'll tell you what I want, Gina – I want to thrash you and turn myself on so much that I come! Right, we've talked enough. Are you ready?'

'No! No, please!'

'Well, I am!'

Raising her arm, the thin bamboo swishing through the air, Brigit struck the older woman's trembling buttocks, the cane landing across her twitching orbs with a deafening crack. Screaming, her tethered body jolting with every lash of the cane, there was nothing Gina could do to halt the sadistic punishment. Her curvaceous buttocks burning as thin weals appeared across her taut skin, she hung her head, her eyes squeezed shut as the cane repeatedly seared her bottom-orbs.

'Hang on!' Larry bellowed. 'I have an idea!' Slipping his trousers down as Brigit halted the thrashing, he grabbed his erect penis and stood before Gina's naked body. 'I'll fuck you while Brigit canes you!' he chortled, easing his solid knob between the woman's swollen cunt lips. 'Every time the cane lashes you, your cunt will tighten and squeeze my cock.'

'When I get out of here . . .' Gina screamed as her cunt sheath yielded to accommodate Larry's solid weapon.

'God, you're almost as tight as your daughter!' Larry breathed, driving his cock deep into her hot vagina, his silky glans resting against the smooth hardness of her wet cervix. 'OK, Brigit, give the interfering bitch the thrashing she deserves!'

The cane repeatedly lashing Gina's shaking buttocks, Larry gasped as her cunt rhythmically gripped his motionless cock, sending electrifying ripples of pleasure through his body. Again and again the merciless tart thrashed Gina's crimson bottom-globes, the woman's screams reverberating around the secret room as Larry began his fucking motions. Grabbing her hips, he quickened his rhythm, fucking her tight cunt as the thrashing continued, taking himself ever closer to his desperately needed climax.

'Tell me when you're going to come!' Brigit cried, bringing the cane down again. 'Tell me when you're going to spunk up her cunt and I'll really give it to her!'

'Now!' Larry panted, biting on the woman's nipples as he drove his cock-head deep into her spasming cunt with a vengeance. 'Now, I'm . . . I'm going to come now!'

Thrashing Gina for all she was worth as Larry's jism jetted from his throbbing glans, Brigit reached her own climax, her vaginal juices flowing from her rubicund love hole and coursing down her inner thighs. Christine's deafening screams resounding through the building, Monica, too, yelled her protests as Larry grimaced and pumped his spunky cargo into his prisoner's abused body.

'Please! Please stop now!' Gina begged as sperm over-flowed from her hot pussy and ran down her thighs. 'Please, please stop!'

'God, I've never had such a good fuck!' Larry gasped, ramming his solid shaft deep into her jismed vaginal duct for the last time. Her inflamed cunny lips taut around the base of his cock, he bit harder on Gina's nipples as Brigit administered the last stinging lash and discarded the cane. Grinning, the sadistic girl grabbed Gina's hair, forcing her head back and gazing into her tearful eyes.

'Well, did you like that?' she purred, her clitoris yearning for a massaging finger, a caressing tongue.

'No! No, I didn't!' Gina sobbed as Larry slipped his penis out of her fiery cunt.

'You can watch me cane your daughter now. You'd like that, wouldn't you, Gina?' Brigit leered, licking the woman's nipple. 'You'd like to see your daughter caned and fucked at the same time, wouldn't you?'

'No, please don't touch Christine! Do what you like to me, but leave Christine alone!'

'But I want to cane her!' Brigit laughed as Larry released Christine's legs. 'I'm dying to cane her bum, and I reckon Larry's dying to spunk up her wet cunt!'

Managing to slip one hand out of her restraining rope, Monica released her other hand as Larry brought Christine's knees up to her chest. Untying her feet, she slipped deftly off the couch and left the room unnoticed as Larry bound Christine's legs to her body. Her labia swollen, ballooning between her thighs, her sex crack gaping, the girl's buttocks were fully exposed, ripe for the caning.

'Right!' Larry laughed. 'I'll straddle her and slip my cock up her cunt, and you'll be able to cane her bum.'

'No, it won't work, Larry,' Brigit sighed, watching him stand behind the girl's buttocks and drive his cock deep into her tight vaginal orifice. 'You're in the way, I can't cane her like that.'

'OK, you fuck her bum with a candle while I fuck her cunt,' her boss suggested in his deepening wickedness. 'You can thrash her after I've spermed up her cunt.'

Turning towards the shelf, Brigit gasped with horror to find Monica missing. 'Larry, she's gone!' she cried. 'She's escaped!'

'Oh, shit! Well, there's nothing we can do about it now. Get the candle and we'll both fuck Christine. We'll do something about Monica later.'

'What if she's gone to the police?'

'Of course she's gone to the police!' Gina hissed, her eyes transfixed on her daughter's cunt lips stretched around the base of Larry's broad cock.

'Shut up, Gina!' Brigit spat.

'No, I don't think she'll go to the police,' Larry observed, withdrawing his cock and driving into Christine's tightening vagina. 'I mean, what would she say, Brigit? Would she tell them that you shaved her cunt? Or that there's an orgy going on?'

'I hope you're right, Larry!' Brigit sighed.

'So do I! Come on, let's give Christine a good seeing to.'

Taking the candle and kneeling behind Larry, Brigit eased the waxen shaft deep into the whimpering girl's bottom sheath, grinning as she watched the delicate brown tissue stretch open. 'God, that's tightened her cunt!' Larry gasped,

withdrawing his solid penis and thrusting deep into her wet love sheath. 'OK, fuck her arse with the candle!'

'I'll see that you're both arrested for this!' Gina cried, watching the candle thrust in and out of her daughter's bottom, Larry's penis driving into her abused cunt. 'I'll make sure that you're both put inside!'

'Shut up, Gina, please!' Brigit snapped. 'If you say another word it'll be you it's put inside!'

His heavy balls swinging, Larry thrust his rock-hard penis in and out of Christine's trembling body. Finding his rhythm with the pistoning candle, taking the panting girl to her enforced climax as her mother looked on in horror, Larry began to gasp. His wet shaft emerging and driving into the girl's tightening pussy sheath, he finally achieved his orgasm, his sperm jetting from his pulsating glans, filling the girl's contracting cunt as her own climax gripped her perspiring body.

Thrusting the candle faster, deeper into her tight arsehole, Brigit managed to reach Christine's throbbing clitoris with her free hand and massage the swollen protrusion, sustaining the girl's multiple orgasm as her cries of sexual satisfaction echoed around the room. On and on Larry and Brigit thrust into their whimpering prisoner's love holes, taking her ever higher to her sexual heaven, plunging her ever deeper into the bottomless pool of depravity.

'Stop it!' Gina cried, only too aware of her daughter's immense sexual pleasure. 'Stop defiling her, you're turning her into a . . .'

'Into a normal girl!' Brigit broke in. 'A normal girl who likes having both her holes fucked at the same time!'

'God, it's heaven!' Christine cried, her naked body

211

trembling as her orgasm peaked again, sending electrifying sensations of debased sex through her quivering flesh. 'Don't stop! Fuck me harder! Oh, oh! Don't stop!'

Larry's balls finally drained, he slipped his wet penis from Christine's steaming receptacle and staggered across the floor to her mother. 'Your daughter's a good fuck!' he breathed, spunk dribbling from his flaccid cock as he tweaked Gina's nipples. 'She's a bloody good fuck!'

'You disgust me, you filthy pervert!' Gina spat as he wiped his cock on her lower stomach, smearing sperm and girl-juice over her smooth skin.

'And *you* disgust *me*, trying to have my practice closed down! Sending that woman here to trick me into taking photographs, threatening me, getting Monica to spy on me, talking that girl, Jane, into testifying . . . yes, Gina Cology, I can safely say that you disgust me!'

'You're evil! You should be closed down and sent to prison for . . .'

'I'm not interested in what you think, Gina,' Larry smiled, walking to the shelf and returning with the depilating cream. 'You see this? This is hair-removing cream, and I'm going to smear it all over your cunt!'

'If you dare to . . .'

'Protest as much as you like, you're going to have a hairless cunt, Gina!' Larry laughed, dropping to his knees and squirting the white cream over her blonde pubic bush.

'I'll go to the police, to my solicitor, to . . .'

'I'll remove Christine's cuntal hair in a minute. Mother and daughter, both with schoolgirlie lookalike cunts – wonderful! I'll fuck you both again when you're hairless.'

Covering the last vestiges of hair with the cream as Brigit

slipped the candle out of Christine's anal duct, Larry jumped to his feet at the sound of the reception bell. 'Shit, who the hell's that?' he breathed. 'Brigit, I'll leave you to sort things out here. Close the wall and clear up the bondage room, and then join me in reception,' he ordered the girl, zipping his trousers and dashing through the door.

'Ah, Mother Barren-Womb!' Larry greeted the old penguin as he breezed into reception. 'And you must be Sister Mary?' he smiled, turning to face a fresh-faced young nun. *The real Sister Mary!*

'Pleased to meet you, Doctor Lickman,' Sister Mary replied coyly, holding her hand out.

'I wasn't going to make an appointment as I'd changed my mind,' Mother Barren-Womb began. 'I didn't think it wise for the sister to come here, but her dizzy spells seem to be getting worse. Are you able to see her now, doctor?'

'Of course. Er . . . if you'd like to go into the waiting room, Reverend Mother, I'll take Sister Mary to my consulting room.'

'I'd rather stay with Sister Mary, if it's all the same to you.'

'Ah, Brigit!' Larry grinned as she approached. 'Would you show Mother Barren-Womb to the labour room . . . I mean, the waiting room, please?'

'I'll stay with Sister Mary!' the obstinate Mother Superior repeated.

'No, that's not possible, I'm afraid. A doctor and his patient require confidentiality, you see. It's only ethical that I see Sister Mary alone.'

'But I . . .'

'I'm obliged to follow BMA rules, you see. If I break the rules, well, I could be struck off.'

'Oh, well . . . if you insist.'

'Yes, I do. Even in my position as proprietor of this establishment, I have no choice in the matter. Right, this way, Sister,' Larry smiled, walking down the hall with the behabited nun in tow.

Leading the trusting daughter of God into the bondage room, Larry bade her lie on the examination couch. 'First of all, I'll need to give you a thorough check-over,' he explained.

'But . . . Doctor, I can't allow you to . . .'

'Sister Mary, how can I help you if you won't let me examine you?'

'What do you want to do?' the young nun asked, climbing onto the couch and lying down.

'I need to check your heart. If you pull your habit up so that I can . . .'

'Pull my habit up?'

'How else can I check your heart?'

'Well, I suppose it's all right.'

Her pale face half smiling, her blue eyes sparkling above her white wimple, the girl was extremely attractive, Larry observed as she raised her buttocks and tugged her habit up over her stomach, revealing her grey woollen knickers. Pulling the garment higher to expose her antiseptic white bra, she gazed at Larry in anticipation. Petite rounded breasts billowing the small bra, her stomach was flat, smooth, her young thighs slim and shapely. Would she allow him to intimately examine her? Larry wondered, imagining slipping his fingers into her tight virginal canal.

'Now then, Sister, these dizzy spells . . . tell me, how often do they occur?'

'Not very often. About twice a week, I suppose.'

'I see. Er . . . would you be good enough to remove your bra?'

'Remove my bra?' she gasped surprisedly.

'Yes, it's in the way. To check your heart, I'll . . .'

'Doctor, I can't take my bra off!'

'Why ever not? I *am* a doctor! Goodness me, I *have* seen women's breasts before!'

'Well, I suppose . . .'

'Larry!' Brigit cried, dashing into the room as the nun was about to lift her bra clear of her firm rounded breasts. 'Larry, there's a man to see you. I think he's a policeman!'

'A policeman?'

'A detective – he looks like a detective!'

Pulling the curtain aside and opening the window, Larry turned to face his hysterical secretary. 'Tell him that I'm out,' he declared, climbing through the window as the exposed nun looked on in astonishment. 'I'll be in touch!'

'You'd better go, Sister Mary,' Brigit blustered, closing the window and pulling the curtain across. 'Come back tomorrow to see the doctor.'

'Yes, I will,' the confused – and almost abused – girl mumbled, pulling her habit down as she slipped off the couch. 'Is Doctor Lickman in trouble with the police?'

'No, no, it's just that they want him to attend the Police Ball and he doesn't want to go. As the habit said to the wimple, I'll hang around while you go on ahead!'

Chapter Seven

'I don't know where Larry is, Lily. He dived out of the window yesterday afternoon and I haven't heard from him since!' Brigit sighed as she leaned on the reception counter. 'It was my fault – a man called to see Larry and . . . I thought he was a detective, but it turned out that he was a bloody pharmaceutical salesman.'

'Oh, no! Poor Larry must be petrified!' Lily gasped, tossing her jacket over a chair. 'What do you think Monica will do?'

'As I said, she escaped and . . . oh, I don't know, Lily! The whole thing's such a bloody mess! Where did you disappear to yesterday?'

'I couldn't find Larry so I went home, I wasn't feeling too well. Thank God it's the weekend tomorrow, I've had enough of all this!'

'You and me both!'

'Are Gina and Christine still here?'

'Yes, I gave them some food last night, and they had sandwiches this morning. They both desperately need the loo but . . .'

'Did they sleep all right? I mean, tied up like that . . .'

'I made them as comfortable as I could. Christine slept on the cross and Gina slept on the floor.'

'What will you do with them?'

'I don't know. I've phoned Larry's house but he's not in. I suppose I'll have to let them go. Without Larry, I don't know what to do.'

'You'd better release them, Brigit. Well, it looks as if everything's come to an end.'

'Yes, there's no way Larry can continue now. The things we did to Monica, Gina and Christine were . . . well . . .'

'I have an idea, Brigit. We'll let them go and we'll dismantle the sliding wall. Get rid of the cross and everything, and no one will believe that there was a secret room.'

'We can't do that! We'd never be able to dismantle the wall! I'll let the prisoners go and we'll just have to hope for the best. I wish Larry would ring, he'd know what to do.'

'I've got it! Leave the wall back, the secret room open, take the cross and things away, put a desk and chair in there and . . .'

'Yes, that's a good idea! OK, let's do it!'

Resting his elbows on his desk, Venereal frowned at Larry. 'Why tell me all this?' he asked suspiciously.

'Eventually, you'd have found out for yourself. I didn't want to waste your time, or mine, so I thought it best that I tell you. Well, you know everything now. Monica Moodie has been stealing money from me, telling you lies, making up fantastic stories . . . I didn't want to see her get into trouble. At heart, she's a good woman but . . . well, there it is.'

'And you say that she's been having sex with your clients?'

'I've caught her with several clients, yes. She . . . I

218

probably shouldn't tell you this but, well, she has severe sexual problems.'

'Really?'

'Yes, she's . . . she's shaved her pubic hair off.'

'Good God! What sort of woman is she?'

'She's very disturbed. She's suffering from post-adolescent regression syndrome.'

'What's that?'

'It's an inexplicable, desperate yearning to return to adolescence. Because she wants to revert to her early youth, she's shaved her pubic hair – the physical appearance of her vulval flesh giving credence to her fantasy about her pre-pubic years. She tells lies about me in an effort to deny the reality of her middle-age.'

'That doesn't make sense. How can telling lies about you bring about a self-denial of her real age?'

'The theory is that the lies block out the reality. Er . . . how can I put it? Lying to you about me in order to see me in ruination has the subconscious effect of a childlike satisfaction of having her own way.'

'Most interesting!'

'Yes, it is. Unfortunately, the syndrome is little understood.'

'But having sex with your female clients is . . .'

'That's all part and parcel of the syndrome. You see, by having lesbian relationships, she's again reinforcing her belief that she's returning to adolescence.'

'How? I don't understand.'

'Young girls play together, older women don't. Lesbianism allows her to play with other females, thus supporting her fantasies about youth. She's had lesbian relationships,

but she's not broken the law. The female clients I caught her with were only too willing to have sex with her. I didn't want this to come to light because I thought you might force me to dismiss her, and I didn't want to have to do that.'

'No, there's no need to sack her. You'll have to keep an eye on her, though.'

'No, I'm afraid it's got to the stage where I'll have to let her go. I didn't want it to come to this but . . . she's taken to masturbating every day. It's simply an additional prop for her fantasy. I wouldn't mind if she did it at home, but she masturbates in reception. Several clients have complained to me about it.'

'My God, that's incredible!'

'It's her husband I feel sorry for. He knew what she was doing and, in the end, he couldn't take the mental pressure, so he left her. He was under immense pressure, as you'll appreciate.'

'Yes, yes. Well, in view of all you've told me, I don't think there's any need for Mr Fullcrack to continue his investigations into your practice. I must admit, I did find the things Mrs Moodie told me hard to believe. She said that there were whipping sessions, bondage . . .'

'She certainly has a good imagination, Mr Venereal! It's all rather sad, really.'

'Apparently, Gina Cology's stories about you and your practice originated from Mrs Moodie.'

'Yes, I know. They'll probably continue to tell you all sorts of dreadful things about me, but you know the truth now. Well, I've taken up enough of your time, I'd better be going.'

'Thank you for coming to see me, Doctor Lickman. You've saved my staff and me a lot of time and trouble.'

'As I said, I thought it best to tell you. I knew that Monica had been in touch with you and . . .'

'Yes, you did the right thing.'

'I'd appreciate it if you'd say nothing to Monica about this. Should she contact you again, just humour her, make out that you'll look into things.'

'Yes, I will. Well, goodbye, Doctor Lickman.'

Pulling up in the car park, Larry wondered what to do with Gina and her daughter. At least Venereal and Fullcrack were off his back, for the time being! The tax man had been satisfied, thanks to Brigit, but he was still in a hell of a lot of trouble, he knew. Entering reception, wondering what hellish problems he'd have to face, he frowned to see Brigit and Lily standing side by side, giggling.

'How are things, Brigit?' he asked. 'Who was the man who called yesterday?'

'I'm sorry about that, Larry, I thought he was a detective. It turned out that he was a bloody salesman!'

'You were wise to be cautious. Good girl.'

'Anyway, come and see what we've done!' Skipping down the hall like a little girl, her red microskirt revealing the gentle curves of her taut buttocks, Brigit could scarcely contain her excitement.

'My God!' Larry gasped as he entered the bondage room and gazed at the desk and office furniture. 'But, where are . . .'

'We let them go,' Lily smiled, standing by his side, her blue eyes sparkling. 'We had to, Larry.'

221

'Yes, I suppose you did.'

'We also have these,' Lily grinned, taking several photographs from the shelf. 'We found them in Gina's handbag.'

'Well, girls, you've certainly done a bloody good job!' Larry beamed, looking through the pictures of the bogus Mrs Cravings, Larry's knob spunking over the woman's grinning face. 'But there's still a problem. If they tell the police about the false wall . . .'

'We took the button away,' Brigit announced triumphantly. 'We ripped the wiring out and took the button away so no one will know about the wall.'

'If anyone looked closely they'd realize that . . . oh well, all we can do is hope for the best, I suppose,' Larry sighed as the reception bell rang.

'I wonder who that is?' Brigit murmured, leaving the room with Larry in tow. 'Perhaps it's . . .'

Her words died as she gazed in horror at Gina, Christine and Monica in the company of a suited, middle-aged man. 'That's him!' Monica screeched, pointing at Larry. 'He's the one!'

'All right, Mrs Moodie, leave this to me,' the man said, stepping forward. 'Doctor Lickman, I'm DI Clarke – might I speak to you in private?'

'Er . . . yes, of course, come this way.'

Leading the detective into his consulting room, Larry closed the door and offered him a seat. Things had never been as bad as this! he reflected, wishing he'd not sexually abused the women. *Hindsight is about as much use as a paper condom!* he mused, watching the sleuth rubbing his chin.

'Three women have made serious allegations concerning you, Doctor Lickman,' he began as Larry sat opposite him.

'Allegedly, two of them were raped by you, sexually abused, and kept here overnight. The other one says that she was stripped, sexually abused, and . . .'

'Sexually . . . I don't understand!' Larry gasped, holding his hand to his head in astonishment. 'For goodness sake, I'm a qualified doctor!'

'Your profession has no bearing on the matter.'

'Well, it should!'

'Whether it should or shouldn't has no bearing either.'

'Why not?'

'Because I'm the detective and I say so. Now, the women say they were taken to a secret room and stripped and bound with rope. Where is your examination room?'

'I'll show you,' Larry replied, rising to his feet. 'This is incredible, it really is!'

'Life *is* incredible at times.'

'Life stinks at times!' Leading the sleuth into the bondage room, Larry smiled, his fingers crossed behind his back. 'This is it. There's the examination couch, minus rope, and the desk over there is where I . . .'

'The women told me that there's a false wall,' the detective interrupted, running his hand along the walls as he walked round the room.

'A false wall?' Larry echoed, his heart racing. 'I really can't think why they're saying these things! Rape, sexual abuse, a false wall . . . mind you, Gina Cology has been trying to have me closed down for a long time. Her practice is going under and she believes that if she can close mine down, she'll have more clients. I suppose there is some logic in her thinking. As for Monica, well, all I can think is that she's in league with Gina because I'm having to dismiss her.'

223

'Well, the walls are solid enough. You say that you're dismissing Mrs Moodie?'

'Yes, I broke the news to her several days ago. She's always arriving late, she takes time off, she's rude to the clients . . . her husband left her recently, which didn't help. I had no choice, I'm afraid.'

'The thing is, Doctor Lickman, I have three women alleging that you sexually abused them. I can understand that one might bear a grudge, but not three.'

'Well, Gina's obviously got her daughter to back her up to try to save her failing business and, as I've told you, Monica . . .'

'Yes, as you've told me. Would you mind coming here, please, ladies?' DI Clarke called, moving to the open door. 'We'll ask the women about the false wall. Right, Mrs Moodie, where is the false wall you mentioned?' he asked as the women filed into the room, followed by Brigit and Lily.

'It was across there,' Monica replied, pointing to the floor. 'There was a padded wooden cross over there, where the desk is, and . . .'

'He tied my daughter to the cross and sexually assaulted her!' Gina broke in. 'And that girl there, Miss Biways, used a candle . . .'

'Used a candle?' Brigit queried.

'She thrashed me with a cane!'

'Does your body bear the marks of the alleged thrashing, Mrs Cology?' the detective asked, raising his eyebrows in anticipation.

'Well, yes, but . . .'

'Would you show the members of the court the marks allegedly caused by thrashing your buttocks?'

'We're not in court!'

'Mrs Cology, your statement has no relevance to the matter in hand. Are you prepared to show the court the marks or not?'

'No, certainly not!'

'They removed our pubic hair!' Monica broke in.

'I cannot accept hearsay as evidence, Mrs Moodie. Please be good enough to show the court the pubic area of your body from where the hair was removed.'

'I can't do that! If you want evidence of the false wall, I'll show you. Look, the switch is here!' Monica shrilled excitedly, moving to the shelf. 'Oh, it's gone!'

Frowning, the bemused inspector rubbed his chin again, his eyes half closing. 'Someone's lying,' he murmured pensively. 'In my line of work, I meet liars daily. But who's lying in this unusual case?'

'You must find your work very interesting,' Larry smiled.

'Yes, yes, I do, Doctor Lickman. Now, if you'll all allow me to sum up. I cannot accept that hair was removed from the pubic regions of these women as I haven't seen the aforementioned pubic regions. As for the marks on Mrs Cology's buttocks, again, I have not seen the evidence and I therefore dismiss it forthwith. We have three women on the one hand, and you on the other, doctor. In my experience, it's the masses who lie, suggesting that you're telling the truth.'

'We're not lying!' Monica protested, shaking the detective's arm.

'Physical violence will get you nowhere, madam!'

'She has a history of physical violence, Inspector,' Larry grinned.

'Is that so?'

'I don't!' Monica shrieked.

'Please, Mrs Moodie, remove your hand from my person and be quiet! So, it's three against one.'

'Three against three!' Brigit corrected.

'Three against four,' Sister Mary rejoined as she wafted silently into the room, her hands clasped between the swell of her breasts.

'Er . . . who are you?' DI Clarke asked.

'I'm Sister Mary, one of Doctor Lickman's clients. I was here yesterday, in this very room, and it was exactly as it is now.'

'You weren't in this . . .' Monica began.

'The Reverend Mother Barren-Womb came here with me. She didn't actually come into this room, but she'll tell you that I'm a nun from The Sacred Bloodied Heart of Our Lady of the Damned Convent, and that I came here to see the doctor.'

'Really?' the sleuth murmured as Brigit dashed out of the room. 'Tell me, Sister, what are you doing here now? What is the nature of your presence in this room?'

'I suffer from dizzy spells and I've come back to see Doctor Lickman. He was called away on an emergency yesterday and he told me to return today.'

'Here's the appointments book,' Brigit grinned as she bounded into the room. 'There, you see, Sister Mary was here yesterday, and there's her appointment for today.'

'This is ridiculous!' Monica bellowed, gazing accusingly at the behabited nun. 'She's lying!'

'I don't believe that a Reverend Mother and a nun would lie, Mrs Moodie!' the detective snapped. 'I've had many dealings with nuns, nunneries and convents

in my time, and I have never known lying to be the Lord's way.'

'Check the wall properly!' Monica cried in desperation. 'Look, you can see the end of the false wall sticking out over there. It slides out, across the room.'

'That's always been like that, Monica!' Larry returned, gazing at the wooden end of the wall. 'It's been there since I bought this place!'

Frowning as he moved to the wall, DI Clarke ran his fingers over the wooden plank. 'This is rather unusual,' he murmured. 'This piece of wood might well be used as evidence against you, doctor.'

'A piece of wood used as . . .'

'As I've said, I was here yesterday, and the room was exactly as it is now,' Sister Mary reiterated, her smiling, angelic face haloed by its frame of white linen.

'Did you see these women when you were here?' the detective asked. 'Did you have communication with any of these women?'

'No, they weren't here. I've never seen them before.'

'She's lying!' Monica screeched. 'I'll bet she's not a nun at all!'

'That will be easy enough to check, Mrs Moodie. I shall consult Rasputin's Directory of Registered Nuns the minute I return to my office. Shall I tell you what I deduce, Doctor Lickman?'

'Who did you juice?'

'What?'

'You said that you'd juiced someone.'

'No, I said *deduced*.'

'You de-juiced someone?'

'My conclusion, Doctor Lickman, that's what I meant!'

'Oh, I see. So, what is your conclusion?'

'I conclude that my time has been wasted, as has yours. But allegations such as these have to be looked into, as you'll appreciate.'

'Yes, of course,' Larry grinned triumphantly.

'As for you three, think yourselves lucky that I'm not going to arrest you for wasting police time!' he growled, glaring at the stunned women. 'You have committed a grave offence punishable by one hundred years' hard labour in a Siberian detention centre. Think yourselves lucky that I'm willing to turn a blind eye to your treachery!'

Beaming as the protesting women followed the detective down the hall and out of the building, Larry turned to Sister Mary. 'I don't understand,' he said. 'What are you doing here, and why did you . . .'

'Brigit rang the convent earlier and asked me to come here. I've been in the waiting room for some time. She explained that there were some women trying to cause you problems, and that I might be needed to help you.'

'I told Sister Mary that Gina and Monica were trying to put you out of business, Larry,' Brigit rejoined. 'I knew that trouble was imminent, so I rang Sister Mary and asked her to help.'

'But you lied!' Larry gasped, frowning at the nun. 'You knew there was a false wall, this room was half this size when you were here.'

'Yes, I did lie. I . . .'

'Damn, now who's ringing the bloody bell!' Larry cursed, dashing from the room. 'Excuse me for a moment.'

*　　*　　*

The man standing in reception didn't look at all friendly, Larry surmised as he approached him. Tall, moustached, with swept-back brown hair, a red face and an angry, twisted mouth, he appeared anything but friendly!

'I'm Doctor Lickman, may I help you?' Larry ventured, forcing a smile.

'Ah, so you're Lickman, are you?'

'Am I?'

'What? You just introduced yourself as Lickman, so you must be.'

'Why ask if I'm Doctor Lickman when I've just told you that I am? I don't understand your line of . . .'

' Because . . . what the hell are you going on about?'

'I have no idea! May I ask who you are? If it's not too difficult a question, that is.'

'My name's Faggot. I'm the father of Jenny, the schoolgirl you sexually abused.'

'Good grief! *Me*, sexually abuse a schoolgirl?' Larry gasped surprisedly.

'Yes, I had it out with my daughter and . . .'

'You had it out in front of your daughter? What sort of father are you?'

'I had it out *with* her!'

'My God! I hope you didn't force her to touch it! Incest is illegal!'

'Listen to me, Lickman! My daughter came here to see you, and you defiled her, you took her virginity!'

'Took her virginity where?'

'In your examination room.'

'Well, perhaps it's still there. Shall we go and have a look?'

'Still there? Are you mentally deranged?'

'I certainly hope not!'

'You deflowered my daughter!'

'I stripped her of flowers? She wasn't carrying any flowers!'

'You fucked her!'

'My God, what sort of language is that to come from the father of a teenaged convent schoolgirl?'

'You'll hear worse than that in a minute!'

'I hope not! I can hardly believe it! You expose yourself to your daughter and force her to touch your penis, you accuse professional men of defiling convent schoolgirls, you use expletives, you . . .'

'Don't mess with me, Lickman!'

'Mess with you? Are you homosexual as well as incestuous?'

'I'll punch your lights out in a minute!'

'And you're violent with it! You need help, Mr Faggot!'

'And you'll need help in a minute – hospital help!'

'My God, I feel for your wife.'

'You feel my wife and I'll . . . what have you to say for yourself?'

'I'm sorry, but your daughter is lying – I am completely innocent of the charge, Mr Maggot!'

'My name's Faggot! She told me that you . . .'

'Listen to me for a minute, Mr Faggot. Teenage girls often have crushes on men in positions of authority – professional men such as teachers, solicitors, doctors, dentists or whoever. I spoke to your daughter here, in my consulting room. The door was left open, there were people milling about, and . . .'

'She told me that you took her to an examination room. How would she know about the room if she hadn't been in there? Answer me that, Lickman!'

'She came here looking for me and wandered into the examination room by mistake. Brigit, my secretary, discovered her in the room and showed her the way to my consulting room. That's how she knows about the examination room.'

'She told me that you had sexual intercourse with her.'

'Good grief! I have never had *any* sexual contact with my secretary, Mr Faggot, let alone full-blown sexual intercourse!'

'With my daughter, you fool!'

'My secretary had sexual intercourse with your daughter? I'll see to it that she's dismissed instantly! Wait a minute, how can two females . . .'

'*You* had intercourse with my daughter, Lickman!'

'Only social intercourse, Mr Maggot.'

'Faggot! I'm having her checked, her hymen, so . . .'

'Mr Faggot, I shouldn't tell you this, it's unethical, against BMA rules, but . . . your daughter told me that she's been having sexual intercourse on a regular basis for over a year now.'

'Rubbish! Of course she hasn't, she's a decent girl. At least, she was until she came here! And another thing, Jenny *never* lies.'

'She never lies?'

'Never!'

'I find that very interesting because she told me that you dress in her mother's clothes. That's true, then?'

'I . . . she didn't say that!'

'She said that when your wife is out, you dress in her clothes, Mr Baggot. Red silk panties, suspender belt, fishnet stockings, six-inch red stilettos . . .'

'No, no, I . . .'

'If Jenny never lies, then you're a cross-dresser, a trans-vestite, a sad . . .'

'She . . . she must have been making it up.'

'But she never lies, Mr Maggot.'

'She must have been mistaken.'

'If your daughter told you that I'd had sexual inter-course with her, then she must have been mistaken about that, too.'

'Yes, yes, she must have been.'

'If I were you, Mr Bollock, I'd leave it at that. Say nothing to Jenny, just let sleeping pussies lie. Of course, if you wish to persist with the matter, then I suggest you bring your wife and Jenny to see me and we'll have everything out in the open. We'll discuss intercourse, cross-dressing, transvestism, women's silk panties and . . .'

'Er . . . no, no that won't be necessary. Well, I'm sorry for . . . goodbye, Doctor Lickman.'

'Goodbye, Mr Maggot.'

Breathing a sigh of relief as the embarrassed man left the building, Larry turned his dirty thoughts to the young nun, wondering why she'd lied to save him. *Right, that's Faggot dealt with!* he mused, walking down the hall to the bondage room. *If only these bloody people would get off my back and let me lead a peaceful life of perverted sex!*

'Ah, Sister Mary!' he smiled as he entered the room. 'Tell me, why did you lie to save me from . . .'

'I've been talking to a couple of the sixth-formers about their visits here,' she smiled sweetly. 'There's one in particular, Jenny, who told me that you'd examined her.'

'Yes, I've just had the girl's father . . . I examined her?'

'Yes, she went into great detail, Doctor Lickman. It was most interesting, most revealing!'

'She told you that I . . .'

'Yes, she did. She told me everything, all the sordid details.'

'Er . . . yes, if my memory serves me incorrectly, I did examine her.'

'She rather enjoyed the experience.'

'Oh, I see,' Larry smirked as Brigit and Lily slipped out of the room and closed the door. 'So, what do you intend to do?'

'I thought you might care to examine me. From what Jenny told me, you're pretty good at examining young women – intimately.'

'But you're a nun!'

'Yes, and I'm also a very lonely girl who's disillusioned with the church. I'm twenty-two, and I've had no sexual experience whatsoever! There was a priest who suggested that I was in need of a massage but he was arrested for gross indecency before the massage occurred. After listening to Jenny's exciting and extremely arousing story, well . . .'

'If it's an examination you're after, I'm sure I can help you!' Larry smiled, his penis twitching at the prospect of penetrating yet another juicy – sacrosanct – pussy.

Locking the door as the nun eagerly pulled her habit over her head and stood before him in her bra and knickers, Larry sensed his penis fully stiffen within his tight trousers.

Incredible! he reflected, surveying the girl's long black hair as she shook her head and allowed her locks to cascade over her shoulders. Not only had she saved him from the police cells and a possible prison sentence, but she was offering him her fresh young body!

'Well?' Sister Mary smiled seductively as she climbed onto the examination couch, deserting her vows. 'Aren't you going to examine me, doctor?'

'Er . . . yes, yes of course! Er . . . I have to ask you this, Mary – do you masturbate?'

'No, I've never masturbated, but I'm more than willing to learn.'

'And I'm more than willing to teach you!'

Tugging the girl's knickers down her long legs as she lifted her buttocks clear of the couch, Larry gazed at her ebony pussy hair, her virginal sex crack. *Here we go again!* he thought happily as he pulled the strangely arousing woollen garment over her feet and parted her legs. *Sex, sex and more sex!* Lifting her bra away from her petite breasts, he grinned. The girl's mammary spheres were small, but extremely firm and well-rounded in youth. Her areolae were dark, with prominent wedge-shaped nipples rising invitingly from her chocolate-brown discs. *Eminently suckable!* Larry adjudicated, squeezing the girl's breasts.

'Have you ever seen a man's penis?' he asked, running a finger up and down her warm, moist sex valley.

'No, never!' the girl gasped, closing her eyes as the new-found sensations of sex rolled through her trembling body.

'Sperm, you've never seen sperm?'

'No, no, I haven't.'

'Then you've obviously never tasted sperm?'

'No, but I'd like to,' she smiled, opening her eyes and focusing on Larry's bulbous glans as he hauled his penis and balls out of his trousers and yanked his foreskin back.

'I'll begin the lesson by introducing you to the fine art of oral sex. I want you to open your mouth and suck my penis, Mary.'

'All right, but you won't stop rubbing me down there, will you?' she asked, gazing in awe at his veined shaft, his large balls.

'I'll rub you after you've swallowed my sperm. Drink my sperm, and then I'll rub you and bring you your first-ever orgasm.'

'It's a funny shape, the top bit, isn't it?' the young nun smiled, her eyes transfixed on his purple helmet.

'That's my knob, the sensitive part that I want you to lick and suck. The small slit is where my sperm will come from.'

'It's very hard!' she exclaimed, squeezing his shaft in her small hand.

'Yes, it is. OK, open wide, I want you to enjoy sucking and licking my knob until I come. I'll come in your mouth, Mary, give you your first taste of sperm.'

Taking Larry's glans into her hot mouth, the unvirginal Mary closed her eyes and moaned through her nose, savouring his salty plum. Pushing his solid penis further into her eager orifice, Larry gasped as the incredible sensations permeated his trembling body. His heavy balls rolling, he slowly rocked his hips, his penis sliding in and out of her mouth, fucking her there.

'You're doing well!' he breathed as she swept her tongue

235

over the silky surface of his throbbing glans. 'Oh, Mary, you're quite contrary! Carry on doing that and you'll soon have my sperm baptizing your tonsils!'

Licking his shaft, his ballooning knob, Sister Mary smiled. 'You taste nice, sexy!' she giggled, engulfing his plum in her wet mouth again.

'I'll taste even better in a minute. In fact . . . I'm coming! God, I'm coming already!'

Fucking her mouth, his knob gliding back and forth over her tongue, pulsating in orgasm, Larry pumped out his sperm. Mouthing and sucking, the girl shuddered, her taste buds alive, for the first time savouring the salty cock-milk jetting from his swollen glans. Swallowing hard as her cheeks filled, she kneaded his draining balls, exploring his twitching shaft with her inquisitive fingers as his orgasm rolled on. Shuddering in ecstasy, Larry watched his spunk overflow from the daughter of God's mouth and run down her cheek as she desperately tried to swallow his jetting communion.

His seminal flow finally ceasing, Mary ran her tongue round his knob, lapping up the remnants of his come, sucking hard to extract more of the aphrodisiacal milk from his sacred cock. She was desperate for more spunk! he mused, focusing on her tautly stretched lips as she took his glans to the back of her throat. Wanking his shaft, kneading his balls, she moaned through her nose and closed her eyes, naively expecting another explosion of spunk to spurt from his fountainhead.

'There's no more!' Larry gasped as she slipped his purple plum from her mouth and gazed disappointedly at his small slit.

'Mmm, that was nice,' she smiled, licking up and down

his glistening shaft. 'This is far better than spending half my life praying!'

'I'm sure it is!' Larry laughed, watching her pink tongue sweep over his silky glans. 'God, you're stiffening me again!'

'Will you give me more sperm if I keep licking you?' she asked excitedly.

'Keep licking and sucking and we'll see what happens,' he smiled, massaging her solid clitoris as she lay with her long legs open wide, her pinken vaginal crack gaping.

'I want to watch it coming out,' she breathed. 'This time, I won't drink it, I want to see it spurting out.'

'OK, I'll tell you when it's coming and you can wank me. I'll spurt it all over your face.'

'No, do it over my breasts, over my nipples!'

'Why, do you want to lick your nipples and lap it up?'

'Yes, yes, I do!'

Sucking on his solid glans, Mary lost herself in her new-found sexual pleasure, her young body trembling as her clitoris throbbed, responding to Larry's rhythmical massaging. She hadn't come yet, he reflected, gazing at her swollen vaginal lips. She hadn't been fucked, either! But she seemed to be more interested in sucking and examining his cock, bringing out his spunk, than in having her vagina penetrated and filled with sperm. There was plenty of time for that! he concluded, returning his attention to his rock-hard organ as Sister Mary gobbled his glans to the back of her throat.

Running his finger down her vaginal crack, Larry paused at the wet entrance to her pussy sheath, wondering whether she'd ever slipped her finger into her cunt, explored the

drenched inner walls of her sex cavern. Slowly, gently, he eased his finger inside her fleshy duct, imagining his knob there, absorbing the wet heat of her virginal sex. Fervently mouthing on his pulsating glans as Larry slowly slipped his finger in and out of her young cunt, Mary was obviously delighting in the sensations, her naked body writhing, her stomach rising and falling.

'God, I'm about to come again!' Larry gasped, slipping a second finger into her wet cunt. 'Not yet, not yet!' he cried as his orgasm welled and his penis ballooned. 'Ah, ah! Yes, now!' Slipping his plum from her mouth, he spurted his come over the girl's petite breasts, her elongated nipples. 'Wank me!' he ordered his starry-eyed pupil, taking her hand. 'Yes, yes, that's it!'

Lifting her head and gazing in awe as the white liquid jetted from his pulsating knob, splattering her breasts, the girl moved her hand faster up and down his shaft, bringing out his orgasm with surprising expertise for a young novice.

'Larry!' Brigit whispered loudly outside the door. 'Larry, Mother Barren-Womb is here!'

'What does she want?'

'Er . . . I've forgotten. Oh, yes, she's looking for Sister Mary!'

'All right, all right!' Larry gasped as the last of his sperm landed on the unholy Mary's breasts. 'Give me two minutes!'

'What shall we do?' the young nun whispered, releasing his cock and propping herself up on her elbows. 'Please, she mustn't know that I'm here!'

'It's OK,' Larry soothed, concealing his spent member and zipping his trousers. 'I'll leave you to lap the sperm

up. You'll be safe enough in here, I'll lock the door behind me and get rid of her.'

Donning a huge grin as he left the room, Larry made his way down the hall to greet the convent superior. 'How are you, Reverend Mother?' he asked. 'It's so lurid to see you again.'

'It's so what to see me again?'

'Lovely, it's so lovely to see you again.'

'Likewise, I'm sure,' the stuffy woman returned stiffly. 'I've discovered that Sister Mary received a phone call asking her to come here.'

'To come here?'

'Yes, although I don't know why as she was here yesterday. The point is, she left the convent earlier, and she hasn't been seen since.'

'Most intriguing!'

'When did she arrive, and when did she leave your establishment?'

'I didn't see her myself, but I was told that she arrived a long time ago, and she left a long time ago,' Larry smiled, leading the old woman into his consulting room. 'Perhaps she went on to . . .'

'She shouldn't have left the convent at all. She knows that it's against the rules to leave without permission, especially unaccompanied.'

'I'm sure she's all right, Mother Fallow-Womb. By the time you return to the convent I'm positive she'll have safely returned with her pink folds . . . to the fold.'

'I have to tell you that I hold you personally responsible, Doctor Lickman.'

'*Me*? Why me?'

'This would never have happened had she not come here in the first place!'

'But *you* brought her here in the first place, Mother.'

'That's as maybe, but I still blame you.'

'Well, I really can't see why. I've been getting on admirably with the sixth-form girls and . . .'

'Yes, and that's another thing – Jenny Faggot's father has been to see me.'

Oh, Christ! 'When was this?'

'Last night. He said that you'd . . . well, that you'd interfered with his daughter's privates.'

'Ah, yes, there was a slight misunderstanding. He came to see me earlier and it's all been straightened out now.'

'A misunderstanding? Having one's daughter's privates interfered with can hardly be looked upon as a misunderstanding.'

'I'm sorry, I don't understand.'

'What don't you understand?'

'I don't understand what you mean about the misunderstanding, Mother Fallen-Womb.'

'What are you talking about?'

'The misunderstanding, I don't understand the misunderstanding.'

'Of course you don't! If you understood, then there'd be no misunderstanding, would there?'

'Er . . . no, no I suppose not, Mother Yard-Broom.'

'You won't be surprised to learn that someone else came to see me.'

'I wouldn't be at all surprised – you're obviously a very popular woman.'

'I mean, in connection with you, doctor!'

'Someone visited me in connection with you?'

'In connection with *you*!'

'That's what I said, Mother Narrow-Womb – in connection with you.'

'No, with *you*!'

'*Me*?'

'Good grief, man, you're impossible to communicate with! I had a visitation from Mrs Monica Moodie in connection with you.'

'There seem to be quite a few people who have connections with me. What was this particular connection in connection with?'

'You don't appear to have a very good command of the English language, Doctor Lickman. You don't understand misunderstandings, you talk of connections being in connection with . . .'

'Well, it's not easy, is it?'

'No, obviously not! Anyway, Mrs Moodie informed me that you've been fooling about with your female clients. She also said that . . .'

'Falling about? I hope she wasn't suggesting that I was drunk?'

'Fooling, not falling! She also informed me that you have a sex room . . .'

'A sex room?'

'Yes, her allegations were of a grave and highly serious nature. The poor woman almost swooned when she was relaying the sordid details to me.'

'I wouldn't take too much notice of Mrs Moodie, if I were you. Sadly, the poor woman's mental state leaves a lot to be desired.'

'Is she ill?'

'Terminally, as far as her brain is concerned! She had an undisturbed childhood which left her terribly disturbed.'

'I find that most disturbing.'

'So does she! It's a great shame that the Lord didn't come into her when she was young, as He did with you.'

'Encourage her to seek redemption for her sins, Doctor Lickman.'

'Oh, I have, Mother. Being a devout catholic myself, I've done all I can to help her follow the Lord's way. I find her lies very worrying. Also, she hears voices, telling her about sex rooms and . . .'

'You have a lot to cope with, by the sound of it.'

'Yes, but I do my best to struggle on.'

'It would appear that I owe you an apology again.'

'No, no, you don't. Well, Mother Board-Room, I wish you luck with your search for the missing sister. I only wish . . .'

'There's one more thing before I go, Doctor Lickman.'

'Oh, what's that?'

'One of the sixth-form girls who came to see you asked me to give you this,' the nun smiled, pulling a small package out of her habit. 'I believe it to be a small gift.'

'Oh, thank you so much, Mother! What a lovely thought! It's at times like this that I realize that following the Lord's way, as I have always tried to do, pays dividends in the end.'

'Indeed it does. Aren't you going to open it?'

'Er . . . no, not now. Well, it's been nice speaking to you again. As I said, I'm sure Sister Mary will have returned to the convent by the time you get back.'

'Yes, I hope so. You don't know who phoned and asked her to come here, do you?'

'No, I'm afraid I don't. According to my secretary, Sister Mary looked around reception and then left without so much as a word. Whether she was looking for me or not, I really have no idea.'

'She's been behaving in a most peculiar manner of late. I wonder who telephoned her, and why?'

'It was probably a mistake, a misunderstanding.'

'Please, don't start that again, doctor!'

'No, no I'm sorry. Well, one must get on.'

'Yes, one must. Goodbye, doctor.'

'Goodbye, Mother Superior.'

Ripping the package open as the Reverend Mother left the building, Larry grinned to discover a pair of wet, cunny-stained school knickers inside. Holding the garment to his face, he breathed in the aphrodisiacal scent of the unknown girl's teenage pussy juice. 'Mmm,' he murmured. 'Very nice!' Examining the crotch, he pictured the fleshy pussy lips the material had shrouded, the youthful vaginal crack that had decanted its maiden cream.

Wondering where Lily and Brigit had got to as he stuffed the knickers into his pocket, he made for the bondage room. *Better send Mary back to the convent*, he decided, opening the door to discover Lily and Brigit naked, attending the nude nun.

'Oh, so this is what you get up to when my back's turned,

is it?' he murmured, focusing on Lily's pink tongue sweeping up Mary's yawning pussy fissure.

'You left the poor girl crying out for an orgasm!' Brigit scolded him, running her wet tongue round Mary's succulent, erect nipples. 'We had to help her.'

'Yes, so I see!' Larry laughed, eyeing Brigit's hairless pussy lips bulging between her shapely thighs as she bent over further and sucked Mary's burgeoning brown bud into her hungry mouth. 'Mother Barren-Womb has just left, she . . .'

'Mother Barren-Womb!' Mary gasped, her eyes wide with fear.

'Yes, she wants to know where you are.'

'Oh, no! What did you tell her?' the quivering girl asked, her clitoris stiffening beneath Lily's caressing tongue.

'I said that you'd left here a long time ago. I think you'd better get back to the convent as quickly as possible.'

'Oh, Larry, don't spoil our fun!' Brigit complained. 'Mary was hoping that you'd fuck her.'

'There's nothing I'd like more, but we don't want the Reverend Mother causing problems. Mary's already in trouble so . . .'

'Yes, you're right,' the young nun sighed as the girls lazily moved their naked bodies into upright positions, gazing hungrily at Mary's gentle curves, her rubicund vaginal valley. 'As much as I'd like to stay . . . I'll come back as soon as I can and you can teach me more about sex.'

'My problem with breasts is a little better,' Lily announced as Mary slipped off the couch and dressed. 'But I'm still not too happy about penises.'

'You're getting there,' Larry smiled encouragingly. 'It'll

take time, but you're getting there. Shit, there's the phone!' he cursed, dashing out of the room.

Flopping into his swivel chair, he picked up the receiver, wondering what on earth would go wrong next. 'Hallo, Doctor Lickman speaking.'

'Doctor Lickman, this is Monica.'

'Monica, how wonderful to hear from you, and so soon after our meeting with DI Clarke!'

'Gina and I are going to put an end to you!' she bellowed. 'You have the photographs back, but there are copies. I have enough evidence to . . .'

'Oh, Monica! I thought I'd heard the last of this nonsense. Listen, why don't you come back to work and . . .'

'Come back to work? After the things you've put me through, I'd never come back!'

'Oh, by the way, your husband came to see me.'

'My . . . what did he want?'

'DI Clarke is a very wise man – he suggested that I certify you insane. The psychiatrist has just left after a meeting with your husband and me.'

'You're the one who should be certified!'

'Well, the ball's rolling – pardon the expression! You'll be picked up and taken to Loony Lane Mansion.'

'Don't be ridiculous! You can't have someone certified without . . .'

'I *have* had someone certified – and that someone is *you*! There's nothing you can do about it, Monica. Whatever you say now will be taken as the ranting and raving of a complete nutter. And if you start going on about sex rooms, whipping, bondage and rape, they'll lock you up and throw the key away!'

Meeting a wall of silence, Larry frowned. 'Monica? Monica, are you still there? Stupid bitch!' Banging the phone down, he laughed. 'Actually, it's not such a bad idea!'

'What is?' Brigit asked as she breezed into the room.

'Having Monica certified insane.'

'Could you do that?'

'No, I suppose not. Well, if I were to have a psychiatrist and a GP ... no, the idea's ludicrous. So, has Sister Mary gone?'

'Yes, and you have a client waiting in reception.'

'Oh, shit! Who is it?'

'Miss Slit, she's a new client.'

'Oh, God! OK, send her in.'

Speculating whether the woman could be a spy sent by Monica or Gina, Larry opened the desk drawer and took a swig from the whisky bottle. There was no telling who the clients were these days, or who had sent them, he reflected wryly, replacing the bottle in the drawer as Brigit showed the client into the room. This one could very easily be a spy!

'Ah, Miss Slit!' Larry greeted the leggy blonde. 'I'm Doctor Lickman, I'm pleased to meet you.'

'Hallo, doctor,' the attractive young woman replied, her full red lips smiling, her delicate blouse billowing, straining to contain her ample breasts.

'Please, sit down,' Larry invited her, moving behind the desk and reclining in his swivel chair. 'So, what's the problem?' he asked as Brigit left the room and closed the door.

'My problem is rather unusual,' the woman said softly. 'I ... I don't really know where to begin. It's all rather embarrassing, you see.'

'Believe me, Miss Slit, I've come across hundreds of unusual problems in my time! Try not to allow your embarrassment to inhibit you. Relax and begin at the beginning. I've discovered over the years that it's usually the best place to start.'

'Well, I . . . I have a fetish about ladies' toilets. I can't keep away from them.'

'I see. When did you first become aware of this fixation for toilets?'

'When I was in my teens. I had a burning desire to hang around in women's public toilets. It's been going on for five years now, and it's getting worse.'

'How do you mean?'

'I spend most of my time in toilets, spying under cubicle doors trying to see the stains in girls' knickers, trying to look at their pussies.'

'You admire the female form, then? You have a fixation for female genitalia?'

'Yes, I just love girls' pussies!'

'Well, if you enjoy your fetish, then I wouldn't look upon it as problematic. Look upon it as a hobby and carry on as you are, enjoying what I'd call a perfectly healthy pursuit.'

'Yes, that's what I was doing until . . . the thing is, I've been arrested twice, once for gross indecency and once for lewd behaviour in a public place.'

'Oh, that does rather change things, Miss Slit. Er . . . before we continue with our fascinating discussion, have you heard of Gina Cology?'

'No, I haven't.'

'Monica Moodie or Christine Cology, do you know of them?'

'No, should I?'

'No, no. It's just that there are people out there trying to get me. They're planning my downfall because they're jealous of my highly successful and lucrative business.'

'How awful! Can't you go to the police?'

'They've already been involved, but the threats are continuing. Anyway, you're here to talk about your problems, not listen to mine. These arrests – were you taken to court?'

'Yes, but I escaped police custody.'

'How innovative! I admire that in a woman.'

'The irony of it was that I was in court, and I escaped through the window of the ladies' toilets.'

'Amazing! OK, so let's get back to your problem. The first time you entered a ladies' toilet, what was your reaction? How did it affect you?'

'It was exhilarating! I was about sixteen at the time. I'd plucked up the courage to go into the toilets on the railway station. I stood there in awe of the cubicles, the wash basins, the tiled walls, the women as they came and went.'

'Were you sexually aroused?'

'Yes, very! Ladies' toilets have an aroma all of their own, an air of female sexuality. The sound of knickers being pulled down emanating from the cubicles is highly arousing. The flushing of chains, the movement of silk panties against inner thighs, the ruffling of women's clothing . . . oh, how I just love public toilets! They're fascinating places!'

'Do you have an overwhelming urge to masturbate in the toilets?'

'Yes, yes, I do. I wait until it's quiet, and then I pull my knickers down and masturbate vigorously.'

'Have you ever been caught masturbating?'

'Yes, a young woman came in and . . . the whole thing was so exciting! I suggested that she masturbate me, but she declined. I offered to bring her off, but she ran away, screaming.'

'I see. How did you feel when she ran off screaming?'

'I had a massive orgasm! God, did I come!'

'How did you feel afterwards? What were your thoughts, your emotions, when you left the toilets?'

'I felt elated! My whole body was quivering, glowing, vibrant!'

'What would your response be if you were to discover a woman masturbating in the toilets?'

'I'd probably come in my knickers!'

'I must ask you this, Miss Slit – do you want to be free of this fetish, or would you be happy to continue if you knew that you were perfectly safe from prosecution?'

'I . . . I'd like to carry on. I've come to see you because I need reassurance, I suppose. I need a kind word, encouragement and . . .'

'There's nothing illegal about a woman entering public toilets. The trouble begins when you spy under the doors and masturbate in full view of the toiletees. I suggest that you speak with Lily, my trainee sex therapist. She has some unusual problems of her own concerning toilets, I'm sure a chat with her will help you no end.'

'Oh, yes, I'd like that very much!'

'I'll show you to the examination room and I'll send her along to see you.'

Showing the busty blonde to the examination room, Larry walked down the hall to reception. 'Ah, Lily,' he smiled. 'Would you go and talk to Miss Slit, please? She has a rather

unusual problem that I think you might be able to help her with. It will also be good training for you. Should you need any help, I'll be in my consulting room.'

'Where is she?' the girl asked.

'In the examination room. She's . . . she's a lesbian, from what I can gather.'

'Oh, good!' Lily beamed, skipping off down the hall.

'Everything OK?' Larry asked Brigit.

'Yes, but I'm fed up with reception. When Monica was here, it was . . .'

'I'll find a new receptionist, Brigit. You won't have to stand in for long,' Larry promised, walking down the hall.

Sitting at his desk, wondering what Monica was up to, Larry took the whisky bottle from the drawer. *Shame I no longer have a secret room*, he mused, recalling Christine's naked body bound to the sex cross as the phone rang.

'Doctor Lickman,' he intoned, pressing the receiver to his ear.

'Ah, Doctor Lickman – DI Clarke here.'

'Hallo, how are you?' Larry asked jovially, fearfully wondering what the detective wanted.

'I've received a complaint from Mother Barren-Womb concerning one of her young nuns, the one whom I met in your examination room.'

Oh, fuck! 'A complaint?'

'Yes, the Reverend Mother alleges that you sexually abused the nun.'

'Oh, no, not another one!'

'Yes, another one. As you can imagine, I'm rather disturbed by the numerous disturbing complaints alleging

your perverted sexual behaviour. I'll be calling to see you concerning the matter in due course.'

'Yes, yes, all right,' Larry sighed. 'I'm always here, so call any time.'

'Thank you, doctor, I will. Goodbye.'

Banging the receiver down, Larry wondered how Mother Barren-Womb had learned of Sister Mary's most intimate and unorthodox examination. *The girl wouldn't have told her!* he reflected. *Unless she's a spy*! Having saved him from DI Clarke, he couldn't believe that Sister Mary had shopped him. Unless it was an elaborate plan to . . .

'Argh!' Lily screamed, running down the hall. 'Argh, a one-eyed monster!'

'What on earth . . .' Larry gasped, dashing into the hall to see Miss Slit chasing Lily, a massive erect penis sticking out beneath her microskirt. 'Miss Slit, you sad transvestite! Come here, Miss Slit!'

'Sorry, can't stop, doc!' the pervert called, leaving the building in hot pursuit of Lily. 'To the toilets, Lily – to the toilets!'

'My God, whatever next?' Larry sighed, returning to his room – to his scotch. 'Thank God it's the bloody weekend tomorrow!' Swigging from the bottle, he ignored the ringing phone. *It'll only be another problem*, he concluded, gulping the liquor down. *Only another bloody problem!*

Chapter Eight

After enjoying a relaxing weekend, Larry sat at his desk and held his head, dreading another week of horrendous problems. 'Monday bloody morning!' he sighed. 'Another week of shit, no doubt!'

'You're right there, Larry!' Brigit grinned, popping her head round the door. 'DI Clarke is here to see you!'

'Fuck me, I can't . . .'

'Good morning, Doctor Lickman!' the detective inspector beamed as he entered the room carrying a large plastic bag.

'Oh, er . . . good morning. Please, sit down. Er . . . Brigit, two coffees, please.'

'Certainly, doctor.'

'So, how can I be of assistance?' Larry asked as the sleuth sat opposite, his face grinning as if he were about to fire a winning shot.

'After being informed of a missing person, a nun, to be precise, I visited Mother Barren-Womb of The Sacred Bloodied Heart of Our Lady of the Damned Convent.'

'Really? Was the nun found?'

'She wasn't missing, she was here, visiting you.'

'Oh . . . er . . . right, yes.'

'It was all rather coincidental, what with the nun making her timely entrance when I was here questioning you – and

the Reverend Mother reporting the girl missing, having no idea that she was here. There are strange things afoot, Doctor Lickman.'

'Are there?' Larry asked, looking beneath the desk at his feet. 'I can't see anything strange.'

'Not at *your* feet!'

'Whose feet, then?'

'It's an expression, a saying. There's skulduggery going on.'

'Good grief, is there?'

'Yes, cloak-and-dagger stuff. As I told you on Friday, the Reverend Mother Barren-Womb has made a serious allegation concerning you.'

'Yes, yes, yes! Look, don't you think this is all getting out of hand?'

'I do, doctor! As you know, I've received complaints of a most serious and disturbing nature from Mrs Cology, Christine Cology, Mrs Moodie – and now from the Reverend Mother. It's *completely* out of hand!'

'Look, Inspector, I'm a busy man so . . .'

'I, too, am a very busy man, doctor. The nun, Sister Mary, came here to see you in connection with her dizzy spells. Allegedly, she was examined . . .'

'Yes, I did have cause to examine her.'

'You admit to examining her?'

'Yes.'

'So far, so good. During the examination, did you interfere with her private parts?'

'It depends on what you mean by *interfere*.'

'Going above and beyond your duty, Doctor Lickman, that's what I mean by . . .'

'Above and beyond my duty?'

'It's one thing for a doctor to physically examine a young lady, and another when he oversteps the mark and the examination becomes sexually motivated, sexually orientated.'

'The nun in question was suffering from a rare vaginal complaint known as *virginitis*. The condition was easily cured, but it necessitated an examination of an internal nature. To put it in layman's terms, I had to push my fingers into her vaginal canal. If you call that interfering with her private parts then, yes, I am guilty as charged – guilty of carrying out my job in a professional manner.'

'I have here in this bag a habit belonging to the nun in question, Doctor Lickman. As you will notice, there's a white stain, just there.'

'Yes, I can see it,' Larry replied, gazing at the garment.

'The stain, as you can see, is near to the neck band, suggesting that whatever produced the substance was close to the nun's head when the smearing of the habit occurred.'

'Yes, a good deduction.'

'I've had the substance analysed.'

'Oh, shit!'

'No, it's not shit, doctor – it's sperm.'

'Sperm? Goodness me, how ever could sperm get onto a nun's habit?'

'That's what I'd like to know. Did the nun remove her habit for the examination?'

'Yes, she did.'

'Where the sperm came from, and why, is a matter I'll deal with later. What I want to know is, was the sperm deposited on the habit while the nun was wearing it, or while she was naked?'

'I fail to see what this has to do with me, Inspector.'

'Please, bear with me, doctor. Now, from my many years' experience, I deduce that the sperm was deposited on the nun's naked body, somewhere near to her head, and the garment was smeared with the liquid as she dressed.'

'Why have you come to that conclusion?'

'Sperm is ejaculated as a result of extreme sexual arousal, as you will know from your medical training. Extreme sexual arousal would not normally arise from handling a nun's habit.'

I wouldn't be too sure about that!

'However, it *would* arise from handling a young woman's naked body in a sexual manner. This suggests that the extreme sexual arousal caused the depositing of sperm on the nun's body, possibly in the region of her neck or face, and the garment was spermed later, as she dressed.'

'Yes, I can see your point, but I still fail to see what this has to do with me.'

'DNA tests, Doctor Lickman, will determine who the owner of the ejaculate was before it was ejaculated.'

'Let me get this clear. The nun, Sister Mary, has obviously taken part in some sort of sexual activity, right?'

'Right.'

'Is that against the law?'

'No, not as such. But . . .'

'Then what is the charge? I mean, if the nun consented to whatever sexual activity took place, there can be no charges brought against her or the man with whom she enjoyed the sexual activity.'

'That's true, but did she consent or not? That's the question.'

'Ask her.'

'I can't, she won't discuss the matter.'

'Then why pursue . . .'

'The Reverend Mother wants me to pursue the case. When one of her nuns, who'd been missing for several hours, returned to the convent wearing a sperm-stained habit, she became alarmed, naturally. Nuns take vows and, during her absence, Sister Mary had obviously broken her vows.'

'Yes, I agree, it does look that way. But I still fail to see what all this has to do with me. OK, a nun has broken her vows, very naughty, very bad – but it's not my problem. Ah, Brigit!' Larry smiled. 'Coffee, just what I need!'

'Will you be long, doctor? We have a busy day ahead, the first client will be here any time now,' Brigit smiled, placing the tray on the desk.

'No, I believe we've just about finished – isn't that right, Inspector?'

'Er . . . yes, yes that's right,' he replied as Brigit left the room. 'Doctor Lickman, I do realize that sexual activity between two consenting adults is legal, but it's the ethics that concern me.'

'Ethics?'

'Suppose a doctor was the nun's sexual partner – I wouldn't deem it ethical for a doctor to take advantage of a patient, especially a nun, would you?'

'No, I wouldn't,' Larry replied, sipping his coffee. 'But it's hardly a matter for the police!'

Taking his coffee from the tray, DI Clarke frowned. He was sure he had his man – but for what? The doctor was right. The law hadn't necessarily been broken, even if the nun's hymen had! Realizing his questioning was

getting him nowhere, the detective finished his coffee and smiled.

'Well, that will be all for now,' he said, rising to his feet. 'I might have cause to question you further, doctor.'

'In connection with what?'

'In connection with . . .'

'What, exactly, is it that you're pursuing, Inspector? What is the case?'

'The case of the defiled nun.'

'If she's been defiled, then it's her own doing, and no one else's concern or business.'

'Apart from the Reverend Mother's, doctor – apart from the Reverend Mother's! Oh, and one more thing. I might have to ask you for a sperm sample. Good day to you.'

Shaking his head as the detective inspector left the room, Larry sighed. 'Bloody man! Oh, Brigit, how are things in reception?' he asked as the girl drifted into the room.

'OK, I suppose. There's a letter for you, it's from the Inland Revenue,' she added, passing him a brown envelope.

'Ah, that'll be my tax demand for zero pounds and zero pence!' Larry beamed, ripping the envelope open. 'Fucking bastards! Fucking cunts!' he bellowed. 'Fifty-five fucking thousand pounds!'

'But I thought Ravenhugh was going to . . .'

'I'll chew his balls off, that's what I'll do! Fucking thieves, perverts, arseholes, pricks, wankers, cunts!'

'Calm down, Larry!'

'Calm down? Calm down? I'll bomb the fucking bastards, blow their fucking Gestapo HQ to fucking bits!'

'There must be some mistake.'

'Mistake? I'll ring that cunt Ravenhugh now and have it out with him!' Larry yelled, flattening the tax demand on the desk and dialling the tax man's direct number.

'Ravenhugh speaking,' the man finally replied.

'Ravenhugh, you dozy fart!'

'I beg your pardon?'

'Brigit sucked your knob off, you fucked the arse off Christine Cology, and then you send me a fucking tax demand for over fifty fucking grand!'

'Ah, Doctor Lickman, I presume. Take no notice of the assessment, it's purely for the record.'

'For the record? For the fucking record? How are you going to bring the bill down from that amount to nil?'

'Leave it with me, I have my ways.'

'You'd bloody well better have!' Larry stormed, banging the phone down. 'Fucking cunt-headed motherfucking bastard!'

'Oh, dear, wrong side of the bed?' Brigit giggled as she sat on the edge of the desk, the tight triangle of her silk panties clearly defining her pussy crack as she opened her legs.

'I'll kill the bastard! Why are you wearing panties?'

'I'm going to sell them – stained panties, thirty pounds a pair.'

'Very lucrative, I must say!'

'The trouble is, I can only produce one pair every three days. Oh, by the way, have you heard from Lily?'

'No, Christ knows where she's got to! That transvestite, the so-called Miss Slit, pulled her penis out – his penis – and terrified the life out of her.'

'She'll be back soon enough. Oh, I almost forgot, your

259

first clients are here – Mr and Mrs Sopping-Gusset. Shall I send them in?'

'Oh, Christ, they're all I need! Yes, yes, send them in, Brigit. And ring Lily, will you? She either works here or she doesn't, I can't have her coming and going as she pleases.'

Swigging from the scotch bottle, wondering whether to close the business down and put an end to the persistent problems, Larry sighed as an uncomfortable-looking middle-aged couple entered the room and stood before the desk. Mrs Sopping-Gusset, with succulent red lips and long blonde hair, was extremely attractive, Larry observed. Her husband, MP for Pissledown South, was well-heeled but something of a prude. The couple had seen him twice before, their relationship rapidly falling apart due to continual arguments over Mr Sopping-Gusset's long working hours. While Larry held out little hope of helping them repair their marriage, their visits paid him handsomely!

'So, how are things?' he asked as they seated themselves.

'As usual, I've been sitting at home all week while John's been working!' Mrs Sopping-Gusset complained.

'And, as usual, I've been working hard to maintain Bunty and her extravagant life style!' her husband rejoined. 'Doctor Lickman, what would your reaction be if you discovered that your wife had a vibrator?'

'Well, I'd be happy in the knowledge that she was enjoying the pleasures of masturbation rather than going to another man for . . .'

'That's what *I* told him!' Bunty broke in. 'What does he expect me to do? He's away in London all day and half the

night, playing about in the House of Commons, leaving me alone twiddling my thumbs.'

'It's not your thumbs you twiddle, is it?' John snapped.

'You're never there to make love to me, so what do you expect me to do, become celibate?'

'I don't expect you to masturbate! I'm an MP, Bunty, I can't have a wife who masturbates!'

'*You* masturbate, so why shouldn't I?'

'That's different, men are allowed to masturbate.'

'And who made that rule? Men, of course!'

'Well, it's the way of the world, Bunty. You masturbate, don't you, doctor?'

'Well, I . . . listen, Mr Sopping-Gusset, female masturbation is perfectly normal – healthy, in fact.'

'Only wanton hussies use vibrators! Streetwalking strumpets, prostitutes, trollops, harlots, hookers, sluts, whores, slag-bags . . . can you imagine the Prime Minister's wife vibrating her clitoris?'

'Well, no, but . . .'

'He'd never win the next election if news spread of his wife's disgusting behaviour with a vibrator! And if it came out that my wife masturbates with a vibrator, I'd lose my seat! What about the Queen? Do you think she masturbates with a vibrator? Oh, oh! One's clitoris is arriving! God for Harry, England and Saint George! Ah, one's arrived!'

'Oh, do shut up, John!' Bunty hissed. 'You don't know what you're talking about!'

'Well, I don't suppose the Queen . . .' Larry began.

'There you are, then!' John cried triumphantly. 'There'd be anarchy if news broke of the Queen's masturbatory habits.

What would the Sunday papers have to say about it? *Lisbet has Buzz in the Boudoir.*'

'Let's leave Her Majesty out of this, Mr Sopping-Gusset.'

'Why? The Queen has a clitoris, she's a woman, so why leave her out of the discussion?'

'Because she has nothing to do with the problems you and your wife are experiencing. Tell me, Bunty, how often do you masturbate?'

'Every day, sometimes twice.'

'Disgusting!' John exclaimed. 'Good grief, it's . . .'

'As you're hell-bent on exposing *my* private life, I think Doctor Lickman should know what *you* get up to!' Bunty interrupted her husband.

'I don't get up to anything!'

'No? What about pulling my dirty panties over your head and masturbating?'

'I have never . . .'

'I've often spied through the keyhole and seen you rummaging through the linen basket! You pull my dirty panties over your face and wank.'

'Bunty, how can you tell such blatant lies?'

'It's the truth!'

'OK, Bunty, let's talk about you and cucumbers.'

'Cucumbers?'

'Yes, I'm pretty good at spying through keyholes, too! What you did with that cucumber yesterday afternoon was obscene.'

'We had cucumber sandwiches for high tea. I used the cucumber to make sandwiches.'

'Yes, and I'll tell you why I didn't eat any – because the

cucumber was still steaming hot from your pussy! What Lord and Lady Sodomite-Brown must have thought, I have no idea!'

'Are you implying that I stick cucumbers up my . . .'

'I'm not implying, I'm stating a fact!'

'Please!' Larry sighed. 'Please, stop bickering! We'll get nowhere by arguing. Now, Mrs Sopping-Gusset, let's play truth or dare.'

'I haven't come here to play silly games!'

'It's not a silly game, it's good fun. Right, truth or dare?'

'Truth, I suppose.'

'OK, did you push a cucumber into your vagina yesterday afternoon?'

'Well, yes, I did.'

'Ha, ha! You see!' John cried jubilantly.

'Now it's your turn, Mr Sopping-Gusset. Have you ever pulled your wife's panties over your face and masturbated?'

'You didn't ask me whether I wanted to tell the truth or . . .'

'I decided for you. Now, tell the truth.'

'I can't tell the truth, I'm an MP – it goes against the grain.'

'Pretend that you're a Catholic priest. On second thoughts . . . Er . . . I've got it, you're a witness in the witness box. Now, have you ever pulled your wife's panties over your face and masturbated?'

'Yes, I have done that but . . .'

'I win!' Bunty trilled.

'There are no winners,' Larry declared. 'You're both as bad as each other.'

'Truth or dare, Doctor Lickman?' Bunty grinned.

'Er . . . truth.'

'Do you masturbate?'

'Well, I . . .'

'Come on, you must tell the truth!'

'Yes, I do.'

'There, you see, John – he masturbates, you masturbate, so why shouldn't I?'

'This is ridiculous! Women shouldn't masturbate with vibrators, it's not normal.'

'It's perfectly normal, Mr Sopping-Gusset,' Larry smiled. 'Look, why don't you masturbate each other? Instead of hiding behind locked doors, do it together, to each other.'

'Well, I'm game,' Bunty grinned.

'I'll give it a try,' her husband conceded. 'I'm not too sure about using a cucumber, though.'

'Oh, go on, John, give it a try! Use the vibrator on my clitty and thrust the cucumber in and out of my pussy.'

'OK, I'll try it. But you'll have to masturbate me, too – while I'm wearing your dirty panties over my face.'

'It's a deal! I'll wear the same pair of panties for a week, and then you can pull them over your face and sniff them while I bring you off.'

'OK, and I'll buy the biggest cucumber I can find!'

'Good, that's that settled, then!' Larry smiled. 'You see how it helps to talk problems over?'

'Yes, you're right, doctor,' Bunty beamed. 'I don't know what we'd do without you, I can't thank you enough.'

'Thank me by paying my fee promptly,' Larry suggested, rising to his feet. 'I'll see you both next Monday and you can tell me how you got on.'

* * *

Showing the happy couple out, Larry frowned at Brigit as she stood behind the reception counter making strange faces. Closing the door after Mr and Mrs Sopping-Gusset, he asked the girl what was wrong.

'Go and take a look in the bondage room!' she squealed hysterically.

'Why, what's in there?'

'It's not what, but who!'

'Who, then?' Larry asked irritably, walking down the hall with the girl running after him.

Entering the room, he held his hand to his mouth and gasped to discover Monica on the examination couch, her limbs spread, her hands and feet lashed with rope, her naked body vulnerable. Eyeing her swollen, hairless cunny lips, a huge candle emerging from her yawning sex groove, he quickly closed the door.

'What the hell . . .' he began. 'Brigit, what on earth have you . . .'

'I had nothing to do with it!'

'The police are on their way!' Monica chuckled, her huge tits wobbling. 'And when they discover me like this, you'll be arrested!'

'The police? Christ, get her out of here, Brigit! Quickly, untie her and I'll play for time when they arrive.'

Dashing to reception, his heart racing, Larry knew there'd be no way out of this one. A woman, naked, bound to the examination couch, her fanny shaved, with a massive candle . . . 'Jesus fucking Christ!' he breathed, wondering who was responsible for Monica's state. *Gina fucking Cology, more than likely!*

'Hi, Larry!' Lily trilled as she breezed into the building.

'Oh, you're back!'

'Yes, I'm sorry about . . . that woman, Miss Slit, was a man, Larry! He pulled his penis out and chased me down the street!'

'My God, what a sad pervert. Look, don't worry about that now, we've one hell of a problem, Lily!'

'Is it to do with DI Clarke? He's just pulled up outside.'

'Fuck me backwards!'

'What's he come back for?'

'Because Monica . . . there's no time to explain. I'll hide in my consulting room and you stall him, OK?'

'What is it he wants? What's the problem, Larry?'

'Just stall him!' Larry cried, dashing down the hall, praying that Brigit had released the woman. 'Stall him for as long as you can, and then show him into my consulting room!'

Swigging from the scotch bottle, Larry was sure that the end had come. The last thing he'd expected was this, he reflected. He realized that Monica and Gina weren't going to give up, but to resort to this? Brigit might be able to untie the woman, but she could hardly dress her and send her out of the building before the detective arrived. Monica, obviously, planned to remain naked and spurt out accusation after accusation. It was down to him to come up with a story – and a bloody good one!

'Ah, Doctor Lickman, we meet again,' DI Clarke grinned as he entered the room.

'Ah, thank God you're here at last!' Larry exclaimed.

'You were expecting me?'

'Yes, of course!'

'Was it you who called the station?'

'Yes, didn't they tell you?'

'No, I was only told that someone had phoned alleging . . .'

'I called and asked that you be sent here straight away. It's that Monica Moodie, she's in my examination room and . . .'

'Let's go and see what's happening,' the detective interrupted, leaving the room.

'My secretary discovered the woman in the examination room, naked! She's gone off her head, Inspector!'

'What's all this, then?' the DI asked in amazement, gazing at Monica's fleshy naked body as she struggled with the petite redhead.

'Please, she's trying to rape me!' Brigit screamed, her blouse ripped open, her skirt round her knees. 'She's gone mad!'

'All right, Mrs Moodie, that'll do!'

'They tried to sexually abuse me again!' Monica cried, pulling away from Brigit and clasping her hands over her bulging, shaved crack.

'I want to press charges!' Brigit bellowed. 'I found her in here, naked, and she tried to rip my clothes off! She said that she wanted to massage my pussy!'

'Get dressed, Mrs Moodie!' the detective ordered the distraught woman. 'I'm arresting you for attempted rape, gross indecency of a grossly indecent nature, causing an affray, and shaving off your pubic hair!'

'You can't do that!' Monica protested as she pushed Brigit away and pulled her clothes on.

'I can, and will, do what I like!'

'It's not an offence to shave my pubic hair off!'

'Ah, a confession! Doctor Lickman, you'll be a witness to the confession.'

'Yes, of course!' Larry beamed.

'I didn't confess!' Monica remonstrated.

'You said that it's not an offence to shave *my* pubic hair off. Being a detective, I look upon that as first-degree confession!'

'I'm sorry that Monica has caused you so much trouble,' Larry smiled.

'She won't be causing anyone any more trouble – not in Holloway!'

'Please, you must listen to me!' Monica cried as the detective grabbed her arm and marched her away. 'No, you must listen!'

Rubbing his hands together, Larry grinned at Lily as she danced into the room. 'Monica Moodie has been arrested!' he cried triumphantly.

'Yes, I heard!'

'What better way to begin the week?'

'There *is* no better way!' Brigit giggled, adjusting her clothing.

'Larry, there's some bad news, I'm afraid,' Lily said dolefully. 'I'm sorry to spoil your moment of victory but the Reverend Mother Barren-Womb is waiting for you in your consulting room.'

'Fucking hell! I can't take much more of this! What does she want, do you know?'

'Yes, she wants to see you about Sister Mary.'

'Again? Christ, I thought that had been settled!'

'And your next client, Miss Shafter, is in the waiting room.'

'Oh, that's good! She's the girl who believes that my spunking up her arse will help to enlarge her tits! Ignorant bitch that she is! Right, Lily, go and tell the Reverend Slagger that I'm out. Tell her to come back later, preferably next week! Brigit, show Miss Shafter in here, I'll be waiting for her.'

Rubbing his hands together as the girls left, Larry felt his penis stiffening at the thought of examining Miss Shafter's tight vaginal sheath, slipping his solid rod deep into her anal canal and filling her bowels with his gushing spunk. *It's time for Lily to join in,* he decided. *Time for her to further her experience of the female breast! And of my knob!*

'Ah, Melinda!' Larry beamed as the timid girl gingerly entered the room.

'Hallo, doctor,' she smiled sweetly.

'Right, we'll waste no time. Clothes off, lie on the examination couch and we'll begin,' he ordered her, eyeing her eternal legs, her shapely thighs. 'Has there been any improvement? Are your breasts any larger?'

'No, I don't think so,' the girl replied softly, unbuttoning her white silk blouse.

'Well, it's early days. These things take time, Melinda. This week, I'm going to ask Lily, my trainee sex therapist, to assist me. A new treatment has just been developed to help enlarge the breasts. It consists of clamping steel rings around the base of each breast and tightening the screws to force the breasts to swell and balloon.'

'Will it hurt?' Melinda asked, her long black hair cascading over her pert mammary spheres as she removed her bra.

'The rings won't hurt too much, but the next stage of the treatment might be a little painful.'

269

Ray Gordon

'The next stage?' the vulnerable patient echoed, her dark eyes wide as she tugged her miniskirt down her naked legs, revealing her bulging panties.

'I'm going to have Lily cane your breasts. A light caning will . . .'

'Cane my breasts? But . . .'

'It's all right, Melinda, calm down. The treatment is designed to firm the breast muscles and stiffen the nipples. It was developed by Professor Brownteat-Bust. The pain will be well worth enduring, believe me.'

'I don't like the sound of that!' the girl gasped, tugging her cunny-stained panties down and displaying her sparse black pubes, her long sex slit. 'Doctor, I don't want my breasts caned!'

'You do want bigger breasts, don't you?'

'Well, yes, but . . .'

'Trust me, Melinda. After the treatment, I'll deposit my sperm in your anal duct. The testosterone will be quickly absorbed into your blood stream, helping your breasts to develop into fine mammary specimens. Right, get onto the couch and I'll call Lily,' he grinned, leaving the room.

Returning with his wary assistant, Larry assured her that she'd be safe, that Melinda's breasts wouldn't attack her. 'You said that your problem is a little better,' he smiled. 'This will further help to cure you of your terrible phobia.'

'What do you want me to do?' Lily asked, her eyes transfixed on Melinda's long nipples, the large brown discs of her areolae.

'Clamp these around the base of each breast,' Larry instructed her, taking two steel rings from the shelf. 'Pull Melinda's breasts through the rings and tighten

270

the screws, forcing her breasts to balloon, her nipples to swell.'

'Are you sure it won't hurt?' Melinda asked fearfully as Lily tentatively placed the rings over her breasts, careful not to touch her nipples – her brown, leering mammary eyes!

'There'll be a little discomfort, that's all,' Larry smiled, gazing at the girl's swollen vaginal lips, her protruding inner petals.

Tightening the screws, Lily gazed in amazement as the whimpering girl's breasts inflated and her nipples distended, standing erect. Tightening the screws further, painfully swelling Melinda's mammary orbs, she stood back, admiring her work as Larry grabbed the thin bamboo cane and placed it on the couch. Melinda should be tied down for the mammary thrashing, he decided. He didn't want her leaping from the couch at the first stroke of the cane!

'OK,' he smiled. 'Open your legs and stretch your arms behind your head, Melinda. Lily, will you tie her ankles to the legs of the couch, please?'

'Yes, doctor,' Lily replied, taking two lengths of rope from the shelf.

'I don't want to be tied down!' the reluctant patient cried as Lily bound her ankles and Larry secured her wrists. 'Please, why are you tying me down?'

'It's part of the treatment, Melinda,' Larry reassured her. 'There's nothing to worry about, I promise you.'

The girl's naked body securely lashed to the couch, Larry reached to the shelf and grabbed a leather strap connected to a rubber ball. 'This is to prevent a condition known as *screamus protestus*,' he smiled, placing the ball in his victim's mouth. Running the leather strap round the back of her head,

he fastened the buckle, securing the gag. 'There, now you're all ready for the treatment. Right, Lily, I want you to cane her breasts. Begin with a gentle caning to ease her into the punish – I mean, the treatment.'

Grinning as she grabbed the cane, Lily was eager to thrash the girl's inflated bosoms. This was her chance to take revenge on female breasts, to vent her anger on the evil mammary spheres! Gazing into Melinda's terror-stricken eyes as she raised the cane high above her head, Lily brought it down, the thin bamboo striking her prisoner's taut breasts with a loud crack.

Struggling and squirming, Melinda was powerless to halt the mammary caning as Lily repeatedly brought the bamboo down, leaving thin weals fanning out across the girl's ballooning flesh. Striking her areolae, her erect nipples, the young sadist lost herself in her revenge, thrashing the menacing, swollen tits with a vengeance.

Her eyes almost popping out of her head as her naked body jolted with every strike of the thin bamboo, Melinda grimaced as Larry forced a huge candle between her vaginal lips and drove the wax phallus deep into her convulsing cunt. Lost in his debauchery, he didn't stop to think of the consequences, of the inevitable reprisals. All that mattered was the perversity of the moment, the breast thrashing, the vaginal abuse – his insatiable craving to commit depraved sexual acts.

Gazing at the girl's face as the cane struck her crimson breasts again, he frowned. Her eyes closed, displaying a faint smile, she appeared to be enjoying the punishment. *Perhaps Lily's breasts could do with a good thrashing?* he mused, thrusting the candle in and out of Melinda's drenched

cuntal sheath. Monica's mammary boulders were certainly in line for a thrashing should she be released by the police and returned to the bondage room!

The rubber ball slipping out of Melinda's mouth, she gasped, begging Lily to tighten the clamps. Discarding the cane, Lily obliged, tightening the screws and forcing the girl's scarlet tits to swell painfully. Grabbing the cane again, she continued with the thrashing to the accompaniment of her prisoner's gasps of sexual fulfilment.

'Do it harder! Cane my tits harder!' Melinda cried as Larry took another candle from the shelf and parted her taut buttocks. Complying as Larry forced the candle deep into the girl's tight bottom sheath, Lily felt her own clitoris swell and throb, her vaginal juices coursing from her hot cunt. Her fear of breasts rapidly fading, she discarded the cane and leaned over Melinda's quivering body, sucking the girl's inflamed nipple into her wet mouth.

Running her hand over Melinda's smooth stomach, Lily located the girl's erect clitoris and massaged the small sex nodule as Larry thrust the candles in and out of her lust holes. Trembling, gasping as her climax approached, Melinda tossed her head from side to side, her black curtain of hair masking her sex-flushed face, her stomach rising and falling.

'Coming!' she sang as her climax erupted, her clitoris pulsating in orgasm beneath Lily's caressing fingertips. 'Oh, God, I'm coming!' Leaving the candles embedded in the wailing girl's love holes, Larry moved behind Lily and lifted her skirt up over her back. Tugging her red knickers down, exposing her rounded bottom cheeks as she fervently mouthed and sucked on Melinda's nipples, he slipped his erect penis out of his trousers.

'D' you want this?' he asked the girl, pressing his bulbous knob between her taut buttocks. 'Do you want this up your bum?'

'Yes, yes!' Lily begged, moving down to Melinda's inflamed pussy lips and standing with her feet wide apart. Lapping at the girl's inner folds, sweeping her tongue over her throbbing clitoris, Lily gasped as Larry's knob pressed against her brown ring, desperate to gain entry to her hot bowels. 'Do it!' she cried. 'Push it right up my bum and fuck me!'

His solid shaft slowly entering her hot anal duct as Melinda's multiple orgasm peaked again, Larry grabbed Lily's hips and drove his knob further into the dank heat of her rectal sheath. Inch by inch of his fleshpole gliding into her tight hole, he drove his knob fully home, completely impaling her on his rigid member, his heavy balls resting against her swollen cunt lips.

'God, that's heaven!' Lily breathed, her face wet with Melinda's sex juices. 'Fuck me, really give it to me!'

'Christ, your arse is tight!' Larry gasped, sliding half his length out of her bottom-hole and thrusting his knob deep into her bowels again.

'Oh, oh, I'm going to split open! Ah, you're so big!'

'Christ, how I love girls' snug little arseholes!' Larry exulted in his crudity.

Her fear of the penis declining, Lily gyrated her hips, delighting in the lewd anal sensations. Reaching between her parted thighs and massaging her solid clitoris as Larry fucked her tight arsehole, she continued to suck on Melinda's pulsating sex button, taking the quivering girl closer to another enforced climax.

'This is somewhat unorthodox, isn't it?' Melinda breathed, her naked body rocking with the sensations of perverted sex as Lily thrust the candle in and out of her drenched cunt.

'It's a tried and tested method of enlarging the breasts,' Larry panted, thrusting his cock deep into Lily's spasming bum-hole.

'I don't understand. How will you doing that to your trainee sex therapist enlarge my breasts?'

'Lily's acting as a catalyst – my sperming into her bowels as she sucks your clitoris will precipitate changes in your breasts. It's known as anal catalytic breast enlargement.'

Ignoring the tethered girl's further questions, Larry increased his rhythm, driving his swollen knob into Lily's velveteen rectal tube, his heavy balls slapping her dripping vaginal lips as his climax approached. His foreskin gliding back and forth over his throbbing knob as he withdrew his penis and thrust into her tight bottom-hole again, his sperm finally jetted from his slit, filling the quivering girl's bowels as her own climax erupted within her pulsating clitoris. Melinda reaching another mind-blowing climax, all three shuddered and gasped in their coming, their cries of sexual gratification resounding throughout the building.

'We must do this again, Lily!' Larry grinned as the last of his spunk gushed deep into her hot anal cavern. 'God, I'll fuck your arse again and again!'

'I've never known anything like it!' the perspiring girl whimpered, massaging her throbbing cherry as she swept her tongue over Melinda's pulsating sex nodule. 'God, it's heavenly!'

Gently slipping his flaccid penis out of Lily's anal canal, Larry zipped his trousers, wondering how Monica was faring

in police custody. 'I'll leave you to enjoy yourselves,' he smiled, gazing at the obvious pleasure depicted in Melinda's expression as Lily sucked the girl's clitoris into her hot mouth. 'Yes, well, as I said, enjoy yourselves.'

Returning to his consulting room, he grabbed the phone and rang DI Clarke. 'Ah, Doctor Lickman,' the detective replied. 'What can I do for you?'

'I was wondering how Monica Moodie was getting on. Has she been charged?'

'Yes, she's been charged and released on police bail.'

'Oh, I see.'

'In view of what she said during her interview, I might have cause to return to your practice to discuss certain matters with you, doctor.'

'Certain matters?'

'Yes, there's the matter of pornographic photographs, allegedly taken by you.'

'Pornographic photographs? I really don't think . . .'

'As yet, I don't have the photographs in my possession, but Mrs Moodie has assured me that they'll be delivered to my office later today.'

'Who by?'

'I'm not at liberty to say, I'm afraid.'

'Right, well, keep me posted, Inspector.'

'Oh, I will, Doctor Lickman – I will! Good day to you.'

Replacing the receiver, Larry frowned. *Gina or Christine will be delivering the photographs*, he mused, wondering how to ambush them. 'Brigit!' he called, hurrying to reception. 'Ah, Brigit, I want you to hang around outside the police station.'

'Whatever for?' she asked surprisedly.

'Gina or Christine will be taking some incriminating photographs of me to the police station later today. I want you to ambush . . .'

'I can't do that! I can't start a fight in the street!'

'Of course you can! It's imperative that you grab the pictures, Brigit – my very life depends on it!'

'OK, but I really don't think . . .'

'Don't fail me, Brigit! Disguise yourself, wear a balaclava, jeans and a jacket so you appear to be a young man. Hide across the road from the police station and leap out of the bushes when you see Gina or Christine and snatch their handbag, OK? Monica might even deliver them, so look out for her, too.'

'OK. I'll go now, shall I?'

'Yes, and do a good job. I'll see you later.'

Watching the girl leave the building, Larry turned his thoughts to Mother Barren-Womb, wondering how to deal with the old bat once and for all. 'Lily!' he bellowed down the hall.

'What is it?' the girl asked, peering round the bondage room door, her face wet with cunny juice.

'I'm going to the bloody damned convent to see Mother Broad-Loom. Hold the fort until I get back.'

'Can't Brigit . . .'

'She's out on an errand of great importance, so you're in charge. I'll try not to be too long.'

Arriving at the convent, Larry parked his car at the foot of the steps to the huge Victorian building and pulled a small plastic bag out of the glove compartment. *I can almost*

smell the sweet scent of cunt-stained schoolgirlies' knickers!
he grinned inwardly as he climbed the steps and entered
the building through a huge oak door. *I wonder where the
laundry room is?*

'May I help you?' a nun asked as she drifted towards
Larry, her pale face smiling sweetly.

'Yes, I've come to see Mother Barren-Womb – my name's
Doctor Lickman,' he replied, stuffing the plastic bag into
his pocket.

'Come with me, I'll show you to her study,' the sister
obliged, turning and walking down the dimly-lit cloister.
'She'll be pleased to see you, she's been wanting to speak
with you for some time.'

'Really?' Larry smiled as the nun knocked on a large
oak door.

'Yes, she's been in a very bad mood since . . .'

'Come!' the Reverend Mother boomed.

'Good luck, doctor,' the nun said softly, lifting her habit
and scurrying down the cloister like a frightened rabbit.

'Ah, Doctor Lickman!' Mother Barren-Womb greeted
him from behind her imposing desk.

'Mother Barren-Womb,' Larry smiled. 'I thought I'd
better come and see you because . . .'

'Sit down, doctor – we have some serious business to
discuss.'

'Oh, do we?' he asked, sitting opposite the grumpy
woman.

'Yes, we do! Firstly, Sister Mary visited your establishment, alone and without my permission.'

'Yes, she . . .'

'Did you examine her?'

'Well, yes, I suppose so.'

'You suppose so? Do you suffer from short-term memory loss, doctor?'

'No, only when convenient.'

'Well, did you or did you not examine the girl?'

'Yes, I did have reason to examine her.'

'Did you remove her habit?'

'No.'

'You're lying! I have it from a reliable source that you *did* remove the girl's habit.'

'No, I'm not lying! I didn't remove her habit – *she* removed it.'

'It amounts to the same thing.'

'As a matter of fact, it doesn't amount to the same thing at all.'

'Be quiet! Can you explain the presence of sperm on her habit?'

Yes, but I'm not going to! 'DI Clarke informed me of the unmentionable stains, Mother Barren-Womb, but I have no idea where . . .'

'Was it your sperm?'

'Good grief, no! I'm a highly qualified doctor, do you think that I'd . . .'

'You're not a qualified doctor, I've checked.'

Fuck me! 'Er . . . checked where?'

'With the British Medical Association. They've never heard of you, *Doctor* Lickman.'

'Oh, I see!' Larry laughed, lolling about in the chair. 'I'm not actually registered with the BMA. I qualified in South Africa, so . . .'

'But the BMA would have you listed as a . . .'

Ray Gordon

'No, no, they wouldn't. Their register only lists doctors who qualify in Britain.'

'I see. Well, that appears to be that matter cleared up. Going back to this dreadful business of the sperm-stained habit, I firmly believe that it was your sperm.'

'And what makes you believe that?'

'Because of the facts that have come to light. Sister Mary visited you and removed her habit, you physically examined her, her naked body, and . . .'

'What bearing does all this have on . . .'

'The evidence might only be circumstantial, Doctor Lickman, but it's more than enough for any court to come to the conclusion that the sperm came from . . . that you deposited the sperm.'

'I've had a vasectomy, Mother Fallen-Doom.'

'Barren-Womb! Vasectomy or not, you'd still be capable of producing . . .'

'Apart from the vasectomy where they cut the vas deferens, they also removed the prostate gland, the Cowper's glands and the seminal vesicles.'

'Why?'

'It was as the result of a deep-seated childhood experience I had with a twelve-year-old girl at school.'

'Really? But I don't see . . .'

'I'm unable to go into detail because of the illegality of the girl's wanton act, but I am unable to produce semen, Mother Barren-Womb. I rest my case.'

'Oh, I see. Well, please forgive me, doctor, I've obviously made a terrible and completely incorrect assumption.'

'That's all right, I quite understand. You weren't to know of my dreadful urological condition. I'm sorry to have to

mention the word in your convent, but I don't possess a penis.'

'Goodness me! Oh, you poor man!'

'I've leaned to live with it, or, should I say, without it.'

'Oh, I'm so sorry.'

'Don't worry. So, as to the stained habit, I'm afraid I can't help you.'

'The police analysed the substance found on Sister Mary's habit and discovered it to be sperm, so who on earth was responsible?'

'Perhaps the police were mistaken and the substance was face cream or . . .'

'I very much doubt that the police made a mistake, doctor!'

'Presumably Sister Mary won't discuss the matter?'

'No, she won't. She's been confined to her room.'

'Oh, has she?'

'Yes, she's been locked in.'

'For how long?'

'Indefinitely! Until I get to the bottom of this, that's where she'll stay, away from men's . . . away from men.'

'Well, I'd better be getting back to my practice, Mother Barren-Womb. I'm pleased that we've cleared the air,' Larry smiled, rising to his feet and moving to the door.

'As am I, doctor – as am I. By the way, Jenny Faggot's father contacted me again. He told me that he'd been completely wrong about you. Apparently, after speaking to Jenny again about her visit to your establishment, he was most impressed with you.'

'Oh, good! So, that's another misunderstanding . . . I mean, another problem sorted out.' Discreetly taking the

plastic bag from his pocket, he deposited it behind a picture of the Pope that stood on a small table by the door. 'Well, I'd better get back to work, I suppose.'

'Yes, thank you for calling, doctor.'

'Not at all, goodbye, Mother Superfluous . . . Superior.'

Leaving the study, the heady fragrance of teenage girlies filling his nostrils, Larry decided to nose around the convent. Although the laundry room with its stained schoolgirlie knickers played heavily on his mind, he went instead in search of Sister Mary's room, wondering whether it would be wise to release her. With her vows broken and the Reverend Mother out to prove her carnal ways, he was sure the young nun would welcome her emancipation.

Creeping up a huge oak staircase, Larry found himself standing at the end of a long hallway lined with doors. *This looks promising*, he mused, tentatively opening each door as he made his way down the hall. Trying a locked door, he smiled, noticing a key hanging on a hook. *This must be it*, he concluded, unlocking and opening the door.

'Doctor!' Sister Mary cried joyfully from her bed, her tearful eyes smiling, glimmering with hope. 'What are you doing . . .'

'Shush! I've come to rescue you,' Larry whispered. 'Do you have any clothes other than your habit?'

'Yes, I have the clothes I wore when I first came here.'

'Good, get changed and we'll sneak out.'

'How did you find me?' the young nun asked, opening a cupboard and taking out a dress and a pair of high-heeled shoes.

'I came to talk to Mother Barren-Womb, she told me that you were confined to your room, so here I am.'

'I'm never coming back here!' she asserted as she tugged her habit over her head. 'Never in a million years! I'm going to get a job and . . .'

'I'm pleased to hear it, but we've got to get you out of here first.'

'There's a fire escape, we'll go that way,' the girl said excitedly, slipping into the tight red dress. 'OK, I'm ready when you are.'

Following her down the hall and through a fire exit, Larry descended the iron steps, praying that the Reverend Mother wouldn't catch him in his act of rescuing the damsel in distress. He knew that DI Clarke would be called in the minute the young nun's escape had been discovered, but he'd cross that bridge when he came to it.

'Quickly, into my car,' he whispered, creeping round the front of the building and opening the passenger door. 'We're out of here!'

'God help us if someone sees us!' the fleeing nun breathed, gazing up at the rows of windows as Larry jumped in beside her and started the engine.

'I don't think God will help!' he laughed, turning the car round and speeding down the winding drive. 'We're in the hands of Satan now!'

Pulling up outside his house, Larry gave the girl the front door key and told her to make herself at home. 'I'll see you around five-thirty,' he smiled as she climbed out of the car. 'Don't answer the phone or the door, OK?'

'OK,' she smiled, dashing up the path.

Returning to his practice and parking his car, Larry wondered how long it would take DI Clarke to pay him

a visit concerning Sister Mary's absconding. Entering the building, he wasn't in the least surprised to discover the detective hovering in reception. Lily making a hasty retreat to the waiting room, Larry approached the besuited man to face the music.

'Ah, Doctor Lickman, might I have another word with you?' the sleuth asked.

'Yes, of course, Inspector – come to my consulting room. I've just been to the convent and had a talk with the Reverend Mother,' he imparted calmly, walking through the door and sitting at his desk. 'We had quite an interesting chat.'

'Yes, I know, she rang me. Doctor Lickman, I'm here because the nun, Sister Mary, has left the convent, yet again. But this time, she had an accomplice.'

'An accomplice?'

'Yes, according to Mother Barren-Womb, she was locked in her room and . . .'

'The Reverend Mother was locked in her room? Oh, the poor woman!'

'No, Sister Mary was locked in her room.'

'What was she doing in the Reverend Mother's room?'

'She was locked in her *own* room. Someone took the key from the hook outside the door and released the nun.'

'Had the nun been imprisoned?'

'Yes, by the Reverend Mother, for her wantonness.'

'Goodness me, it sounds as if the convent's a prison!'

'The Reverend Mother had good reason to lock the sister in her room. The reason that I'm here is because the nun's disappearance coincides with your visit to the convent.'

'Well, all I did was talk to the Reverend Mother in her study, and then leave the building and drive straight back

here. I've had nothing to do with disappearing nuns, I can assure you!'

'*I*'ll decide whether or not you've had anything to do with disappearing nuns, Doctor Lickman. Now, you say that you drove straight back here?'

'Well, not straight back, exactly.'

'Ah, so you went somewhere else first?'

'No, I didn't.'

'But you just said that you didn't come straight back.'

'I had to go round corners, follow the road – it's the law. I thought you would have been aware of that, seeing as you're a . . .'

'Please, don't play games with me, doctor!'

'Sorry.'

'Did you notice anyone in the vicinity of the convent when you left?'

'Yes, there was a young woman walking down the drive.'

'What was she wearing, can you remember?'

'Er . . . a dress, a red dress.'

'That's what Sister Mary was wearing when she escaped from the building. You didn't offer the woman a lift, did you?'

'A lift? Good grief, no!'

'Why put it like that?'

'I never offer young women lifts, Inspector! What with the things you read in the papers, well, I . . .'

'Yes, quite. I've ordered a manhunt to . . .'

'Don't you mean a girl cunt . . . girl hunt?'

'I know what I mean, doctor! My men are combing the area, searching for the girl, as we speak. Did you climb the stairs to the nuns' nunneries?'

'The nuns' nunneries?'

'Their rooms, their bedrooms.'

'No, no, I didn't. I had no reason to climb the stairs to the nunneries.'

'This is all too coincidental for my liking, doctor. We have several cases all appertaining to one nun. There's the case of the nun who visited you and removed her habit for an examination, the case of the spermed habit, the case of the missing nun, and now the case of the escaping nun. I'm none too happy, as you can imagine.'

'Indeed, I can, Inspector. In my considered opinion, I'd say that . . . oh, excuse me,' Larry smiled as the phone rang. 'Hallo,' he replied, lifting the receiver. 'Yes, he's here. I'll put him on. It's for you, Inspector.'

Taking the phone, DI Clarke cleared his throat. 'Clarke speaking. Attacked in the street? In broad daylight? Did she get a good look at her attacker? Damn it! So, the photographs were stolen? No, no, leave it to me. All right, goodbye.' Replacing the receiver, he frowned at Larry. 'It would seem that Mrs Cology was attacked a short distance away from the police station. Her handbag was snatched.'

'Good grief!'

'The bag contained the pornographic photographs, allegedly taken by you.'

'Bloody thugs!' Larry grunted. 'I blame the parents.' *One up the bum for Brigit!*

'Again, rather coincidental, don't you agree?'

'How do you mean, Inspector?'

'Well, the nun escaped when you were at the convent, her habit was sperm-stained during the time she was away from

the convent visiting you, the bag containing the photographic evidence of you was stolen . . .'

'I can see that you're pointing the finger at me, but . . .'

'I don't point fingers, Doctor Lickman. And I must say that the long arm of coincidence isn't *that* long!'

'May I ask you something, Inspector?'

'Yes, of course.'

'If you were to discover a man and a woman naked together in a cornfield, what would you suppose they were doing?'

'That's easy – in my considered opinion, I'd say they were planning an armed robbery.'

'If you saw two men entering a public toilet cubicle together, what would you think they were up to?'

'Fighting over the only available cubicle and causing an affray. I'd be obliged to arrest them and charge them accordingly.'

'So what are your conclusions as far as Sister Mary is concerned?'

'I conclude that she's up to something of a grim and sordid nature.'

'Have you come to any conclusions where I'm concerned?'

'Yes, I have. I always look for a common denominator, doctor, and in this case, the common denominator is you.'

'But, surely, it's the nun?'

'No, the nun had nothing to do with the bag snatch.'

'Neither did I!'

'And she had nothing to do with the accusations Mrs Moodie made, or Mrs Cology and her daughter, for that matter.'

'But you've already taken Mrs Moodie in and charged her with . . .'

'Can you explain these, Doctor Lickman?'

Gazing in horror as the detective removed a pair of convent knickers and red panties from a plastic bag, Larry cringed. Obviously, he'd ransacked his desk drawer and come up with the spoils – or soils!

'Yes, I can explain them,' Larry smiled. 'The red panties belong to my secretary, Brigit, and the grey knickers were left here by a sixth-form girl from the convent.'

'Why would she leave her knickers here, doctor?'

'Because . . . because she'd changed to go on to a netball match and she dropped them on her way out. I put them in the drawer for safe keeping.'

'The name tag reads Jenny Faggot. You do realize that I'll have to check your story of the alleged netball match, don't you?'

'Yes, of course.'

'I'll have a word with the Reverend Mother about netball matches and ascertain whether Jenny Faggot is in the team and when she last played. I'll be in touch, doctor. Good day to you.'

'Yes, er . . . good day, Inspector.'

Watching the man stuff the incriminating knickers into the plastic bag and leave the room, Larry grabbed the bottle of scotch from the drawer and took a swig. 'Hell's bells!' he cursed. 'I'm fucked – well and truly fucked!' At least Brigit had managed to snatch the bag containing the photographs, he consoled himself. But what with the police hunting for Sister Mary, and Jenny's convent knickers, things weren't looking too good. *I'm well and truly fucked rotten!*

Chapter Nine

Answering the phone as he entered his consulting room the following morning, Larry wasn't at all surprised to hear Monica's angry voice bellowing in his ear. 'I've really got something on you now!' she hissed. 'I can't prove that you arranged to have Gina's bag snatched as she was on her way to the police station with the photographs, but I've got something far better on you now!'

'Goodness me, Monica, you don't give up easily, do you? Why don't you . . .'

'I never give up! I know that you've had two wives, and that you weren't divorced from the first one when you married the second!'

Fucking bloody hell! 'Er . . . two . . .' *Fuck me backwards!* 'Two wives, Monica?'

'Yes, two wives – you bigamist!'

'I think you must have your knickers in a twist! Try pulling them out of your arse crack!'

'My God, you disgust me!'

'As always, I aim to displease, Monica. You're not ringing from Loony Lane Mansion, are you?'

'Of course I'm not!'

'Tell me, how's your lesbian relationship with Gina?'

'I don't have a . . . I've just been in touch with your wives

and told them where you are, where you work and where you live. They were very eager to talk to you. In fact, they're on their way to see you now.'

'From whom did you hear these slanderous lies of a most disturbing and malicious nature, Monica?'

'From the private detective Gina and I employed. Apparently, you have a string of debts, too.'

'I'm only indebted to you, Monica.'

'What?'

'I'm indebted to you for the years of joy and happiness you brought me when you worked for me.'

'Joy and happiness?'

'My mistake, I meant sorrow and grief.'

'You brought me more sorrow and grief than you'll ever know!'

'Why, thank you, Monica!'

'It also appears that several teenaged girls' fathers want to know of your whereabouts.'

Oh, my God! 'Fathers? What would teenaged girls' fathers be wanting with me?'

'Surely you don't need to be reminded of your sordid and disgusting past?'

'Yes, please remind me, Monica.'

'You defiled them, as you do every young girl who's unfortunate enough to come your way!'

'Defiled them? There, you see, you're leaping before you've looked again!'

'I have more on you, much more!'

'Please, do enlighten me.'

'I know about those falsified certificates hanging on the wall in reception . . .'

'Falsified? They're my qualifications, Monica!'

'They're not worth the paper they're written on, and you know it! I'll see you in court, as they say! Goodbye, *non-doctor* Lickman!'

Replacing the receiver, his hands trembling, Larry took a deep breath and rummaged in his desk drawer for the Bell's. Monica was far more resourceful than he'd imagined – and revengeful! Realizing the full extent of the horrendous consequences of sexually abusing Monica and Gina, he gulped down a quadruple scotch, wondering what the hell to do.

'Hi, Larry!' Brigit beamed as she breezed in. 'Did Sister Mary sleep well?'

'Yes, she did.'

'Christ, why are you on the scotch at this time of the day?'

'Monica just rang. She . . . she's dug some dirt up, I'm afraid.'

'On you, presumably?'

'Yes. You see, I was married, twice, and . . .'

'I didn't know that!'

'When I married my second wife, I was still married to the first.'

'Oh, shit!'

'Exactly! Monica has hired a private dick, and he's come up with some pretty sordid stuff from my sordid past. I really don't know what to do.'

'Well, it depends on what Monica plans to do.'

'She's told my wives where I am. Also, there were several teenaged girls that I . . . well, their fathers are after my blood.'

'Christ, Larry, talk about a checkered life! Is there anything else?'

'Yes, I have several massive debts, and Monica knows that I have no qualifications. If she tells everyone where I am, I'll be right in the shit!'

'You shouldn't have taken Sister Mary back to your house. If that cop decides to call at your place, he'll . . .'

'Sister Mary is the least of my problems! Anyway, she's not there any more, she moved out this morning.'

'Where to?'

'A flat in town. What am I going to do, Brigit? What the fucking hell am I going to do?'

'Stay calm, for one thing. Should any debt collectors turn up, I'm sure Lily and I can do a deal with them, if you get my meaning.'

'Where is Lily?'

'In the toilet trying to stick her foot up her pussy.'

'God, she needs help!'

'I did offer to help her but she said that she could manage. As for your wives . . .'

'As for my wives, they'll kill me!'

'No, they won't. I'll tell them that you're living abroad. I've got it, I'll move into your house and say that I'm renting the place while you're away.'

'What about the practice?'

'I'll say that I'm running it.'

'And my falsified qualifications?'

'Seeing as everyone will believe you to be out of the country, they can't question the certificates.'

'Oh, I don't know, Brigit! I can hardly go into hiding, can I?'

'Why not? Just lie low for a few weeks, until the dust settles, and things will be OK. You can move into my flat, no one will go there.'

'All right. I'd better get out of here, I've a feeling that the storm's about to break. Shit, there's the reception bell! I'll escape through the window! Here, take my car key, and there's my front door key.'

'There's a spare front door key to my flat beneath the flowerpot by the gate. Make yourself at home. Oh, and don't go rummaging through my bedside cabinet – the shock might kill you!'

'OK, thanks, Brigit. Oh, by the way, should DI Clarke turn up, tell him to search Mother Barren-Womb's study. Tell him that rumour has it that she's into cannabis.'

'Cannabis?'

'Just tell him, OK?'

'OK.'

'Right, I'll be in touch.'

Composing herself as she watched Larry dash across the car park, Brigit closed the window and returned to reception to be confronted by an attractive brunette in her late twenties. *One of the wives?* she speculated, eyeing the woman's full red lips.

'Where's my bloody husband?' she demanded of Brigit.

'I have no idea, Mrs . . .'

'Lickman, Carole Lickman. Where's that bigamistic bastard, Larry?'

'Oh, you mean Doctor Lickman. He's living abroad, in Brazil.'

'Brazil? But I was told that he . . .'

'He left yesterday. He'll be gone for a year or so, I'm afraid. I'm Doctor Biways, Doctor Lickman's assistant. Can I help you?'

'Who's in charge of this place?'

'During Doctor Lickman's absence, I am.'

'Did you know that Larry was married?'

'No, he never discussed his private life.'

'I'm not surprised!'

'He's a very private man.'

'I'll give him bloody private when I catch up with him! Now, you listen to me, young lady – Larry is a bigamist, a liar, a thief, a two-timing bastard, a . . .'

'What is it you want, Mrs Lickman?'

'I want . . . well, I want . . .'

'What do you plan to do?'

'Larry married me when he was already married to another slut!'

'You don't look like a slut.'

'I'm not a slut! What I meant was, he was married to a slut when he married me.'

'So, you want to cause trouble, is that the idea?'

'Trouble? I'll kill the bastard!'

'If you don't mind my saying so, you look rather pale, Mrs Lickman.'

'Pale? What are you talking about?'

'Your complexion . . . you appear to be somewhat liverish. I'm a qualified doctor so, if you'd like me to take a look at you, I'd be only too happy.'

'It's stress, that's what it is!'

'You look run down, quite ill, in fact.'

'I *do* feel a bit queasy, I must admit.'

'Are you taking medication for anything?'

'No, I'm not.'

'Look, you and I have no argument, so let's have a chat about your husband while I'm examining you.'

'I want to know all about him. Tell me everything.'

'Yes, I will. I'll tell you all you want to know while I'm examining you.'

'I've been feeling strange lately, I could probably do with a thorough check-up.'

'If you'd come this way, Mrs Lickman.'

'Please, call me Carole.'

'And I'm Brigit.'

Leading the way to the bondage room, Brigit knew she wouldn't be able to restrain herself, to suppress her insatiable craving for women's naked bodies. The thought of getting her fingers up Carole Lickman's pussy stiffened her clitoris, wetted her vagina, as she ushered the unsuspecting woman into the torture chamber and locked the door.

'Slip your clothes off and I'll give you a head-to-toe examination, Carole.'

'You want me to take *all* my clothes off?'

'I might as well give you a thorough examination while you're here, while I tell you all about Larry. You appear to be anaemic, and I don't like the look of your pupils: they're dilated.'

'Are they?' the woman asked, slipping out of her dress, revealing her curvaceous body to Brigit's wide eyes. 'My husband, Roger, said that . . . my partner, I mean, he's not my husband. He's been saying for some time that I don't look well and that I should see a doctor.'

'He's right, Carole,' Brigit smiled as her patient, her victim,

peeled her black satin bra cups away from her firm mammary globes, her succulent nipples. 'Your areolae don't look right to me.'

'Don't they?' the woman asked, looking down anxiously at her rounded breasts, the chocolate-brown discs of her areolae.

'No, they're the wrong colour. You see the way your areolae are puckered – that's a sign of traumatic vaginal distress,' Brigit said authoritatively, assuming Larry's convincing bedside blurb.

'Traumatic vaginal distress?' Carole echoed, slipping her shoes off and tugging her matching black panties down her long legs.

'It's a rare condition, but there are still several cases reported every year in Britain. Lie on the couch and I'll take a good look at you.'

Watching the gullible Mrs Lickman climb onto the couch, Brigit decided that if she could befriend her, reason with her, she might be able to save Larry. After all, the woman now had another partner, so why pursue him? Opening her patient's legs and parting her fleshy labia, Brigit felt her stomach somersault, her clitoris stir in anticipation as she gazed greedily at Carole's deep-pink sex nodule. Tentatively slipping her finger into the naked woman's hot vaginal sheath, she smiled.

'Bring your knees up to your chest, please, Carole,' she instructed, ogling her patient's outer pussy lips bulging around her finger as she took her position. 'That's it, now I can examine you properly,' she smiled, slipping a second finger into her slimy sex duct.

Grinning as she moved her fingers in and out of Carole's

tight pussy sheath, Brigit focused on her inner lips, the pink petals dragging along her pistoning fingers, leaving creamy sex sap in their wake. *Tie her down and thrash her?* she contemplated, slipping a third finger into the woman's tightening sex hole. What Larry would say if he knew that she had one of his wives naked on the examination couch, about to be caned, she had no idea!

'There's something not quite right,' Brigit murmured, slipping her fingers out of the woman's drenched cuntal sheath. 'I'd like to take a look at your cervix,' she added, taking a vaginal speculum from the shelf.

'I'm all right, aren't I?' Carole asked, her blue eyes reflecting her concern.

'I'm not sure. OK, bring your legs down, that's it. Now hang your feet down on either side of the couch.'

'I don't think I can open my legs that wide!'

'If I'm to examine you properly . . .'

'All right, I'll try.'

Watching her victim's vaginal crack open as she parted her legs and lowered her feet on either side of the couch, Brigit decided that befriending her, trying to reason with her, wouldn't be half as much fun as sexually abusing her naked body, caning her taut buttocks until she screamed and begged for mercy. Recalling caning Gina's delectable buttocks, she sensed an overwhelming urge to commit the most vile and debased sexual acts she could think of on her latest victim.

'So, how long has Larry been in business?' Carole asked as Brigit sank three fingers into her open sex hole.

'Abut six years,' Brigit smiled, eyeing a length of rope on the shelf.

'Does he have a woman?'

Yes, several every week! 'No, not at the moment.'

'Does he have money? Is his business lucrative?'

'No, he's stone broke, I'm afraid.'

'Oh, that's a shame, I was going to take him for every penny he's got!'

'I'm going to tie your feet together to check your muscle reflexes,' Brigit digressed, grabbing the rope and kneeling down. 'The idea is . . .'

'Tie my feet together? But . . .'

'There, that's it!' the sadistic young redhead grinned, securing the rope between the woman's ankles and standing up. 'You have a nice body, a really nice body.'

'I don't understand why . . .'

'Now I'm going to tie your hands so that I can examine your breasts properly.'

'I really don't see why you have to tie me down!' Carole protested shakily as Brigit bound her wrists and secured the ropes to the legs of the couch.

'With your arms in this position, behind your head, your pectoral muscles will tighten, allowing me to check your breasts properly.'

'I'd rather you didn't do this, Brigit!'

'I have to tie you down so that I can sexually abuse you, Carole – lick and finger-fuck your beautiful cunt!' Brigit giggled, leaning over and sweeping her tongue up her prisoner's yawning sex crevice. 'Mmm, you taste good!'

'Please, what *do* you think you're doing!' Carole yelled.

'Licking your cunt.'

'Release me this minute or I'll . . .'

'Unless you stop screaming at me, I'll gag you!'

'Gag me? What sort of girl are you, for Christ's sake?'

'An insatiable bisexual pervert!'

'You can't do this! I'll . . . *mmmf!*'

Grabbing Carole's panties, Brigit stuffed them into the woman's mouth, halting her screamed protests. Resuming her vaginal licking, her mind swirling with wicked ideas, she imagined Larry cock-fucking his wife's tight vaginal canal, his knob sperming into her hot cunt. Stretching the woman's pussy lips wide apart, exposing her clitoris, her intimate inner flesh, she lapped up the aphrodisiacal cunt milk oozing from her gaping hole.

'God, you taste sexy!' she breathed as Lily entered the room and gasped. 'I love drinking girlie juice from wet cunt holes!'

'Brigit, who . . . what are you . . .' Lily stammered, holding her hand to her open mouth.

'This is Carole Lickman, Larry's wife – well, one of his wives. Come and play with her.'

'Does Larry know about this?'

'No, he's . . . he's gone to Brazil.'

'Brazil? When did he . . .'

'I'll tell you all about it later, Lily.'

'Brigit, Sally Peabody's in reception. She wants to see Larry.'

'Oh, God, not her!'

'I'd better get rid of her, tell her that Larry's out.'

'Bring her in here and she can enjoy an hour or so with our prisoner.'

'Brigit, are you sure that . . .'

'Of course I'm sure! Go and get her.'

Running her fingertips round Carole's stiffening nipples,

Brigit considered ringing Larry and getting him to come back and fuck his wife. But realizing that her plan would end in ruination if Carole knew that Larry wasn't abroad, she wondered where she could find two men to abuse the woman. Picturing two solid penises driving into her prisoner's love ducts, filling her cunt, her bowels with spunk, she contemplated ringing Ravenhugh. *Or three men!*

'You're going to have three girls attending you, your cunt, your tits,' she giggled, grinning at Carole. 'We'll finger your cunt, vibrate your clitty, suck your tits, your long nipples . . . Ah, Sally, how are you?' she asked, turning to face the scruffy little tart.

'Fuck my fuckin' arse 'ole! What the fuck . . .' the girl gasped.

'She's yours to do with as you wish. You can do anything you like to her.'

'Anyfink? Fuck me, I'll start by finger-fuckin' 'er wet fuckin' cunt 'ole!'

Struggling to escape, Carole squirmed and wriggled as the cunt-thirsty slut pushed four fingers into her defenceless vagina and began her fervent thrusting. Watching Lily tweaking their victim's elongated nipples, Brigit felt her clitoris swell. *There are four of us*, she contemplated. *Eight tits, four clitties, four bum holes* . . . Dashing across the room as the reception bell rang, she locked the door behind her and ran down the hall.

'Oh, DI Clarke!' she exclaimed surprisedly, praying that he wouldn't hear the cries of female orgasm when they emanated from the bondage room.

'Ah, Miss Biways, isn't it?'

'Yes, Brigit Biways.'

'Is Doctor Lickman available?' the detective asked, his eyes lowering to the girl's shapely thighs.

'No, he's not here. May I help you?'

'I've come to see him about a netball match. Or, I should say, a nonexistent netball match and a girl who allegedly played netball in the nonexistent netball match who isn't a member of the netball team.'

'Er . . . I'm sorry, I'm not with you.'

'Knickers, Miss Biways.'

'*Knickers?*'

'Convent schoolgirl knickers, to be precise. Knickers, red panties, a sperm-stained nun's habit, stolen photographs, a nonexistent netball match, a missing nun . . . a catalogue of unexplained incidents and serious allegations all centring on Doctor Lickman, Miss Biways.'

'I'm still not with you, Inspector. Photographs, nuns, netball matches . . . what is this all about?'

'Crime, Miss Biways – crime of a most serious and depraved nature.'

'Crime? But . . .'

'Crimes of the flesh, crimes of a debased sexual nature. I have also been informed that Doctor Lickman has two wives – that he's married to two women.'

'Larry's not married!'

'He is, twice over! Tell me, Miss Biways, when will he be back?'

'I . . . I don't know. Look, Inspector, I'm sure we can sort this out. I know a lot about Larry, the practice, his clients . . . why don't you come to the consulting room and we'll have a chat?'

'Yes, that might be a good idea. There are many

unanswered questions playing on my mind. I don't like questions of an unanswered nature, they disturb me.'

'Come with me and I'll try to answer each question in turn, Inspector.'

Entering Larry's consulting room and sitting on the edge of the desk as the detective settled in a chair, Brigit parted her thighs, displaying her hairless pussy lips to the wide-eyed man. Policemen, tax men . . . they were all the same, she reckoned, opening her legs further. They'd all succumb to the offer of a young girl's pussy slit, no matter what their profession!

'So, Inspector, where shall we begin?'

'Er . . . I . . .' he stuttered, staring at her moist, pinken inner lips protruding invitingly from her cunny crack. 'Let's start with the case of Jenny Faggot. She came here to see Doctor Lickman and . . . do you mind closing your legs, Miss? I can't concentrate with you sitting like that!'

'Closing my legs, Inspector?' Brigit smiled innocently, cocking her head to one side and parting her thighs further. 'Don't you like my body?'

'It's not a question of whether I like your body or not – I'm a married man and I can't . . .'

'Do you get on with your wife?'

'Yes, of course I do. Now then, Jenny Faggot visited Doctor Lickman and, allegedly, dropped her knickers as she was leaving the building.'

'Does she shave her pussy?'

'I beg your pardon?'

'Your wife, does she shave her pussy?'

'No! Please, Miss, I . . .'

'I prefer mine shaved,' Brigit smiled, lifting her skirt up

and opening her legs as wide as she could. 'Look, nice and smooth! Why don't you feel my pussy lips, feel how soft and smooth they are?'

'I really don't think I should, Miss!'

'Oh, please!'

'Well, I . . .'

'You're not gay, are you?'

'Of course I'm not!'

'Well, feel my pussy lips, then.'

Reclining, Brigit lay with her feet dangling in front of the desk, her legs wide apart, her miniskirt hoisted up over the creamy plateau of her stomach, her cunt gaping above her suspendered black stocking tops before the steaming sleuth's bulging eyes. He'd succumb, she knew, as she parted her fleshy sex hillocks with her slender fingers, exposing her glistening inner folds, her open sex hole. What normal man could resist such a blatant offer?

Placing his chair between the harlot's stockinged legs, the detective tentatively stroked her swollen outer lips, running his fingers over her warm, smooth skin. Probing between her splayed lips, he slipped a finger into the wet heat of her tight cunt, licking his lips as he thrust his sex-juiced finger in and out of her vaginal sheath.

'Mmm, that's nice!' Brigit breathed, her exposed clitoris swelling. 'You can lick me, lick my cunt out, if you want to.'

'I . . . I really don't . . .'

'Oh, go on! You're fingering my pretty cunt, so why not lick her out?'

Sensing the man's warm breath between her legs, Brigit closed her eyes, waiting in anticipation for his wet tongue

to sweep over her inner folds and lap up her pussy milk. Gasping as he pressed his lips against her stretched flesh, she shuddered as he sucked her clitoris into his hot mouth and ran his tongue over the sensitive tip.

The aphrodisiacal smell of victory accelerating her rising arousal, she shuddered. She'd won! Got the fly exactly where she wanted him – in her glistening sex-web. Now all she had to do was lie back and let him enjoy himself, and he'd leave Larry in peace. It was too easy, she mused as her clitoris pulsated. Her cunt, her weapon, could bring down any man – have any man eating out of her pussy! Or woman, for that matter, she reflected.

'I like you licking my pussy!' she purred. 'Why don't you get your cock out and give me a good fucking?'

'You're not a prostitute, are you?' he asked, slipping his fingers from her drenched hole and licking around the entrance to her lust duct.

'No, I'm not. And if I was, I could hardly charge a policeman for sex!'

'Why are you doing this, then? What is it you want?'

'I want to be fucked, fucked good and proper. And I want you to get off Larry's back.'

'Ah, I might have guessed! So, he's guilty as charged, then?'

'All Larry's guilty of is working hard and enjoying a good sex life. So, are you going to give me the fucking of my life?'

Spying through her eyelashes, watching DI Clarke rise to his demise, Brigit grinned as she heard him unzip his trousers. Praying that he was big, that he'd fuck her senseless, she quivered as she felt his bulbous knob press against the wet

flesh surrounding her open cunt hole. His swollen glans gliding into her vaginal sheath, she gripped the sides of the desk, gasping as her cuntal sheath bloated, stretching to accommodate his huge truncheon.

'I shouldn't be doing this!' he gasped as he began his rampant fucking motions. 'I'm on duty.'

'You're on the job!' Brigit laughed, wrapping her long legs around his body, forcing his solid cock deep into her hot cunt.

'I shouldn't be on the job while I'm on the job.'

'On the job or not, you're doing a good job. There's nothing like breaking and entering! Christ, you've got a big cock!'

'And you've got a tight cunt!'

Thrusting his solid weaponhead in and out of Brigit's spasming cunt, the sleuth grabbed her legs, holding them high in the air, forcing her outer labia to swell around his glistening shaft as he fucked her. Emitting low moans of sexual pleasure, he grimaced, his knob ballooning, throbbing as his sperm jetted into her inflamed vaginal sheath, bathing her cervix as her own climax erupted.

'God, I'm there!' Brigit wailed, her body quivering uncontrollably as her orgasm peaked, erupting within her pulsating clitoris, transmitting electrifying ripples of debased sex deep into her contracting womb. 'Ah, God! Coming! Coming! Ah, my cunt, my beautiful cunt!'

His spunk lubricating the girl's tightening sex cylinder, the detective made his last probing thrusts, ramming her hot cervix with his throbbing glans, draining his heavy balls. Massaging the last ripples of orgasm from her solid clitoris as he slipped his penis out of her brimming cunt, Brigit lay

trembling on the desk, her vaginal lips drenched, inflamed, swollen.

'I . . . I shouldn't have done that,' the man said remorsefully. 'I've overstepped the mark.'

'It was great!' Brigit gasped, her fingers gently caressing her pink cumbud. 'God, you're bloody good!'

'Yes, but now what?' he asked, zipping his trousers. 'This puts a new light on things. Our relationship, detective and criminal, has now become . . .'

'I'm not a criminal!' Brigit protested as she sat up.

'Well, detective and . . .'

'Our relationship is now fucker and fuckee!' she giggled, slipping off the desk and covering her dripping fanny with her microskirt.

'I'd better be going, Miss.'

'You won't be bothering Larry again, will you?'

'The sexual act we have just enacted cannot be allowed to prohibit my investigations into Doctor Lickman's alleged sexual acts, Miss Biways.'

'In that case, all I can say is, the sexual act we have just enacted will have to be revealed to Mrs Clarke.'

'Mrs Clarke? Er . . . that will be enough of your threats, young lady!'

'It's not a threat, Inspector, it's a statement of fact.'

'I'll run you in for prostitution if you're not careful!'

'All right, have it your way. You go and carry on with your investigation, and I'll do as I think fit.'

'As you think fit?'

'I might decide to cry rape. After all, my cunt *is* full of your sperm, isn't it?'

'Er . . . I'll give your proposal some thought, Miss Biways.

You've placed me in a somewhat awkward situation, to say the least!'

'You placed *me* in a somewhat awkward position! Half-naked across Doctor Lickman's desk!'

'Er . . . yes, well, I must get back to the station. Good day to you.'

'Good day, Inspector. And do bear in mind what I said. Oh, I almost forgot! Search Mother Barren-Womb's study, she's into cannabis.'

'Cannabis?'

'Yes, one of the convent girls let it slip when she was here – I thought you ought to know about it.'

'Right! Thank you, Miss – thank you very much!'

'Not at all, Inspector.'

Sighing as her latest hush-cunt victim left the building, Brigit was about to return to the bondage room to see how her prisoner was faring when the phone rang. 'Brigit, it's me!' Larry whispered as she pressed the receiver to her ear. 'What's happening, anything of interest?'

'DI Clarke just fucked me over your desk.'

'Jesus fucking Christ! Have you won him over?'

'It's hard to say, Larry. I asked him whether he'd get off your back now and . . . well, he's thinking about it.'

'Thinking about it? Didn't you threaten him?'

'Yes, but he also threatened to run me in for prostitution. Anyway, forget about him, there's more bad news, I'm afraid.'

'Oh God, now what?'

'Carole Lickman is tied to the examination couch with Lily and Sally Peabody giving her a good seeing to.'

'What? Brigit, you shouldn't have . . .'

'I didn't know what else to do! Besides, she's got a lovely cunt – she tastes really sexy.'

'Fucking hell! Look, I'd better come back. I can't sit in your flat all day doing nothing while . . .'

'Did you look in my bedside cabinet?'

'Yes, I did, and I have to say that I have never seen such a massive double-shafted vibro in my life! Christ, Brigit, you're a dirty little bitch! And as for the assortment of church candles! Where did you get them from?'

'I nicked them from the local church, where else?'

'Good grief! Didn't the vicar mind?'

'Not after I stuffed one up his arse and then swallowed his holy seed! He was OK about them after that.'

'Bloody hell, whatever next? Look, I'll come back and try and sort things out with Carole. Oh, is it OK if I bring the double-shafted vibro with me?'

'Yes, why not? You can shove the shafts up Carole's tight holes!'

'God, no! Look, I'll be there as quick as I can. What we do about Carole, God only knows!'

'We could always kill her.'

'The bitch will kill *me* if I'm not careful! I'll see you soon, Brigit.'

'OK. Bye, Larry.'

Returning to the bondage room, Brigit gasped to discover Carole with heavy weights hanging either side of the couch, connected to her nipples with metal clips. Her breasts painfully stretched into taut cones of flesh, her face grimacing as the girls thrust a massive candle in and out of her hairless pussy, Brigit gazed in awe.

'God!' she cried, moving to the couch. 'You've shaved her cunt!'

'Yes, good, isn't it?' Lily smiled, her face glistening with fanny milk in the light as she looked up.

'And she can't fuckin' say nothin' 'cause I stuffed me fuckin' knickers in 'er fuckin' mouth along with 'er own fuckin' knickers!' Sally chuckled, slipping her T-shirt over her head and exposing her firm, braless breasts.

'Larry's on his way here,' Brigit imparted, eyeing Sally's wedge-shaped nipples. 'What he'll say about this, I really don't know!'

'Oh, good!' Sally squealed, tweaking her erect nipples. 'He can give me fuckin' bum a good fuckin seein' to!'

'I don't think he'll be in the mood for that – not when he sees his wife tied to the couch!'

'Course 'e'll be in the fuckin' mood! There ain't nothin' what 'e likes better than fuckin' me bum 'ole!'

'God, Sally, your language leaves a lot to be desired!' Lily laughed as she thrust the candle in and out of Carole's bloated vaginal cavern.

'Me language leaves a lot of fuckin' what?'

'Nothing,' Lily smiled. 'Well, are we going to cane her tits or not?'

'Fuckin' right we fuckin' are!' Sally grinned, snatching the cane from the shelf.

Shaking her head as Sally began the mammary thrashing, Brigit frowned. Larry would go mad, she knew, as she gazed at Carole's grimacing face, the horror mirrored in her wide eyes. This was no way to deal with the woman, she reflected, wishing she'd never tied her to the couch. Her nipples distended, thin weals forming across the taut

skin of her breasts, her fanny shaved, a huge candle thrust deep into her abused cunt . . . this was no way to deal with her at all!

Leaving Carole to her fate as the reception bell rang, Brigit locked the door and wandered down the hall, her mind spinning, wondering why the practice had become such a disastrous mess. Raising her eyes to the ceiling as she saw Mother Barren-Womb hovering at the reception counter, she sighed. *Now what the hell's going on?*

'May I help you?' she asked the elderly nun.

'Where is Doctor Lickman?'

'Er . . . he's out at the moment.'

'Well, it's not good enough!'

'Well, I'm sorry, but there's nothing I can do about it! He's out, and that's that!'

'Don't you raise your voice to me, young lady! Now, listen – one of my nuns has gone missing and I want to know where she is. Doctor Lickman helped her to escape from the convent yesterday, and I want to know what he's done with her!'

'I'm sure he hasn't *done* anything with her.'

'He was seen leaving the convent with the girl. He drove her away in his car and I want to know what he's done with her. When will he be back?'

'He'll be ages, there's no point in waiting.'

'I *will* wait, in his office – if it's all the same to you!'

Watching the portly penguin stride down the hall, Brigit realized that the practice had become more than a disastrous mess – it was a bloody nightmare! Larry should never have become involved with the young nun, she reflected, leaning on the reception counter. There

again, *she* should never have become involved with Carole Lickman!

'Brigit, what's happening?' Larry asked nervously, creeping through the main entrance clutching the double-shafted vibrator, his dark eyes darting this way and that.

'Larry! Christ, thank God you're here! Mother Barren-Womb is in your study, and she's in a foul mood.'

'Oh God, things are going from bad to bloody worse! Here, take your vibro, you'd better hide it somewhere. Right, I'll deal with Mother Barren-Womb first and then I'll confront that bitch, Carole,' he sighed, holding his head as he ambled down the hall.

Entering his consulting room, he summoned a weary grin for the black blob seated at his desk. 'Mother Barren-Womb, how lovely to see you – yet *again*!'

Turning, her face scowling, the Mother Superior rose menacingly, her fists clenched on her ample hips. 'Where's Sister Mary?' she demanded to know. 'She was seen leaving the convent with you yesterday. What have you done with her?'

'Sister Mary?'

'Yes, Sister Mary! She got into your car and you took her away. Where is she?'

'But I *walked* to the convent, Mother Doom-and-Gloom.'

'My name's Barren-Womb! What do you mean, you walked?'

'I used my feet. It's an ingenious design feature of the human body – if you repeatedly put one foot in front of the other, you'll find that you move along the ground.'

'Don't be ridiculous!'

'No, it works! Watch, I'll show you.'

'I know how to walk, you stupid man! What I meant was, I thought you'd driven to the convent.'

'Oh, I see. Well, as Satan . . . I mean, as God had blessed us with such a lovely day, I thought I'd walk rather than use my car. What with the Chinese laundries, there's more than enough pollution in the air without me driving to the convent and making matters worse.'

'Oh, well, in that case . . .'

'You say that she was seen leaving in a car?'

'Yes, one of the sisters saw her through a window. She left with a man fitting your description.'

'How odd. The plot thickens!'

'Indeed, it does, doctor!'

'Mind you, all men fit my description.'

'No, they don't.'

'Well, all men have two legs, as I do – and a head and two arms and . . .'

'Stop acting the fool!'

'Sorry, I was only trying to be unhelpful. I suggest you contact DI Fart . . . I mean, Clarke, and see what he has to say.'

'He's already on the case, useless man that he is. He can't solve a simple case such as a sperm-stained habit, let alone discover the whereabouts of a missing person!'

'I'm sure he's doing his best. Why not return to the convent and leave him to solve the case?'

'Yes, I suppose I have no choice. Are you sure you didn't drive to the convent?'

'I'd remember if I had, wouldn't I?'

'It might have slipped your mind.'

'No, nothing ever slips my mind. I'm blessed with an airtight mind, Mother Sexterior ... Exterior ... Mother Superior.'

'Airtight? You can't even remember my name!'

'I'm pisslexic ... dyslexic.'

'Are you?'

'Yes, I'm of a dyslexic disposition. I inherited the condition from my sister's father.'

'From your sister's father? Surely, you and your sister had the same father?'

'Did we?'

'Don't you know?'

'We didn't have the same mother, so ...'

'How can she be your sister if you were born of different women?'

'I don't know. Wait a minute! Perhaps I haven't got a sister!'

'You must know whether you have a sister or not!'

'Must I? Yes, I suppose I must. In that case, I can't have a sister.'

'Why not?'

'Because I've never seen her.'

'This is ridiculous, doctor! You're talking utter rubbish!'

'Yes, I do seem to be, I'm so sorry.'

'Well, I'll get back to the convent. Goodbye, doctor.'

'Goodbye, Mother Posterior.'

Grabbing the scotch bottle from the drawer as the troublesome woman left the room, Larry took several gulps to prepare himself for what was bound to be a horrendous confrontation with Carole. He'd not seen her for eight

years, and he'd prayed that he'd never see her again. *Prayers obviously don't work for the wicked!*

'Carole!' he beamed as he jollied into the bondage room. 'How ghastly it is to see you again! Oh, I see the girls have shaved your cunt, how nice for you! Now, what I need is some dirt on you, something to blackmail you with.'

'Hang on!' Brigit gasped as Sally slipped the candle out of Carole's inflamed cunt and lapped up her sex juices. 'I've just remembered that she said she had a husband. Roger, that was it – and then she called him her partner.'

'Really?' Larry grinned. 'Carole, you haven't committed a bigamistic act of bigamy, have you?'

Her eyes reflecting her hatred for her husband, Carole managed to spit the panties from her mouth and scream. 'Release me this minute or I'll . . .'

'Or you'll what?'

'When you married me, you were already married to that slut, Sarah!'

'Carole, my marriage to you was dull and devoid, and now it's null and void, so let's not drag the past up.'

'I'm going to tell . . .'

'Tell your husband, Roger, that you're already married?'

'He's not my husband!'

'That'll be easy enough to check. Lily, for goodness sake, leave her nipples alone for a minute and go and ring the registrar of births, miscarriages and deaths.'

'Miscarriages?' the girl echoed as Carole's sore nipple slipped out of her mouth.

'In my opinion, marriages are miscarriages of justice. Just go and make the call. Ask whether Carole Lickman . . .'

'There's no need to do that!' Carole spat. 'All right, I'm

guilty, we're as bad as each other. Let me go, and I promise you that you'll never see me again.'

'Don't let the fuckin' slag fuckin' go, Larry!' Sally protested. 'She ain't fuckin' licked me fuckin' cunt out yet!'

'I have to let the fuckin' . . . I have to release her, Sally. We have a deal, so she's free to go.'

'It ain't fuckin' fair! I wanted to sit on 'er fuckin' face and bring me fuckin' cunt off in 'er fuckin' mouth!'

'Good grief, Sally, you really are . . .'

'She's a filthy, dirty, disgusting, vile, debased slut of a lesbian!' Carole hissed.

'Oi, no fuckin' slag-bag of a fuckin' slapper fuckin' talks to me like that!'

'You're the most despicable, loathsome, trollop of a girl I have ever come across!' Carole hissed.

'Larry, you ain't fuckin' gonna let 'er talk to me like what she fuckin' did, are you?'

'Sally, Sally! Please, try and make an effort to clean up your language!' Larry sighed as he released Carole's wrists. 'You must stop your incessant swearing!'

'Stop me fuckin' what swearin'?'

'Incessant, perpetual, continual, unending, persistent . . .'

'What the fuckin' 'ell are you fuckin' goin' on about?'

'Nothing, it doesn't matter. Lily, untie Carole's feet, will you?'

'If she's the sort of girl you employ, then I feel very sorry for you, Larry,' Carole remarked as she hauled her aching body upright and covered her weal-lined breasts with her folded arms.

'She's a client, Carole, not an employee. Now, get your clothes on and get out of here!'

'I will, don't you worry!'

'Sally, you'd better go. I'll see you on Thursday as usual. Lily, tidy this place up and then man reception. Brigit, come to my consulting room – I want a word with you. Goodbye, Carole. Please, don't ever let me see your ugly face here again!'

'Walking out on you was the best thing I ever did!'

'I walked out on you, if you remember. Goodbye, Carole!'

Heading back to his consulting room with Brigit in tow, Larry sat in his swivel chair and grabbed the bottle of scotch from the drawer. Shaking his head as Brigit sat opposite him, he smiled at his pretty secretary.

'Well, quite a fiasco!' he chuckled, suddenly seeing the funny side of the dreadful situation.

'Yes, quite!' Brigit grinned, provocatively licking her full red lips.

'So, hopefully, Ravenhugh has been taken care of, Fullcrack and Venereal have backed off, Carole's been dealt with . . .'

'DI Clarke might keep away now, too.'

'Yes, thanks to you and your pretty pussy!'

'That just leaves Mother Barren-Womb.'

'I think she might well be taken care of by now!' Larry laughed.

'Why, what have you done?'

'Did you tell DI Clarke to search the old bat's study?'

'Yes, I did. What have you done, Larry?'

'Planted a plastic bag in her office – a plastic bag full of cannabis!'

'Christ! She'll be arrested!'

'Yes, with any luck! But I still have the debt collectors to face, and my other wife, Sarah. Oh, and several teenaged girls' fathers!'

'Yes, but things are looking better, aren't they?'

'Indeed they are, Brigit – indeed they are! Shit, the bells, the bells! OK, you go and see who's in reception and I'll finish off the scotch.'

'Right, I'll see you later.'

Grinning as he reclined in his chair, Larry contemplated the recent events, and the satisfactory outcome of most of them. Gulping down his sustenance, he imagined the Reverend Mother trying to explain away the bag of cannabis. She'd point the finger of blame at himself, he knew, but there was no proof. He doubted very much that the woman would be arrested – but it would certainly ruffle her cunny-stained grey woollens!

'Doctor Lickman, Miss Kitty Clittie is here to see you,' Brigit smiled, showing a young Japanese woman into the room. 'I'm sorry, but I forgot to check the appointments book.'

'Ah! Er . . . yes, Miss Clittie. Please, take a seat,' Larry invited, slipping the bottle of scotch into the drawer and rising to his feet. 'I'm pleased to meet you.'

'Hallo, doctor,' the exquisite doll smiled, shaking Larry's hand as Brigit slipped out of the room and closed the door.

'This is your first time isn't it, Kitty? Oh, you don't mind me calling you Kitty?'

'No, not at all.'

'Good – I'm Larry. So, this is your first time?'

'Yes, I hope I haven't called at an inopportune moment?'

'No, no, you made your appointment and you kept it – it's just that my secretary forgot to tell me that you were coming. Well, not coming, exactly. Er . . . so, what's the problem, Kitty?'

'Well, I can't achieve orgasm. I've tried everything, but I just can't do it.'

'It's a common problem in women of your age. I've come across it many times, the problem, that is. How old are you?' Larry asked, gazing at the girl's lustrous long black hair framing her exotic face.

'I'm twenty-two.'

Ah, tight, wet, hot! 'Have you ever been able to achieve orgasm, Kitty, or has this problem only recently come . . . I mean, come about?'

'I've never had an orgasm in my life.'

'How do you know that?'

'Well, I'd know if I'd experienced an orgasm, wouldn't I?'

'Not if you don't know what an orgasm is like. If you've never experienced an orgasm, then it stands to reason that you don't know what it's like to experience one. You might have had one, and not known what it was.'

'Well, yes, but . . .'

'You say you've tried everything. What have you tried?'

'My boyfriend, he . . . he's tried oral sex.'

'Tell me the sordid . . . the details of this act of oral sex, Kitty.'

'He licked me, between my legs.'

'What, he licked your thighs?'

'Well, no, between my . . . my vaginal lips.'

318

'Ah, good, good! Have you tried to achieve orgasm on your own, by masturbating?' *By frigging your solid clitty?*

'Yes, he bought me a vibrator, but that didn't work.'

'The vibrator didn't work?'

'No, I'm afraid not.'

'Were the batteries OK?'

'The thing worked, it buzzed and vibrated, but I didn't have an orgasm.'

'Oh, I see. OK, we'll start with the basics – you know where your clitoris is, don't you?'

'Not really.'

'Er . . . obviously, you know where your vagina is?'

'Yes.'

'Your clitoris, Kitty, is situated between your vaginal lips, at the top of your vaginal crack. You can easily identify it with my fingertip . . . with *your* fingertip – it's hard, somewhat like a small pea. If you stretch your vaginal lips apart, pull them up and apart as far as you can, you'll see your clitoris hiding in the top of your sex valley.'

'Shall I try it now, Larry?'

'You don't mind pulling your panties down in front of me?'

'No, you're a doctor, aren't you? Anyway, my father always used to say "Kitty, your body is the body of a woman, and as a woman, you are to offer your body to men for their pleasure".'

'Right, shall we take a look at your clitoris, Kitty?'

'Yes, of course. I do hope I've got one.'

'Don't worry, because if you haven't got one, I have knowledge of a special treatment that will cause the finest clitoris to grow in a matter of weeks.'

319

'Really?'

'Yes, the treatment's called *clitorus fertilisus cum spunkus*. OK, let's have a look.'

Standing, the young woman pulled her tight satin minidress up and tugged her black lace-frilled panties down to her knees, exposing her trimmed, triangular thatch of black pubic hair, her long, oriental pussy crack to Larry's mesmerized eyes.

'I can't see it,' she breathed despondently, yanking her cunny lips wide apart. 'Perhaps I haven't got one?'

God, she's fucking beautiful! 'Er . . . if you'll come round here and allow me to show you,' Larry grinned, his penis swelling as he gazed at her pinken inner sex folds. 'That's it, stand with your feet wide apart. OK, let's have a proper look at you.' Taking her fleshy outer lips between his fingers and thumbs, he stretched her delicate flesh, her clitoris popping out from beneath its protective pink bonnet. 'There it is! Have a look, just there, you see?'

'What, that small pink lump?' the girl asked incredulously, lowering her head and gazing at her neglected cumbud.

'Yes – that, Kitty, is your clitty . . . I mean, your Kitty . . . your clitoris.'

'Oh, so I have got one! But what's it for, what does it do?'

'It will bring you orgasms, when you know how to . . . it might be an idea to go to the examination room and look further up your . . . *into* your problem.'

'How will it bring me orgasms?'

'Well, you see . . . come with me, Kitty, and I'll explain everything to you,' Larry smiled, releasing her cunt lips and rising to his feet. 'I'll instruct you in the fine art of female masturbation.'

'Oh, thank you!' Kitty beamed, tugging her panties up and almost skipping like a lamb after Larry to the bondage room.

The pleasure's all mine!

Closing the door as the girl stood by the examination couch, Larry gazed lustfully at her pert breasts swelling her black satin dress, her nipples clearly outlined by the erotic material. She was a real stunner, he surmised, and he wasn't going to waste any time in getting his fingers, his solid penis, deep into her tight little pussy!

'OK, climb onto the couch,' he smiled. 'Oh, you'd better remove your dress and panties.'

'I do hope this is going to work, Larry,' she said pensively, tugging her dress over her head.

'Oh, it'll work all right!' he assured her, feasting his eyes on her straining black bra, the gentle swell of her suntanned stomach. 'Believe me, I've brought many a woman to . . . I mean, I've helped many a woman in your predicament.'

I've fucked them to orgasm!

Slipping her panties down, Kitty kicked them aside along with her shoes and climbed onto the couch. Her long legs open as she lay down, Larry focused on her pink inner lips protruding between the fleshy hillocks rising either side of her moist pussy crack. *The makings of a good schoolgirlie lookalike!* he mused, imagining her mons, her swollen pussy lips, unveiled of hair.

'OK, we'll start by . . . I think you'd better take your bra off, Kitty.'

'Oh, why do I have to do that?' the girl asked, her alluring slit-eyes looking up at him.

'Well, because . . . because your breasts should come into

321

play during masturbation. Slip your bra off and I'll begin the lesson.'

Sitting upright, she unclipped her bra and peeled the cups away from her succulent breasts. 'There,' she smiled, reclining and resting her head on the couch. 'Now I'm completely naked.'

'Indeed, you are! Er ... right, so ...' *Jesus, I'd give anything to fuck her!* 'OK, drop your feet down either side of the couch, Kitty.'

'I don't know if I'll be able to ... oh, yes, I can!' she declared, opening her legs as wide as she could and lowering her feet by the sides of the couch. 'There, now what?'

What indeed? 'OK, your clitoris, as you have seen, is situated at the top of your sex crack. Your nipples ... during orgasm, Kitty, it's best that your nipples are stimulated. Now, what I'm going to do is attach metal clips to your nipples to add to the sensation of your climax.'

'Metal clips?' the girl echoed in surprise. 'Is that normal?'

Nothing I do could ever be considered normal! 'Perfectly normal, Kitty. Most women have a trinket box or a small velvet bag where they keep their nipple clips.'

'I didn't know that.'

'You see, you're learning already!'

'You're a good teacher, Larry.'

'I am that, Kitty – I am that!'

Taking two metal clips from the shelf, Larry attached them to the girl's elongated nipples, watching her pretty face grimace with the mixture of pain and pleasure as they bit into her sensitive brown milk teats. *Better not use the weights!* he decided, his eyes transfixed on her

darkening areolae as the pinching sensations permeated her firm mammary globes.

'OK, now I'll begin the lesson,' he smiled, running his finger up and down her gaping vaginal fissure. 'During masturbation, the vaginal muscles convulse, rhythmically tightening and relaxing. To add to the debased sensations . . . the *heavenly* sensations, I'm going to give your muscles something to grip on.'

'Such as what?' the girl asked, lifting her head and staring at the metal clips squeezing her aching nipples.

'A candle, Kitty. I'm going to shove a . . . *slip* a candle into your vaginal orifice to give your muscles something to hold on to.'

'A candle? Is that normal? I mean, surely, women don't use candles?'

'They use anything they can get their hands . . . yes, they do, Kitty. In fact, I was reading in the *Medical Journal* only the other day that doctors are now being advised to instruct their patients to push candles into their vaginas daily.'

'Whatever for?'

'To firm and tone the muscles. Many women, as they become older, tend to suffer vaginal problems due to the slackening of the muscles. Now, your cunt's very . . . your vagina, no doubt, is very tight, but later in life . . . suffice to say that regular use of candles will keep your vagina tight, youthful, hot, wet . . . er . . . in good shape.'

'OK, whatever you say, Larry.'

Taking the largest candle from the shelf, Larry held the girl's swollen sex pads wide apart and gently pushed the

candle deep into her tight cunt. Gasping as her inner flesh stretched to accommodate the massive phallus, she closed her eyes. The candle finally coming to rest against her cervix, she arched her back, the sensations of crude sex already beginning to permeate her naked body.

Larry grinned smugly. This was all he wanted out of life – to be alone in the bondage room with a beautiful fresh girl naked on the examination couch, a candle pushed deep into her wet cunt, her nipples painfully pinched by metal clips. Tax men, the police, the health authority, Gina Cology . . . they could all go to hell as far as he was concerned! Jumping as the door suddenly burst open, his stomach sank as he focused on Sarah, his first wife – his wife!

'Ah, er . . . Sarah, how are you?' he stammered, releasing the candle and jumping back from Kitty's blatantly abused naked body.

'So, I've caught up with you!' the attractive blonde hissed as the girl leapt off the examination couch, the candle shooting out of her cunt and rolling across the floor as she grabbed her clothes and fled the room. 'My God, you haven't changed, have you? Sexually abusing innocent young girls, as always!'

'She happens to be a client!' Larry returned angrily, disappointed at the premature loss of his latest plaything.

'A client? What, with clips on her nipples and a candle up her . . . you owe me money, Larry! Twenty thousand pounds, to be exact!'

'Er . . . what a lovely day!' Larry grinned, opening the window. 'We're having a lovely summer. Well, I must dash, Sarah! Bye!'

Leaping through the window, he sprinted across the car park, his wife's environmentally unfriendly words wafting on the wind.

'Larry! Larry, come back here – you adulterous, two-timing, perverted, thieving bastard!'

Chapter Ten

'One from the fucking tax man, one from the electricity board, one from . . . this looks interesting, Brigit,' Larry said, showing the girl the envelope. 'A hand-delivered pink envelope, that's strange! Ah, it's probably from some horny young hussy who's dying to have my cock spunking up her hot, tight, wet cunt!' he chuckled.

'You shouldn't have come in this morning, Larry. I thought you were going to lie low for a while?'

'I haven't come this morning!'

'This is serious, Larry!'

'At the end of the day, when all's said and done, when we've lived and loved and fucked and climbed out of the shit-pit again and again – nothing's really serious, is it?'

'I still think you should have stayed away for a few days! Anyway, I haven't heard anything from your wives this morning, and DI Clarke has been ominously quiet. He's probably feeling guilty about fucking me rotten over your desk!'

'Yes, let's hope your beautiful, succulent, hot, tight, wet pussy has done the trick! God, I need a fuck!'

'You can fuck me later, give me a good seeing to! God, my cunt's so wet!'

'The wetter the better! Are you wearing panties?'

'No, I'm not. I've given up the idea of selling dirty knickers, it takes far too long to soil them – and I prefer to have my pussy bare.'

'So do I! When did you first start creaming your panties?'

'I suppose I was about twelve when I started juicing my knickers. When I was in my early teens I used to lie in bed at night and finger my cunt and then suck my juices from my wet fingers. Actually, I still do!'

'God, you're a horny little bitch, Brigit!' Larry laughed.

'Oh, I'm becoming wetter by the minute!'

'I'll drink from your cunt later! Did anyone come nosing around after I'd left yesterday?' Larry asked, ripping the envelope open.

'No, nothing happened at all. No girls' fathers, no debt collectors . . . not even a call from Mother Barren-Womb.'

'She's probably been banged up for possession of cannabis!'

'Imagine that in the papers – Reverend Mother arrested for . . .'

'Christ!' Larry gasped. 'This letter's from Monica! Look, she wants to come back to work!'

'Don't be daft! She wouldn't come back here for all the sperm in China!'

'She says that she was wrong about me and she's sorry for all the trouble she's caused.'

'Obviously it's a trick!'

'I'm not so sure, Brigit. She says that . . . bloody hell, she reckons she really likes me!'

'She's gone off her bloody head! She's obviously set this up with Gina. I reckon she thinks that, by working here again,

she'll be in a position to get hold of some inside information. She won't give up, Larry, I know that much!'

'Yes, you're probably right. She wants me to ring her. Trick or not, I'd better call the old bat and discover what her game is.'

'OK, call her now. I'll be in reception.'

'Right. Where's Lily?'

'In the toilet.'

'Jesus Christ, I really must do something about that girl!'

'She's beyond help, Larry!'

'I'll have to think of a new form of treatment for her. How about having three men fuck her three orifices? That would induce a subconscious reaction, although I'm not sure what kind!'

'That's something I've always dreamed about – having three men fuck my three holes, all spunking into my naked body.'

'Really? Well, I'm sure I can arrange it for you! Talking of debased, filthy, disgusting, wonderfully perverted sex – are there any clients booked in for this morning?'

'Yes, Molly Molest. I was going to deal with her myself but, as you're here, perhaps you'd . . .'

'When's her appointment?'

'She's due any time now.'

'Oh, God, I was hoping to have a quiet morning.'

'I'll deal with her, if you like.'

'No, it's OK, I'll see her. Send her in when she arrives. Right, I'd better go and ring the Moodie witch.'

Sitting at his desk, Larry read the puzzling letter again, contemplating its contents, wondering why Monica had

suddenly decided that she liked him. After all the woman had been put through, tied to the couch, having her fanny hair removed, her cunt licked out, he couldn't understand why she wanted to see him again, let alone work for him. *She knows about my wives, my false qualifications . . . it must be a trick!* he reflected, lifting the phone and dialling her number. *It must be!*

'Monica, it's Larry.'

'Oh, hallo, Larry,' she replied sheepishly. 'You . . . you got my letter?'

'Yes, I've just read it. What's this all about? You say that you really like me, and you want to come back to work?'

'Yes, I . . . I've been thinking and . . . since my husband went, I've been pondering on your words.'

'Which words?'

'All the things you've said about sex and Catholics and . . . well, naked people in cornfields and men entering public toilet cubicles together. I realize how very wrong my thinking has been. As you said, I've not been looking before I've leapt.'

'I see. Well, I'm not sure that it would be a wise move, you coming back to work here, Monica. After all you said yesterday about my wives, my qualifications . . .'

'I've been very wrong about you. I really enjoyed the work, Larry, I'd love to come back. I've also come to realize that my life has been so dull and dreary. Compared to the life you lead, I might as well be dead!'

'But, Monica, after all the damage you've done . . . listen, I have a client arriving any time now – come and see me later and we'll talk about it.'

'All right, I'll do that. And I'm sorry for . . .'

'Yes, I know. Just come and see me.'

'Yes, I will. Goodbye.'

'Bye, Monica.'

'Would you credit it?' Larry gasped, replacing the receiver and rubbing his chin. 'Would you fucking credit it?' Deciding that it would be far better to have Monica working for him so he could keep an eye on her, he decided to take her back. 'I suppose I *do* miss the old hag!' he chuckled, opening the letter from the Inland Revenue. *I miss taunting the inorgasmic old witch! I'd better give her a good thrashing when she arrives!*

'Right, that's fucking it!' he stormed, banging his fist on the desk. 'You fucking bastard, Ravenhugh! You fucking, cunting, spunk-bubble of a fucking arsehole!'

'God, what *ever* is the matter?' Brigit cried as she burst into the room. 'Larry, what the hell . . .'

'Fucking Ravenhugh, that's what's the fucking matter! He's reassessed my fucking tax demand and the cunt wants thirty thousand fucking pounds!'

'After all I did for him? I sucked him off, he fucked Christine . . . what a cunt-faced bastard!' Brigit stormed.

'What this bloody country needs is a revolution!'

'Let's get him back here, and Lily and I will tear his cock off and chew his balls to a pulp!'

'Yes, yes, that's a bloody good idea, Brigit!'

'What, tearing his cock off and chewing his balls to a pulp?'

'No, getting him back here. We've got the photographs, remember? OK, Brigit, find out his wife's phone number and arrange for her to come here. I know, tell her that her husband has been taken ill. Tell her that he's here and he

wants to see her. Also, get Ravenhugh here to coincide with his wife's visit and we'll . . .'

'And we'll make sure she catches him fucking my wet cunt!'

'Yes, brilliant! God, what a fucking brilliant plan! Christ, with my brain, I should be running the fucking country! Revolution, here I come! OK, get onto it. Oh, and get that dodgy photographer in the High Street to develop the film.'

'OK, I'll do that first.'

'Power to the masses! Storm the Inland Revenue! Bomb Customs and Excise HQ! I know, let's commandeer St Thomas's Hospital!'

'Why?'

'Because it's right opposite Parliament. If we set cannons up in the wards, one in the labour ward, one in geriatric, one in the canteen . . . don't you see, Brigit? We could fire shells across the Thames and . . .'

'We can't do that, Larry!'

'Why not?'

'Well, it would disturb the patients! Think of some poor woman giving birth with a fucking great cannon going off by her bed, firing shells through the window.'

'Oh, yes, I hadn't thought of that. I know, we'll hijack a pleasure boat – you know, one of those glass-topped boats. We'll install the cannons, machine-guns, missile launchers, and sail past Parliament and let them have it!'

'You've gone mentally insane, Larry!'

'Oh, I thought it was a pretty good idea. It would solve my income tax problem.'

'Yes, but you'd be better off taking less extreme measures, like murdering Ravenhugh, for example.'

'Yes, yes, you're right. OK, you set him and his wife up, and we'll deal with him that way. It's a shame, it would have been fun sailing up the Thames and . . .'

'I'll leave you to daydream, Larry!'

'Oh, yes, right. OK, Brigit – go, go, go!'

Pacing the floor as Brigit dashed from the room, Larry grinned. 'Right, what's on the agenda?' he mused excitedly, his stomach somersaulting in his elation. 'OK, destroy Ravenhugh's marriage, that's a good start. Get Lily out of the toilet – no, I haven't got the mental energy to waste on the daft girl! Ah, yes, kill Sarah . . . no, I'd better not do that! At some stage, I'd better catch up with the latest news on Mother Barren-Womb.'

Grabbing the ringing phone, he perched himself on the edge of his desk. 'Doctor Lickman speaking.'

'This is Mother Barren-Womb!' the woman bellowed in his ear.

'Ah, good morning Reverend Mother – I was just thinking about you.' *About ripping your clitoris off!* 'Tell me, how's the executive director keeping?'

'Who?'

'The chairman of the world.'

'What *are* you talking about?'

'Your boss, God – how is He?'

'Blasphemy!'

'I'm sorry if you feel that I've blasphemed, I only asked how . . .'

'You'll be cast into the eternal fires of hell! Now, you .

listen to me! I know that you planted cannabis in my study, and I . . .'

'*Me*, Reverend Mother? I can assure you that . . .'

'Your assurances are worthless!'

'Are they really? Good grief, I'd better get onto my life assurance company at my latest inconvenience and defile a complaint! I'll add them to my list of targets.'

'Don't be ridiculous, you know very well what I mean! You've caused me a lot of trouble, Doctor Lickman. I've had the police and sniffer-dogs roaming all over the convent.'

'Was there a smell?'

'A smell?'

'The sniffer-dogs, were they sniffing out a smell?'

'Only from your lump of cannabis! Now ten sixth-form girls have been arrested for possession! What do you have to say about that?'

'It serves them right, Mother Bar Room!'

'You know very well that my name's Barren-Womb!'

'Oh, yes, of course – I do apologize. Put it down to my pisslexia.'

'Pisslexia?'

'Yes, I . . .'

'The parents are up in arms and the . . .'

'Are they revolting?'

'Revolting?'

'Goodness me, word gets round pretty fast when there's talk of a revolution!'

'What revolution?'

'Er . . . nothing. God, the phone's probably tapped! I'd better be careful what I say. So, the parents are up in arms – I mean, they're upset.'

'They're understandably distressed by the arrests of their daughters!'

'Young girls shouldn't be smoking cannabis – it's not natural. Come the revolution, I'll . . .'

'Natural or not, the convent's reputable reputation has been irreparably wrecked.'

'That's quite a mouthful! Try saying it faster.'

'What *are* you talking about now?'

'Tongue twisters.'

'Tongue . . . listen to me, Doctor Lickman!'

'I'm surprised that you allow the girls to smoke dope in school, Reverend Cover.'

'I *don't* allow them!'

'Oh! So you're saying that you have no control over your pupils? Your position of authority carries no weight whatsoever when it comes to exerting authority?'

'I am *not* saying that! What I'm saying is . . .'

'What I fail to understand is why you allow the girls to smoke cannabis. It's hardly teaching them the Lord's way, is it? Apart from that, it's against the law – until I get in, that is!'

'I have already told you that I do *not* allow them.'

'Mind you, what with that burning bush episode in the Bible, perhaps it *is* the Lord's way.'

'The burning bush has nothing to do with . . .'

'I'll bet the burning bush was a huge cannabis plant and old Moses went staggering off on a high, having hallucinations of angels and . . .'

'Don't be ridiculous, of course the burning bush wasn't a cannabis plant! Anyway, the girls know full well that it's against the rules.'

335

'Why were they in possession of cannabis, then?'

'Because they *broke* the rules!'

'Rules are made to be broken. Not many people realize it, but that's the twelfth commandment – rules shalt be broken.'

'The twelfth? What's the eleventh, then?'

'Women shalt mastur—'

'There are only *ten* commandments! And I doubt very much that you adhere to one of them!'

'I adhere to them all, Reverend Mother. Have I coveted your wife?'

'My wife?'

'Have I killed you, stolen from you, worshipped a false Reverend Mother, been unfaithful to . . .'

'You don't know what you're talking about! Burning cannabis bushes, Moses hallucinating . . .'

'Don't I? Many a true word, Mother – many a true word!'

'Listen to me, you troublemaker – DI Clarke is going to deal with you. He isn't stupid, he knows that you planted the cannabis in my study.'

'Can he prove it?'

'He'll find a way, don't you worry!'

'Oh, I never worry, Mother Wooden Spoon.'

'I see little point in continuing this futile conversation, Doctor Lickman!'

'Ah, we agree on something, at least!'

'Yes, we do! Goodbye!'

'Goodbye, Reverend Brother – and may your Devil go with you!'

'I hope you burn in the eternal . . .'

Banging the phone down and walking to the window, Larry contemplated his next move. What was DI Clarke up to? he wondered, gazing at a young woman pushing a pram along the street. *Christ, I'll bet she fucks something rotten!* The reception bell resounding through the hall, he turned and left the room, wondering how many teenaged cunts were in the world at any one time. *Talking of cunts, I must contact DI Clarke.*

'Good morning, Molly!' he greeted the petite brunette as he entered the foyer. 'And how are you on this fine summer morning?' *Juiced up and ripe for a fuck?*

'Hi, Larry,' the pretty girl smiled. 'I'm all right.'

More than all right! 'OK, let's not waste any time, Molly – to the examination room!'

'I . . . I have a problem, Larry. I need to talk to you before we . . .'

'Oh, right. Er . . . come into my consulting room and we'll have a chat,' he smiled, walking down the hall.

Seating the girl at his desk, he scrutinized her ballooning white blouse, the profile of her long nipples clearly defined by the tight silk material. Her pretty mouth half open, as if about to speak, she offered a nervous smile as she twisted her long chestnut hair round her slender fingers. Wondering what her problem was, why she'd not dived into the examination room for her fortnightly vibrator-induced multiple orgasm – the cure for *clitorus insensitivus* syndrome – Larry returned her smile and reclined in his swivel chair.

'So, Molly, what's the problem?'

'I can't sleep at night,' she confessed softly. 'I lie awake thinking of penises.'

337

Ray Gordon

And I lie awake thinking of juicy cunts! 'I see. How long has this penile-induced insomnia been going on?'

'For several weeks now. I've always had a fixation, a fetish, I suppose, for penises. Since I first saw a boy's stiff penis behind the bike sheds at school, I've not been able to get the vivid pictures of male organs out of my mind.'

'Where was this stiff penis, Molly?'

'I've told you, it was behind the bike sheds.'

'What, lying on the ground, hanging on a rusty nail?'

'No, it was attached to the boy's body.'

'Oh, yes, I see. For a minute, I thought you meant . . .'

'I really don't know what to do! At night, I close my eyes and see an image of a huge erect penis, and I can't get to sleep.'

'So, there's one penis in particular?'

'There used to be several, but now there's just the one.'

'Do you recognize the penis? I mean, are there any distinguishing marks to enable you to identify the owner of the organ in question?'

'Well, I suppose I like to imagine that I know who it belongs to. I . . . I can't tell you who I imagine it belongs to, it's too embarrassing.'

'The man in question, you've never actually seen his penis?'

'No, I haven't seen it, I just imagine it to be his. It's magnificent! I lie in bed at night, the image of the wonderful organ clear in my mind – and I masturbate until the early hours.'

'Yes, you do look a little tired.'

'What can I do, Larry? I can't go on night after night like this!'

338

'Don't distress yourself, Molly. This is a rare condition known as *penisus erectus maniacus*. Roughly translated from old Lickuanian, it means a maniacal craving for the erect penis. You'll be pleased to hear that there's a cure for this peculiar condition . . .'

'I want to be able to sleep at night but . . . well, I don't want the penis to go away. I mean, I'd miss it, wouldn't I?'

'Yes, but if we're to . . .'

'I know what the answer is. The man I imagine to be the owner of the penis, if he were in my bed with me, we'd make rampant love until I was sexually satisfied, sexually fulfilled – and then I could sleep.'

'The man you imagine to be the owner of the penis – is he married?'

'No, he's not married.'

'Is he aware of your feelings?'

'I haven't felt him! If I had, then . . .'

'No, what I meant was, is he aware of your feelings for him, your emotions?'

'Oh, I see. No, I can't bring myself to tell him.'

'You must, Molly. You must tell him of your emotional torment without further delay.'

'No, I can't. I wish I hadn't told you about the penis now.'

Desperate to examine the young girl's exquisite vaginal folds, Larry sighed. The last thing he needed was a boring discussion about another man's penis! But Molly was obviously distressed, and the only way he'd get his fingers inside her hot, wet cunt was to play along with her, put her mind at rest. Racking his brain, he suddenly had an idea.

'Molly, I'm going to show you *my* penis,' he smiled. 'I

want you to touch it and fondle it. The theory is that my penis will replace the imaginary penis.'

'But I . . .' she began hesitantly as Larry leapt to his feet and whipped his erect organ out.

'There, what do you think of it?' he asked proudly as he stood before her, his huge weapon pointing skywards, only a foot away from her popping green eyes.

'It's . . . it's wonderful!' she gasped, reaching out and pulling his foreskin back. 'Oh, it's so wonderful!'

'Molly, this psychological approach necessitates . . . how can I put it? Have you ever taken a penis into your third vagina?'

'My third vagina? Where's that?'

'It's your mouth.'

'Oh! So where's my second vagina?'

'Your bottom-hole.'

'My bottom-hole? But, surely, my vagina is . . .'

'Not many people realize that females have three vaginal orifices, Molly. Think yourself lucky that I've imparted this little-known fact to you. So, have you ever taken a penis into your third vagina, into your mouth?'

'Well, I . . .'

'The reason I'm asking you is because I believe you to be suffering from penile deficiency.'

'No, I've never taken a penis into my mouth.'

'Ah, I thought as much! What about your second vagina, your bottom-hole?'

'Certainly not!'

'It's so sad to see women blatantly neglecting their vaginal orifices. In fact, it's verging on criminal! You'll have to change your ways, Molly.'

'Yes, I'll try.'

'Right, I'm pleased to hear it. Now, penile deficiency is a condition usually only found in nunneries. The nuns, being chaste, suffer penile deficiency as a result of years of penis denial.'

'I didn't know that!'

'Oh, yes! In monasteries, the monks suffer from vaginal deficiency due to years of vaginal denial. Mind you, unlike the nuns, they make up for it by replacing the vaginal sheath with each other's . . . yes, well, I won't go into the sordid details of the sexual behaviour of monks. I want you to take my penis into your mouth and suck it, Molly.'

'Suck it?' she asked surprisedly, examining his silky-smooth glans.

'Taking my penis into your third vagina, into your mouth, will have a beneficial subconscious effect. You see, sucking my penis and swallowing my sperm will re-educate your subconscious, it will bring about a deep-seated subconscious transformation.'

'Oh, I see. But . . .'

'Trust me, Molly. And believe me, I'm not doing this for *my* benefit! I very rarely go to such lengths to serve my clients.'

'It's very good of you to go out of your way to help me, Larry.'

'There are times when going above and beyond my duty is deemed well within the line of duty, and this is such a time. Now, open your third vagina and suck my penis and swallow my sperm.'

'All right, if you think it will do me good.'

'I *know* it will do me good . . . I mean, do *you* good.'

Watching the delectable girl part her full red lips and take his knob into her hot mouth, Larry gasped, his penis twitching as she explored his glans with her wet tongue. Her lips stretched around his solid shaft as he thrust out his hips. Driving his purple plum to the back of her throat, he hooked his heavy balls out of his trousers.

'Fondle my balls!' he breathed, his warm scrotum pressing against her chin. 'Ah, yes, that's it! Good girl! Run your tongue around the end of my penis, that's it! Ah, God! Think about what you're doing, Molly, think of my knob in your mouth, think about my sperm coming out, filling your beautiful third vaginal orifice!'

Sucking, rolling her tongue over his throbbing glans, Molly closed her eyes, concentrating on her act of oral sex, waiting in anticipation for his sperm to gush from his cockhead and fill her cheeks, desperate for her first taste of salty spunk. His body becoming rigid, his face grimacing as the beginnings of his orgasm stirred, Larry took the girl's head in his hands. *She's not going to escape my spunk!*

'Ah, here it comes, Molly!' he gasped as his sperm coursed up his penile shaft and jetted from his pulsating glans. 'God, I'm coming!' His spunk bathing her sweeping tongue, filling her cheeks, her eyes bulged as she tried to pull away. 'You must drink it all!' Larry breathed, driving his orgasming knob to the back of her throat. 'You must swallow my spunk!'

Gripping her head and rocking his hips, Larry fucked the pretty girl's mouth, shooting his jism down her throat until he'd drained his rolling balls. His shaft glistening with her saliva as he slipped his purple knob out of her baptized mouth, he stood trembling before

her as she lapped up the droplets of white liquid from his slit.

'My God!' Monica cried as she entered the room to gaze in horror at the lewd scene. 'I have never witnessed such a vile and debased act!'

'Monica!' Larry gasped, concealing his penis and hurriedly zipping his trousers.

'Good gracious! You're a dirty little slut, forcing the doctor to commit such a vile and degrading act! Get out of here!'

'No, Molly, don't go!' Larry pleaded as the distraught girl fled the room with sperm running down her chin.

'Doctor, are you all right?' Monica asked concernedly.

'Of course I'm all right! What do you mean by . . .'

'Oh, you poor man! I've met her type before, luring professional men to commit vile sexual acts. Fancy coming here and forcing you to commit such a depraved sexual felony! Despicable, that's what she is!'

'But I thought . . . Monica, you usually blame me!'

'That's where I've been going wrong, Larry. I now realize that these young hussies have been forcing themselves upon you, coercing you into committing filthy, disgusting, degrading sexual acts.'

'What? I don't understand.'

'It's all right, Larry – I'm here to look after you now.'

'But . . .'

'I'll make sure that these despicable hussies leave you alone. Right, I'll go and man reception. Are you sure you're all right after your horrendous experience? It must have been a terrifying ordeal!'

'Yes, yes, I'm fine.'

'Good, let's hope nothing like that ever happens again! I'll be in reception.'

Shaking his head in disbelief as the woman left the room, Larry frowned. 'What sort of trick is this?' he breathed. Whatever Monica's game was, he had no idea. All he could think was that she was feigning her allegiance only to expose him when she'd gathered enough evidence of his debauchery to nail him once and for all. Realizing that he should tell her to go, that she'd be nothing but trouble, he decided to have a lengthy and hopefully enlightening chat with her later.

Ringing the police station, Larry asked to be put through to DI Clarke, praying that Brigit and her alluring pussy had done the trick. If the detective was still hell-bent on persisting with his investigations, he decided he'd take a leaf out of Monica's book. *Side with the enemy,* he mused. *Feed him more false information concerning Mother Barren-Womb and her convent.*

'DI Clarke,' the sleuth finally replied.

'Inspector, it's Doctor Lickman.'

'Ah, Doctor Lickman, you've been conspicuous by your absence of late.'

'Yes, I . . .'

'Well, I'd better fill you in on the latest allegations made against you.'

'Allegations, Inspector?'

'Cannabis.'

'No, I'm sorry, I haven't got any.'

'I do not wish to purchase . . .'

'I know a man who . . .'

'Do you, now? Give me his name and address.'

'No, I meant, I know a man who . . . well, I know a man, that's all.'

'Doctor Lickman, Mother Barren-Womb alleges that you planted a quantity of cannabis in her study.'

'I haven't planted cannabis in her study! You'd need a greenhouse to plant it in, not a study – and it's the wrong time of the year. The spring is the best time to . . .'

'Planted as in placed, doctor – not sown!'

'Placed? Why would I place cannabis in her study?'

'Why indeed? The convent . . .'

'Talking of the convent, has the missing nun been found yet, Inspector?'

'No, she's still at large.'

'From what I remember of her, she was slim, petite and . . .'

'At large as in on the loose! Are you always so difficult to converse with?'

'When in oral communication, I must say that my conversation is completely converse to your allegation.'

'What?'

'Opposite, Inspector. My conversational skills don't prove to be difficult, they are converse to your statement stating that I have difficulty conversing.'

'What *are* you . . . can we please move on, doctor? Let's discuss the convent schoolgirl's knickers I have in my possession.'

'Oh, yes, let's!'

'There *was* no netball match. The girl, Jenny Faggot, *was* not in the netball team, *is* not in the netball team, and has no chance of *join*ing the netball team.'

Ray Gordon

'Then why did she change into her netball kit, Inspector? The cream thickens . . . I mean the slot . . . the plot . . .'

'She didn't change into her netball kit because she *has* no netball kit, and she cannot play netball and does not even *attempt* to play netball.'

'She can't play netball?'

'No, she can't. She doesn't own a netball skirt, a netball top, netball socks or netball knickers.'

'Are you saying that she left my establishment knickerless?'

'Yes, that's exactly what I'm saying.'

'Good grief! I really can't believe that I've actually had a knickerless schoolgirl in my long-established establishment!'

'You'd better believe it because I can tell you that the judge will!'

'The judge? Was there a knickerless judge in my establishment?'

'Please, Doctor Lickman! Now, you say that you found the girl's knickers on the floor?'

'Yes, that's right – in the hallway.'

'I put it to you, doctor, that you removed the girl's knickers. Now, come on, let's be having the truth.'

'Yes, I did remove them.'

'Ah, so you confess to removing the aforementioned knickers?'

'I can't deny it, Inspector.'

'Are you prepared to sign a sworn statement to that effect?'

'Yes, of course. I removed the girl's knickers from the hall floor.'

'What?'

'I removed the girl's knickers from the . . .'

'Yes, yes, I heard what you said.'

'Then why . . .'

'I can see that this conversation is leading nowhere. I'd better come and see you, doctor. By the time we've finished our conversation, your phone bill will have run into thousands of pounds!'

'Oh, right. Well, I'll look forward to your visit.'

'Good day, doctor.'

'Yes, I'm hoping it will be. Goodbye, Inspector.'

Replacing the receiver, Larry rubbed his chin. DI Clarke obviously had no intention of abandoning his enquiries into his escapades. *There's only one thing for it*, he reflected. *Brigit will have to open her pretty pussy again!* Walking to reception, he decided to feed Monica some false information to discover whether or not it found its way back to the prying detective. *They're probably in this together!*

'Ah, Monica!' he smiled as he approached the counter. 'Jenny Faggot is on her way to see me. I'm going to examine her, an internal examination of a vaginal nature, so will you make sure that I'm not disturbed when I'm locked in the examination room with her?'

'Locked in the . . . yes, of course.'

'Thank you. The last thing I need is someone hammering on the door trying to find out what I'm up to!' he chuckled.

'Er . . . yes, right. Oh, by the way, talking of being locked in, Lily has locked herself in the toilet and she won't come out.'

'Yes, I know. Leave her in there, it's the best place for her while she's encountering one of her toilet-induced mental traumas.'

'Yes, of course.'

'Jenny Faggot will be here any minute now. Er . . . would you pop across the road and get me some stamps from the post office, please? Take the money from petty cash.'

'Oh, er . . . what, now?'

'Yes, please. I'll cover reception while you're gone.'

'Yes, of course. You say that Jenny will be here any minute?'

'Yes, that's right. Oh, by the way, keep this to yourself, Monica. I'd rather Mother Barren-Womb didn't know about the girl's visit – or DI Clarke, come to that!'

'Yes, I see. I missed working here, it's so good to be back, Larry.'

'And it's good to have you back, Monica.'

Grinning as the woman took some change from the petty-cash box, Larry watched her leave the building, his plan formulating perfectly. 'Lily!' he yelled, dashing to the toilets. 'Lily, quickly, I need your help!'

'I'm not coming out!'

'You'll come out this instant or I'll kick the door down and thrash your vaginal lips with the cane!'

'Shan't!'

'Lily, I'm warning you! Come out now, or I'll have my entire army of revolutionaries queue up to fuck your arse!'

'Shan't!'

'Unless you open the door, I'll tie you to the examination couch and have ten women rub their nipples all over your naked body!'

'Shan't!'

'And ten men wank and splatter their spunk all over your face!'

'What do you want?' the neurotic girl asked, sliding the bolt back and emerging from the cubicle.

'Come to the examination room and I'll tell you. I've just devised a plan so devious, so shrewd, so cunning, that I have to say that I'm a bloody mastermind! Come on, Monica will be back any minute.'

Locking the door as he entered the bondage room with the morose girl, Larry smiled. 'OK, when I tell you, I want you to make whimpering noises, sexual noises, orgasmic noises.'

'You want sex with me?'

'No! Well, yes, but not now. Pretend, Lily – pretend that you're on the couch with a candle up your cunt, a finger up your bum and a vibrator pressed against your clitty bringing out the best orgasm you've ever had.'

'Why pretend? Why can't I . . .'

'Because I've a strong hunch that someone is going to come bursting through the door.'

'Bursting through the door? Who would do a thing like that?'

'Detective Inspector Clarke, accompanied, no doubt, by Monica Moodie!'

Explaining the situation to Lily, Larry wondered where Brigit had got to. She'd only gone to the High Street, he reflected. She should have been back long ago! Thinking it a shame that the girl wouldn't be around to witness his moment of glory, he paced the floor, praying that Monica was ringing the detective and telling him of his imminent debauchery.

'I wonder how Gina Cology's doing?' he asked Lily, checking his watch.

'I don't know, but I'd like to have Melinda here again and cane her breasts. It really helped me with my problem, whipping her breasts.'

'I'll have to arrange it for you, Lily. I wouldn't be surprised if the time comes when Monica is tied to the couch again. You can cane her huge tits, if you like.'

'Oh, yes, I'd love that!'

'Hang on!' Larry breathed, dashing across the room and pressing his ear to the door as he heard movement in the hall. 'OK, Lily, that's your cue!' he whispered, recognizing the sleuth's distinctive low voice. Murmuring, moaning, whimpering, Lily assumed her role of an orgasming female with remarkable zest – and authenticity!

'Oh, God, it's heavenly! Ah, ah! Ah, don't stop!'

'That's great, keep going!' Larry grinned, noticing a shadow through the drawn curtain. *Good, they've got the place surrounded!* 'Really scream with sexual pleasure, Lily! You're coming as you've never come in your life before!'

'Ah, God, my cunt! Ah, oh, oh, my beautiful clitty!'

The door suddenly shattering, splinters of wood scattering across the floor, DI Clarke flew across the room, crashed into the far wall and crumpled to the floor. 'Shit!' he cursed, climbing to his feet and rubbing his head. 'Shit, fuck and shit!'

'Inspector Clarke!' Larry gasped, concealing a wicked grin as Monica made her timely appearance in the doorway. 'What on earth do you think you're doing?'

'I ... er ... I tripped and fell through the door,' he stammered, holding his bruised arm as he gazed at Lily, his suspicious eyes frowning to see the girl fully clothed.

'You really should be more careful, Inspector! You

could have broken something! As it is, you've broken my door.'

'Yes, yes I'm sorry about that. Er . . . are you all right, Miss?' he asked Lily.

'Yes, I'm perfectly all right.'

'I . . . I thought Jenny Faggot was . . . was coming to see you,' Monica stammered, turning to face Larry.

'She cancelled.'

'What were you doing in here, Miss?' the detective asked Lily. 'What was the reason for you being in this room with the doctor?'

'She was helping me to tidy up, Inspector,' Larry smiled. 'As Monica's been away, the place was in dire need of a woman's touch, so I commandeered Lily.'

'We heard screaming and moaning!' Monica gasped.

'Yes, I heard that, too,' Larry replied. 'I thought it was someone outside the building, I was about to go and take a look.'

'My men are . . .' the detective began. 'I mean, there's no one outside. Well, I'll be getting back to the station.'

'Didn't you want to see me?' Larry asked.

'Oh, er . . . no, it can wait. I'll see to it that you're reimbursed for the cost of the repairs to the door, doctor. Er . . . good day to you all.'

Waiting until the inspector had left, Larry turned to Monica. 'Well, whatever next?' he quipped. 'Fancy tripping over and crashing through the door like that!'

'Yes, yes, I saw him trip as he approached the door.'

'He must have been running down the hall to hit the door hard enough to smash the lock. Oh, well, at least he's going to pay for the damage.'

'Why did Jenny Faggot cancel her appointment?' Monica asked suspiciously. 'It's rather odd that she cancelled at the last minute, and just when I'd gone to the post office.'

'There's nothing odd about a client cancelling an appointment while you're at the post office, Monica!'

'No, no, I suppose not. Well, I'll get back to reception. Has the girl made another appointment?'

'Yes, she's booked in for next week. Right, I have another sixth-form girl arriving shortly. Lily, would you be good enough to clear up in here, please?'

'I need the toilet.'

'What for?'

'To try and get my foot . . . I mean, to go to the loo.'

'You can do that after you've cleared up,' Larry smiled, leaving the room. 'Knowing you, you'll spend the rest of the day in the toilet!'

Contemplating matters while sitting at his desk, wondering whether Monica would believe that another convent girl was due, Larry pondered on the woman's next move. *She might call the sleuth back*, he mused. But, her plan having failed miserably, she might not try the same trick again. Putting himself in her shoes, he reckoned her next move would involve Gina Cology. But how, he had no idea. Gina had been ominously quiet of late – perhaps she was formulating new plans for his downfall?

Hearing voices emanating from reception, Larry leapt to his feet and crept across the room. Spying round the door and gazing down the hall, he gasped in horror to see Sarah. 'Jesus, my fucking wife's back!' Dashing to the window, he was about to make his escape

when the woman burst into the room and slammed the door shut.

'Oh, Sarah!' Larry grinned sheepishly, closing the window. 'I was just getting some fresh air. How nice to see you again.'

'I'll give you nice!' the woman spat, folding her arms and scowling menacingly.

'Yes, we did have some nice times together, didn't we? Do you remember when we went to Spain on holiday? Oh, happy, happy days!'

'Happy days? You screwed the chambermaid!'

'Well, yes, I suppose I did. But it was an innocent accident, my angel.'

'Don't you angel me! What do you mean, an innocent accident?'

'Well, there I was changing into my swimming gear, and she came in and threw her naked body across the bed and demanded crude sex.'

'You didn't *have* to screw her arse!'

'No, you see, I thought it was you, my loveliness. It was dark and . . .'

'It was in the middle of the day!'

'Yes, but the curtains were drawn. They're very thick, Spanish curtains. Anyway, that's how the accident happened.'

'Accident, my fanny!'

'You've had an accident with your fanny? Would you like me to take a look?'

'You keep away from me! What about the time when I caught you screwing our next-door neighbour's daughter in the potting shed?'

'Ah, yes . . . I was looking for some six-inch flowerpots for my geranium cuttings when she wandered into the shed by mistake.'

'By mistake?'

'Yes, the silly girl, she thought she was in her own garden, in her father's shed! Again, it was pretty dark, and when she pulled my dick out and sucked my knob into her hot, wet . . .'

'You screwed her!'

'Well, sort of.'

'What do you mean, sort of? You either screwed her or you didn't!'

'Well, I did, but only by accident, my sweet.'

'I am *not* your sweet! You deliberately screwed the poor girl over the workbench!'

'Well, put that way . . .'

'I suppose you're going to tell me that the illegal and debased incident up at the sheep farm was an innocent mistake?'

'Yes, you see, I was in the lambing shed trying to help a sheep . . .'

'All right, I don't want to hear the sordid details! What I *do* want to hear is how much money you're going to give me.'

'Ah, money, yes! As it happens, I don't have any money, my little petal.'

'Don't lie! And stop calling me ridiculous names!'

'Sorry, my little . . .'

'I've discovered quite a lot about you over the last couple of days. For starters, you own a nice house.'

'I rent it.'

'No, you don't! Secondly . . .'

'Would you like me to fuck you in lieu of . . .'

'My God, you get worse!'

'It was only an idea, Sarah. I was trying to resolve your problem for you.'

'*You*'re the one with a problem!'

'We *all* have problems, Sarah. So, how have things been? I expect you were devastated when I walked out on you?'

'I left *you*, if you recall.'

'Oh, yes, of course – the schoolgirlie incident in the park.'

'*Incident?* Is that what you call it?'

'That's what the police called it. Do you have a man at the moment, Sarah? Several men, perhaps? Several hundred . . .'

'I have *a* partner, yes. He's a decent man, a hard-working . . .'

'What's his name?'

'Ian.'

'What would Ian say if he discovered that you'd been coming here for several months to have your cunt screwed by my bloody great cock?'

'Oh, no! Don't think you can . . .'

'Does he know you're here now?'

'Well, no he doesn't.'

'I have witnesses to the alleged screwing sessions, Sarah.'

'What do you mean?'

'Well, there's my secretary, Brigit, and my trainee sex therapist, Lily. They'd both be willing to . . .'

'I'm going, Larry!'

'Oh, so soon?'

'Yes, but I'll be back – you can be sure of that!'

Sighing as the distraught woman left the room and slammed the door shut, Larry held his hand to his head. *God, whatever next? One minute things seem to be getting better, and the next* . . . Gulping from the scotch bottle, he swung round on his heels as Brigit opened the door.

'Sorry I've been so long,' she smiled. 'He developed the photographs while I waited.'

'Oh, good, good!' Larry beamed, taking a large brown envelope from the girl.

'They've come out really well. I'm going to contact Ravenhugh and his wife next and arrange the end of their marriage.'

'Great! OK, what I'll do is . . .'

'I see Monica's back.'

'Yes, and she's up to her old tricks already!'

'Larry, there's a young woman at reception talking to Monica.'

'Is there? What about it?'

'She looks suspicious to me. They were laughing, as if they were old friends. When I came in, they went quiet.'

'I've a pretty good idea what Monica's up to, Brigit.'

'I really don't think you should have taken her on again.'

'I didn't, she sort of took herself on.'

'She'll be trouble, Larry, you mark my words! Well, I'll go and organize this Ravenhugh business.'

'OK, see you later.'

Scanning the photographs as Brigit left the room, Larry grinned. *Got you now, Ravenhugh!* he thought happily, gazing at a shot of the tax man with his erect penis driving deep

into Christine's wet cunt hole. Slipping the incriminating evidence into his desk drawer, he wondered what Monica was up to in reception. This was another set-up, he was sure as he made his way down the hall and smiled at the pretty blonde chatting at the counter.

'Doctor Lickman,' Monica began, smiling nervously. 'This is Holly Holdall.'

'Hallo, pleased to meet you,' Larry greeted the girl, shaking her hand.

'Hi! I was just saying to your receptionist that I'm in a desperate situation. I haven't got an appointment, but I was wondering whether you had the time to see me now?'

I wouldn't mind seeing what you've got inside your panties! 'Yes, as it happens my next client hasn't turned up so I'm free. If you'll follow me.'

Leading Holly into his consulting room, Larry closed the door and offered her a seat. She was in her early twenties, he reckoned, and decidedly fuckable! But, sure that he'd been set up, he knew that he had to be very careful. Monica, no doubt, had planned to catch him in the examination room with his solid cock embedded deep within the girl's tight cunt. One slip, and he'd not only find himself deep in the girl's wet vagina but deep in the shit as well! Who had Monica lined up as a witness? he wondered, admiring the swell of the girl's firm breasts through her tight T-shirt. Who was waiting to pounce the minute he'd impaled the little beauty on his rock-hard cock? DI Clarke and his merry men, no doubt!

'So, Holly, what's the urgency to see me?' he asked, sitting opposite her.

'I have a problem,' she began, tossing her golden locks

357

over her shoulder and provocatively licking her glistening red lips. 'For some reason, I've suddenly become a nymphomaniac.'

'Suddenly? When did this happen?'

'About three weeks ago.'

'What, just like that?'

'Yes, literally overnight.'

'I see. Tell me, what events led up to the fateful night in question?'

'I'd been out with a girlfriend for a drink. Nothing unusual happened, we had a drink and a chat and then went our separate ways. When I got home, I realized that I was in a state of acute sexual arousal.'

'How did you feel, exactly?'

'Acutely sexually aroused.'

'What did you do?'

'I did something that I'd never done in my life before – I masturbated.'

'You'd never masturbated before? Not even when you were a teenager?'

'No, never.'

'Was it nice?'

'Yes, very! I lay in the chair with my legs over the arms and masturbated for several hours.'

'How would you describe yourself before the night of literal overnight transformation?' Larry asked, sure that he recognized the girl, her features strangely familiar to him.

'Well, I wouldn't describe myself as a prude, but I was never particularly sexual.'

'What have you been doing, sexually speaking, over the last three weeks, since the as yet inexplicable transformation?'

'Taking man after man home for nights of crude sex, masturbating eight or nine times every day, buying porno magazines . . .'

'Yes, yes, I see. As a psychosexual sexual therapist of sexology, it's all becoming very clear to me, Holly. Tell me, how's your relationship with your parents?'

'OK, I suppose – about average.'

'What does your father do for a living?'

'He's . . . he's a . . . what's my father's profession got to do with my problem?'

'It might have everything to do with it,' Larry smiled. 'I'd say that this was a parental-based problem. I'd better physically examine you. Although this would appear to be a psychological problem of a psychologically based nature, I'll check you physically before we go any further.'

'What does that entail, exactly?' Holly asked, her blue eyes locked to Larry's.

'Basically, it entails a physical examination. Er . . . would you mind waiting here for a moment?' he smiled, rising to his feet. 'I have something to do before I take you to the examination room.'

Leaving the room, Larry wandered down the hall to reception, sure that he knew the girl from somewhere. Monica wasn't at the counter, which fuelled his suspicion that he'd been set up. *Is this a trap?* he wondered, going down the hall into the bondage room. What was the plan? And where were Monica and DI Clarke hiding?

'Brigit!' he called, walking back to reception. 'Lily! Where the hell is everyone?' Leaving the building, Larry scanned the car park for his staff and the boys in blue. 'This is crazy!' he breathed, walking back through the main door

and checking the waiting room. 'Brigit! Lily!' Wondering whether the detective could be holding the girls, keeping them at bay while the raid took place, he decided to take Holly to the examination room. To take another step closer to the trap – without falling in!

'Right, if you'll come with me, Holly,' he smiled, peering round his consulting-room door.

'Oh, right!' the girl trilled, leaping to her feet. Grinning as she followed him, she seemed overly eager to go ahead with the examination, Larry observed. Feeling uneasy, sensing that the entire police force were about to storm the building and catch him red-knobbed, he suddenly had an idea.

'Holly, I've just remembered that I have an appointment with my bank manager,' he said apologetically, leading the girl into the bondage room. 'I'm sorry, but I'm unable to examine you now.'

'Oh, that's a shame,' she replied disappointedly, sitting on the examination couch, her short skirt riding up to expose the triangle of red silk covering her swollen sex.

'I'd completely forgotten about it. I've a head like a sieve!'

'Can't you just take a quick look at me?' the bad blonde asked forlornly, parting her shapely thighs further.

'No, I'm afraid there's no time. Look, I feel bad about this, Holly. I'll tell you what I'll do. I don't normally see clients during the evenings but, if you're able to come here this evening at, say, eight o'clock, I'd be only too happy to examine you and continue with our discussion.'

'Eight o'clock, yes, that should be all right,' she agreed, slipping off the couch and tugging her miniskirt down to conceal her panties. 'Er . . . will we be alone? I mean,

normally there'd be a nurse or someone present during an examination, wouldn't there?'

'I have a trainee sex therapist who's usually present during examinations – I'll make sure she's here this evening, OK?'

'No, it's all right – I don't mind being alone with you. Right, until eight, then,' Holly smiled, leaving the room.

'Yes, until eight.'

Frowning as he watched the girl make her way down the hall, Larry was sure that there were eyes spying at him, people lurking, waiting to pounce the minute he'd slipped his fingers into her tight sex hole. *Why does she want to be alone with me?* he wondered. Brooding on her familiar features, he returned to his consulting room and took the bottle of scotch from the drawer.

'Come the revolution . . . I still say it's a bloody good idea! Parliament is right opposite St Thomas's Hospital. If we take out Westminster Bridge and . . . what the fuck am I talking about?' *Oh well, all I do now is wait*, he mused, flopping into his swivel chair and swigging from the bottle. *Wait and see who asks searching questions about Holly's untimely departure!*

Chapter Eleven

Larry'd dialled Brigit's and Lily's numbers several times during the early evening without success. Where his staff had mysteriously disappeared to, he had no idea. Even Monica hadn't answered her phone, and he wondered whether they'd all felt that things had become too dangerous and done a runner. *To hell with them!* he thought, lolling back in his chair as he swigged from the Bell's. *I have young Holly to look forward to!*

The time nearing eight, he was becoming increasingly positive that Holly wasn't being used as bait in DI Clarke's trap – if there was a trap. Her familiar features still worried him, but he was determined to enjoy the pleasures of her naked body without the fear of a police raid spoiling his fun. He'd examine her, he mused, his penis swelling agreeably – tie her naked body to the couch, cane her taut buttocks, and then fuck her senseless! *I'll remove her cunt-hair first, though!*

Leaping to his feet as the reception bell rang out, he rubbed his hands together, his rampant cock now solid at the prospect of abusing the young delicacy. 'Ah, Holly!' he beamed as he left his consulting room and walked briskly down the hall.

'Hallo,' the girl smiled, her tight miniskirt doing little to

conceal her scarlet panties, bulging with their warm, fleshy cargo. 'I'm not too early, am I?'

It's the early bird who catches my stiff worm! 'No, no. Right, let's go to the examination room!' Larry beamed, rather too impatiently.

Leading the girl down the hall, he thought it might be an idea to check outside the building before stripping and abusing her curvaceous young body, before cleansing her sweet cunt with his sinuous tongue and slipping his wily penis deep inside! *Just a quick look round for DI Clarke and his gang*, he decided, imagining rifle-wielding police hiding behind their cars, bellowing through loud hailers.

'Right, Holly, if you'll remove your clothes and lie on the couch, I'll be with you shortly,' he smiled, gazing at her ballooning T-shirt, her nipples pressing alluringly through the tight material. *God, I'm looking forward to this little tart!* 'I'll only be a minute.'

'Where are you going?' she asked, stepping out of her shoes and yanking her T-shirt over her head, revealing her straining white lace bra.

'I'm only going to . . . I won't be long.' *Cleavage sex? Yes, why not?*

Checking the car park before walking round the building, Larry was satisfied that there were no spies, no one waiting to pounce the minute he'd slipped his erect penis deep into his victim's tight pleasure centre. Entering the building and bolting the main door, he locked the toilet and waiting-room doors as an added measure of security. Making his way back to the examination room, he locked his consulting-room door. *That'll take care of the bastards!* he chuckled inwardly. His stomach somersaulting, he imagined his solid glans

embedded inside Holly's tight anal duct, his gushing spunk filling her bowels. *Jesus, what an evening of perverted filth this is going to be!*

Returning to his waiting feast, he gazed hungrily at the girl's naked body laid out on the couch – the swell of her firm breasts, her dark areolae and udder-like nipples. His eyes roaming over her smooth, flat stomach, the neat indent of her navel, he focused on his favourite area of the female form – her pink vaginal crack, clearly visible through her sparse blonde pubes. She was a rare beauty, he adjudicated, licking his lips. A rare beauty indeed, and no one was going to spoil his evening of debauchery – no one!

'Right, Holly, I'll begin with an internal examination just to make sure that things are in order,' he explained, parting her long legs and grinning as her vaginal slit opened, gaping invitingly, exposing her moist, unfurling inner petals.

'I think I'm physically OK,' she murmured, focusing on Larry's beaming face as he peeled her succulent pussy lips apart, laying open the wet entrance to her tight cunt. 'I mean, everything's working properly.'

'As I said earlier, I'm sure that this is a psychologically based psychological problem, but . . .'

'What do you mean, a psychologically based psychological problem? Surely, all psychological problems are psychologically based?'

'Not necessarily, Holly. Some psychological problems are physically based.'

'Physically? But how can they be?'

'I won't bore you with the technicalities. Suffice to say that I want to eliminate the slight chance of a physical defect causing a psychologically based psychological problem

leading to . . . leading to what, I don't know now. I seem to have confused myself, psychologically, I mean.'

'Something physically wrong wouldn't turn me into a nymphomaniac, would it?'

No, I suppose not. 'Oh, yes, that *can* happen,' Larry asserted, his finger sliding into the wet warmth of her pinken sex orifice. 'For example, should your G-spot become overdeveloped, the electrical impulses sent from your vagina to your brain would trick your pleasure centre, and you'd become extremely sexually aroused.'

'Really?' she gasped as he slipped two more fingers into her tightening lust hole.

'Oh, yes – I've come across many an overdeveloped clitoris in my time, too.' *Spunked over dozens of clitorises!* 'What happens is, the abnormally numerous clitoral messages confuse the brain, leading to rampant and completely uncontrollable psychological sexual arousal resulting in a perpetual physical craving for orgasm.'

'Oh, I see – I think! Is my G-spot OK?'

'Yes, perfectly. Right, now for that small but very important organ, your clitoris,' he smiled, taking the vibrator from the shelf. 'I'm going to stimulate your clitoris with the clitoral massager and piston my fingers in and out of your vaginal canal to determine your sexual response.'

'You're going to use a vibrator on me?' she gasped surprisedly.

'Well, it's listed in the gynaecological instruments catalogue as a clitoral massager but, seeing as it vibrates, I suppose you could call it a vibrator.'

'Do you usually use a vibrator on your clients' clitorises?'

'Oh, no, I only use it when I need to determine clitoral

response.' *When I want to juice up their cunts before I fuck them!*

'How many women do you examine each day?'

'It depends – sometimes one, sometimes ten.'

'You enjoy your work, do you?'

'It's just a job, Holly – just a job. Someone has to do it, and that someone's me.' *What's this? The bloody Spanish Inquisition?*

Switching the vibrator on, Larry pressed the buzzing tip against the girl's already swollen sex nodule, grinning as she immediately responded by emitting low moans of pleasure. Thrusting his fingers in and out of her wettening vaginal sheath as she arched her back, he realized that she was quickly nearing her climax. *The more comings you sow, the more you reap!* he mused, his penis now painfully ballooning within his trousers.

'Ah, God!' Holly cried, her head tossing from side to side, her golden tresses veiling her flushed face as her orgasm welled within her young womb. 'God, it's . . . it's heavenly!'

'You're responding very well,' Larry praised his gullible client, gazing at her areolae darkening in her arousal, her nipples like bullets.

'I'm . . . I'm coming! Oh, God, I'm coming already!'

'It's the vibrator . . . I mean, the clitoral massager. It's designed to . . .'

'Ah! Yes, yes! God, I'm . . . I'm there!'

Her naked body shaking violently, her mouth open, gasping, the girl screamed as her orgasm gripped her, sending electrifying pulses of sex through her perspiring flesh. The vibrator sustaining her incredible pleasure, the

orgasmic shockwaves rolled through her curvaceous body, taking her ever higher to her sexual paradise. His thrusting fingers drenched with her girl-come, Larry held the vibrator against her pulsating clitoris, gazing in awe at her inflamed outer lips as they reddened and swelled to an incredible size. *She really is a nympho!* he mused happily as she sang out in her coming. *A real, live nympho!*

'Oh, God! Please, no more!' Holly begged, her knuckles whitening as she gripped the sides of the couch. 'Please, please, no more!'

'You did very well,' Larry smiled, moving the vibrator away from her aching clitoris as she propped her exhausted body up on her elbows.

'That was beautiful!' she gasped, her pretty face flushed. 'God, that was quick! I've never come so fast before! What are you going to do to me next?'

'I'll examine your breasts.'

'While you're down that end of my body, perhaps you should examine my bottom?' she grinned, seductively licking her succulent red lips.

Frowning as he slipped his fingers out of her drenched love duct and switched the vibrator off, Larry thought again about the girl's familiar looks. Suggesting that he examine her bottom set alarm bells ringing in his mind – but his insatiable craving to lust over girls' naked bodies would get the better of him, he knew!

The girl was more than overly eager to be examined, he reflected as she rolled onto her stomach and lay with her long legs wide open. Was this a set-up? he wondered again as she turned her head and flashed him a salacious grin. *Who the hell is she?*

'I've just got to nip into my consulting room, I won't be a minute,' he said, eyeing her rounded, taut buttocks, her long vaginal fissure nestling between her parted thighs, her succulent, swollen outer labia irrigated with cunt milk. Walking into the hall, his suspicion rising, he left the building and checked the car park again. *Nothing!* he mused, rubbing his chin pensively as he walked round the building. *No DI Clarke, no Monica . . . nothing!*

Closing and locking the main door, he became confused. Brigit had said that Holly had been laughing with Monica, as if they were old friends, and yet . . . *Shit, I can't let an opportunity like this slip through my fingers*! Back in the bondage room he decided to go for it, to use the girl's vulnerable body to satisfy his ever-rampant craving for debased, perverted sex – despite the consequences!

'OK, I might as well check your anal canal,' he said, taking the jar of honey from the shelf and parting her firm buttocks. 'You might well have an anal tract problem causing you to become dangerously sexually aroused.'

'That doesn't follow!' Holly argued, turning her pretty face and gazing into his deep-set eyes.

'It's very common in lesbionic nymphomaniacs. You see, the anal sphincter muscles spasm, sending impulses to the clitoris, causing the erectile orgasm to swell and yearn for the relief that orgasm brings.'

'Oh, right,' she murmured, resting her head on the padded couch.

Pouring a good quantity of the golden honey over her tightly closed bottom-hole, Larry imagined his penis penetrating her there, bloating her tight rectal duct as he drove his knob deep into the very core of her young

body. Had she ever had her bum fucked? he wondered in his deepening perversity. One thing was for sure – she wouldn't leave the bondage room until he'd taken her anal virginity!

'Oh, what's that?' she asked surprisedly as the thick liquid ran down her anal valley to her bulging sex lips.

'It's called Honeylube. It's a special lubricant I use for anal examinations,' he replied, replacing the honey jar and taking the largest candle from the shelf. 'Have you ever had a rear end . . . I mean, an anal examination before?'

'No, no, never.'

'OK, I'm going to insert my rectal dilator into your bottom, Holly. It might hurt a little, but it has to be done.'

'You must do whatever's necessary, doctor – I'm completely in your hands.'

Completely at my mercy!

Stretching her rounded buttocks wide apart, exposing her small brown hole, Larry pressed the pointed end of the candle against her anal ring, grinning wickedly as the wax piston glided into her tight rectal cylinder. Gasping as her bottom-hole progressively yielded to the tapering shaft, Holly parted her legs further, projecting her buttocks, offering the very sexual core of her young body to the depraved quack. Wondering whether the time had come to lash her naked body to the couch with rope and fuck her tight arsehole, Larry thought again about the girl's familiar looks, sure that he knew her from somewhere.

'God, that feels heavenly!' Holly gasped as he pushed the candle fully home, the delicate brown tissue surrounding her hole opening to at least two-and-a-half inches. 'I'm sure you don't do this to all the girls you examine!'

'This is the recommended method of examining anal canals,' Larry replied. 'Right, while the dilator is doing its job, I'll massage your vaginal walls to relax your muscles and we'll continue our discussion.'

'Oh, oh!' the girl trilled as he drove four fingers into her hot lust duct and kneaded her sex-drenched inner flesh. 'Oh, that's . . . that's nice!'

'I'm only doing this to relax your vaginal muscles, Holly. Tell me, when did you first discover masturbation?'

'I began masturbating when I was thirteen.'

That's a lie! She said the first time was three weeks ago! 'How did you discover the fine art of female masturbation?'

'I was in the bath washing when . . . I was rubbing the soap between my legs, between my vaginal lips, and it felt really good. I lay on my back in the hot water with my feet resting on the edges of the bath and kept rubbing. Suddenly, I shuddered and my whole body became alive and – woosh! I masturbated every day after that – I have done ever since. Oh, that's nice, keep rubbing inside me!'

Lying bitch! What the hell's she up to? 'This may seem like an odd question but it's important that I know if I'm to help you. At what age did your pubic hair grow?'

'Er . . . I was about twelve, I suppose.'

'Tell me the sordid . . . the details, Holly.'

'The details?'

'Yes, where they first sprouted, what you thought, what your . . . your vulval flesh looked like.'

'They grew just above my vaginal crack. Just a few hairs, about a dozen at first, and then they spread.'

'And your breast buds, tell me about their development.'

'Well, first my nipples became larger, sensitive, and then my breasts swelled.'

'I see. Have you ever sucked your nipples?'

'Oh, yes, many times.'

'Again, this may sound like an odd question but have you ever had a lesbian relationship?' he asked unashamedly, gently twisting the candle, massaging her velveteen anal flesh.

'Yes, with a girl I knew at school. We were in my bedroom one weekend, just playing around, fighting on the bed – and she kissed me.'

'And then what happened?'

'She pushed her tongue into my mouth and it made me feel all funny, really sexy.'

'Was this after you'd discovered masturbation?'

'Yes, I was about fourteen. She lifted my skirt and slipped her hand down the front of my knickers and masturbated me. God, did I come!'

'Did you masturbate her?'

'Oh, yes, I did. We got completely carried away and licked each other's clitties. My parents were out and we ended up naked on the bed doing anything and everything to each other.'

'Did you enjoy sex with her on a regular basis?'

'Yes, most weekends, until we left school – then I lost touch with her.'

'You've not had a lesbian relationship since?'

'No, but I've often thought I'd like to.'

Slipping his long fingers out of her rhythmically tightening sex sheath, Larry took several lengths of rope from the shelf. The girl had described herself as not particularly sexual before her sudden transformation into a nymphomaniac,

he reflected – yet now she'd revealed that she regularly masturbated and often thought she'd like a lesbian relationship! There was something very strange going on, he concluded. Either she was a genuine nymphomaniac, or the bait for the trap – but which? If this *was* a trap, then he'd taken the bait. So why wasn't DI Clarke reeling him in? Trap or not, his penis yearning for the welcoming heat of her wet cunt, the time had come for the real fun to begin.

'OK, I'm going to massage your feet to check your anal reaction.'

'Anal reaction? How will massaging my feet . . .'

'It's reflexology, Holly,' Larry replied patiently, tying lengths of rope to her ankles. 'You see, particular points on the feet correspond to certain parts of the body. Your big toes correspond to your nipples, your little toes to your vaginal lips, your heels to your clitoris, your insteps to your anal canal . . . there, that's it!' he grinned, securing the ropes to the legs of the couch.

'Oh! You've tied me down!' the girl cried, turning her head and trying to lift her naked body.

'It's all part of the examination,' Larry reassured her. 'Lie flat and stretch your arms out so I can secure your wrists.'

'But . . .'

'Holly, you *do* want me to help you, don't you?'

'Well, yes, but . . . I've never heard of a doctor tying his patients down before!'

Neither have I! 'It's a new method recently devised by the BMA,' he smiled, spreadeagling her arms and tying her wrists to the couch legs. 'They not only highly recommend it, but they supply the ropes free of charge. There, now you're ready for the *real* examination!'

'Real examination? What do you mean, *real*?'

'You're ready to have my knob examine your cervix!' he chuckled. 'You'd like my big cock stuffed up your hot, wet cunt, wouldn't you?'

'Oh, God, yes!' Holly breathed, much to Larry's surprise. 'Really give it to me!'

This was definitely a set-up! he thought fearfully. He knew that he should send her packing before the storm broke. But, his penis thirsty for her wet sex hole, his heavy balls rolling, his lechery outweighed his better judgement. Eyeing the candle emerging between her taut, unblemished bottom cheeks, he decided that a good thrashing was in order. Taking the cane from the shelf, he raised his arm, bringing the thin bamboo down with a resounding crack across her twitching buttocks.

'Argh!' she screamed, trying to struggle free of her bonds. 'No, please, what are you doing?'

'Caning your beautiful bum!' Larry laughed, striking her tensed orbs again.

'No, you can't do this!'

'I can and I am! There's nothing I like better than thrashing young girls' bottoms!'

Chuckling as thin pink weals began to fan out across her twitching flesh, Larry brought the cane down again and again, delighting at the helpless girl's cries for mercy. With no one around, no chance of Monica hammering on the door and demanding to know what was going on, he was in his element, and he thrashed his young prisoner with a vengeance.

'Oh, oh! Please, that's enough!' she whimpered, her naked body squirming beneath the cane. 'Ah, God, my bum!'

'Your bum's lovely, Holly! I'll fuck your hot bum-hole after I've thrashed you!'

'Ah! Oh, please, please!'

'Ah, you're begging for more! Yes, I like that!'

Continuing the merciless thrashing as Holly's buttocks turned bright scarlet, Larry brought the cane down again and again. Spurred on by her incessant screaming as the candle shot out of her spasming anal sheath and flew across the room, he thrashed the backs of her legs. Almost incoherent words of sexual pleasure bubbling from her pretty mouth, Holly began to emit low moans of satisfaction.

'Ah, so you *do* like it!' Larry grinned, thrashing the soft skin of her legs just below her burning bottom orbs.

'My bum, do my bum again!' she pleaded. 'Ah, yes! Harder, cane me harder! God, I'm . . . I'm coming!'

Her lust juice pouring in torrents from her open sex hole, Larry thrashed Holly's stinging bottom to the accompaniment of her cries for more. *A first-rate nymphomaniac!* he decreed, bringing the cane down as hard as he could, the deafening cracks resounding round the room. His arm beginning to ache, he administered the final blow, breaking the cane in two as it struck her crimsoned bum cheeks.

'Well?' he grinned. 'Did you like that?'

'My clit!' the girl whimpered. 'Please, I'm coming, rub my clit!'

'Like this?' Larry chuckled, reaching between her warm thighs and parting her wet pussy lips. 'Is this what you want?' he breathed, massaging her solid clitoris.

'Ah, yes, yes! Don't stop! Oh, God, my cunt! Coming, coming! Ah, God, I've come!'

'I'll fuck your cunt in a minute!'

'Yes, please, fuck me now!'

Grabbing another candle from the shelf, Larry forced it deep into her rectal sheath, stretching her delicate brown tissue wide open before whipping his solid penis out and climbing onto the couch. Positioning himself between her splayed thighs, he retracted his foreskin, exposing his silky, purple knob in readiness for the vaginal fucking.

Working his ballooning glans between her honey-sticky cunny lips, Larry located the entrance to Holly's cuntal sheath and drove his swollen shaft into her hot lust duct. Gasping as he withdrew and thrust his knob into her tight sheath again, his belly slapping her taut, weal-lined buttocks, he managed to grab the end of the candle and phallus-fuck her tight arse.

'Like it?' he panted, thrusting into her two lust holes.

'God, yes – it's incredible!' she gasped, her naked body rocking with the double pummelling. 'Is this what you do to all your clients?'

Might as well play her game, whatever it is. 'Yes, I screw all clients.'

'Has it ever caused you problems?'

'How do you mean?'

'Well, clients reporting you for . . .'

'No, never. Do you mind if we chat later – it's not easy to discuss clients and fuck at the same time!' he breathed, his knob ballooning within her accommodating cuntal duct.

Repeatedly driving his solid organ deep into the girl's juicy receptacle, Larry sensed his climax quickly approaching. *I'll fuck her pretty mouth next!* he decided, ramming the candle deep into her hot bowels. *Her cunt, then her mouth, and then her tight arse!* His shaft wet with her juices of sexual arousal,

he continued his fucking motions, bringing out her second shuddering orgasm.

'I'm coming again!' she wailed, her tethered body shaking violently. 'God, I'm coming again! Harder, fuck me harder!' On and on Larry drove his huge organ, deep into her tight vagina, until her sex sheath gripped his cock like a velvet-jawed vice as his spunk gushed from his pulsating glans. Filling her hot cavern with his copious flow of sperm, he fucked her until his swinging balls had drained and she almost passed out in her sexual delirium. Finally withdrawing his girl-wet penis, he hauled his trembling body off the couch and stood by her side, swaying in the aftermath of his incredible climax.

'Jesus Christ! God, you're fucking good!' he gasped, slipping the candle out of her abused anal canal.

'So are . . . so are you!' the girl whimpered, lifting her tear-streaked face. 'Never in my life have I come like that! God, I could have you fuck me all night long!'

'I might just do that!' he laughed, zipping his trousers and releasing the trembling girl. 'Have a rest, and then I'll fuck your bum-hole!'

Jumping at the sound of smashing glass, Larry dragged the girl off the couch. 'Fuck me! Quickly, get dressed!' he ordered her. Bolting out of the room as another pane of glass shattered, he stopped outside his consulting room. 'What the fuck . . .' he gasped, hearing moaning noises emanating from the room. Pressing his ear to the locked door, it was evident that someone was in there. But who? he wondered as the intruder climbed to his feet, pieces of broken glass tinkling to the floor.

'You all right, Sergeant?' DI Clarke's unmistakable voice whispered.

'Yes, Guv, I think so. This is the wrong room.'

'The wrong room? Jesus, you blithering idiot!'

'You told me to break into this room, Guv!'

'It doesn't matter what I told you, you're a bumbling idiot! Go and let me in through the main door!'

'This door's locked, Guv.'

'Bloody hell, what a botch-up! All right, you'd better get out of there. We'll try the window round the side.'

Holding his hand to his head, Larry suddenly realized why Holly's features were so familiar to him. 'The inspector's bloody daughter!' he breathed, dashing into the bondage room as she finished dressing. 'Your name's Clarke, isn't it?' he accused the cowering girl.

'Er . . . no, no, it's . . .'

'You're that copper's bloody daughter!'

'No, I . . .'

'Right, come with me!' he hissed, grabbing her arm.

Marching his prisoner down the hall, he bundled her into the waiting room and opened the window. 'Get out of here!' he whispered angrily, pushing the girl through the window. 'And don't come back!'

'No, please, I don't want to go!' she protested, peering through the window at Larry. 'You're right, he is my father, but . . . the plan was . . .'

'Yes, I know what the bloody plan was!'

'I've changed my mind! I liked the things we did. Please . . .'

'Changed your mind, my arse! Go on, piss off out of here!' Larry hissed through gritted teeth, closing the window and

watching the girl run off into the night. 'Thank God for that! Right, now I have to face DI bloody Clarke!'

Dashing into the bondage room, Larry opened the window as the sergeant was about to lob a brick through the glass. 'Fuck me!' he cried, leaning out of the window. 'What the fuck do you think you're doing!'

'Ah, Doctor Lickman! Open the main door, I'll meet you there,' DI Clarke called, emerging from the shadows. 'Sergeant, you keep an eye on the building and make sure that my . . . that no one leaves.'

Opening the main door, Larry frowned at the detective as several of his men filed into the building and began searching for the girl. 'What on earth is going on?' Larry demanded angrily. 'You've smashed my window, and now . . .'

'The girl you have here, she's my daughter! Due to the incompetence of my incompetent sergeant we were delayed and . . . I hope you haven't touched her, Doctor Lickman!'

'Girl? Your daughter? What *are* you talking about? There's no girl here, Inspector!'

'No girl? But . . . my men will find her, don't you worry!'

'Has she gone missing?'

'I sent her here as part of my plan to catch you red-handed. You've been set up, doctor. If I find that you've done anything to her, I'll . . .'

'There's no one here, Guv,' the sergeant interrupted as he emerged from the bondage room and walked down the hall.

'Of course she's here, you incompetent fool! Look again, man!'

'Inspector, talking of missing people, my staff seem to have disappeared,' Larry said. 'I don't suppose you know anything about their disappearance, do you?'

'I might, and there again, I might not.'

'Ah, so you've obviously abducted them as part of your plan, whatever your crazy plan is.'

'My crazy plan, as you put it, is to arrest you for committing grossly indecent sexual acts of a grossly indecent nature against several innocent young women – including a nun, a convent schoolgirl, a . . .'

'What?'

'You heard. So far, you've been one step ahead of me, but now . . .'

'Will you *please* tell me what all this is about, Inspector? My staff have gone missing, you break down the door to my examination room, you've smashed the window in my consulting room, and now you're talking about indecent sexual acts involving nuns and schoolgirls!'

'She's not here, Guv,' the sergeant repeated as he emerged from the waiting room.

'Look again!'

'But, Guv . . .'

'Look again! Where is my daughter, Doctor Lickman?'

'I have no idea! I didn't even know you were the proud owner of a daughter!'

'If she's come to any harm, I'll . . .'

'Look, let's calm down, Inspector. Now, you say that you sent her here?'

'Yes, as part of my . . .'

'Well, all I can say is that she didn't arrive. I locked up at five, as usual, and I've been catching up with

paperwork ever since. I can assure you that no one has been here.'

'She came here earlier, doctor. She called herself Holly Holdall and . . .'

'Ah, yes, a girl named Holly was here earlier. I was unable to see her as . . . so, Holly is your daughter?'

'Yes, and you told her to come back at eight this evening.'

'No, I didn't. I never see clients during the evenings, it's a rule I made some years ago, and I've rigidly adhered to it.'

'Are you suggesting that my daughter, a detective inspector's daughter, is lying?'

'No, I'm just saying that she hasn't been back since she left earlier today. I was unable to see her without an appointment, and I told her to phone and book an appointment with my receptionist. Have you tried the pub?'

'The pub?'

'Yes, she might have gone for a drink.'

'Of course she hasn't, she doesn't drink!'

'Sorry, it was only a suggestion.'

'She's not here, Guv!' the sergeant broke in as he emerged from the toilets.

'All right, tell the men to get back to the station. Now, doctor, I'm going to get to the bottom of the matter if it's the last thing I do!'

I've already got to the bottom of the matter! 'Good, and I wish you luck with the search for your daughter. Now, Inspector, please tell me where my staff are.'

'They'll be released shortly.'

'Why did you arrest them?'

'I arrested them on a whim.'

'On a whim? You can't do that!'

'I can do what I like.'

'Are you of a whimsical nature?'

'Far from it, I'm rock-steady! I'll be back tomorrow, doctor, and if my daughter isn't at home . . .'

'If she isn't at home, then it has nothing to do with me.'

'We'll see about that! And when I do find her, I shall physically examine her for signs of . . .'

'You can't physically examine your daughter, it's illegal.'

'Due to the nature of the allegations brought against you by Mrs Cology, I shall examine my daughter's bottom for weals. I shall also examine her pubic region for missing pubic hair.'

'Incest!'

'It's within my power, doctor. Good night, to you.'

Sighing as the sleuth left the building, Larry made his way to his consulting room and unlocked the door. Switching the light on, he gazed at the shattered window. 'Bloody cops!' he cursed, taking the bottle of scotch from the drawer and slumping in his swivel chair. 'Bloody cops!'

Wandering into the consulting room, the morning sun streaming in through the broken window, Brigit shook Larry's shoulder. 'Larry, wake up! What the hell are you doing? Wake up!'

'What? Er . . . Brigit! Oh, fuck!'

'Did you sleep here all night?'

'Er . . . yes, yes, I did. Jesus, look at the bloody window!'

'Yes, I've seen it. Lily and I were taken to the police station. What happened here?'

'DI Clarke and his men raided the place. God, my head! I was screwing his daughter and . . .'

'Screwing his daughter? Bloody hell!'

'It's all right, it turned out OK. What happened to you?'

'We were taken to the police station and kept there for hours.'

'Monica too?'

'No, I don't know where she got to.'

'Bloody woman, she set this up with the cops!'

'You should never have taken her back, I told you that it was a mistake!'

'Yes, yes, I know, Brigit! Did the police charge you with anything?'

'No, they said that they were protecting us. God, you say you fucked the inspector's daughter? How come he didn't catch you?'

'He was delayed, thankfully! I managed to bundle the girl out of the waiting-room window while the cops were round the front of the building. The thing is, when he questions the girl, he'll realize what happened. He reckons he's going to examine her for weals and shaved pubic hair! Shit, I'm really in it!'

'He can't examine his own daughter!'

'He can and he will, believe me!'

'I can't understand why he persisted. I mean, after screwing me over your desk, why ever did he . . .'

'Your threats obviously didn't bother him. Did you set Ravenhugh and his wife up?'

'No, they're ex-directory – I couldn't get their phone number.'

'Fuck, so he'll still be on my back! At least Fullcrack and Venereal have left me in peace.'

'I checked the appointments book when I came in, we've a really busy day ahead, Larry.'

'Oh, God! When's the first client arriving?'

'There's a new client due in about ten minutes. She made the appointment yesterday, just before we were carted away by the police.'

'Fuck it, all these bloody problems! OK, I'll wash and smarten myself up. Er . . . coffee would be nice.'

'Right, coffee it is. By the way, Lily isn't here.'

'Thank God for small mercies!'

Grabbing his battery-operated shaver from the desk drawer Larry ambled to the toilets to wash, wondering why the debt collectors hadn't swooped – and the teenaged girls' fathers! *Shit, what a bloody cock-up!* he reflected, shaving the stubble from his chin.

'Larry, there's a phone call,' Brigit called as he walked through reception combing his dark hair back.

'OK, I'll take it in my room. Who is it?'

'A man from the local paper.'

'Bloody hell! What the fuck does he want?'

'I don't know, he just asked to speak to you.'

'OK, switch it through.'

Sitting on his desk, Larry lifted the receiver, wondering what on earth the local paper wanted with him. 'Doctor Lickman speaking,' he said authoritatively.

'Ah, Doctor Lickman, my name's Meddler, Dick Meddler. We're running a piece on your practice and I wondered whether . . .'

'On my practice?'

'Yes, I've already interviewed several of your clients and a member of your staff and I was wondering whether you'd like to react to their comments.'

'Who was the member of my staff?'

'Mrs Monica Moodie.'

'She's no longer a member of my staff. What were her comments?'

'She's made some pretty strong allegations about you, that's why I thought it only fair to give you the chance to retaliate. As for the clients, I've interviewed Mrs Cravings, Miss Jane Churcher, Christine Cology . . .'

'She's not a client!'

'Well, she says that she visited your practice and that you examined her, Doctor Lickman. I see no reason to disbelieve her. Funnily enough, we were contacted by the Mother Superior of The Sacred Bloodied Heart of Our Lady of the Damned Convent. She also had some very interesting things to say about you.'

'No comment!' Larry snapped, banging the phone down. 'Shit and double fucking shit!'

Pacing the room, he kicked the broken glass across the floor as he cursed Monica. 'It's no wonder the fucking old cow hasn't turned up today!' What he could do to stop the paper running the article, he had no idea. Obviously, once word was out about his unorthodox examination techniques, the allegations of enforced bondage and whipping sessions, he'd be ruined. *Time to call it a day!* he decided as a loud knock sounded on the door.

'Come in!' he called irritably.

'Doctor Lickman?' a besuited young man carrying a

briefcase asked as he entered the room. 'Oh, your window's broken!'

'How observant of you. What do you want?'

'My name's Basket, I'm from Customs and Excise.'

'Are you now? And what the fuck are you doing here? Why aren't you fucking well customing and exercising?'

'Oh, there's no need for that attitude, Doctor Lickman!'

'Isn't there?'

'No! Might I take a seat?'

'Are you also a bailiff?'

'A bailiff? No, why do you ask?'

'In that case, no, you cannot take my office furniture!'

'Oh, yes, er . . . it's come to our notice that you aren't VAT-registered.'

'That is correct, I am not VAT-registered. And I never have been, and I never will be bloody VAT-registered!'

'From the figures I've received from the Inland Revenue, your turnover would indicate that . . .'

'May I say something, Basket?'

'Yes, yes, of course.'

'I'm going to count to five, and if you're not out of my establishment by then, I'll rip your cock off and stuff it down your fucking throat!'

'Oh, Doctor . . .'

'One!'

'But . . .'

'Two!'

Holding his head as the man fled the room, Larry sighed. 'God, what the fucking hell's going to happen next?' Taking the whisky from its hiding place, he gulped down a mouthful and left the room. 'Brigit!' he yelled, bounding down the hall

and swigging from the bottle again. 'Brigit, where the fucking hell are you?'

'What? What is it, Larry?' the girl asked, peering over the counter. 'Should you be drinking scotch at this time of the morning?'

'I have nothing else to drink! Where's my bloody coffee?'

'Oh, yes, I was just . . .'

'Did you let that cunt of a VAT man in?'

'VAT man? But he said he was a salesman from Garry's Gynaecological Gadgets.'

'Lying, fucking, thieving bastard! Where the fuck's Lily?'

'She's just come in. She's . . .'

'Don't tell me, she's in the toilet! Right, this is what we'll do . . .'

'Your first client's in the waiting room, Larry.'

'Shit! The local paper are on to me, Brigit! They've spoken to Monica and . . . shit, what the hell shall I do?'

'You'd better see your client and then we'll talk about it.'

'OK, OK. Right, send her to the examination room. I can hardly use my consulting room now that cunt-faced wanker Clarke has smashed the fucking window!'

'Right, I'll send her in.'

Clearing the ropes away from the examination couch, Larry decided that, as this might well be his last client, he'd really put her through it. 'I'll fuck her arse, I'll fuck her mouth, I'll fuck her cunt, I'll . . . oh, hallo!' he smiled as a pretty ginger-haired girl drifted silently into the room.

'Hallo, doctor. Your receptionist sent me along to see you. My name's Oral Orifice.'

'That's an unusual name.'

'Yes, my parents named me after the way I was conceived, but I've never understood what they meant.'

'After the way you were conceived? I don't see how oral . . . anyway, how can I help you?' he asked, gazing at her extremely short blue miniskirt.

'Well, I've been suffering from a vaginal complaint for some time now, but my GP tells me that it's psychosomatic.'

'Yes, some vaginal complaints are psychomatically psychosomatic. What is the complaint, exactly?' Larry asked, patting the couch. 'Lie down and I'll have a look at you.'

'It's strange, but I have a sort of numb feeling around my . . . well, around my clitoris,' the girl said coyly, lying on the couch.

'Numb? That's unusual for such a sensitive area. Is your clitoris numb, or just the surrounding flesh?'

'My clitoris is fine, as sensitive as ever!'

'OK, lift your skirt up and slip your panties down,' Larry smiled. *Here we go again!*

Gazing in awe at her shaved pussy crack as she tugged her skirt up over her stomach and pulled her knickers down to her knees, Larry frowned. His suspicion rising as she began to unbutton her blouse, he moved to the window and peered through the gap in the curtain. *The coast seems clear*, he mused, returning to the girl's side. But it had seemed clear the night before!

'Er . . . you don't seem to have any pubic hair,' he said pensively, eyeing her full vaginal lips, her long dividing

groove, as she opened her blouse and lifted her bra clear of her pert young breasts. 'Is there any particular reason for that?'

'Yes, it never grew.'

'That's most unusual!' *So fucking unusual that I don't believe it!* he mused, observing a fine stubble covering her swollen sex lips, the rising flesh on her mons. *The lying bitch has shaved!*

'Yes, that's what my GP said. The numbness is all around my clitoris,' she explained, unashamedly parting her soft outer labia with her slender fingers and exposing her pink cumbud, her moist inner sex folds to Larry's appreciative gaze. 'All around there, round the base of my clitoris. Do you think the lack of pubic hair and the numbness are connected?'

'Possibly, I have come across such a phenomenon before. OK, let me take a look,' he murmured, moving her hand away and holding her pussy lips wide apart, examining her succulent, pinken lust hole.

Breathing heavily and twisting her long nipples as Larry examined her clitoris, the girl appeared to be highly sexually aroused. Massaging her stiffening sex button, Larry was sure that this was yet another girl sent as bait to lure him into a trap. *Fuck me, they don't give up!* he reflected, slipping two fingers into her drenched cunt. *Right, I'll teach the little slut to come here and trick me into fucking her!*

'Wait there a minute, I'm just going to get a vaginal speculum,' he smiled, withdrawing his sticky fingers from her vagina and leaving the room. Dashing down the hall to reception, he called out for Brigit, grabbing her arm as she approached him.

'What is it?' the girl asked.

'That girl in there, she's a fucking spy!' he whispered. 'Don't let anyone come into the building. Lock all the doors and don't let anyone in. Don't even answer the phone.'

'All right. How do you know she's a spy?'

'I recognize the bitch – she works for the local paper.'

'Fuck me! How come you recognize her?'

'I remember her being pictured in the paper a couple of years back. She was their top reporter of the year or something. I remember her because the article was next to an advert I tore out of the paper. I'm positive that it's her.'

'Christ! What are you going to do?'

'Well, I reckon we're totally fucked, what with DI Clarke, the newspaper, Ravenhugh, the VAT man, my bloody wife . . . get Lily out of the toilets and keep watch while I thrash the girl's buttocks and fuck her tight bum-hole!'

'But, Larry . . . what are we going to do, long term?'

'As yet, I don't know. It would seem that everyone is closing in – I really don't know what to do. Right, if there's a problem, ring the reception bell. Keep your finger on the button and don't stop ringing until I get here. OK, I'm going to deal with the reporter of the fucking year!'

Returning to the bondage room, Larry wasn't surprised to discover the girl lying naked on the couch. Scrutinizing her shapely, suntanned body spread invitingly before him, he concealed a wicked grin. *The last supper*, he mused, wondering which vile and debased act to savour.

'Right, stand up and lean over the couch, Oral,' he instructed his unsuspecting victim, his penis stiffening as

she climbed off the couch and bent over. 'That's it, stand with your feet wide apart. I'm pretty sure I know what the problem is, so I'll check your spinal alignment. Lean right over the couch with your arms stretched out.'

'What about the vaginal speculum?' the girl asked, taking her position, her rounded buttocks projected, vulnerable – perfectly placed for a whipping!

'There's no need for the speculum now. You see, if your spine's slightly out of alignment then your pubic hair would never grow and you'd sense a numbness around the base of your clitoris. Tell me, do you ever feel tempted to push a finger into your bottom? I ask you that because it's another sign of rampant spinal misalignment.'

'Why, yes, I do feel the urge to do that!'

Lying fucking bitch! 'Ah, I thought as much.'

Taking a long length of rope, Larry secured it to one end of the couch. Hauling the rope over the girl's back, he pulled it tight and quickly bound the other end to the head of the couch, grinning evilly as she struggled to stand up. Ignoring her hysterical threats, he bound rope to her ankles, pulling her feet wide apart and securing the ends to the couch legs. Her bottom crease gaping, her brown anal entrance exposed, defenceless, he grabbed a leather strap from the shelf and began lashing her taut buttocks.

'Please, what are you doing?' she cried, her body jolting with every deafening crack of the strap. 'Ouch! Ah! God, no! Please, don't!'

'What's the matter, reporter of the year? Suddenly got cold feet, have you?'

'Please, I'm not a . . . argh! I'm not a reporter!'

'You're in for the thrashing of your life, and then for the

arse-fucking of your life!' Larry stormed, wondering how the trap was to be sprung, who was going to try to enter the building and catch him red-knobbed. A newspaper photographer, perhaps?

'I don't understand! Why are you beating me? What have I done?' Miss Orifice screamed as the leather strap cracked loudly across her tensed bottom orbs, leaving wide pink stripes in its wake. 'Please, you're hurting me!'

'Hurting you? I'll thrash your bum until the pain turns into pleasure and you come all down your thighs!'

The lashing continuing unabated, Larry lost himself in his debauchery, the girl's crimson buttocks and screams for mercy only serving to drive him on. Eyeing her cunny cream coursing down her inner thighs, dripping from her gaping cunt and pooling on the floor, he decided to fuck all her holes one after the other – again and again and again until she passed out with sexual pleasure.

'Christ, Larry!' Brigit exclaimed, gazing at the girl's scarlet bottom cheeks as she joined Larry. 'I think she's had enough!'

'Never!' he cried, bringing the leather strap down again, causing the girl to jolt and scream. 'Never! Never! Never!'

'That's enough!' Lily shrieked, grabbing his arm to halt the punishment. 'God, you'll kill her!'

'That was the idea!' Larry panted, rubbing his aching arm as he discarded the strap.

'Christ, she's soaked!' Brigit observed, kneeling behind the sobbing girl. 'Look at her cunt milk, it's streaming out of her hole!'

'God,' Lily breathed, kneeling beside Brigit. 'I'd like to lick her out!'

'And me!' Brigit rejoined as Larry leaned against the wall, his penis bulging his trousers.

Watching the cunt juice-thirsty girls lapping at Oral's inner thighs, their tongues trying to slip into her gaping vaginal entrance, Larry sighed, wondering why everything had gone so terribly wrong. *It was only a matter of time, I suppose*, he reflected, looking back over the years of perverted sex with one client after another. *Only a matter of time.*

'What's the plan, Oral?' he asked the whimpering girl as fingers delved deep into her drenched cunt, her bottom-hole. 'You're from the local paper, so what's the plan?'

'I'm not from . . .'

'I recognize you, so there's no point in lying any more. Now, what's the plan?'

'I was . . . my colleague was going to come here and . . .'

'Is the main door locked, Brigit?'

'Yes, it's locked.'

'So, Oral, your colleague was going to come bursting in, with a camera, no doubt, and . . .'

'Yes, yes! Please, can I go now?' she sobbed as Lily's tongue slipped into her open vaginal sheath. 'Just let me go and I'll say nothing about . . .'

'Not until I've fucked you!' Larry laughed. 'OK, girls, make way for my big cock!'

Standing behind his prisoner, Larry grinned as Brigit grabbed his solid penis and guided him into her dripping cunt. Beginning his fucking motions, his lower belly slapping her crimson buttocks, he gasped as the girls kneaded his swinging balls.

'God, she's wet!' he cried, grabbing her hips and driving

his cockhead deep into her tight sheath, battering her cervix. 'I'm going to miss fucking my young clients!'

'We won't have to close the practice, will we, Larry?' Brigit asked, slipping a finger deep into the girl's hot anal canal.

'Yes, we might have to. Jesus, I've never known such a hot, tight, wet pussy!'

'I wouldn't have a job if you closed down!' Lily complained, licking Oral's buttock.

'Jesus Christ, I'm coming!' Larry gasped. 'God, I'm coming!'

His sperm jetting from his throbbing glans, he fucked the young girl with a vengeance, his heavy balls rolling, swinging as he repeatedly drove his knob into her spasming sex duct. Whimpering, Miss Orifice reached her enforced climax, crying out with sexual pleasure as her curvaceous young body shook violently.

Massaging her pulsating clitoris, Lily sustained the girl's shuddering climax, her own clitoris in dire need of a caressing finger, a sweeping tongue. Brigit, too, needed the relief of orgasm, her cumbud swelling between her bulging vaginal lips as she finger-fucked Oral's bottom-hole.

'This is the police!' a voice bellowed through a loud hailer. 'Come out with your trousers up!'

'Fucking hell!' Larry gasped as his balls finally drained and he slipped his wet member from his last client's delectable cunt. 'What the fuck . . .'

'What shall we do?' Brigit cried, slipping her finger out of the girl's tight bum and leaping to her feet.

'Christ knows!' Larry breathed, zipping his trousers. 'Christ bloody knows!'

'Doctor Lickman, come out with your trousers up!'

'Bloody hell!'

Dashing to the main door with Brigit and Lily in tow, Larry held his head as he gazed through the glass panel at DI Clarke and his men, Mother Barren-Womb, Fullcrack, Venereal, his two wives, Ravenhugh, the VAT man, a Press photographer and two dozen or so other men gathered in the car park. This was it, the end!

'Quick, through the waiting-room window!' he cried, dashing across the foyer. 'We'll escape through the fucking window!'

'Escape to where?' Lily snivelled, chasing after Larry and Brigit.

'France. We'll set up in Bordeaux, it's lovely down there. There are dozens of suitable properties for sale. We'll take the ferry and . . .'

'What about money?' Brigit interrupted as Larry opened the window and peered cautiously outside. 'And your car's in the car park, so how are we . . .'

'I've a bank account in another name, money's no problem. As for my car, I thought something like this might happen so I parked it in the back street.'

'We can't just leave the country!' Lily gasped as Larry bundled her through the window, his hands up her skirt, groping her firm buttocks as she fell to the ground. 'What about my flat, I owe rent on it!'

Pushing Brigit through the window as the police force hammered on the main door, Larry knew there was little time. 'Sod the rent! Why can't we leave the country? We have each other, money, a car – and a brilliant future full of sex! Why not go for it?' he cried, making his own escape.

Dashing round the back of the building, the three

Muffateers cut through the bushes into a side road and bundled into Larry's car. Speeding down the road as DI Clarke's men stormed the building, they made their timely escape.

'We'll pick our passports up and nip into the bank!' Larry grinned. 'Then it's down to Dover to catch the ferry!'

'God, what with all this excitement, my cunt's really wet!' Brigit giggled.

'And mine!' Lily rejoined.

'Don't worry, girls, there are plenty of French sticks where we're going! *Sacré bleu*, think of all the French pussy awaiting us! Soixante-neuf! Stuff the system! Stuff the French tarts! Bienvenue, la France!'

Fuck!